Blue

Bayou

DICK
LOCHTE

SIMON &
SCHUSTER

NEW YORK LONDON TORONTO
SYDNEY TOKYO SINGAPORE

SIMON & SCHUSTER
Simon & Schuster Building
Rockefeller Center
1230 Avenue of the Americas
New York, New York 10020

Designed by Laurie Jewell
Manufactured in the United States of America

1   3   5   7   9   10   8   6   4   2

Library of Congress Cataloging-in-Publication Data

Lochte, Dick.
Blue bayou/Dick Lochte.
p.   cm.
I. Title.
PS3562.0217B5   1992
813'.54—dc20   92–3506
CIP

ISBN: 0-671-74711-8

For Dr. Jane and the Little Kingfish

Soft and slow, the funeral band moves on,
Feet dragging toward heaven's ground.
The sun shines bright on brass and tears,
Another soul is heaven bound.

"Burial Society Blues" (circa 1903)
Georges Sagrette

Prologue

●

CROAKER SAT in his parked black Thunderbird listening to the midnight opera on FM and thinking about murder. He was a big man with a case-hardened body that looked as if it wouldn't bend easily. He was wearing a seven-hundred-dollar featherweight gray suit from Yves St. Laurent's Paris shop that fit him the way a seven-hundred-dollar suit, even with the current rate of exchange, should. But with his lifeless, dull brown hair and a face that might have been hammered out of granite, he did not convey the cultured mid-Atlantic businessman image he was seeking.

His T-Bird rested, engine and air conditioner thrumming, on one of the less lively residential blocks of St. Ann Street in New Orleans's Vieux Carré. Outside, the heavy, humid night supported a symphony of good and bad Dixieland, barkers' spiels, genuine and forced laughter, and drunken yells that echoed around corners and along damp alleyways from the teaming tourist blocks of Bourbon and Royal. Croaker didn't hear them, thanks to the car radio.

He smiled approvingly at some unknown programmer's choice of Ravel's *L'Enfant et les Sortilèges*. Though he loved opera in general, he preferred the French to the Italian, just as he preferred the French to the Italians, a bias not totally uncommon in the city of New Orleans.

While he hummed along to a libretto by Colette, no less, his eyes panned from the empty street to an apartment building's recessed doorway where a sweaty, stocky man in baggy khaki trousers and a bright Hawaiian-print shirt fiddled with the lock.

The door opened and the stocky man turned and flashed an idiot grin of triumph before entering the building.

The man in the T-Bird frowned.

Croaker was not his real name, of course. His employers, famous for their colorful aliases, had tagged him with it, discovering to their dismay and discomfort just how profoundly it annoyed him. After profuse apologies, they continued to use it behind his back because it fit him so well. There was his Cajun French heritage. His frightful hoarse voice that resembled Clint Eastwood's with a touch of the croup. And finally, there was his occupation.

He used a small can of talc to powder his hands, careful to keep the white dust away from his suit. Rolling on a pair of membrane-thin rubber gloves, he leaned forward to get a better view of the balcony above the building's entrance. He stared at the closed shutters behind the balcony's elaborate grillwork. Now, if the fool they'd saddled him with remembered the signal . . . As if in reply, the shutters shifted slightly and a small white light blinked twice.

Croaker turned off the car's ignition, silencing engine, air conditioner, and opera. He reached back to grab a cheap, uncovered pillow from the rear seat.

The humid night air engulfed him as he crossed the street. He discovered that it was just as unpleasantly warm and moist inside the building, except that a faint odor of garbage was added to the package. On the second floor, the door to apartment 2-B was open an inch. He went through it quickly and silently, surprising the stocky man who was seated at a desk, tying a shoelace. He stared at Croaker as if he'd been caught in an obscene act.

"What's your problem?" Croaker rasped.

"Nothin'," the stocky man protested. In the moonlight, beads of perspiration glistened on his forehead and upper lip.

"Find anything interesting?"

The stocky man played his penlight on an open desk drawer.

"Just bullshit stuff. No files. Nothing like that. They were all in the other place the guy was using for an office."

"Take your time," Croaker suggested sarcastically, placing the pillow carefully on the desktop. "You're not in any hurry, right?"

The stocky man began opening and closing drawers. He moved rapidly about the darkened apartment.

Croaker watched him for a few minutes, then paused to study the spines of books in a floor-to-ceiling shelf behind the desk. Mainly mysteries. A few volumes on New Orleans history. The man who lived in the apartment was obviously no intellectual.

The room was hot and smelled of stale, sweet pipe tobacco smoke. The stocky man, perspiring heavily, strolled toward Croaker. "No business stuff," he said. "No files, like I said. But the old guy had a broad up here. I found this little bikini outfit in the clothes hamper."

"He was keeping a young woman," Croaker said. "Anything else of hers around?"

"No."

"Good. Maybe she's moved out. Makes it easier."

"Here's something you can maybe use," the stocky man said. It was a Smith & Wesson .357 Magnum heavy barrel.

"Where was it?" Croaker asked.

"Bedroom closet, hanging on a hook."

"In the holster?"

The stocky man nodded. "First chamber empty."

"Fine," Croaker said. "Just drop it on the pillow."

He watched the stocky man nestle the pistol with care, as if it were an objet d'art. Then he scowled and pointed to a lump poking from the man's pants just below his left hip. "What's that? A little lagniappe?" The stocky man was known as an expert locksmith. But his reputation included a disquieting habit of snatching worthless souvenirs.

"Aw, hell. It ain't anything much."

Sheepishly, the stocky man reached into his pocket and withdrew a snowfall paperweight. Croaker shook his head sadly.

"You want me to put it back, huh?"

Croaker looked at the object. Inside the glass ball was a miniature beer bottle. The ersatz snow floated down onto it. A caption read, "Dixie Beer on Ice." Croaker said, "Keep it. If the cops find it, you can always say the guy gave it to you. And when they don't believe you, you can tell them how you came here tonight with me. And then we could wind up sharing the same cell and . . ."

"I'll put it back."

Croaker's throat felt slightly sore from all the talk. He withdrew an atomizer from his pocket. The stocky man returned; he made a nervous hand-washing motion and his rubber gloves squeaked. "I guess I'll be going, if that's all."

"Have a nice evening," Croaker told him. "And don't forget to lock the door behind you."

Alone in the apartment, Croaker removed a penlight from his coat pocket and checked the pistol. Then he searched the desk until he found a little red cardboard box containing canceled checks. He studied the signature on them before plucking a pen from its desktop holder.

Nearly two hours later, at 2:35 A.M., Croaker heard someone coming up the stairs. One man, humming softly. Croaker could have adjusted his plans to take care of an unexpected second party. But his target was alone, which was preferable.

He positioned himself by the door. A key turned in the lock and the door opened. A tall, thin man paused briefly, then entered. As he shut the door, Croaker expertly tapped the back of his skull with a rubber tube filled with buckshot. The thin man grunted and fell too quickly for Croaker to grab him.

Croaker paused, waiting to see if the thud of the body would result in any neighborly concern. The old building seemed quiet. At that time of night, the average French Quarter denizen was either out, drunk, or asleep.

The man was slumped forward, his upper body and face pressed against the door. Croaker slid the body until it was draped along the floor on its back. He shined his penlight onto the man's face, to make sure no damage had been done during the fall. There was a red patch on the cheek, a scrape from the rough wood of the door. No problem. He checked the limbs. No breaks. There had been a time in New York when a broken ankle nearly destroyed what he liked to think of as his Design for Dying.

Croaker placed a throw rug under the man's feet. Lifting the upper part of the man's body, he used the rug to carry/slide him across the dark wood floor.

When he had positioned the body in the desk chair, he picked up the gun and the pillow. The target's face was a series of bony crags and peaks, with an almost too delicate mustache. He'd been trying to hide his high forehead with a comb-down. A fellow Frenchman, Croaker thought wistfully.

He placed the Smith & Wesson into the man's hand, raised the hand until the gun barrel entered the man's mouth. He covered hand and gun and face with the pillow and pulled the trigger. The report of the gun was muffled by the pillow. But it was still possible that someone in a neighboring apartment might have heard the noise. Croaker waited, listening. He didn't particularly care if a neighbor was calling the police. He'd be gone by the time they arrived. He merely wanted to make sure that the hall would be empty.

Satisfied that no one was about to knock on the door, Croaker turned on the desk lamp and surveyed his latest workmanship. The suicide note he'd forged earlier was in the middle of the desk. He bent forward and positioned the note just a bit closer to the lamp. The gun was on the floor, lifeless fingertips barely touching it. Perfect.

The pillow had leaked a few feathers and he plucked them from the body and the floor, depositing them in his coat pocket next to the sheets on which he'd practiced the dead man's handwriting.

He took a final look at the corpse and its surroundings. It was, he thought, one of his most successful creations.

1.

TERRY MANION was in the lounge watching a movie on videocassette when the voluptuous Miss Sonnerbend, wrapped in a minimal swimsuit as always, entered, glided across the floor, and whispered in his ear, "Dr. Courville wants to see you."

Manion waited until the effect of her warm breath on his ear dissipated, then pulled himself away from the film, a thriller titled *The Ipcress File*. He had seen it before. Seven times, to be exact. The first time, in 1965, he'd been a shy, skinny, tow-haired, myopic lad of seven. His father had thought he might profit from a movie with a protagonist who was, as portrayed by a youthful Michael Caine, thin, blond, nearsighted, and heroic.

The remaining viewings had all occurred during the past twenty-two days of his stay at Evangeline Spa, a pricey rehabilitation center located near the town of St. Martinville in the arch of Louisiana's swampy boot. The establishment boasted every known amenity except a selection of videos to satisfy Manion's movie buff taste.

"What's up?" he asked, admiring the muscles in the woman's bare back as she led the way.

"You've got visitors," she said.

"I didn't think visitors were allowed."

"They aren't, usually," she replied, her gait remaining constant.

Just before he entered Dr. Courville's office, Miss Sonnerbend gave him a wink and said, "Don't forget. We've a date by the pool in thirty minutes."

He watched her walk away. She expected him to.

*   *   *

The therapist, Dr. Courville, was a diminutive man with a narrow, shadowy face that was saved from the appearance of malevolence by large brown eyes that radiated kindness. Manion did not trust Dr. Courville's eyes.

The little man rounded his large desk and met him at the door. "Terry, some policemen have come about your trouble in Los Angeles. You don't have to talk with them now. It's up to you."

"You're the doctor," Manion said. "What do you think?"

"I think it's up to you." Dr. Courville smiled and his eyes softened into caramel. "You're capable of making your own decisions."

"What if I decide to rely on your decision?" Manion waited, but when the doctor remained silent, refusing to play the game, he sighed and asked, "Where are they?"

"In Group Room two."

"I'll give it a try."

"Ah, Terry, I didn't see your journal in the stack last night," Dr. Courville said, with only the faintest hint of admonishment.

They were supposed to keep a daily journal in which they answered four questions—"What was the most significant event of the day?" "What did I learn about myself today?" "What did I get from group today?" and "What did I get from lecture today?"

"You may find this hard to believe, Doc," Manion replied sincerely, "but I seem to have misplaced it."

Dr. Courville's eyes lost none of their kindness. "You're so near the end, Terry. You're not going to fight us now, are you?"

"I've been writing in it every day, haven't I? I just couldn't find it."

Dr. Courville nodded. "I'm sure you will, if you want to. On another matter, I believe I have a sponsor for you when you return to New Orleans."

Manion regarded him suspiciously.

His eyes dripping with warmth and understanding, Dr. Courville went back to his desk, shifted a stack of papers, and found a book. He handed it to Terry.

It was a thick volume with a glossy black dust jacket interrupted by a colorful tropical plant growing in the shape of a skull. Manion recognized the cover. The book had been a best-seller a few years ago. *In Salvador,* by Marcus Steiner. "You might want to read this, Terry," Dr. Courville suggested.

"Why?"

"I've convinced Marcus Steiner to be your sponsor." Dr. Courville made it sound as if Terry's ship had just come in.

"I thought we members of the Narcotics Anonymous club didn't deal in last names," Manion said lazily as he accepted the book.

Dr. Courville's kind eyes blinked. "With celebrities like Marcus," he said, careful to use the first name now, "anonymity is impossible. In any case, he went public with his problem long ago. It's in the book."

Manion opened the back cover of the novel and studied the author's photo on the inside flap. Steiner appeared to be a burly, supremely confident man in his fifties whose scalp had replaced most of his hair and whose full white beard surrounded a wry smile. The smile looked practiced.

"Do I get a vote on this?" Manion asked.

"Certainly," Dr. Courville said, a bit puzzled. "Do you know Marcus Steiner personally?"

"No."

"He's a fine writer. Humorous. A man's man. I thought you'd be a perfect match."

"The guy's a reformed addict, isn't he?" Manion asked.

"Of course," Dr. Courville said.

"Well, I'm not sure I want to leap right into an association with an ex-junkie."

Dr. Courville frowned. He said, "But surely you understand that any sponsor would be . . . ah, another of your little self-amusements."

"Sometimes, it's all we've got," Manion replied.

The two men in Group Room 2 turned to stare at him as he entered. One was a thin, almost prissy fellow in his late forties, garbed in a dark suit. His shirt collar was tight enough to cause a fold in the loose skin around his neck. He was perched on a chair at a round table. A strange object like an adding machine was on the table in front of him. The other man was a big, heavy-boned gent in a rumpled seersucker suit who sat on a chair at a window, exhaling a cloud of smoke around the cigarette in his thin lips. Something about him struck Manion as familiar.

The big man looked up from the sports page of the New Orleans *Times-Picayune.* "Wal, hello, Manion. Thanks for coming so quickly. I don't suppose we've been here more than thirty, forty minutes." His accent was the New Orleans specialty that combines the worst of Brooklyn and Biloxi. Leo Gorcey mixed with Tennessee Williams.

He surveyed Manion, from his bare, sandaled feet to his walking shorts to his purple polo shirt. He glanced at the book in his hand. "Doin' a little light reading, huh?"

When Manion did not answer, he said, "Pull up a chair, why don't ya? This might take a while."

"I've got a swimming date at three," Manion said.

The big man grinned and shook his head. "Goddamn amazing. You take a lickin' and keep on tickin'."

Manion placed *In Salvador* on an end table and draped his thin bones over a chair facing the big man. Past him, through the window, he got a glimpse of rolling lawn and trees laden with moss.

"Yes sir. A lot of people are taking dirt naps out L.A. way, but here you are, making swimming dates, readin' pop novels, sitting on Shit Hill."

Manion said, "Dirt naps. Shit Hill. Rude poetry."

The big man folded the newspaper neatly and tossed it onto the floor as if he never wanted to see it again. "Is your mind clicking on all cylinders, podnah?"

Manion realized with certainty that he knew him. "Eben Munn?" he asked.

"That's mah name."

They had been classmates at Mater Dolorosa grammar school. Mother of Sorrows. By name alone worth two or more chapters in the Book of Catholic Guilt. Young Munn had been a redneck rowdy with a buzz cut and a jaw like a steam shovel. On a class trip to the Evangeline Country, Manion had watched in silence as he filled his pockets with souvenir postcards from a shop near the famous mighty oak, while a yahoo buddy kept the ancient saleslady occupied. That had taken place not ten miles from where they both presently breathed the country air. Ten miles and twenty years. Munn still had the buzz cut and the jaw.

"So you're *compos mentis,* after all, huh?" Munn asked. "Well, me and Maurice Jobert, sitting at the table there, we had to drive for over two hours to get to this spa or rehab center or whatever the hell they call this dry-out clip joint. Then we been sittin' here for another forty minutes, like I said. Just to hear your story on what went down out in California."

He looked at the prissy man with obvious distaste and said, "You ready, Big Mo?"

Wincing at the nickname, Jobert pressed a button on his little machine and nodded. His fingers paused within an inch of the keys.

Manion noticed that Munn had picked up a habit of biting the inside of his mouth. He asked casually, "What'd you ever do with those postcards?"

Munn ignored the question. "Hold on, Maurice," he said. "You wait for my signal to begin."

Jobert stared at him without expression, fingers poised.

To Manion, Munn grumbled, "They got you tranked up?"

"No. That's not the part of the treatment. You remember taking those postcards?"

Munn smiled. He asked, "They put you through a lot of bad times out west, huh?"

"Enough. I don't understand what you're doing here."

"I'm with the New Orleans Police Department, NOPD. Homicide," the big man said. "Thought you knew that."

"Maybe I did. Read it in the paper. Something."

"And you, with a PI license. You coulda knocked me over with a Manale's breadstick when they laid that one on me. Hot Lunch Manion, Uptown Manion, pickin' a nice, clean occupation like private dick."

Miss Sonnerbend strode into the room without knocking. She'd put an unbuttoned chambray shirt on over her swimsuit. Her green eyes moved from Jobert to Munn to the floor where Munn had ground out several cigarettes. She asked Manion, "Ready for that swim?"

"Swim'll have to wait," Munn muttered, "until we're finished here."

Miss Sonnerbend, who had been a physical therapist for nearly fifteen years and as such had put up with the worst sort of behavior from the worst sort of people, immediately recognized in Munn a personality that was one step beyond anything she had encountered previously. "Mr. Manion is scheduled for pool therapy," she said icily. "We have very strict schedules here, sir. We try to adhere to them."

"Not now," Munn said flatly. "G'wan. Beat it, Esther. Go practice your breaststroke or something."

Miss Sonnerbend stared at Munn without blinking. Then she said very slowly to Manion, "I'll be at the pool." She took her time leaving the room.

Munn wiggled his thick eyebrows at Manion. "Why, you ol' fox. Doin' a little snorkelin', I sure as hell bet." He chuckled, lighting another cigarette.

"Did you ever graduate from grammar school?" Manion asked.

Munn gave him a long, appraising look. "Grammar school, high school, and got a B.A. degree all framed hanging just behind my desk, Loyola University of the South. But with all that education, I still can't figure out why any sane man would do that to himself."

"Do what? Go swimming?"

"That, too. But no, I was talking about sticking shit up your nose or in your arm. I used to work Vice and, Jesus, that gives you the picture faster'n Polaroid. Kids from good fam'lies. Catholics. Hebes even, and when we were kids, the Hebes wouldn't so much as drink beer. Makes no diff'rence now. Pack your nose or feed your arm and, zip-ola, you wind up low tide on Pontchartrain Beach."

"You are definitely a rude poet," Manion said again.

"I don't suppose that's a compliment."

"Depends on where you are," Manion said, shifting his view back to the window and the grass and the trees. He wiggled his toes in the sandals.

Munn scowled and turned to the prissy man. "Let's try it again, Maurice." He leaned forward and said, "Okay, Manion. Why were you out in L.A.?"

"Why should I tell *you*?"

Munn exhaled heavily and shook his head. He wanted Manion to realize that he was being extremely patient with him. He said slowly, as if talking to a child, "Because we got a request from a Fed named Gildcrest for a deposition. They're putting together a little trial out in California and they think they got a solid case against the crowd who messed up your head for you. Gildcrest is willin' to let you rest here and get all bettah, but he does want your deposition. Though the word of a cokehead can't mean all that much, huh?"

A sudden chill passed through Manion's body. The Creoles would have said a rabbit just jumped over his grave.

"You can start anywhere you want," Munn prompted.

Manion stood up. "Not just now," he said. "Maybe after my swim."

"No swim. You might be going to the goddamn jail to make a statement. But you definitely aren't going for a swim." Munn shook his head in wonder. "You haven't changed even one itty bit, Manion, have you? You were a snotty bastard as a kid. And you're still one. Only now you're a shit-outta-luck PI who's pickin' with the chickens. No big bucks. No big daddy. No big nothin'."

There wasn't much Manion could say about that. Munn went on, "If I went to all the trouble to drive out here with Maurice, who I gotta tell you is not the world's most scintillating traveling companion, I sure as hell ain't gonna go back without something to make it worthwhile. You understand?" His tone was not quite angry, but his enunciation had improved.

The past few years had turned Manion from idealist to realist. The policeman wanted information. The policeman was going to get information. Easy or hard.

So he took the easy way. He sat down again and gave Munn an abridged version of the story. He had traveled to Los Angeles on the trail of a runaway teenager and badly underestimated the complexity of his assignment. He had paid for his mistake by being captured by a group of murderers who kept him in a drugged state for several weeks. He wound up in the detox ward of a hospital in Bay City, California, just a few Quaaludes this side of vegetable life. Upon his release, a West Coast private detective named Leo Bloodworth had flown with him back to Louisiana and arranged for ground transportation to the Spa. *C'est finis.*

Jobert's nimble fingers kept his little machine clicking steadily the whole time. Finally, Munn stood up and shook his pant legs until they covered his skimpy black socks and rubbed against his scuffed brown shoes. He nodded to Jobert, who turned off his machine and gathered the little strips of paper that were now filled with electronic shorthand symbols.

"So you go out hunting a kid," Munn said, "and you wind up in a joint like this." He looked around the room.

"I've been in worse," Manion told him.

"Yeah. I guess we both have."

Munn turned to the stenographer and said, "Maurice, why don't you head on out to the car? I'll be right along, soon's I say goodbye to my old classmate."

Jobert hesitated and for a moment Manion thought the man would actually speak. But he didn't. He picked up his gear and left.

Munn asked, "You been in contact with anybody in New Orleans lately?"

"No. Isolation from the outside world is part of the therapy. I'm surprised they let you in here."

"I can be pretty irrepressible when I wanna be."

Manion stared at him. "No kidding."

Munn asked, not casually enough, "Who's taking care of your case load while you paddle around here?"

"Why?"

"Is it some goddamn secret? Hell, I never saw a guy who plays it so close to the vest for no reason."

Manion said, "An old friend is taking care of the office."

"He got a name?"

"J. J. Legendre. I used to work with him a few years ago, before he retired."

"When was the last time you talked to him?"

Manion cocked his head to one side. "Months ago. Just before I left for California. What's this all about?"

"Geez, you're suspicious. Nothing for you to get all het up over. Just finishing touches." The homicide detective offered his hand and, without thinking too much about it, Manion shook it.

"Gimme a call when you get back to Nola," Munn said. "We'll go out and tear up the town." Then, remembering where he was, he added, "Or maybe not. Anyway, you keep it outta the mud, you heah?"

And he was gone. Manion felt confused and on edge. He was ready for a swim with Miss Sonnerbend.

2.

DURING THE drive from Evangeline Spa to New Orleans and the Criminal Courts Building, Maurice Jobert sat in the suicide seat of Eben Munn's stifling unmarked sedan in complete discomfort, sweating under his dark suit and feeling his shirt collar dig into his neck. No matter how many times he complained to the laundry, the shirts continued to arrive stiff as cedar planks, with collars sharp as steak knives. He suspected his wife requested the extra starch out of pure maliciousness.

During the whole trip, Munn barely acknowledged his existence. No words of comradeship. No apology for the cigarette smoke blown in his face, or the gaseous bellows from high and low. No insipid discussion of the weather or the political climate.

Nor did Munn allow Jobert a choice of radio fare. The steno was forced to endure a call-in show featuring a doctor whose book, *Sexual Dysfunctions, Their Cause, Their Cure,* prompted a vigorous discussion rich in listeners' personal case histories. Munn seemed totally enraptured by the material, laughing wildly as each poor soul described his or her hellish failing, and treating each sad tale to his own crude commentary.

Actually, the trip was a nightmare of Jobert's own choosing. Ordinarily he would have handed the assignment to one of his assistants. But for reasons unknown to him, the brief, apparently routine interrogation of Terry Manion was of some consequence to a mysterious benefactor. The time spent would be worth his while.

As soon as Munn's car pulled to a stop at the Criminal Courts

Building, Jobert was out of it like a shot, feeling oddly free in the heavy evening humidity. The policeman growled at him through the car window, "Don't sleep on that transcript, Jobert. I want a copy on my desk tomorrow morn."

Jobert almost smiled. He was definitely not going to sleep on the transcript. In fact, it took him only forty-five minutes to get it transcribed and Xeroxed. Then he was back on the sidewalk, heading for a downtown bus, a folded copy of the transcript forming a bulky bulge in his coat pocket.

He disembarked from the bus on the corner of Canal and Royal, blissfully happy to be away from his moist fellow passengers. He took stock of his location, then walked hurriedly into Rubenstein's Men's Store, where, in air-cooled comfort, he bought a hat. He thought that the stiff off-white straw boater with the blue-and-yellow-striped band made him look like an idiot, but he bought it anyway.

Critiquing his appearance in every reflective surface he approached, he crossed Canal Street and moved along the narrow sidewalks of the French Quarter, avoiding panhandlers, tourists, and local shoppers with equal disdain.

He paused at the dusty window of Orlybert's Antiques, adjusted the boater to a vaguely rakish tilt, and entered the store.

The wooden floor creaked under his feet as he moved past French Provincial chairs and Early American writing tables and a dreadful red maple dining set that he rather fancied. The store was even less populated than usual. There were only two customers that he could see. They were at the far end of the shop, standing beside the polished desk where Loretta Pruitt sat, closing a sale.

She was a small woman, almost as tiny as his wife, who stood no higher than five three and weighed a hundred and ten on a very inactive day. Loretta was in no other way like his wife. She was some seventeen years younger and dressed accordingly. At the moment, she was in simple white frock with a bright orange and purple scarf tied around her shoulders. Also unlike his wife, she behaved like a . . . well, like a sprite, which is what Jobert finally had had the nerve to suggest by way of a compliment on that miraculous afternoon when she entered his life.

He'd been in the midst of his usual trout meunière lunch at the Dixie Diner, near the Criminal Courts Building, when she'd wandered in and asked to share his table. There'd been other empty tables, but she chose his. Demurely, she inquired as to his opinion on the Dixie's *spécialités de la maison*. Less demurely, she wondered why such an attractive, cultured person was dining alone on such a beautiful spring day. He'd been too charmed and flustered to ask her the same thing. The next day they had lunch again. In a hotel room.

The memory of that more intimate introduction warmed him as he snooped around the antique shop, not really noticing any of the odd pieces of furniture. Finally, Loretta concluded her transaction and ushered the couple out.

She paused at the door and locked it. With a dainty fingernail, she positioned the hands on a cardboard clock until they reflected seven P.M., allowing them a half hour together before the shop would reopen for the predinner trade.

Then, with a shy little smile, she turned to Jobert, whose straw hat was in his hand. "Put it on again," she ordered.

He put it on.

"I was right. A hat makes you look ten years younger."

He grinned at her, wondering what would happen next. One never knew with Loretta.

She pressed her pointed chin to her chest and moved forward like a shy schoolgirl, her brown eyes staring up at him through long lashes. When she was only inches away, she said, "You'd better take a breath."

He had, indeed, forgotten to breathe. He inhaled and giggled nervously. "You . . . take my breath away," he said, hoping that the comment might conceivably be thought of as suave.

"Little me?" she said, turning her heart-shaped face to him.

"Little you."

"Of course, I'm not so little here." She took his trembling hand and placed it on her right breast.

He pulled her to him and kissed her. Awkwardly. He could feel his back straining. He unlocked his knees, and that gave him some relief.

Loretta's mouth became more demanding. Her painted fingernails moved to open the buttons of his shirt.

When she had removed his coat and tie, and his shirt was unbuttoned and dangling on the outside of his rather tented trousers, she asked, "Did Mr. Bear bring me something?"

Jobert nodded. "In my coat."

She looked down at the suit coat tossed carelessly on the carpet. The edges of the transcript poked from its inside pocket. She smiled and leaned close to him, tickling his hairless naked chest with her nails. "Which bed shall we use today, my jolly bear, the Louis Quatorze or the Early American?"

"You pick."

"The Louis then. I'm feeling very . . . French."

Jobert had no idea why this beautiful, intelligent, sexually demanding young woman should want him so passionately. But he did not for a moment doubt that she did. Judging by the way she warmed to her task, one could not exactly fault him for his folly.

Sitting at the window of an oyster bar across the street from Orlybert's Antiques, Eben Munn smiled at the waitress who deposited a frosty beer bottle on his table.

"No glass. I remembered," she said, wetting her lips. "I guess you must like the scenery around here, or something."

It amused him how wrong and how right she was.

He sipped the beer and sighed. "Ah, the first kiss of the day."

She smiled. "Bartender says it's on the house."

Munn raised his bottle to the bartender. He turned to look at the antique shop, and the waitress looked at it too. "Closed already, huh?" she asked. "Business must be lousy. It's the goddamn depression."

"You know who owns that place?" Munn asked.

She shook her head.

"You know who owns this place?"

"Sort of," she said.

"Same guy," Munn told her.

"No shit?"

"No shit."

She paused in thought. "Then I guess he ain't feeling the depression."

"I guess not," Munn agreed. "And I don't suppose it'd kill him to part with another Bud now, would it?"

"Another Bud," she called to the bartender.

Munn had to admit that the job had stuck him in worse places. He shot the rest of his beer, belched as politely as he was able, and tried to figure out how Manion fit into the whole mess.

3.

MANION RETIRED early that night. At approximately eleven P.M., he awoke from an unbearably happy dream to find that instead of lying in the embrace of his former wife, Gillian, he was alone in the bed. But not alone in the room.

He could hear breathing and the pad of soft soles on the floor. He opened his eyes. There was a vague shadowy lump near the foot of his bed. Slowly, he reached out his hand and found his glasses. He put them on.

There was enough Louisiana moonlight for him to see a man in white coat and trousers heading toward the door.

Manion reached out again and turned on his bed lamp.

The man spun around, startled by the light. He had a red, babyish face under unruly black hair. He was a few inches shorter than six feet and thick enough through the chest to strain his white orderly coat.

Manion said, "Can I help you with something?"

The man's ruddy face paled, but he replied, "I'm sorry. I'm new here. I got screwed up. Wrong room. Sorry."

He backed away, bumped into the door, opened it, and ran into the hall.

Manion decided not to try and catch him. What purpose would it serve? He had seen the nametag on the man's coat. "Oscar." Tomorrow was another day.

He got out of bed and propped a chair under the doorknob, just in case Oscar decided to return. There were no locks on the doors.

He wondered what Oscar had been after. Not money. He kept a ten-dollar bill on a table in plain view. His mentor, J. J. Legendre, had explained that that was the best way to tell if somebody had been messing with your room. The bill was still there.

As he walked toward the bed, he saw *In Salvador* lying on the floor. He bent to pick it up. And there—under his bed—was his missing daily journal. It was the sort of place he might have mislaid it. Except that it had not been there earlier when he made a thorough search of the room for it.

He picked it up and took it and Marcus Steiner's novel back to bed. He flipped through the journal. It seemed to be in the same condition as when he'd last seen it. He tossed it onto the chair, then plumped up his pillow, settled back, and opened *In Salvador.*

It began with an author's note.

I wrote my first novel, *In Saigon,* after returning from the hell that was Vietnam. It was part of my rehabilitation, my cleansing of mind and body from the effects of drugs that dulled the proximity of death. My next two books, *The Twilight Toll* and *Women of Manhattan,* were completed in the States, under conditions that were, in every aspect, blissful. That time of happiness was short-lived. The book you are now reading is, once again, the result of a rehabilitation from an addiction. Love is as powerful as any drug. And as destructive. But, with a little luck, you can come away with your ass intact.

Manion yawned, dropped the book to the floor, put out the light, and flattened the pillow. Before long he was asleep again, dreaming about his ex-wife, Gillian. He didn't need Marcus Steiner to tell him anything about addiction—drug, love, or otherwise.

The next day he strolled the grounds, trying to find Oscar, the mysterious orderly. Failing that, he visited the personnel office; its sole occupant, a rather bored young man, sat at a desk reading the morning paper. "Was there some problem with this Oscar?" he asked.

"No," Manion lied. "He did me a favor and I'd like to thank him."

"Oscar, huh?" The young man shook his head sympathetically.

"Unfortunately, this Oscar charactah, Oscar Saville, apparently decided we weren't for him. He packed up in the middle of the night. I saw it on the gateman's log. Saville left the premises at twelve forty-five A.M."

"Isn't that sort of unusual?" Manion asked.

"A bit," the young man agreed. "But some of the guests can be very demanding. There are problems with,"—he wrinkled his nose—"incontinence, upset tummies. That sort of thing. Every so often a new employee discovers that the work wasn't as, well, as mentally and spiritually uplifting as they'd hoped. And they vamoose."

Manion asked him if he had a forwarding address for Saville. The young man smiled. "I'm afraid that'd be against policy, suh."

Manion reached into his pocket and withdrew a ten-dollar bill. He folded it and placed it on the young man's desk.

"For just the address?"

Manion took out another bill, placed it beside the first. "And maybe the references that got him hired."

The young man left the money on the desk, moved to a file cabinet, and rolled open a drawer. He flipped through folders, frowned, flipped through them again. "It's gone," he said.

He returned to his desk, rooted through the in and out boxes. "I don't understand this at all. It'll be my tail if the file is missing."

Manion picked up the ten-dollar bills and put them back into his pocket. "Thanks anyway," he said.

The young clerk was too disturbed to notice. He went back to the cabinet. "Maybe I misfiled it."

On his way out, Manion stared at the lock on the door. Tiny scratches. First Eben Munn, then a phantom orderly. It was definitely time for him to be going home.

4.

IN A weight room in a fitness club in the heart of New Orleans, Reevie Benedetto sat with his back pressed against a leather slab, his stomach cinched in a heavy strap, his bare legs tucked behind and captured by a padded metal bar. He stared at himself in the floor-to-ceiling mirror, noted the fine layer of sweat on his tanned forehead and was pleased. He was a big, handsome man of twenty-seven, with dark eyes and a deceptively friendly smile. He took a deep breath and raised his legs, lifting the bar, which in turn raised seventy pounds of lead weight. He lowered his legs slowly. The weight felt too comfortable, so he increased it to eighty. Much better. He went through a set of twelve leg extensions, delighting in the gathering and tightening of muscles in his upper thighs and calves. He let a grunt of pleasurable pain escape his lips as he rested briefly.

A brutish, hulking young man with a tiny, close-cropped head on which a pair of earphones perched like pincers moved behind Benedetto. He flicked an earphone off his right ear and said, "Mind if I work in?"

Benedetto answered, "Yes, I do."

The young hulk, surprised at this breach of weight room etiquette, took a backward step. Then he moved forward and reached out to place a huge hand on Benedetto's shoulder. Benedetto's eyes held his in the mirror. "Don't even consider it," he said in a not unfriendly way.

The big hand fell away, but the young hulk glowered at him.

"There are at least three other leg extenders in other rooms in the gym," Reevie told him, continuing to pit his strength against the weight.

"This is the only Eagle," the young hulk complained. He was quite correct. Reevie had stocked this smaller workout room with Eagle machines, which were his preference, too. He shifted his attention to the message on the young hulk's shirt, reversing the letters of the mirror image. "Crack the backs and suck the heads," it read. The instructions on peeling and eating crawfish. Benedetto was amused enough to say, "I'll make it fast."

He finished another set at his leisure, totally ignoring the waiting hulk's sullen glare. Then he unbelted and disengaged his legs and moved on to a machine designed to expand the chest. He thoroughly enjoyed the two hours he spent each day at the Sports Plantation, a modern coeducational gym in the shadow of the Superdome on Poydras Street. It provided weights, saunas, a swimming pool, courts for racquetball, five large carpeted areas for mass aerobic exercises, and a number of rooms where masseurs and masseuses literally worked their fingers to the bone.

For nearly eighty years the building had been the home of the Crescent City Athletic Club, where many of New Orleans's respected and affluent gentlemen had gathered to take steam, swim nude in salt water from underground wells, and down a few cocktails prepared by Leroy, a renowned mixologist, before heading for the office or for hearth and home.

Reevie bought the place in 1985, the year after his graduation. He went to work immediately to rid the establishment of the older CCAC members, employing various methods of intimidation. He began by denying them the little amenities they'd come to expect over the decades. No more hot towels, for example. No more busboys to bring them their favorite refreshments poolside. Then he hired a local artist to create a logo—a cartoon pelican, the state bird, wearing a headband, gym shorts, and tennis shoes—that was sure to cause even more complaints from the conservative element. His next step was to open the doors to Latins, Orientals, blacks, and women, in that order. Finally, he retired Leroy and turned the bar into a health food cafeteria.

His legal name was Reeves Bennett. His mother's doing. After the divorce, the court had awarded her custody of six-year-old Reeves, the only child resulting from a basically loveless marriage. Mother and son had moved to Virginia to stay at first with her parents and then later with her new husband, a likable drunk named Thilo Van Hooten who was heir to the Van Hooten and Thayer tobacco empire.

Reeves had been brought up in the right circles, gone to the right schools, been in with the right crowd. It was not until his second year at Choate that his real father invited him to spend his spring break in New Orleans.

The Van Hootens often traveled in limousines, but none was so wonderfully garish as the silver stretch Mercedes that awaited him that spring day at New Orleans International Airport. The conveyance was stocked with champagne, cigars, and a redhead named Larice who claimed his virginity on the Airline Highway as the car roared into the city. Reeves came up for air just in time to see a billboard exhorting travelers to try the Mississippi Gulf Coast for the vacation of a lifetime. He laughed at the suggestion. His dad had already given him the vacation of a lifetime and it had only just begun.

From that visit on, he spent every spare weekend he could in New Orleans with his father, a short, overweight fellow with sallow complexion and sad Sicilian eyes, and with Larice, whom he nicknamed Licorice. He had wanted to skip college altogether, but his father, for perhaps the first and only time, agreed with his mother that a degree was crucial in today's marketplace. Jerri Van Hooten had her heart set on Harvard. But Charlie Benedetto had heard about this place in Switzerland where European captains of industry sent their young men to sharpen their business skills.

"It's amazing," Emilio Vargas, one of the world's leading exporters of cocaine, had told Charlie Benedetto one balmy French Quarter night. "You send them a little boy and they send back a cold-blooded barracuda. Now you may ask yourself, why do that to your kid? And the answer is, families got more use for a barracuda than they got for a little boy." Vargas had then smiled, explained to Reevie's father precisely how he had taken advantage of him in their last negotiation, and concluded, "My graduation class from St. Croydon's included three Euro princes, a member of British royalty, a guy who is a key player in the present administration in D.C., and a Chinaman who now owns half of Beijing. Happy functioning sociopaths, one and all. You owe it to the boy. You owe it to yourself."

So Reevie had a wonderful and productive four years in Switzerland, sharpening his business skills during the week and spending each weekend building on the sexual foundation that Licorice had laid on that fateful first trip to New Orleans. On the day he graduated, eager to put all of his newfound knowledge into practical use, he hopped aboard the first jet heading in the direction of America's Southland.

The night after Reevie's arrival, diploma in hand, Charlie Benedetto officially welcomed him to the city with a dinner in the largest private room of Bordeaux's restaurant, one of the city's oldest and most respected. There he was introduced to an interesting assortment of men, including his father's rather raffish friends and business associates, several judges, local celebrities, politicians, and even a few high-ranking members of the New Orleans Police Department.

It was his uncle Johnny "The Wolf" Benedetto, a gangly lummox with a high forehead and a flat nose, who started calling him Reevie. Johnny, a mildly retarded fellow who performed odd jobs for his elder brother—such as breaking the feet of a drunken tourist who in a stupor had urinated on the tire of the wrong limousine—had run his hand through the boy's carefully combed hair and said, "The kid can't have a name like Reeves, for Chri'sake. He gonna wind up in the Boston Club with all those fuckin' society snobs."

"He winds up in the Boston Club the day I buy the fuckin' Boston club," the senior Benedetto replied.

"Irregardless," Johnny insisted, "I ain't gonna call my only nephew *Reeves*." Giving it an effeminate twist.

Then a drunk suggested, "What about Li'l Crawfish?" Reeves's father was on the verge of ordering the man's death, when he considered the occasion, calmed down, and merely had the fellow tossed into the alley. Not until weeks later did Reeves discover that "the Crawfish" was not a nickname people usually called his father to his face. The reference was to Charlie Benedetto's left hand, which was missing its two middle fingers, shot off by a sadistic NOPD vice cop who, it was rumored, shortly thereafter became part of the foundation of the Hot Times Lounge in Fat City.

"Reeves Benedetto." His uncle Johnny stood there shaking his head in mock sadness. "Mother pin a friggin' rose on me. How's about Reevie? What d'ya think, Chawlie?" Johnny looked to his older brother for approval, and he got it.

And so it became official. The Crawfish's son was thereafter to be called Reevie.

He was in his private lounge when Lonnie Mason, his secretary, buzzed him to say that Larice was on hold.

Ordinarily he might have left her on hold. Her initial usefulness had ended some time ago, when he discovered that college girls could be just as much fun sexually and were on the whole better conversationalists. But that day he was expecting her call.

"Yes?" he asked, keeping any hint of anxiety from his voice.

" 'Reta just sent me an envelope, Reevie honey."

"Fast work," he said in a complimentary tone.

"You want me to bring it around?"

"I'll send Johnny."

"Oh." She paused. "Tell him I'll tack it to the door."

Tack it to the door? What the hell did she think it was, a laundry list? "No, honey. You wait for him to get here and you put it in his hand."

"He'll want to put something in my hand. You know Johnny. I'll bring it over."

He could feel his temper rising, but this wasn't the moment for it to blow. As they had told him time and again at St. Croy's: *Anger wins no battles.* "Okay. Leave it with Lonnie in the office. Tell her to put it in the safe."

"You're not gonna be there, huh?"

He was not flattered by the disappointment in her voice. "Nope," he said. "Sorry."

"Well, you know where I live, Reevie. Drop by any time you're hungry for a little Licorice."

"Right," he said, hanging up before she thought of something else to keep him on the line.

He waited in his private lounge until Larice was gone, then went to the office safe and withdrew the creased envelope she had brought. Not only creased but damp from her perspiration. He opened it with his fingertips and shook out the pages.

He read them carefully, twice, then buzzed Lonnie to come in. She was a strangely quiet girl with large, dark eyes. His speculation was that she might be attractive if she'd do something to her hair other than cut it in bangs, and if she used makeup and wore dresses that showed off a body he suspected was considerably more shapely than the frumpy sacks she hid it in. He wondered if she purposely dressed down for the office, to keep guys like his uncle Johnny from getting ideas. She'd never even given *him* a second glance. Maybe she liked women. He didn't really care as long as she handled the job.

He gave Lonnie the limp pages. "Put those through the shredder, would you?" he said, watching her as she exited, imagining a jut of hip here, a curve of breast there.

Finally, he picked up a phone, dialed a number, and waited while a distinctive, hoarse voice unnecessarily identified itself. Ignoring the loud operatic music in the background, Reevie Benedetto said, "I think we can forget about Manion. He's been out of the city for months."

"There still may have been some contact."

"It's not very likely. Manion apparently had his hands full with something else entirely, in California."

"Suppose I find evidence to the contrary?" came the gruff reply.

Benedetto sighed. "If I'm wrong, no big deal. You can always kill him."

5.

FIVE DAYS after his encounters with Eben Munn and the sneak-thief orderly, Oscar Saville, Manion's stay at Evangeline Spa drew to a close. By ten A.M., some four hours before the official checkout time, he was packed and ready to leave. He had filled out the "Continuing Recovery Planning" sheet, had answered the questions pertaining to the "newly recovered"—questions about his self-discovery, his proposed daily activity, his spirituality, and his sobriety.

Manion filled in the blanks satisfactorily, though he was not sure he really believed the things he wrote. All he knew for sure was that he wanted to resume his life and put the past behind him.

But that would not be for another four hours. So he read Marcus Steiner's book. Its hero, he discovered, was a journalist who travels to Guatemala in 1982 to cover the fighting. He falls in love with a Salvadoran woman and marries her. While he is in Nicaragua, sharing beans and philosophy with the Sandinistas, she goes back to her old boyfriend, a drug dealer, who takes her to Costa Rica. The reporter returns, searches for her, finally finds her a year later in a filthy hotel in San Salvador, dead. She is lying in the hotel's only bathtub where, just minutes before, she had slashed her wrists. Before dying, she managed to scrawl a note in Spanish. Translated, it reads, "I have nothing more to lose." The reporter spends another two years tracking down the dope dealer who abandoned the woman. He has many adventures, sees a great deal of the suffering and pain of civil war. He finds the dope dealer and kills him, and he emerges from Salvador a stronger, better man.

Manion slammed the book shut and went "Whew!"

He looked at his watch and found to his relief that it was time to go.

In the reception area, Dr. Courville and a few of the other staffers were bidding their farewells to those re-entering the outside world. Manion was disappointed to see that Miss Sonnerbend was not there. Doing her laps, probably.

Dr. Courville shook his hand and asked, "Have you given any more thought to Marcus Steiner acting as your sponsor?"

"I just read his book," Manion said.

"Yes?"

"I think he needs more help than I do."

Dr. Courville's eyes lost their warmth, but only for a moment. "He'll be good for you."

"Why?"

"Because he has had similar problems to yours and he seems to have overcome them."

"How much of the book was autobiographical?"

Dr. Courville smiled. "You two can talk that over. Good luck, Terry. I hope we don't see you back here again."

"No chance of that, Doc," Manion told him. "Unless you get a better selection of movie videos."

Manion walked out to find a bright, not too humid afternoon that smelled of magnolias and freshly cut grass. The slate-gray Cadillac sedan was waiting just outside the main gate, as expected. Its windows were dark enough to keep its occupants hidden, but Manion knew that a leather-skinned fossil name Felix would be behind the wheel.

The passenger door opened and a square, heavy-shouldered man rolled out of the car. He was wearing a light blue suit and an even lighter blue shirt, unbuttoned so that at least two inches of undershirt and a gold crucifix showed past the collar. His round face, with its bluebeard stubble and dark, connected eyebrows, broke into a grin at the sight of Manion. "Hey, T-bone," he shouted in a voice heavy with phlegm. "You need some he'p with your sootcase?"

"I can handle it, Buddy," Manion said, carrying his flight bag to the car. Buddy Lapere's huge, hairy first grabbed the canvas bag and tossed it easily into the open trunk. It landed with a thud, jostling a large hamper that was covered with newspaper.

Buddy looked into the trunk and chuckled. "Whoa, Mistah Hawdshell, where you think you goin'?" He bent over and reached beside the hamper, pulling out a live freshwater crab, being careful to keep his fingers away from its snapping claws. He lifted the newspaper and tucked the crab neatly among the others in the hamper. "Felix sure don't want none of them crabbies crawlin' up inta his car ta expire. You never get rid of dat smell, no. C'mon, T-bone. We got us a two-hour ride back to th' land o' dreams."

Manion, who had accepted Buddy's nickname for him without question years before, opened a rear door and settled onto the sedan's soft leather seat. The conditioned air was icy, the way Felix liked it. Without turning his head, Felix said glumly, "You evah gonna learn, Terry?"

Manion shrugged. "I'm kinda slow, I guess."

"That's for damn sure," Felix said, starting the car's engine. "There's some Black Jack back there on a tray, if you feel like a drink," he added nastily.

Manion smiled at him. "The way you drive, I may be forced to have one."

Felix chose not to reply. He knew Manion was joking. He had been a chauffeur for forty years, serving the same mistress, who never once complained about his driving. And she was not known for her forbearance.

Buddy plucked a cigar from the ashtray and chewed on it because Felix did not allow him to smoke on long trips. "Hey, T-bone," Buddy asked in his Cajun singsong, "you want some comp'ny back dere? We could play us some gin."

"You guys," Manion said. "If you're not talking about bourbon, you're talking about gin. I've been dry for nearly two months. Give me a break."

Buddy looked stricken. "Hey, T-bone, I didn't mean the booze gin—"

"He's pullin' your leg, Boudreaux," Felix cut him off. "You know how Terry likes to have his little joke."

Buddy looked at Terry, who said, "No cards today. I'm not ready to test my luck just yet."

"Okay, man." The round, blue-bearded face relaxed. "You callin' th' tune, heah?" With one activity closed to him, Buddy leaned forward and played with the radio dial until he found WWL, a clear-channel station from New Orleans that was using its wattage to transmit middle-of-the-road music. Buddy began to sing along with Jo Stafford about shrimp boats.

Manion stared through the smoked windows at moss-covered trees and swampland. The poet Longfellow called the area "the forest primeval" and mentioned specifically "murmuring pines and the hemlocks." Manion had no idea what a hemlock tree looked like, or if there were any in that part of the world. He knew better than to take Longfellow's word for it. Sister Dominica had noted—on that infamous Mater Dolorosa field trip during which Eben Munn stole the souvenirs—that the poet had never set foot on the land he made so famous. Nathaniel Hawthorne had heard a tale about an Acadian girl named Emmeline Labiche who had traveled to America only to be driven mad by the discovery that her fiancé had given her up for dead and married another. Hawthorne told a minister friend the story, and the minister had repeated it to Longfellow. Manion had no idea why this particular literary vignette had stayed with him over the years, when so many considerably more crucial matters had escaped his memory. Thinking about it prompted a yawn.

Buddy consulted the steel Rolex on his wrist. "You gonna be late for dinnah. The lady ain't gonna like that."

"How's the old girl doing?" Manion asked.

"You call her the ol' girl and she'll part your hair for ya," Buddy replied. "She's egg-zackly the same, T-bone. She never changes. Like the Mississippi."

"The Mississippi changes all the time, you goddamned Cajun," Felix grunted.

"Well, *she* sure don't," Buddy said.

"Is there any chance J.J. will be at the house?"

Buddy stared at Felix, who shook his head. Buddy said, "Prob'ly not."

"How's he been doin'?"

"Like always," Felix said. But his voice sounded strange.

Manion started to ask another question about J.J., but Buddy broke in with a long, pointless story about a bank robbery in Harahan.

Five miles out of Breaux Bridge, as Felix aimed the Cadillac onto Interstate Highway 10—or as the locals preferred, I-10— Manion fell into a confused sleep.

6.

THE BENEDETTOS, *père et fils,* were having their after-
dinner demitasses at Toddy White's, a soul food restaurant that had
in the past few years, thanks to a number of overeffusive articles in
New York–based magazines, expanded its clientele from middle- and
lower-income black locals to upwardly mobile young white tourists
and a few of the more adventuresome white New Orleanians. Dining
at Toody White's had not been the Crawfish's idea. He had, in fact,
fought tooth and claw to change their venue to Antoine's or Arnaud's
or some other bastion of gourmet pride where he would be served by
waiters who knew and feared him. But Reevie's will prevailed, mainly
because he had some definite purpose in mind other than just an
evening meal, while the Crawfish cared only about filling his stomach.
And the Crawfish, too, read New York magazines from time to time.

It was only six P.M., early to have already finished dinner, particularly in a city where people don't usually sit down to dine until
eight-thirty or nine. But the elder Benedetto liked to sup very early
and then spend the next few hours visiting his various strip joints,
nightclubs, and illegal gaming parlors—places where he would not be
caught dead eating the food.

They were alone at a large table that had been set up expressly
for them in a low-ceilinged basement room adjoining the restaurant's
modest wine cellar. Meals usually were not served in that room, but
Reevie had selected it because he knew that his father would not dine
in the same area where blacks were eating. As he suspected, Toody

White, an imposing, solemn woman with skin the color of mocha, had leapt at the chance to keep the infamous Charlie "the Crawfish" Benedetto out of the sight of her respectable customers. It was an example of racial coexistence at its most harmonious.

Reevie had also arranged for a specific waiter to take care of them. Toody White had been curious, of course, since her establishment was not exactly Antoine's, where having your own server was a matter of status. But Reevie had made her a gift of two crisp new fifty-dollar bills to curb her curiosity and to ensure that she not inform the waiter of their arrangement.

For the better part of an hour the young Benedetto had watched as his father devoured two bowls of shrimp and crab okra gumbo, a dozen fried oysters, and enough cassoulet Toody—a mixture of pork, lamb, sausage, and goose—to feed a carful of button men. To top off the extensive meal, he was working his way through a mound of bread pudding with brandy sauce.

Charlie Benedetto spotted his son's smile. "What?" he asked, slightly irritated.

"You're amazing," Reevie told him. "What's your cholesterol count?"

Charlie "the Crawfish" Benedetto made a shooing motion with his pudgy left claw. "Save that bullshit for the clucks who go pound their guts in your gym. Perriggi says I'm in great shape. And you can ask any of those million-dollar lawyer bastards you hang around with what they think of Perriggi. The best goddamn heart man in the city."

Reevie shrugged. He rather liked his father, but if the old man wanted to clog his arteries with sludge, it only meant that he, Reevie, would be taking over with less effort than he anticipated. He said, "Let's get a pot of coffee that's a little warmer."

He turned to the open doorway and raised one finger, and Rillo, Charlie's bodyguard/chauffeur, bounded into the room like a paranoid puppy. Reevie told him his needs and Rillo grabbed the pot and exited. Scarcely a minute passed before their waiter arrived with a new pot of steaming, aromatic black liquid.

While the Crawfish was engaged in his nightly food frenzies, he rarely noticed the hand carrying the plates. But the meal had been an exceptional one and he was feeling expansive. He lifted his hooded eyes to the waiter and said, "You people put on a pretty good feed."

The waiter replied, "Thank you, sir." It was the sharpness of the "sir" that caused the Crawfish to emit a little grunt. Reevie regarded his father bemusedly as the fat man glared at the bespectacled young waiter. He had seen how quickly the temper could rise in that corpulent frame, how easy it was to inflame that narrow mind. He watched as the glistening pupils behind those hooded lids took in a light-skinned black man in his early twenties, neatly shaved, hair cut close to the scalp.

Reevie had already scrutinized the waiter, approving of the care the young man had taken with his appearance. Crisp white apron, fresh white shirt, bow tie that was not a clip-on. Meticulous in both dress and the serving of the food. And he seemed to be physically fit, carrying himself with the grace of an athlete.

The waiter was testing out quite well, Reevie thought. But this was definitely a moment of truth. The Crawfish growled, "You know who you're serving, boy?"

The waiter paused mid-pour and appeared to concentrate on the question. There was no expression whatsoever on his light-skinned, oddly delicate face. His dark eyes remained guileless behind rimless glasses. "Yes sir," he answered without a trace of a southern accent. "You're a very famous gentleman. Mr. Charles Benedetto."

The Crawfish continued staring at the waiter. Reevie watched them both, wondering if it would become necessary for him to defuse the situation.

Then the old man grinned suddenly. Grunting, he pulled out a roll of bills, peeled off a twenty, and stuck it into the patch pocket of the waiter's white apron. "You give the right answer, you get the prize. Just like on the quiz shows."

The waiter stared at him for a few seconds. His face was completely immobile, except for little knots that worked by his jaws. Finally, he smiled politely and said, "Thank you, sir. Will that be all?"

The waiter hadn't done or said anything to set the Crawfish off, but he had an attitude. The fat man said thunderously, "It's 'all' when I fucking say it's 'all.' Okay with you boy?"

The waiter understood that the Crawfish was losing control, but he was not sure how to answer his question without inciting him further. He turned to Reevie and asked him, quickly and unhesitatingly, "Is there anything more I can do for either of you gentlemen?"

Reevie grinned affably and lifted one eyebrow. "What's your name, waiter?"

"Leon, sir."

"Have you ever considered leaving this establishment, Leon?"

"I am most happy here, sir."

"And you make what? Three, four hundred a week in tips?"

Reevie saw Leon's face close up a bit. That was a fine, natural reaction—annoyance. A man's take-home pay was his own business, and not the subject of idle conversation. But Reevie was not making idle conversation.

"The specific amount isn't important, Leon," he said. "But I assume we're in the ballpark. And that's before estimated taxes and Social Security and maybe even some splits with the dishwashers."

Leon remained silent.

"Well," Reevie went on, "suppose I were to offer you five hundred a week? In undeclared cash?"

The Crawfish grumbled "Bah" and pointed to his cup.

Frowning, Leon topped their china cups with the thick, black coffee. "What would my duties be?" he asked Reevie.

"Act as my, ah, representative at my home."

Leon allowed himself a smile. "You mean, be your butler?"

"Nothing that formal. Make sure the maid cleans under the bed and the cook doesn't use margarine. If you're looking for a title, let's call you my domestic assistant."

"When would you need my answer?"

Reevie looked at the thin, gold-bordered square on his wrist. "How's about in ten minutes?"

Leon nodded and gave them both a half-bow before exiting. He moved at double speed.

The Crawfish scowled at his son. "What the fuck you do that for?"

"I like his style," Reevie said.

"The guy's a smart-ass, high-yella spade. He pisses me off."

Reevie tried to keep the annoyance out of his voice when he said, "You're the one doing all the pissing, Dad."

"You know, son, sometimes you piss me off too." The Crawfish picked up a spoon and tossed it through the door. Rillo retrieved it immediately. "Get that high-yella waiter to bring me a stick for this coffee. And a clean spoon."

"Make that three sticks," Reevie added.

Rillo nodded and moved swiftly from the room. The Crawfish growled, "Well, you got yourself a butler, Big Stuff."

Reevie shrugged a what-can-I-say? shrug.

"I wish you were . . ."

"What?" Reevie asked.

"I dunno. Less like your mother maybe. More like me. You need to be tougher."

"I'll be okay."

The Crawfish shook his big head. "Listen to me. I ain't gonna be around forever. Ten years maybe. Twenny at the outset. Hell, maybe twenny-five. Then what? I want you to step right in. I don't wanna see no young banana nose with a set of steel chinies step in and take the ball away, the way I took it away from Joey Scalise, his old man died."

Reevie's face grew solemn. Twenty-five years. Jesus. Not very likely. "I wouldn't worry about it, Dad. When the time comes, I'll be ready."

"But you don't take no interest in the way the business works. You screw around with that low-rent exercise place, which maybe'll keep you in beans and rice, but sure as hell ain't no ticket to Fat City. You don't seem to have no ambition at all that I can see."

Reevie almost choked suppressing the laugh. When he was sure he could keep a straight face, he said, "The time is far off—twenty or so years, like you said. By then I'll be ready."

Charlie Benedetto nodded, but he was far from convinced.

Leon returned with a tray on which three shot glasses filled with bourbon were balanced. He faced Reevie. "I go to school three nights a week," he said. "So I'd need to be free to leave at six."

Reevie looked up at him. He'd already known about Leon's schooling.

"Assuming that's no problem, I could start tomorrow, if that's what you want."

Reevie smiled. "It is indeed, Leon."

"You gonna hang on to that booze all night, boy?"

"Excuse me, sir," Leon replied, placing a shot glass in front of the Crawfish, who grabbed it and poured it into his demitasse.

Leon put a shot glass in front of Reevie, then pointed to the remaining glass with a questioning look on his face.

"That's for you," Reevie said. "To seal the deal."

Leon hesitated, then said, "Thank you, but I don't drink when I'm working."

"But you do take a drink every now and then?"

Leon nodded.

"Fine," Reevie said. He removed a pen and a business card from his pocket. It had the cartoon pelican emblem of his athletic club, the Sports Plantation, on its front. He turned it over and printed his home address and phone number, then dropped it onto Leon's tray. "Give that whiskey to my father," he said. "By the way, once you work with me, you won't have to put up with his bullshit anymore, okay?"

Leon's face showed nothing as he served the liquor and quietly left the room. The Crawfish exhaled mightily and wheeled on Reevie. "I think you're fucking confused about something, boy. I don't take that kind of shit from anybody, not even you. All I do is clear my throat and Rillo uses your new *assistant* for crab bait in the Rigolets. Don't *evah* talk back in me in front of a nigger again, or so help me, it'll be the last time you ever do."

Reevie successfully suppressed his smile. It was almost too easy to get the old man going. One more nail in the coffin. "I'm sorry, Dad. Sometimes I don't know what gets into me. I love you, though. You know that, don't you?"

Charlie Benedetto's eyes filled with tears. He reached out his arms. Reevie had to stand and bend forward so that his father could embrace him. "Dammit, son. Sometimes, hell, most times, I don't know what makes you tick at all."

"Like what?" Reevie said, easing away from the plump, moist hands and taking his seat again.

"Like that shit with the booze," the Crawfish said.

"It was a test. I wanted to see if he drank."

"You don't drink either, but you got booze in front of you."

"That was to make the test more effective." He pushed the shot glass until it was lined up with the others in front of his father.

The Crawfish shook his big head. "I drink three sticks and Rillo'll have to roll me home."

"Then don't drink them."

"They're on the goddamned bill," the Crawfish said. "I sure as hell ain't leavin' 'em for the coons in the kitchen."

The second shot of bourbon filled his cup to the lip. He looked from it to Reevie and smiled. "I swear to Jesus I am proud of you, boy. You got your weird little ways, but you get the job done. I just wish you'd set your sights a little higher, is all."

"You worry too much."

The Crawfish emitted a strange sound, somewhere between a belch and a hiccup. His version of a chortle. "I was just thinking about something this guy told me once about that fancy-schmancy school where I sent you."

"St. Croy's? What about it?"

The Crawfish waved his digitally inadequate hand in dismissal. "Nothing. Just that it don't seem to live up to its rep in all cases."

The comment nettled Reevie. His deep feelings for his alma mater almost led him into a discussion of the effectiveness of a St. Croy education. But he recalled the words of one of the masters at St. Croy's, a thin, bloodless fellow named Twining. "In the course of any negotiation," Twining had explained, "one should be particularly careful not to provide any information of substantive value other than that necessary to close the deal. If, for example, one were to announce to one's adversary—and any business opponent most certainly qualifies—that he or she was looking particularly fit, that information, gratuitous or not, might come back to haunt one in the form of bravado, overconfidence, and, in general, aggressive behavior. If, on the other hand, you tell them that they are looking particularly un-well, they may be so dismayed that they postpone or cancel all ne-gotiations. Even the most innocent comment may prompt unwanted consequences. *Say nothing more than must be said.*"

So Reevie settled back in his chair, quietly watching as his father, glassy-eyed now, lifted the third shot glass with an unsteady hand and got some of it into the coffee cup. Twenty years! Two more would be too many.

7.

TERRY MANION awoke on the back seat of the Cadillac to Buddy's phlegmatic voice announcing, "Hey, Lafayette, we almos' dere."

Manion raised himself, rubbed the sleep from his eyes, and ran his fingers over the car seat until he located the glasses that had slipped from his face during his nap. He adjusted them and stared out at what appeared to be a golf course. "Where are we? City Park?"

Buddy chuckled. "You bettah believe City Pawk. You ain't been away so long dey went and changed the pawks."

Felix guided the car off the divided highway onto Moss Street, heading away from Lake Pontchartrain. To their right flowed, slightly *en retard,* Bayou St. John. More than a century earlier, the waterway had earned its vague infamy by serving as a site for orgiastic dances and rituals presided over by the city's most popular voodoo queen, Marie Laveau. Now the area looked particularly tame, except for the traffic that was piled up all the way from Esplanade Street, waiting to enter the Fairgrounds for an afternoon of racetrack fun and desperation under the hot southern sun.

While the Caddy sedan crept along, Manion stared blankly at a cemetery that separated Moss Street from the track for several city blocks. St. Louis Cemetery No. 3 had been built on a stretch of high ground in the mid-1800s when the considerably more prestigious St. Louis Nos. 1 and 2, located near the French Quarter, filled to capacity with victims of yellow fever. To Manion this one looked pretty crowded too. Its densely packed crypts always reminded him of a stone housing project. A project for the dead.

Buddy pointed to a large apartment complex that had been constructed on the corner of Esplanade and the Bayou. "Ever' time we drive pass dat place, I wunner how dey get anybody to rent de apawtments overlookin' de cemertery. How'd'ja like to look at dead bodies ever' mawnin' wit' yo' coffee and sweet rolls?"

"That's why they sell venetian blinds," Felix told him.

"But that'd cut off the Fayh Grouns, podnah. Hell, as long as you stuck facin' stiffs, you might as well get sumpin' out of it. Watch the hossies go round."

Felix sighed, then went through the familiar ritual of cursing himself, sotto voce, for even bothering to talk to Buddy. Manion continued to stare at the crypts. It had been a while since he'd been to Cypress Grove to visit his father. His mother was there too, but he'd never known her, exactly.

Suddenly, he heard the faint sounds of a brass band playing a dirge. He lowered a window, and a trumpet solo on "Just a Closer Walk with Thee" drifted over the traffic noise. Manion spotted a funeral procession consisting of nearly a hundred friends and family. The deceased was residing in what appeared to be an ivory casket being carried by a quartet of bucketmen. Judging by the size of the crowd it was a burial of some importance to the community.

"Any idea whom they're sending off?" he asked the two men in the front seat.

Felix didn't bother to turn his head to look. He said, "Joe Sylvestre. Came that close to going up against the Brown Bomber. All he had to do was knock Tony Galento on his butt. But he didn't. End of story. Still, he was a damn game heavyweight. And a real crowd pleaser.

"He was seventy-eight. Ticker went out on him. Had a nice obit in the *Picayune* this morning."

Buddy nodded, impressed. "Some send-off!" he acknowledged. "Th' Basin Street Brass Band, in full swing." He pointed to a group of black men in black suits and black peaked caps playing trumpets, saxes, cornets, and even tubas, all highly polished and catching the still-hot waning sun. They swayed to the beat of the music. So did the rest of the mourners, many of them carrying furled umbrellas. It was like a choreographed movie scene, all that swaying. Later they would turn the body loose with a drumroll, and the mood would change. The umbrellas would be opened. The beat would pick up. The sorrow over death would be edged out by the joy of life.

"I hope th' Crawfish is footin' the bill," Buddy continued. "He sure as hell owed it to Joe. Fo' twenny years he shagged as much as ninety percent of th' gate and gave 'at poah sonofabitch a dollah a night to get his brains beat into gumbo. Hell, it wasn't a month ago I seen ol' Joe over at Charlie's Steak House, rootin' inna garbage."

"Well," Felix said dryly, "if I was going to root in garbage, I'd probably head for Charlie's too. Best beef in town." He found a hole in the traffic that took them around the Fairgrounds snarl.

Manion watched through the rear window as the mourners and the band and Joe Sylvestre, the almost contender, were swallowed up by the traffic and crypts and tombstones. He said, "The Crawfish isn't paying for the band. The burial society picks up the tab, for the music and for the funeral. That's what a burial society is all about. It's the only way blacks could make sure they'd get a proper funeral."

"I nevah heard that befo'," Buddy said. "But it makes sense. Hey, T-bone, maybe we oughta start our own burial sa-siety, the way some of us been droppin' lately."

"Oh?" Manion asked. "Did somebody die?"

Buddy glanced at Felix, who shook his head in disgust. "Naw, T-bone. Nobody lately. Jus' in general."

Manion sighed. He began to hum a tune as the Caddy made its way around a bend. He was almost surprised to realize it was "Oh, Didn't He Ramble," the song usually played by the funeral bands after the corpse had been laid to rest.

He was still humming it five minutes later when the sedan turned into a drive that led between gnarled oak trees to a two-story home about a hundred yards from the barely flowing Bayou. The house, of antique brick and gray-painted wood, was covered by an amazing assortment of plant life. Ferns and palm leaves and ivies worked their way up and around the brick, pressing against window screens that in some instances bore patches indicating that the vines had gained at least temporary entry. Bright red flamingo plants and yellow Golden Trumpet buds found room among the vines to break the shades of green. At ground level were a variety of aloe and succulents, with begonias for color.

Felix pulled up by a carport housing a pearl-colored Chrysler and a shiny green Jaguar four-door. "She's home," Manion said, indicating the Jaguar.

"Hell, T-bone," Buddy growled, "where d'ya think th' lady's gonna be wit' you back on yo' feet? Out eatin' ersters at the Acme? You th' proj-u-gal, man. You bettah get inside."

As Manion stepped from the car, Felix started the engine.

"Aren't you guys coming in?"

Felix shook his head. Buddy said, "Th' lady don't say for us to come in. So we don't. Th' lady'll tell us when to come give you a lift home, T-bone. You be good, heah?"

The lady in question was named Nadia Wells. She was, as best Manion could calculate, in her early seventies. She lived with her dapper, straight-backed husband, George, who was several years her senior, and a fourteen-year-old schnauzer named Louie who looked considerably more ancient than either of them. From this tranquil, oak-laden, pastoral spot, aided by a sixtyish secretary named Olivette and a series of ever changing cooks and housekeepers, Nadia Wells operated the Wells Agency, a company with a solid-gold reputation when it came to guard services and repossessions. Approximately thirty men and women were employed full-time by Nadia Wells, who relayed their assignments to them herself by phone from the screened-in back porch of her home along the sleepy Bayou.

She established the agency just before World War II, after shuttering two of her bordellos on South Rampart. She had been as famous locally as those other French Quarter madams, Gertie Yost and Norma Wallace, and at least as financially successful. But, as she once explained to a *Times-Picayune* reporter, "I just got tired of listening to all those young ladies complainin' about life and old men complainin' about their wives. And my hubby George's a deMolay and never was comfortable with me in the profession. So I said, That's it! I'd made some good money and some good friends. And I used them both to start a new business. And with *it,* I made me some more money and some more friends."

Manion's path crossed Nadia Wells's when he was at rock bottom. Raised by a single parent who had given him anything that money could buy, he'd grown up a bookish, somewhat aloof young man who felt his mother had deserted him by dying at his birth and who made very few friends for fear that they would desert him too. Instead, he would spend his hours alone, reading, or traveling great distances by streetcar and bus to movie houses where afternoon films were unspooled. If his real life was shy of friends, his fantasy life was rich with adventurers and spies and cowboys and private eyes.

Thinking back on it later, he wondered if it hadn't been the entirely fictional code of fair play instilled in him by movies and books that prompted him to dismiss out of hand the career in the diplomatic corps his father had arranged for him. He enlisted in the army, pushing himself through the rigors of basic training at Fort Leonard Wood in Missouri and moving very proudly into Army Intelligence, a name that his father insisted was a contradiction in terms.

It was while studying German at the Defense Language Institute in Monterey, California, that he met, at an after-hours club in nearby Seaside, the beautiful Gillian Duplessix, a lively and flirtatious young woman from his home town who was then keeping company with a wealthy Army lieutenant who was rumored to be CIA and whose studies in Kurdish, Baluchi, Tajiki, and, of course, Farsi, did much to legitimize the rumor.

Manion's service stint placed him in West Germany at a time when most of the action was in Iran, but the experience gave him needed confidence and toughened him, mentally and physically. Still, he was not quite tough enough to handle the double desertion that fate tossed his way seven years later. First had been his father's suicide, prompted, everyone assumed, by a combination of illness and certain improprieties discovered at his bank, the Century National. Almost immediately, Manion's wife of barely three months—the former Gillian Duplessix, whom he'd met again at an elaborate dinner party the previous debutante season—left him, because he was "too much of a southern gentleman for her," according to a hastily scribbled note taped to the liquor cabinet. Rather than ponder the precise meaning of her critique, he'd opened the cabinet and removed a bottle of Cabin Still whiskey.

He left the house only twice during the next few days. The first time was to clean out his desk in the sun-bright space he'd occupied as head of security of the Century National Bank. The new officers of the bank had terminated his contract—quite correctly, he thought, all things considered. The second time he left the house was to pick up a case of Cabin Still.

He was in a hazy, half-drunk state the day that Nadia phoned. He had heard of her, had in fact seen her once—copper hair upswept, thin as a Giacometti sculpture—dining with her quiet, soft-spoken husband in the good room at the old Arnaud's and being attentively catered to by the maître d', Billy Spino.

She got to the point right away. Her strong yet musical voice informed him that she had been a friend of his father's. Imagine that! An infamous courtesan and his banker father! But then the old man had been full of surprises, none of them particularly amusing. She wanted to know how she could help. Manion hung up on her.

One night, as he staggered from the Absinthe House, eighty-sixed for probably the final time, two men pushed him into a gray sedan and drove him to a private hospital on the River Road, where a doctor name Farber, since deceased, supervised his drying out.

On what he called his Final Day of Atonement, the two bruisers, Felix and Buddy, arrived to escort him to the house on the Bayou. They had seemed to be the most hardened of thugs. But in Nadia Wells's presence, their faces beamed like schoolboys'.

Manion, of course, behaved badly. He insulted the two men. Then he insulted Nadia, telling her precisely how much he resented her interference. She in turn, without ever dropping her lilting southern lady accent, gave him a tongue-lashing that would have done a river pilot proud.

"You're a useless, disgusting, arrogant little shit," she wound up. "But you'd better drop that spoiled rich kid act like a bad habit, sonny. You're no longer rich and no longer a kid, and that leaves only the spoilage. Not a commodity currently in demand. So get in step or take the pipe. That decision's yours. If, however, you feel you must raise your voice against me one more time, I'll have Buddy and Felix drag you out to that bayou and drown you like a skunk. Now, while you're thinking that over, how about a good stiff shot of hooch? No? Then maybe you've still got enough brain cells left to learn a thing or two."

Manion had enough cells left to realize that he was in the presence of someone worthy of his obedience. At her request, he went to work for the Wells Agency as an apprentice, dogging the tracks of an operative named J. J. Legéndre, a tough old bird who'd been a cop and a con man and a lot of things. Legendre taught him as much about the gumshoe business as anyone could. At the end of three years, Nadia Wells fired Manion.

She nudged him into opening his own office, even found the

vacant house on Merchant Place for him. He suspected that she'd sent most of his first clients his way, but never knew for sure.

All that had been years ago, and it had been at least six months since he'd visited her house on the Bayou. It looked the same as always. Husband George was resting in a hammock down near the water. Olivette was in the kitchen supervising a black girl who couldn't have been over eighteen in the preparation of a dinner that had been delayed at least an hour waiting for him. And Nadia was in her favorite wicker chair on the porch with Louie, the ancient schnauzer, wheezing at her feet.

She was wearing a blue gingham shirt and a denim skirt, no stockings, and tiny black penny loafers, one of which dangled from a foot that rested on the edge of a footstool with a needlepoint top. Her short, cropped hair, which for some of her life had been a bright henna and for much of her life an elaborately coiffed copper, was now as white as shampoo suds. Her triangular pink face was wrinkle-free, even when she was distressed as she was then, speaking harshly into the mouthpiece of a no-nonsense, standard-issue Southern Bell telephone.

"Well, I hope you realize that the muffaletta cost you a day's pay, you idiot boy!" Her swimming pool–blue eyes, as cold as Freon at the moment, spotted Manion over the rimless glasses that she wore low on her aristocratic nose. The hand not holding the phone waved him forward. She gave him a wink.

"Not applicable," she said sternly into the phone. "It is not enough just to repossess the vehicle. You've got to hang on to it, boy. You don't stop for some goddamned sandwich when there's even the remotest chance somebody's on your tail, waiting to take the car back. . . . Now, stop trying to make me think you're anything but a dumb coonass, and get back to that fella's house and repossess that car again." She paused for a beat, listening, then added, "Well, of course he'll be waiting. And all I can say is, if he uses his shotgun, you better damn well get in the way of the pellets. I don't want that Porsche damaged."

She slammed down the receiver and smiled at Manion. "The ordeals of being in the business world, hon." Her blue eyes crinkled as she looked him up and down. "Well, you appear to be downright healthy and remarkably fit for a fella who couldn't hit the bed with his bottom a couple of months ago."

Manion winced. "You saw me then?"

"Who do you suppose took you off that plane and drove you to the Spa?"

"I . . . I thought it was the detective, Bloodworth."

"I sent him home after he delivered you. No sense paying his freight all the way to the Spa."

"You paid him?"

"The agency did. What did you think?"

"I thought Margee had." Margee was his former sister-in-law.

"Oh?" Nadia Wells looked down her nose through the glasses at him. "Whatever gave you that idea?"

"I was working for her when . . . when I did what your repo guy just did. When I lost control of the situation."

She nodded. "That happens sometimes in our line. You ran into a case where there were too many variables."

"Anyway," he said, "I assumed that Margee was taking care of my, uh, rehabilitation."

"I'm afraid Mrs. MacElroy hasn't any particular feeling for workmen's compensation. And, in fact, there isn't a whole lot of money left in that particular family."

"Then you picked up the tab at Evangeline Spa?"

"The agency did. Now you come over here and give an old dame a little sugar."

She held her smooth cheek out and he kissed it. Her skin was dry but surprisingly firm. It smelled of lilac powder.

He was about to take a wicker chair across from her when he remembered that it was a very rickety, almost perilous perch where Nadia placed visitors who were not to be encouraged to stay too long. He selected the wicker couch instead.

Since Nadia had mentioned that it was the agency and not her personally who paid for his rehabilitation, Manion realized that she had some sort of quid pro quo in mind. He wanted to clear that up right away. "Exactly how would you like me to repay the agency?" he asked.

"We'll talk about it before you leave. Right now"—she turned away from him and raised her voice—"If Miss Olivette can stop running around like a chicken with its head cut off, maybe our very late dinner might proceed!"

"Any time you all are ready, Queenie, Lou-Ruth and I have this end covered," came Olivette's cigarette-and-cognac rasp from somewhere inside the house.

Her expressive face registering mock surprise, Nadia rose easily from her chair. She picked up a long-handled bell—the kind school-marms in western movies used to ring—and gave it a few shakes. This prompted her husband George to slide off his hammock and move toward the house, yawning.

Within minutes, they were seated at a long birchwood table in a brightly lit room with dark green walls and pale wooden trim. Nadia was at one end of the table. George, who'd taken the time to put on a tie and a dark blue blazer, was at the other. Olivette sat across from Terry, her flat, wide-eyed face with its sharp, upturned nose focused on the closed kitchen door. She was a big woman, with massive breasts that protruded like gunwales pressing her silk blouse to its limits and beyond. Her unnaturally jet-black hair was tucked under a turban that more or less matched her mauve pleated slacks. Manion wondered where in New Orleans a woman might purchase a turban in this day and age. Maybe she made them herself. Maybe they were antiques from the forties, when Olivette, then a very young woman, had been one of Nadia's most popular hostesses.

Olivette held her breath while Lou-Ruth, the latest cook, carried in the huge redfish courtbouillon and placed it on the table in front of Nadia. Nadia's eyes paused briefly on the girl's T-shirt, a bright or-ange one that read; "Stop Apartheid Now." Then she stared at the fish, sniffed at the red sauce, and trailed a fork through it.

Nadia broke off a hunk of redfish and sampled it daintily. She paused, then smiled at the girl. "Not half bad, honey."

The girl smiled back and said, "Wait'll you try the corn bread," curtsied, and returned to the kitchen.

Nadia snapped at Olivette, "Was that curtsy your idea?"

Olivette shrugged.

"She's too good a cook to have to curtsy to anybody, even Paul Prudhomme. No more curtsying around here, unless it's done for ironic effect. And that T-shirt, it goes. I have no complaint with its message, but I don't want to have to look at Day-Glo orange before I eat."

"Maybe she's got one in simple black or white," Olivette grum-bled sarcastically.

"That'd be just fine," Nadia said. "Now, before George passes out from hunger, perhaps he could say grace and we'll dig in."

They ate heartily. It was the best food Manion could remember. George, who had taken up art a few decades ago, expounded for a while on some exhibit at Delgato Museum that he'd recently visited. Olivette discussed a few household problems that needed solving. Nadia mentioned a book she'd read about religious wars through the ages. From time to time, Manion would look up from his plate to find the old woman staring at him with a strange smile on her face.

After the green salad and fresh strawberries, Nadia asked Manion to carry their two demitasse cups to a small room off the dining area. There were several places in the house where she conducted business. This was her study/office, wood-paneled, with bright red filing cabinets against a far wall and soft suede-covered furniture. She sat at her desk and Manion picked a chair that he remembered as being moderately comfortable.

"Is this when we talk shop?" he asked.

"I'm trying to make up my mind if you're ready for it."

"I'm fine," Manion said, eighty-five percent convinced.

"You know, sonny, that I don't believe in candy-coating the pill when there's medicine to be administered."

He gave her a puzzled look.

"It's some goddamned awful news," she said. "Can you take it?"

His mind spun through the list of people who meant something to him. It was a remarkably short list, and he'd been given hints. He asked, "J.J.?"

"He's dead, sonny."

The breath went out of Manion as if he himself were giving up the ghost. He had never considered the possibility of J. J. Legendre's mortality. During that period that they had worked together, J.J, though he had edged past middle age, had been able to outrun, outtalk, outbluff and outlast him. A man of boundless energy and big, bony physique, he seemed as durable as any of the movie legends that had had as much to do with the molding of Manion's character as his own family. Of course, John Wayne had met his fate too, and Cary Grant . . . and his father.

"How?" Manion heard himself ask.

Nadia hesitated, her eyes locking onto his. "He ate the gun," she said almost wistfully. Then she added, "Or so they say."

"Is there some doubt?"

She sighed. "J.J. never struck me as the kind of fella who'd go out that way."

"No," he agreed. "When did it happen?"

"Two weeks ago. Your doctor advised against my—"

"The funeral . . ."

"We sure as hell didn't make a big thing of it. George, Olivette, and me, a couple of the fellas J.J. bummed around with—Gorman, Lucerno, Pos Fouchette, and that crowd—Felix and Buddy, of course, and some sad-looking little gal who was the latest in a line of J.J.'s 'nieces.' Couldn't have been more than a teenager, with the brain of a three-year-old. Oh boy, it was worse than depressing. No priest, of course, on account of the suicide."

Manion nodded. "I remember how that works," he said.

Nadia knew that Manion was replaying his father's funeral in his head. She had done the same thing. That one had been much worse. She had not even been able to join the mourners at the grave site but had remained in her rented limousine, hiding herself and her tears behind tinted windows.

Manion took a sip of coffee. It was thick and black. The chicory added its own bitter kick. Coffee had not been allowed at the Spa. He said halfheartedly, "Maybe there was a reason."

"You mean like cancer or heartbreak?" Her voice took on a hard edge. "J.J. wasn't one to give in to adversity of any kind. Oh, he might edge around a difficult situation, but he wouldn't crawfish away from it."

"Then what? You think somebody killed him?"

"It's as much a hope as anything," she admitted.

He tugged at his ear, trying to look at least half as skeptical as Humphrey Bogart, who'd created the gesture. "I suppose you managed to get a copy of the pink sheet?"

"And the yellow sheet," she replied. Her left hand went out to her desk and found Xeroxes of both the investigating officer's and the coroner's reports, which she passed to him.

What they told him was that Jaime Jarrod Legendre, age sixty-four, had, on the specific night in question, died of an apparently self-induced gunshot wound to the head in his rented apartment in the Alligrette Building, the bullet piercing the palatine and continuing on through various bits of tissue, gland, and muscle before exiting through the parietal bone, eventually lodging in the spine of a book resting on a shelf across the room: John Chase's *Frenchmen, Desire, Good Children,* a humorous history of New Orleans's streets that became a local best-seller in the early fifties.

Manion's optically enhanced blue eyes scanned the reports without blinking. When he looked up, he said, "There was a note, and everything else seems to indicate suicide. If it was murder, the killer knew the game."

Nadia placed a burning-hot hand on his. "If it was murder, I want you to find out."

He stared at her. "Why? A Catholic burial?"

"Oh, the hell with that, sonny. J.J. was as lapsed as they come. And it's just a bunch of decaying flesh and bones buried out there at St. Louis Number One. I just want the satisfaction of knowing that I wasn't wrong about *him,* too."

The words were out before she realized what she'd said. She scowled, searching Manion's face to see if he'd understood the implication.

His expression didn't change. It was one of the things that annoyed her about him, his poker face. It was an invaluable asset to his occupation. But at times it was damned aggravating.

"What about his will?" he asked.

"None was found."

Manion cocked an eyebrow. "Did he mention anything in his suicide note about what he wanted done with his possessions?"

"Nothing like that, sonny. Just a few scribbled words about having nothing more to lose."

"He used those words, 'nothing more to lose'?"

Nadia nodded. "The obituary in the *Picayune* said the note may have been a reference to a song. It was a nice obit, by the way. I had a talk with the editor."

"J.J. wasn't a loser," Manion said, "and I can't believe he'd have thought of himself as one."

"Well," she said, "his checking account at the Hibernia Bank didn't indicate he'd been winning much lately. It didn't quite cover his bills and the funeral." She opened a file drawer. "The little girl took one of his pipes as a remembrance. I scored something for you that might be a bit more practical." She placed the object on her desk. It was a thin leather pouch that Manion knew contained an assortment of instruments that could open almost any lock. He had watched while the picks paved the way for numerous car repossessions over the years.

He thanked her and slipped the pouch into a pocket of his sport coat. Then he asked, "What's the name of J.J.'s last niece?"

"Slo. Slo Bentine."

"Is that some kind of nickname?"

"According to her mom, she was christened Ursula. They're from the Ninth Ward, where they sort of make up the language as they go along. So maybe in Ninth Wardese, you might abbreviate Ursula as Slo."

"Did she go back home to the Ninth Ward?" he asked.

"Pos would know. I think he saw to it she got back home after the funeral."

Manion excused himself and went through the house to a library where Nadia had a private line that wouldn't interfere with incoming business calls. He dialed a number and, while waiting for his party to respond, studied a series of amateur artist George Wells's pastels that hung on the wall between two bookcases. They seemed to be depictions of pale, round pinkish blobs. He couldn't figure out what they were supposed to be.

Pos Fouchette answered on the fifth ring. There was a lot of noise in the background—music, men's voices shouting, the tinkle of ice cubes against glass. Fouchette sounded as if he had a cold in his long nose. He also sounded drunk. "If this be Cherie, get your ass ovah heah, girl. We outta brew."

"This not be Cherie," Manion said, mocking Pos's singsong voice. "This be Terry Manion. And you've had enough brew."

"Terry Manion, by damn? Wel, mah fren'. Well-come back to de lan' of the liv-ring. Buddy's ovah heah tol' us you back in action. We got us a bourrée game goin', Terry, make you a fortune in a hour. You come on ovah."

Manion smiled in spite of the situation. "Not tonight, Pos. I'm a little tied up."

"Got some fine berled crabs, Terry. Buddy brung 'em and we seasoned 'em with everythin' in de pantry."

"Pos, I'm looking for Slo Bentine."

Pos Fouchette hesitated a few seconds. Then: "You don' wanna have nuthin' to do with her, Terry. She's just a silly kid."

"I want to talk to her."

"Why?"

"Ask her about J.J."

"You can ask me," Pos said. "I know as much about the man as that dumb *femme* Slo."

"Then *we* can talk tomorrow," Manion told him. "Where does she live, Pos?"

"You sumpin', Terry. Got that one-track mine, just like the old witch." The reference was to Nadia Wells, and it was not made bitterly, though years before she had fired Pos for sleeping on the job. Pos called Nadia a witch because he sincerely believed she practiced voodoo in her house on the Bayou.

"I understood you had the girl's address," Manion said. "But I suppose I could call around . . ."

"No, Terry. I know where she live. It's on Roclay, just this side of Arabi. I . . . uh, she's liv-ring with her mama, Terry. Her mama dint wanna take her back after J.J. passed on. So she keepin' a kinda low profile. I wouldn't go out there tonight, fo' instance. Just cause her trouble an' you ain't gonna get no talk in. Yoah bes' bet is to get her to meet you away from home."

"You have a phone number?"

Pos hemmed and hawed some more and finally gave him the number. They ended their conversation without Pos providing Slo Beatine's address. Manion decided not to press it. He wondered if Pos had some sort of relationship with the girl.

Manion replaced the receiver, frowning. Nadia stood in the doorway. "You don't have to get the whole job done tonight, sonny. J.J's not in any hurry. You want to stay over here? Your place is gonna seem a mite lonely."

"Thanks, Nadia, but I'm anxious to get home and start putting things back in order," he said. One of George's globular pastels caught his eye.

"What are these things?" he asked.

The old woman smiled. "What do they look like to you, sonny?"

Manion shrugged. "I have no idea."

Nadia said, "Considering you were once a married man, I'd expect you to be a bit more knowledgeable about such things. They're women's breasts. D cups, I would imagine. When George was younger, he was a real tit man."

8.

POS FOUCHETTE was having trouble concentrating. Since the game of bourrée was a fast-moving combination of poker and bridge in which cars and homes had been known to change hands, inattention could be costly. "You bou-ray, you sonofabitch!" Lee Gorman shouted at him across the card table. "Match the goddamn pot, 'fore I gets angry."

Pos shook his head, trying to clear away the boozy fog. "How much we got in there?"

"How much?" Buddy Lapere exhaled, in between massive bites of a soft-shell crab poor boy dripping with hot sauce. Buddy put down his sandwich and reached out to slap Pos behind the head. "You bettah wake up, Possum, or you gonna lose your pirogue an' your pole, too."

Pos dodged the hand and stood up angrily. He took a wad of bills from the pocket of his plaid shirt and peeled off two tens, throwing them onto the pile of money in the center of the table. "That enough, dammit?"

Gorman's big, thick fingers separated the bills. "Another twelve, Pos."

Pos carefully removed a five and a ten from his roll, placed them in the pot, and extracted three dollar bills. He backed away from the table. "Deal you out, Pos?" a tall redhead named Steiner asked as he shuffled the cards.

"The man jus' bou-rayed, Steinah," Buddy said. "He gets a chance to win his money back."

"Naw," Pos said. "I'm out for a few hands. Gotta make a call."

Buddy stared at Pos, who was his cousin and whom he had known since he was a small boy. "What's goin' on?" he asked.

"Nothin', Buddy. Jus' sumpin' I gotta do. Dammit! I fed the goddamn pot. I gotta get an excuse from you to leave the table?"

"Not from me, cou-san," Buddy said, and reached for his poor boy, obviously stung.

Pos coughed and backed away from the suddenly silent table. "I didn't mean to take your head off, Buddy. I just gotta do somethin'."

"So do it," Buddy said, gesturing with his sandwich.

Pos went into his bedroom, ignored the Leroy Neiman prints that decorated the walls, and sat down on his Cajun King Size bed, which was still rumpled from the night before. He dialed a number, then decided to light a cigarette while he waited for somebody to answer.

The response came so quickly he did not have time to get the Zippo into place. "Yes?" Slo Bentine's dazed child's voice cooed in his ear.

"Hi, honey, this be Pos Fouchette."

"Oh! Hi."

"Your mama home?"

"No," Slo replied. "She's at the movies, with Mrs. Tamonia from next door."

As if Pos cared who the hell Mrs. Tamonia was. The important thing was that Slo was alone. "I bettah come by," he said.

"Why?"

"To see you, of course."

"What for?" Pos knew she was not acting coy, that she really had no idea why any man would want to see her.

" 'Cause you be a pretty little thang."

"Oh," she said, then added, "I don't think that's so good an idea."

"What's not good about it?" He got the cigarette lit, finally. But the tobacco tasted as bitter as crabgrass.

"I mean, you were a friend of J.J., and he and I were . . . you know. And I don't think it would be right, him being dead only a few weeks. Besides . . ."

"Now, darlin', I can assure you J.J. won't be givin' a good goddamn if we see each othah. He has got his mind on othah thangs, like do his wings fit and how's he gonna keep the dirt off that white gown."

She giggled. "It's good to think of him looking like that, with wings and all. He was a great man, Pos. Best I ever knew."

"I be a pretty good man too, hon. You'll see."

"Not like him, Pos."

He stubbed out the cigarette. "I guess not. Anyways, I be there in a half hour."

"My mama'll be home in an hour." It was a warning.

"I'll hurry," Pos said, strangely elated but not certain he wasn't doing something stupid.

Two decades before, an eighteen-year-old Pos and his twenty-two-year-old brother, Foster, had bade farewell to Ciel Bleu Bayou, the smell of their father's sun-dried nutria and muskrat pelts still in their nostrils, and made their way to the Crescent City. Since then Pos had fallen in love infrequently. With bar women mainly. But those affairs of the heart had soon been terminated either by him or by them. Slo Bentine had seemed quite different from the others, ever since their meeting at J.J.'s apartment.

He had stopped by to drop off some surveillance photographs of a transvestite who had supposedly stolen a ring from J.J.'s client, another transvestite. What use the detective had for the photos, Pos couldn't imagine. His assignment had been to take the pictures, and that's what he did. J.J. had been on the phone and Slo, dressed in a bright yellow bikini, had been taking the sun on the balcony, lying on a large black and white Saints towel with tiny little plastic eyecups covering her lids. She looked like the Cat Woman or something.

She must have sensed his presence because she sat up suddenly and removed the cups, exposing eyes the color of emeralds and the depth of the Gulf at high tide.

It was the first time in Pos's memory that he actually envied another man. He envied J. J. Legendre with all his heart and soul. He confessed it to his priest and to his brother, Foster. The priest told him to pray for the strength to overcome temptation and the near occasion of sin. Fos, in typical fashion, suggested that Pos simply take the girl away from the old fart. But Pos could not do that. J.J. was his friend.

When he received word of J.J.'s death, his first thought had been of Slo. Only later did he begin to realize that J.J. would never have taken his own life, that someone must have gone to a lot of trouble to make it look as if he had. With that revelation came the dreadful suspicion that he, Pos, may have been an unwitting party to the death. Because of his lust for a beautiful young girl, he may have said the

wrong thing to the wrong person. He was afraid to find out if this was
so. Instead, he chose a self-imposed penance: he would not see Slo
Bentine again.

But that was changed now. The girl could be in danger. Which
was why he kicked the Trans-Am's speedometer to seventy, almost
flying along St. Claude Avenue. He'd take care of her, smooth things
out.

Within twenty-five minutes, record time, the polished red
Trans-Am was rumbling down Tupelo Street and onto Roclay, cruis-
ing through a flat patch of unremarkable residential neighborhood, its
inhabitants settled in for the night. He braked in front of a house so
white it seemed to glow in the moonlight. He was disappointed that
Slo had not met his expectation, was not waiting for him. She had not
even turned on the porch light—for him or for her mother.

He shuffled his feet nervously as he waited for her to respond to
the door chime. Then she was standing in the crack of the door,
wearing a sweet summer dress of powder blue patterned with little
yellow flowers. She peered out suspiciously. "Is that you, Pos?"

"Maybe if you turned on the light . . ."

"It's burnt out. Wait a sec and I'll go get my purse."

She was more than a second, but less than five minutes. When
they were in the car, she asked where they were headed.

"A movie, maybe. There are guys playing cards at my place, but
I tol' 'em to be gone in an hour."

"Then what? You don't expect me to go to your house?"

"Apartment," he said. "Yeah. You see, you got a problem you
don't know about."

She sat forward anxiously, apparently ready to spring from the
car. "It's you who's gonna have the problem."

He shook his head. "No, no. You don't unnerstan', *cher'*." He
looked at her helplessly, then blurted out. "If you knew J.J. good
enough to love him, you must know he dint do that to hisself."

She slumped back against the plastic seat cover and started to
cry.

"There's this fella, name Terry Manion. He's a good enough
fella, but he was real close to J.J.—"

"I know about him," she interrupted, sniffling. "J.J. talked about
him a lot."

"Well, Terry's been away."

"I know where he's been."

"Anyways, he wants to talk wit' you about J.J."

"So?"

"I think he means to set the record straight on J.J., which is fine, except that he thinks you might be able to help him."

"Me?" Her pretty, puffy lower lip dropped in surprise.

"Well, *cher'*, you be J.J.'s girlfriend. Terry figures if anybody knows what he might of done to get hisself killed, it be you."

"But I don't know anything."

"You don't have to convince me, Slo. An' it's not Terry you got to worry about. But if he starts to stir thangs up, maybe somebody else figure you know thangs. Then it won't be so healthy for you."

She stared at him, understanding fully what he was saying but trying to find some way of refuting it. Finally, she said, "What can I do?"

"I'm 'onna he'p you," he said. "We go to the movies firs', then to mah place on Gen'l Pershing. I make a phone call or two and we get this worked out. Okay?"

"You can do that?"

He nodded, proud to be able to contribute to her salvation.

"Why?" she asked.

"Why what?"

"Why are you getting involved in something that might get you in trouble, too?"

"Because I . . ." He took his time with the words. "I care for you."

"That's silly," she said. "You don't know the first thing about me."

"I know enough," he said.

"That's silly," she repeated. But she was studying his face now. He felt good, as if his life were suddenly on the upswing.

9.

AT PRECISELY eight o'clock, Felix deposited Manion on the cracked sidewalk in front of his office/apartment on Merchant Place. The dour driver's nose twitched as he surveyed the short, three-block street that was almost hidden on the far edge of the French Quarter. At its beginning, where it met Canal Street a block and a half away, two gentlemen were staggering out of a dim barroom called the Captain's Curse. Several semicomatose human shapes were spending the night huddled in doorways. Manion's two-story building was flanked by darkened shops of dubious enterprise—the Crescent City Finance Company, a Mafia front; and Plauche's Old Gold, a temporary repository for stolen goods—and was itself faintly ominous, with a shop window draped in black. At its center was an easel on which was displayed a faded poster for the film *The Third Man,* a tale of betrayed friendship and failed romance that was one of Manion's favorites. "You need any help with your bag?" Felix asked.

Manion knew Felix well enough to realize that he did not want to leave the cherished Cadillac to the mercy of the neighborhood. "I'm fine, Felix. Thanks for the lift."

"Part of the job, Terry," Felix said, obviously relieved. "If you need me, just give a holler. Buddy'll be available too, soon as the bourrée game plays out. Of course, that could take a week."

Manion grinned and waved as the car pulled away. He carried his luggage up the stairs to his building and had just inserted his key in the lock of the dark blue front door when he heard a thumping on the display window of the old-gold shop to his right. Its owner, Plauche, stood there, a bizarre figure framed in backlight, gesturing him over.

First, Manion unlocked his front door, releasing a cascade of fliers and advertisements that had been wedged into the jamb. He ignored them and deposited his luggage.

Plauche was a large oblong box of a man with a wide, loose-skinned white face and thinning lampblack hair. He was dressed for the evening in a floor-length silk Oriental gown of reds and yellows and greens. His shark's mouth contained more gold than his entire window display, and he gave Manion full benefit of its glittering wonder. "Welcome back home, neighbor. Your mail has been piling up." His voice was something between a whine and a croon.

Manion followed him inside the shop. It was meticulously clean, with sparkling glass counters under which an array of ancient coins, belt buckles, rings, cuff links, and other golden geegaws winked in the overhead light. There was a tap-tapping sound from an open door in the back of the shop that grew louder until a small, almost hairless dog appeared. It was a mutt, possibly a mixture of dachshund and fox terrier, that looked to Manion as if it were on its last legs. It waddled over to Plauche, who hunkered down to allow it to leap into his arms.

"Ah, that's Daddy's boy," he said, grinning at the pathetic creature. "My little Tokay-Mokay."

He carried the dog back to Manion, shifted its weight to one arm, and reached under the pristine counter. He lifted a cardboard box embossed with the name of Gus Mayer's department store. It was filled with Manion's mail.

"There was a Mr. Legendre who said he had permission to use your quarters?" Plauche said, making it more a question than a statement.

"I was away longer than I'd planned. He was helping out."

"Ah. Well, had I been notified, I could have provided him with this—it appears as if some of these bills are urgent. But, as you may recall, that was not your instruction."

"You did just fine. There's nothing that can be done to my credit rating that hasn't been done."

Plauche nodded, but his normally placid face seemed troubled. "Something more?" Manion asked.

"Your Mr. Legendre. It was in the *Picayune*. He did the Dutch."

Manion nodded.

"He was a close friend?"

"Close enough."

"I'm sorry." Plauche's eyes shifted from Manion's to his display counter. He took a little sidestep with his dog, as if to distance himself from the awkwardness of the situation.

Manion turned to leave.

"I, ah, should inform you," Plauche said, frowning. "You had two . . . visitors."

Manion stared at him, waiting. Plauche's discomfort increased. His face twisted. "I hate this sort of thing, but I feel I must tell you."

"Please do."

"Two men. I'm afraid they may have robbed you."

Manion's mind spun. The orderly at Evangeline Spa and now this. Was it some spillage from the business in Los Angeles? He thought not. That had been a fait accompli. "When?" he asked.

"Possibly two weeks ago. Just before the witching hour. I'd closed up the shop and was in back, engrossed in an intriguing little book titled *The Second Coming: Satanism in America*. Perhaps you have read it? No? In any case, I heard them pass in the alley. One had a particularly gruff voice, as if he'd had surgery on his throat. He was complaining that the other man had kept him waiting. I turned out the light and moved to the front of the store. Through the window, I saw them forcing your door and going in. I watched for an hour before giving in to sleep. I never heard them leave."

Manion understood that it would never have occurred to Plauche to call the police. Fences did not maintain open lines of communication with law enforcement officials. "People wander down that alley all the time," he said. "What made you check out these two guys?"

Plauche gave him the barest hint of a smile. "The voice of the second man," he said. "I recognized it. I . . . have had business dealings with him. The hoarse man was a complete stranger."

"Your . . . associate, he did the jimmying?"

Plauche nodded. "They're not supposed to work this neighborhood. I am most emphatic about that. I consider this a breach of faith."

"What's his name?"

Plauche hesitated. "I am confused by conflicting loyalties. In my business, one does not bandy information about one's clients. On the other hand, I am adamant in my wish to ensure the tranquillity of my neighborhood. You notice that the drunks from the Captain's Curse never behave badly in this block. It's because of Tokay, of course, my little killer dog."

It was a new one on Manion. He stared at the sickly dog, wondering if Plauche was joking. The pale man was evidently serious, because he continued, "It's something I read in a book on home security. You feed your dog a very, very small amount of arsenic powder, increasing it until his system can carry it without harm. Unfortunately, it isn't very kind to his coat, but eventually, the animal has enough poison in his bloodstream that his bite will cause real damage, possibly death."

Manion frowned. "That sounds a little, ah, theoretical."

"Of course. But who among us would care to test the theory, eh? New Orleanians are a superstitious lot, always eager to believe something new. Since word of Tokay's dark side has spread, there has been considerably less bother in the neighborhood, less noise from the inebriate clientele of the Captain's Curse."

"But it didn't stop two men from breaking into my apartment," Manion said.

Plauche sighed. "Alas, no. The little twerp had the effrontery to violate my neighborhood. Odie Shecksnyder is the name he gave me. It has the ring of truth."

"Know where he lives?"

Plauche shook his head. "No, but . . ." He plucked a red notebook from the pocket of his kimono, turned its pages, grunted in self-satisfaction, and scribbled something on a square pad next to his phone. "His phone number," he said, handing the scribble to Manion. "Five months old, but it may still be current. These fellows *do* move about, however. I hope they went easy on you, Mr. Manion. You know I couldn't interfere."

"Thanks for the information," Manion said, pocketing the paper.

"No trouble. No trouble doing a neighbor a favor." Plauche's eyes searched Manion's face. "Try brewer's yeast for that."

"For what?"

"Bad diet. I can tell by your skin tone. From my experiments I have learned what poisons in food can do. You have not been eating well. Put two tablespoons of brewer's yeast into your morning o.j. Makes the flesh more elastic."

"Right," Manion said to be polite, trying not to focus on the dewlaps hanging from Plauche's jawline. He moved uncertainly out to the sidewalk. He could feel the fence's eyes following him all the way back to his building.

It was impossible to tell that the door lock had been picked, and the advertisements and junk mail littering the door were a nice touch, assuming they'd not been jammed there since the break-in.

The interior of the building was neater than when he'd left it. The downstairs office area had never been so tidy. The framed film posters—Robert Mitchum looking wearily at a neon caricature of Charlotte Rampling for *Farewell, My Lovely*, Alan Ladd giving Veronica Lake the benefit of his dreamy *The Glass Key* smile while Brian Donlevy observed them both bemusedly—were perfectly level, not tilted slightly as they had been in the past. The various odds and ends, from an antique Stork Club ashtray to a huge model aircraft that appeared to have been constructed around the skeleton of a small animal's head, had been rearranged to best advantage. An even patina of recent dust covered desktop, files, and visitor chairs. The books on the shelves were neatly aligned.

Upstairs, a brown spread had been removed from the closet and draped crisply over the bed. Three books were stacked on the floor beside a stuffed chair and an ugly gooseneck reading lamp. Nothing seemed to be missing. He dropped his luggage on the chair's matching footstool and removed the pouch containing J. J. Legendre's lockpicks from his pocket, placing it carefully on top of his dresser. Then he wandered into a small bathroom with dark purple walls, where he discovered the first missing item: his grandfather's straight razor, which he'd kept in the medicine cabinet beside his own Gillette.

He retraced his steps to the downstairs office and opened the drawers to the desk. The case records did not appear to have been disturbed. Four of them were tagged in a familiar hand that was not his own. J.J. had evidently initiated a few odd jobs out of boredom or curiosity or both.

Manion placed the quartet of new case records on his desk, opened the long front drawer, and pawed through a variety of papers and receipts until he found a slightly battered photo. It had been taken by one of J.J.'s "nieces," a brunette he vaguely recalled. In it, he and J.J. were standing in front of Laffite's Blacksmith Shop on Bourbon Street, shaking hands like two businessmen congratulating each other on a smart piece of work. What they had actually been celebrating was Manion's somewhat involuntary emancipation. Nadia

Wells had just given him his walking papers, pushing him into business for himself. The smile on J.J.'s face looked more than slightly
rueful, as if Manion's youth were a reminder of his approaching
retirement. The smile on Manion's face radiated confidence and ea-
gerness. Army Intelligence had taught him the basics, and his work as
head of security at his father's bank had introduced him to the intri-
cacies of white-collar crime. But it was J.J. who'd exposed him to the
down-and-dirty tricks of the trade, had trained him in the skills of
secret and open surveillance, had honed his technique in hot-wiring
cars for repossession, planting bugs, covering his tracks, had clued
him in on the con man's art of employing a variety of names and
occupations to gather information, including the use of a portable
printing press to create credentials in his car in a matter of minutes.

J.J. had doubted the wisdom of Nadia Wells's decision to try and
turn a self-indulgent, lazy, overeducated alcoholic college boy into an
effective, shrewd working detective. He'd been amazed at how quickly
and enthusiastically Manion had warmed to his new occupation, had
in fact begun to elaborate successfully on the lessons he'd learned.
What J.J. never understood was that while the world of private investigation was somewhat different from anything Hollywood or
crime novels had led Manion to expect, it still had one similar, powerful appeal. It forced him to concentrate on people and problems
that had nothing to do with his own rather empty life.

At least that's what Manion had thought when his picture was
taken with J.J. on that bright and cheery afternoon. He gave the
photo a final wistful look before placing it back in the drawer. He
turned his attention to the case folders and flipped through them. A
foreign-car dealer had needed someone to help his repo men through
an unusually busy weekend. A Hattiesburg woman had wanted her
brother followed discreetly during his two-day visit to New Orleans;
he was only a sophomore at Ol' Miss and she was afraid he might
come to harm in the "notorious" French Quarter. An elderly man had
requested an armed companion for an overnight trip to New Iberia.
A restaurant owner had sent J.J. to the bayous looking for a missing
oyster opener whom he considered "the best in the business." J.J. had
not been able to find the guy. But he had closed out the other files to
the clients' satisfaction.

Manion wondered how much time his late friend had spent in the
apartment. Had he cleaned it? Had the thieves?

Manion spread out the mail on the desktop and picked through it. Once the brochures and fliers and duplicate bills had been deposited in the wastebasket, he was left with seven overdue invoices and two letters, one business, one personal. He smiled wanly at what that said about his social life.

In his minuscule kitchen, he tested and tossed out a carton of spoiled milk. He took an opened can of French Market coffee from the fridge and used it to fill the top portion of a porcelain dripper. There were several inches of Abita Springs water left in a plastic jug which he poured into a dented pot. He set it to boil on a four-burner stove with a surface no larger than a chessboard, then spent the next fifteen minutes ladling the boiling water, tablespoon by tablespoon, over the chicory coffee grounds. From time to time, he glanced through the door to the desk with its unopened letters. He was only mildly curious.

Finally, he carried a cup of thick black coffee to his desk. He removed his checkbook and methodically paid his bills. Only then did he treat himself to an examination of the two letters.

They were not really worth the wait. The first envelope contained a check and a note from Mrs. Anna Lamotta Bruns, a client who had hired him earlier that year to follow her father, a widowed wholesale food magnate who had taken up with a woman one third his age. Mrs. Bruns did not want her father to marry this woman and, with the mumbling of a few legal and binding words, make her the heiress to half of his produce empire. Mrs. Bruns had hoped that Manion might be able to provide her with some hard proof that the woman was not a manicurist, as she proclaimed, but a prostitute or worse. Mrs. Bruns mentioned a sum far in excess of his regular fee if he would guarantee results. Manion had agreed to snoop around but with no guarantees. As it turned out, the woman seemed to be exactly what Mr. Lamotta thought she was—a rather pleasant, affectionate manicurist.

Mrs. Bruns's note informed him of her dissatisfaction with his report. The check was for services rendered. It was in the amount of ten dollars, roughly one fiftieth of the price Manion had quoted her.

He folded and tucked the check into his shirt pocket. Then he slid open the file drawer, removed the folder marked "Bruns," and neatly stapled the letter to its inside cover.

The second letter was from his sister, Suzanne, his senior by four years, a single woman who lived in Alexandria, Louisiana, where she did something or other with computer graphics for the city. Her message was short. She wondered why she'd not been able to reach

him by phone. She was worried about him. He traced her Spencerian
hand, which he found totally unfamiliar. He didn't think she had ever
written to him before.

Annoyed with himself for having forgotten to inform her of recent developments, he picked up the telephone, pleased that it was
working (one of the strongest dunning letters had been from Southern
Bell), and dialed her number. After three rings, Suzanne's recorded
voice notified him that she was not at home. He would have been
disappointed if she had been. He left a message that he hoped would
reassure her about his physical and mental health and ended by in-
viting her to dinner in New Orleans, date to be determined.

Replacing the receiver, he suddenly realized that there was no red
light on his answering machine. Someone had turned it off. And the
mini-tape containing incoming messages was missing.

He found a blank tape in the desk and recorded a new outgoing
message. As he moved his hand toward the telephone again, he paused
to activate a small FM radio beside it. Almost immediately, the room
was filled with the painful if melodic sounds of Rigoletto discovering
his dead daughter. Manion winced and spun the dial to WWNO and
the live sounds of a local progressive jazz group.

He lifted the receiver, waited a beat, then dialed a number it had
cost him a case of Jack Daniels to learn. At the sound of an electronic
tone, he punched in Odie Shecksnyder's phone number. There was a
whirring sound broken by a mechanical voice that responded with the
phone's location. A Henderson Parish address.

Manion replaced the receiver, clicked off the radio, eased himself
from the chair, and headed toward the front door. Dr. Courville had
warned him about pushing himself too soon after leaving the Spa. But
he felt better than he had in months.

Before leaving the house, he thought a minute, then turned and
climbed the stairs. He opened the closet door and found his Colt .30,
removed it from the holster, and checked to see that it was fully
loaded. He dropped it into his coat pocket as he descended the stairs.

It had been so long since he'd carried a gun that it felt like a
sandbag dragging down his coat. But the confidence it gave him was
worth the weight.

His mood was so high he speed-walked the three blocks to Zohran's
Garage, where he kept his 1964 Mustang convertible. Timo, the night

man, was deep into a TV crime program when Manion marched in on him. He was a big, bald black man with a Dizzy Gillespie goatee. His eyes shifted toward Manion behind gold-framed aviator glasses and he brought a huge hand down flat on the desktop.

"I be damned. The man has come to reclaim his chariot. Finally."

"I hope you've been taking good care of it, Timo."

"Good care, my man? I personally been driving it to Slidell every weekend to see a fine girl over there. Probably put at least five thousand miles on it."

Manion smiled, but he wasn't sure that Timo was kidding. The black man pushed his chair back to where an assortment of key rings dangled from hooks on the wall. He lifted one with the tips of two fingers and tossed it through the air to Manion.

"In all serios-ity," Timo went on, "the ever beneficent Mr. Zohran was wondering when he might see a check for the past three months."

"I just got back," Manion said. "I'll drop it off tomorrow."

"Mr. Zohran will be mellowness personified," Timo said, winking and returning his attention to the small TV screen.

The Mustang had belonged to Manion's father, who had kept it in mint condition. Its top rattled, as convertible tops will. And there were none of the contemporary touches, like seat belts or headrests. But it *was* air-conditioned, and that was all that counted when you drove through a New Orleans summer. Manion couldn't imagine owning any other vehicle.

Timo had taken good care of it. Its original racing-green paint glistened spotlessly under the naked ceiling bulb. Manion slipped behind the wheel and experienced a momentary dizziness. Dr. Courville had prepared him for that. He shook it off, started the engine, and eased the car from its slot and out of the garage.

The Mustang handled better than he remembered, but driving seemed almost a new experience. He worked his way through the French Quarter's noisy and anxious traffic to St. Louis Cemetery, where he picked up a faster-paced Claiborne Avenue. He stuck with that as it jutted southwest pasts the Superdome, then made a large half circle and headed in the general direction of Joanelle Street, just over the Henderson Parish line, where he might find Odie Shecksnyder if his luck was with him. Or not with him, as the case might be.

10
.

REEVIE BENEDETTO and his father caught the early dinner show at Charlie's Place, the Crawfish's ridiculously overpriced nightclub in the heart of the French Quarter. The bill that night consisted of an all-white Dixieland band that did its best to duplicate Louis Armstrong's charts, followed by a pneumatic canary-blond songstress from northern Louisiana who belted Stephen Sondheim show tunes while writhing seductively in skin-tight spandex.

The singer had barely begun a medley of numbers from *Sweeney Todd, the Demon Barber of Fleet Street* when Johnny the Wolf joined their table. Leering at the songstress, he said, "Look at the nay-nays on that broad. I gotta get some of that."

The Crawfish, who was still drunk from the shots of bourbon he'd had with his after-dinner coffee, chortled and said, "Try not to mess up her vocal cords, huh?"

Reevie took a deep breath and managed to keep the disgust he felt for both of them under wraps. He said, "I'd better be going."

"Sit a minute," his father said, He too was watching the singer. Suddenly, his face twisted in confusion. "What the fuck's she singing about? Meat pies? That broad's singing dirty songs in here?"

Reevie said, "It's from a Broadway show about a barber and a woman who sells meat pies. It takes place in London in the nineteenth century."

"Yeah? I still don't like it. Johnny, when she's finished, you go talk to her and tell her to forget about the fuckin' meat pies, huh? It's disgusting. We got people eatin' here."

"I'm heading out, Dad," Reevie said.

"Hold on. I wanna get something straightened out. Johnny tells me you been usin' Croaker."

Johnny reluctantly turned his attention from the singer to Reevie. He had a lazy alligator smile on his face. Reevie said, "I had a problem and Croaker helped me with it."

"Johnny tells me you had a guy zipped because of a dame."

Reevie nodded. He had twisted the truth a bit when he'd explained his need for Croaker to Johnny.

"It never occurred to you to mention this to me?" his father asked indignantly.

"I thought he'd cleared it with you, Chawlie," Johnny whispered.

Reevie knew this was not a time for weakness. "It wasn't important enough to bother you," he said. "It was a personal thing."

"Personally, son, it is my belief that only a dumb fuck zips a guy because of a broad, no matter how fantastic she is in the sack."

Reevie was suddenly amused by the thought that he killed a man for a woman. But that wasn't why he'd ordered Croaker to do away with J.J. Legendre. He said, "I guess I'm more of a romantic than you, Dad."

The Crawfish blinked. "So tell me the details. Johnny here ain't much for details."

"I dint know any details," Johnny winced.

"This guy was a two-dollar snoop," Reevie said easily. "He was blackmailing this woman I know and I decided to help her out. I asked Johnny to take care of—"

"Croaker wasn't my idea," Johnny interrupted. "I don't like that son'bitch. He's too fuckin' arrogant."

"Yes," Reevie admitted. "I told Johnny to use Croaker, because it was Croaker who helped me when I was in college."

The Crawfish nodded and said, "I remember. He's a pro."

"Well, he wasn't such a pro on this one," Johnny said. "I had to personally take care of a loose end. And now I hear there may be more."

"Is this true?" the Crawfish asked his son.

"No," Reevie said with conviction. "It's all done. If there'd been anything for you to worry about, I'd have brought the matter to your attention."

Charlie Benedetto looked from his son to his brother. "Johnny," he said, "go do your thing with Miss Meat Pies, huh?"

Johnny gave him a nervous smile and left the table without meeting Reevie's eyes.

Reevie said, "It's too bad Johnny's IQ isn't on a par with his sex
drive."

"You shoulda told me you were using Croaker," the Crawfish
said.

Reevie nodded. He stood up. "I have to run."

"Me too," his father said. "I've had enough culture for one
evening with the meat pie song. Jesus!"

As they walked through the brightly lit front door area into the
steamy night, the Crawfish asked, "You need a lift?"

"No, thanks."

"I gotta limo."

"No. It's okay. I'm just walking a few blocks."

"A few blocks? What the hell you gonna do? Get laid?"

"Eventually, maybe," Reevie replied.

"In the Quarter? Not one of *our* bimbos?"

"No."

"The others, you riskin' a bunch of disease. Hell, with ours you
riskin' a bunch of disease."

"I'm not seeing a hooker, Dad. You should know me better than
that."

"Ah. This is the dame who's been causin' all the trouble?"

Reevie nodded.

The Crawfish shrugged. "So you let this woman walk by herself
in the Quarter at night? With all the panhandlers and coons?"

Reevie was finding it increasingly difficult to ignore his father's
prejudices. "She's having dinner with friends. I'll take a little stroll,
give them time to finish their meal. Then I'll have a demitasse with
them, and she and I will go off on our own."

The Crawfish pretended to look hurt. "Well, if you prefer pussy
to an evening wit' your old man . . ."

"Anytime," Reevie said.

The Crawfish laughed wetly. "Yeah. I would too, if my plumbing
was as rust-free as yours." He was still laughing inside his garishly
elongated Mercedes when it pulled away from the curb.

As it turned the corner, Rillo, seated behind the wheel, gave
Reevie a two-finger salute. Reevie waited until the car was out of sight
then looked at his watch. He was running late.

11

•

ODIE SHECKSNYDER'S address on Joanelle Street in Henderson Parish belonged to a clapboard building surrounded by a shell yard and a twelve-foot-high chain link fence. No light to be seen. No sign of humanity. Across the ruptured asphalt street squatted a HiTex gas station, looking equally lively. But a bare yellow mosquito bulb just over the pumps gave the impression that, sooner or later, somebody might stagger by to unlock the office door. The station's fenced-in neighbor held no such promise.

Manion parked his Mustang near the gas station and studied the shadowy clapboard. At some point in history, it had been painted royal blue, but too many rainy nights and relentless sunny days had bleached it and decorated it with Rorschach patterns of flaked enamel. An ancient sign on its dark display window read, sans irony, "Faron's High Times Lounge."

As Manion approached the chain fence, he saw that the padlock on the gate had been sheared off. Why anyone would have gone to that much effort to enter the place, he couldn't begin to imagine.

He did not trespass immediately. Instead, he walked to the gas station, where a phone booth was outlined in the dim yellow light. Its glass panels were punched out, initials had been carved on every square inch of its standing interior, and its city directory was long gone. But the phone worked. Only a second or two after he dialed Shecksnyder's number, he could hear an echoing response from somewhere within Faron's High Times.

Leaving the pay phone dangling, he went to his car and removed
a pencil flash from the glove compartment. He walked to the fence
gate, and pushed it open with his foot. He paused, listening for the
sound of an animal—a slavering dog, perhaps—racing toward him in
the darkness. But all he could hear was the ceaseless ringing of the
telephone coming, it seemed, from the rear of the building.

Manion sloughed through the weeds and wild grass that tufted
the potholes in the shell covering. The ground-floor windows were
painted black. As he trudged on, the ringing grew louder, vibrating
through the building. He discovered that the sound was escaping into
the night through the rear door, which was open an inch or two.

Manion shoved the door tentatively with the toe of his shoe. It
creaked. He tried to ignore the hairs that stood on the back of his
neck. He remembered his gun, removed it with some difficulty from
his pocket. He was not actually a gun person. He might be able to hit
a man at four feet, but probably not where he wanted to; beyond that
distance, firearms only frustrated him. Their main appeal was the
often false security they provided. Though in truth he did not feel
particularly secure. Gun in one hand, penlight in the other, he entered
Faron's High Times.

The first room he encountered was unhealthily humid. There was
a damp grittiness to the cement floor. The pungent odor of stale beer
and ancient seafoods settled on the heavy air so naturally it might
have grown there, like mildew on old sneakers. Manion cast a pale
light over the long, mottled sinks hugging both walls, probably used
for opening oysters when the High Times was in its prime.

To the right was a storeroom cluttered with crates—factory-
packed items like TV sets and VCRs, microwave ovens, the odd disc
player. Manion assumed they were selections from the Odie Shecksnyder stockpile.

The ringing phone was in a dusty alcove beside a pool table
covered by a soiled mattress and pillow. His penlight picked up an
assortment of freshly laundered slacks and shirts with colors and
patterns appropriate to a Hawaiian betting parlor, all hung on a wire
formerly used for keeping score of the pool games. Manion poked at
them with the barrel of his gun, before he spotted a pair of black
suede loafers on the pool table.

He lifted the left, then the right. As he replaced the right shoe, he
felt a faint shifting within it. A lift, perhaps, or a heel cushion. It was

actually a sheet of paper, folded and refolded. Manion put the Colt into his coat pocket and spread the sheet on the pool table. It was a handwritten list, scrawled in obvious haste. He shined his light on the page and felt the adrenaline start to pump in his veins. It was J.J.'s handwriting, scrawls mixed with block letters. He had seen it a thousand times on notes and instructions and critiques of his reports.

It had never been easy to decrypt J.J.'s personal shorthand, of which this was a prime example. It read like a list of unconnected nonwords: "Gay-no," "New At C," "Wash in Basin Bur So," "Baton Gay," "Gallig, LaP & Fur-no." There were other, even less decipherable squiggles. Manion refolded the sheet and stuck it into his coat pocket.

Moving slowly, he found a standing trunk that contained Odie Shecksnyder's undershorts and socks and colored T-shirts. A handsome leather two-suiter rested by the trunk. In it were both clean and dirty underwear and white socks, two colored slacks and three white slacks, four white shirts and a pair of white tennis shoes. There was also a Dopp kit brimming with electric razor, a toothbrush, and toiletries, including a plastic bottle containing Zantac pills, which, according to the druggist's label, were "to be taken as needed for stomach disorders, not to exceed 300 milligrams a day." Shecksnyder had apparently not unpacked from a recent trip. His ulcers must not have been acting up.

More toiletries—another razor, various hair treatments, deodorants—were in what was once the male customers' lavatory. The heirloom straightedge razor that had been stolen from Manion's apartment was not there. The detective picked up a toothbrush, ran his finger over its bristles. They were as dry as fallen leaves.

The main room of the High Times was furnished in Depression Barroom chic. Rough hardwood tables, nicked and notched by bored patrons and the passing years. Chairs that wobbled and creaked. A workingman's bar with dust a half-inch thick on its pocked surface, and past it, empty shelves with paint eaten away by cheap booze and even cheaper solvents.

Manion moved behind the bar, tested the faucet and found that it worked. Someone, Shecksnyder probably, had added the shiny new microwave oven that rested on a counter next to the empty cash register. Dirty plastic plates lay in the sink collecting mold.

Manion found the dead man in the walk-in freezer in the kitchen.

His murderer had thoughtfully activated the refrigeration, so that the body, resting on its back, had been more or less preserved, a ghastly blue white, except for the crusted-brown cut across its neck from beneath one ear to the other. Frost covered the man's babyish face. His eyes were open, glassy. His black hair was a hard, icy cap. He was wearing dark slacks and one of his Hawaiian shirts. The last time Manion had seen him, he'd been dressed as an Evangeline Spa orderly, using the name Oscar Saville.

Beside the body lay the razor that had belonged to Manion's grandfather. Brown stains on its blade showed under the patina of ice.

Dizziness ebbed and flowed through Manion's brain. Dr. Courville had mentioned possible bouts of light-headedness. Brief little warnings to slow down.

Manion steadied himself against the doorjamb, his fingers momentarily sticking to its surface. He yanked them free, but they stung as if they'd been kissed by flames. The sensation brought him around, cleared his head. Distaste wrinkled his nose as he moved toward the dead man and hunkered next to him, feeling chilled both physically and mentally.

He reached out a hand in the direction of the man's pants pocket and paused. The phone had stopped ringing.

Manion rose too quickly and dizziness overtook him once again. He stepped awkwardly from the freezer. He was vaguely aware of someone standing at the door. Then a hard substance—a leather sap filled with lead pellets, he was told later—smashed against his skull. There was no immediate pain. Merely shock, surprise, fear. Then nothing. The pain came later.

Faron's High Times looked as if it were back in business. The main room was filled with people. Manion was lying on his back on the long bar, with a blanket folded under his head for a pillow. Beside him, a young woman in a white smock was waving a small bottle of ammonia under his nose. He sniffed and tried to rise. His head felt sore and soft, a Halloween pumpkin slightly past its prime.

The woman drawled, "What's yoah name, please?"

"Huh?"

"Do you know yoah name, suh?"

"Terry Manion."

"That's fine. Now, how many fingers do you see?"

"At least three."

"More than three?"

"No. Just three."

A loud voice rang out across the room. "Guess that lets you off the hook, Landry. You didn't scramble Manion's brains after all."

Manion raised onto one elbow and swung his legs down, lowering himself to the floor.

"Sir, you really should . . ." the woman in white began.

"Don't worry about Manion, honey. He's had enough lying down to last a normal man a lifetime."

Eben Munn grinned at Manion. "Boy, you sure do get in the thick of it, don't you?"

Over Munn's shoulder, Manion saw cops of various stripes trying to look busy while the crime scene team sleuthed about collecting evidence. One tall plainclothes cop with a pinched, stubbled face and a diamond stuck in his left earlobe stared at him warily with steady, appraising eyes. Manion guessed him to be Landry, the man who'd sapped him.

A short, red-face, balding man in his early fifties with a fringe of graying dirty-blond hair and brown sun bumps on his forehead joined Munn at Manion's side. He was wearing an open-neck white sport shirt and a shiny gray suit with a leather ID pouch taking the place of a display handkerchief in its top pocket. "What exactly was you doin' in here, cap'n?" he asked Manion.

Manion stared at him without expression.

"This here's Joe DeLongpre, Manion," Munn offered by way of introduction. "He's been with the Henderson Parish Sheriff's Office so long he remembers the name of Delancey's horse." The reference was to Kevin Delancey, a sheriff of Henderson Parish in the late nineteen-forties who somehow was able on his meager salary to build a huge mansion in Kenner, complete with private stable. The "reform candidate" who eventually replaced him built his dream castle in Mandeville. The following election, Delancey ran on his own reform ticket, declaring that he had amassed so much money that he could finally afford to give the people an honest ride. In the spirit of Louisiana politics, he was reelected.

DeLongpre winced at the mention of Delancey, glared at Munn briefly, then turned back to Manion. "I axed you a question, cap'n."

"I was looking for a man named Odie Shecksnyder," Manion

answered. His mouth was dry and he looked wistfully at an ancient Jax Beer sign on the wall.

"Oh, you found him, Manion. Sure as hell did," Munn said, chuckling.

"Why was you lookin' for the man?"

"He was a housebreaker," Manion said.

"So?" DeLongpre asked.

"He broke into my house."

"Ah. So you slit his throat?"

Munn shook his head. "C'mon, Joe. Like I tol' you, Manion just got out of the box today and little Odie's been cooling off for a couple days at least."

DeLongpre wheeled on the bigger man. "What the fuck makes any of this your business, Munn? You guys don't have enough homicides in the city you got to branch out?"

Munn assumed an air of mock innocence. "Gee whiz, Joe. I was just toolin' around when I heard the name of my old classmate Manion coming from the squawk box. I figured I had some information crucial to the homicide, namely that Manion has been out of commission until this afternoon. Maybe save you from jumping to some wrong conclusions, wasting time while the real perps beat a path to Miami or Cuba or wherever the hell they go these days."

DeLongpre stared at Munn, then switched his attention back to Manion. "I'll still need a statement from you, cap'n. And we got some other things for you to sign."

Munn said, "I wouldn't sign anything that looks like a release, Manion, until you get your head checked out by your doc. My guess is, Landry used an illegal sap on you."

"That's it, you sonofabitch," DeLongpre spewed at Munn. "You don't come around here fucking with our business. You don't have no reason. You don't have no right. And you don't know what the fuck you're talking about. Landry"—he pointed with his thumb to the earringed detective, who was by then sitting on a tabletop near the door talking to a uniformed officer—"is a goddamned good cop, mister. Better than most you got on the NOPD. He sees a broken lock on the gate, comes in, and finds your old pal here standing over a stiff. What's he supposed to do? Shake his hand?"

Munn shrugged. He asked Manion, "Did Landry identify himself?"

Manion shook his head.

"Well, that would have been a good icebreaker," Munn said to DeLongpre. "You know, like they do on TV—'Police officer, freeze.' Considering the circumstances, that'd have been damned appropriate."

"I've had it up to here with you, Munn."

"Up to where?"

DeLongpre's eyes nearly popped as he struggled to get himself under control. Breathing loudly through his nose, he turned to the room and shouted, "Billet!"

A lugubrious fellow with a blue stubble lumbered forward. "Yeah, Joe?"

"Get this Manion guy's statement. What he was doing here. Where we can reach him we need him, like that. And find out where he's been spending his days. But don't take any guff off that asshole." He indicated Munn.

"Sure, Joe," Billet said, looking at Munn curiously. When De-Longpre had steamed off, he said, "You shouldn't ought to do that, Lieutenant. He's hard enough to put up with when he ain't angry."

"Don't believe that act," Munn answered. "Joe's just like all the girls. He loves me. Really."

Billet rolled his eyes and took a small tape recorder from his pocket. He thrust it out to Manion and began, "Last name first, first name last. And spell it please, for the steno."

"Just like all the girls," Munn repeated, waving across the room at DeLongpre and sending him an elaborate pantomime kiss.

12.

REEVIE BENEDETTO hurried past the dawdling tourists and Quarter denizens to the Hotel Rue Royal. He ignored the cluster of men in dark suits and ten-gallon hats milling around the front desk and took the elevator to the fourth floor. At room 407, he knocked once, paused, knocked twice.

The door to room 408, across the hall behind him, clicked open. He looked over his shoulder at a thick-chested young man whose tight-fitting sport coat did little to disguise the fact that he was a good old country boy, through and through. The country boy raised an Uzi until it pointed at him, sniffed air past clogged sinuses, ran a large red hand through his straight wheat-colored hair, and closed his slack jaw just enough to emit a sharp, quick whistle.

The door to 407 opened on a different breed of gunman. This one was South American, in white shirt and slacks, his hair in a ponytail. He had flat eyes. A small teardrop had been tattooed on one of his prominent cheekbones, the right one. He used *his* Uzi to wave Reevie into the suite.

It was the sort of overdecorated room one might except from a self-described modern luxury hotel. Smoked-mirror walls, the furniture all monochromatic leather and dark wood and chrome. Floor-to-ceiling windows facing the muddy Mississippi in all its dubious beauty.

Two men were seated in the room. A spindly old codger, wrapped in a loose-fitting seersucker coat and denim pants, perched on a black leather couch drinking something pale green and watching Robert De Niro posturing on a silent TV screen. His white hair, wispy as corn silk, framed a sun-baked, creased face. A cigar the size of a child's baseball bat poked past thin, pursed lips.

The other man—the one on the white leather chair—was poised gracefully, but he was soft through the middle, a fact that his expensively cut gray silk suit failed to hide. He looked like an overindulgent gigolo. His name was Emilio Vargas.

Both men turned to Reevie. The old man squinted at him through the smoke from his cigar. Vargas rose and approached with his right hand extended. "Reeves, *mi amigo.*"

As Reevie shook the offered hand, the Latin's other hand clasped his elbow. He permitted himself to be led around the couch until he was facing the old man. "Reeves, it is my pleasure to introduce you to Farmer Brown."

The codger did not stand. But he raised a thin arm and allowed Reevie to clasp a hand that was as strong as wood but just as inanimate. "Sorry about that stupid-ass name. But I ain't about to use mah real one in an unfamiliar room."

Reevie shrugged. He didn't give a damn about names.

The old man grumbled, "You a little late ain't cha, boy?"

"I was dining with my father. He's not happy with anything less than six courses."

"No kiddin'? I eat light myself. Simple fare. Homegrown." He chuckled. Reevie looked at Vargas, who shrugged a what-can-you-do? shrug.

"Like this hotel, for instance. Seen-yore Vargas was kind enough to have dinner sent up. All I can say is this here's the most expensive hash house I ever et in."

"I could suggest a few restaurants . . ." Reevie began.

"Screw that, Slick. Boyd and me didn't drive here to wine and dine. Seen-yore Vargas says you got a business venture to discuss. Let's be about it."

Reevie smiled. "You don't mind if I sit down first?" He took the chair farthest from the television set. He wanted no competition from Robert De Niro. He said. "The new legalized gambling bill is going to be passed."

"Yeah?" Farmer Brown was not impressed. "But we probably won't live long 'nuf to see it."

"The state is on the verge of bankruptcy," Reevie said flatly. "Some sort of substantial revenue is needed to pump up the treasury."

"Hell, boy. That's what they was saying years ago, back when oil got cheap as dog shit and this state started to bottom out. Only nothing happened."

"Nothing happened?" Reevie asked incredulously. "There's a lottery now. The state legislature has already approved riverboat gambling on the Mississippi."

"Maybe," the Farmer acknowledged the truth begrudgingly. "But are they making any money with that stuff?"

Vargas settled back in his chair, watching Reevie intently. Reevie was more conscious of hm than of the old coot, to whom he replied slowly, as if to a child, "The lottery giveaway is more than a half-million dollars. So it must be doing fairly well. And several very smart businessmen are betting a great deal of money that the gambling boats will pay off. I wish that I'd carved a piece of that pie. But since I didn't, I certainly don't want to miss the next opportunity which is casino gambling."

"Okay," the Farmer said. "So maybe it comes to a vote. And John Q. Public likes the idea of corner casinos. Then what?"

"Quite simply, we will be in control of the entire operation."

"How you gonna swing that?"

"There's not much doubt how the public will vote, once we get the whole business on the ballot. In two weeks, the state legislature will decide that it goes on the ballot."

"You know how the legislature's gonna go, huh?"

"Do you know if grass will grow after a rain?"

The old man sucked his teeth while he thought. "Granted it gets on the ballot and gets voted in," he said, "you still got one more hurdle to jump."

"The same committee that will recommend the gambling bill to the legislature will also be awarding the contracts. Five honest men and true. Would you like to hear their names?"

The old man leaned forward, impressed. "You bought every one of 'em?"

"Just three," Reevie told him matter-of-factly.

The old man thought that was hilarious. "That's all, huh? So, what do you want from the Farmer?"

"Money, of course."

"Your daddy's got more money than me."

"That's right. But it's his, not mine."

"You ain't willin' to risk your daddy's scratch, but you ask me to risk mine?"

"Risk has nothing to do with it. My father's not involved in this."

The old man raised a feathery eyebrow. "You cuttin' your daddy out?"

Reevie sighed. "He was never in. Is that a problem?"

The old man squinted, sucked his teeth again, and shrugged. He turned to Vargas. "You know that Charlie Benedetto ain't a part of this, *amigo?*"

"Of course. That is why we came to you."

Farmer Brown grinned at them. "I'll be damned. You gents are somethin.' Last year, when the seen-yore here and me worked out a marketing plan for my crack, I kept wonderin' what made the Crawfish change his mind about lettin' a little homegrown product into his precious New Orleans. Now I realize maybe he didn't change his mind at all. Maybe he don't know about that neither."

"You are not unhappy with our relationship?" Vargas asked.

"Hell, seen-yore, would I be here now if I was unhappy? No way. I don't give a crocodile fart if the Crawfish is in or out. But I can't help wonderin' . . ."

"What, *amigo?*"

"What would Benedetto do if he found out what you boys are up to?"

"Do we look worried?" Reevie asked.

"No. But that could be 'cause you're stupid. It's not just him, it's . . . you know, the whole organization."

Reevie stared at him, unblinking. "What makes you think the organization is still counting on *him* to run this part of the country?"

The smile left Farmer Brown's face. Here was something he hadn't considered. His long fingers rose to remove the cigar. He stared at Reevie for nearly a minute, then asked, "How much cash you need?"

"A million seed, to grease the chute, change a few minds, hire a few people. Nine million for the riverfront real estate, the architects' plans for the casinos, construction costs. A final two million for advertising and promotion. A total twelve million, which will buy you thirty percent of the net receipts."

"I put up one hundred percent of the money and receive only thirty percent of the net? Mister, there are men fishing for boots in the Bayou who are still waiting to collect net profits."

"Then let's say twelve percent of the gross."

The old man sucked his cheeks. His face looked as if it might cave in.

Reevie stood up. "It's my best offer. *We're* doing all the work. The only thing you have to do is make sure the money has some acceptable history. I understand you're good at that."

"I got a working farm. The government is happy as can be when I turn a nice profit."

"We're not talking about a fortune here. Only twelve million dollars. That barely buys a livable house in Southern California."

The Farmer stood creakily. He put out his hand and he and Reevie shook again. This time there was more power behind his grip. "It's a deal, podnah. You'll get the first five mil in two days. Free and clear."

Reevie smiled. The old man shook Vargas's hand too. Vargas nodded to Ponytail, who rushed to unlock the suite door. The door across the hall opened and the good ol' boy flanked the Farmer in the hall, his arm and his Uzi hidden inside a small piece of luggage.

When the door was shut and secure, Vargas flopped onto his chair, picked up the remote control, and clicked off the TV. Reevie asked, "Wherever did you find that obnoxious Neanderthal?"

"See! I have been saving you from the dark side of our business. The Neanderthal I discovered on a medium-sized farm near the Texas border just this side of Shreveport. I sought him out because I had to. Crack is rapidly becoming your country's drug of choice. I particularly enjoy the way it is being hawked: 'Buy American! Why should the filthy Colombians profit from your drug habit!' As a filthy Colombian, this offends my sense of . . . profit."

"But out of all the guys with farmland crack houses, why him?"

Vargas shrugged. "He was convenient. Able to supply four states. We do quite well."

"You're not breaking any records in New Orleans," Reevie said.

Vargas gestured with his hands. "Assuming you were merely amusing yourself with the Farmer, and that your father is still *número uno* in this part of the world, I would say we're doing okay. Were he not so, ah, influential, we could operate more openly and more efficiently."

"What will your people say if they find out you're underselling their white powder with the Farmer's rock?"

"The situation with my people grows more tenuous each day," Vargas said. "It is their own fault. Blowing up judges. Flouting the law. Making international enemies. They are reaping the whirlwind of bad public relations. Unlike us, they have not learned the importance of quiet power. Or of diversity." He smiled. "Enough economic philosophy. What are you drinking? Still Glenlivet?"

"I'd love to, but there is a beautiful woman . . ."

"With you, there usually is, *amigo.*" Vargas rose.

Reevie paused before leaving. "You know," he said, "we don't need the Farmer's money. You could easily finance this operation yourself, Emilio."

Vargas clucked his tongue. "How quickly we forget the words of our infamous alma mater. *'Never . . . never invest your own capital when you can invest someone else's.'* "

Reevie nodded and smiled.

"You know, it was I who convinced your father to send you to St. Croy's."

"I am well aware of that. I owe you for what I am today," Reevie said sincerely. "Thank you, *amigo.*"

He allowed himself to be embraced by the Latin. "Sorry I have to run. But the woman . . ."

Vargas smiled and nodded that he understood such things.

When the door to the suite had shut behind Reevie, Vargas walked to the bar and poured himself a tequila on the rocks. He took a sip and said to Ponytail, in Spanish, "The boyish Mr. Benedetto is so impressed by his own superiority. If his father is too foolish to kill him, someday we may have to."

Ponytail shrugged. Vargas envied the man his clarity and simplicity. You kill. You don't kill. It was all the same to him.

13

●

IT WAS nearly midnight when the Henderson Parish policeman, Joe DeLongpre, returned Manion's gun and told him he could go home. Eben Munn trailed along with him to the Mustang. "Hot wheels," the plainclothesman exclaimed. "Well, Manion, the night's still a youngster. Let's grab a quick one at this joint I know in Jazz City."

"I just came off of a chemical dependency program eight hours ago and you want me to grab a quick one."

"I thought you were in there for drugs," Munn said.

"Gosh, the psychological training you men of the law go through must be quite extensive, Eben. 'Dependency' is the key word. Drugs, booze—it's all poison."

"You mean you don't *drink*?"

"Nope. Not for a while. But when I did drink, when I was so looped I'd throw up on myself and fall asleep in alleys, I still prided myself on staying away from Jazz City."

"What the hell's wrong with Jazz City?"

"I remember when it was a warehouse area, ugly, rat-infested, dull," Manion told him. "Now it's block after block of boutique bars and theme restaurants. That's not my idea of an improvement."

"Maybe, but it's got this kind of anonymous quality."

"Fine," Manion said, getting into his car. "You need anonymity. I need sleep."

"Hold on, podnah." Munn loped around the car and slipped into the bucket seat beside Manion. "We ought to talk."

"About what?"

"C'mon, let's us go to Jazz City. As long as you're not drinkin', you can be the designated driver."

"Forget it," Manion said. "The self-help part of my treatment is that I stay away from bars."

"It's like the nuns used to tell us about the near occasion of sin, huh?"

"Exactly."

"Well, you're gonna shake hands with temptation tonight, podnah. Let's get rollin'."

Manion didn't move. "My head's sore where that bastard sapped me."

"I'll fix you up with a couple aspirin, you'll feel like doin' the 'gator."

"Forget it."

Munn's large head slumped to his chest. "C'mon, Manion. For ol' times' sake? You and me. You don't have to drink. Just sit there." When Manion still made no attempt to start the car, he added, "There's something you don't know about your pal J. J. Legendre's death."

"You lied to me at the Spa, when you asked about him."

"That was that crackpot shrink, Courville. He told me not to mention it. Me, what do I care?"

"What about J.J.'s death?"

"I'll tell ya. All I ask in return is a very small portion of your evening. I'll ask you some questions. You ask me some questions. All very friendly. In a nice anonymous place like Jazz City."

Manion started the engine.

It was edging toward one A.M. when they entered the Nola Olé! a dim, noisy, smoky nightclub filled with drunken, desperate strangers. It was Eben Munn's idea of heaven. He found them a table away from the frantic pickup action at the bar and out of direct earshot of the blaring sound system. He ordered a *cerveza*, then translated the word for the waitress. Manion ordered a Barq's root *cerveza*.

Surveying the room, Manion said, "This was an excellent choice."

"I knew you'd like it," Munn replied, ignoring Manion's sarcasm. "Well, podnah, suppose you tell me about Mr. Shecksnyder."

And Manion did.

"He went to all the effort of getting a job at that Evangeline place, just to steal a look at some kind of notebook/diary you were keeping?"

"That's the best I can figure."

Munn smiled at the waitress as she delivered their order. When she'd gone, he asked, "How did you know he'd broken into your house, too?"

Manion hesitated. "A neighbor told me."

Munn nodded. "A neighbor who recognized him, huh? Probably the fence."

"You know my neighbors?" Manion asked, annoyed.

"You'd be surprised the things I know about you, podnah. I'm thorough. I know more shit than you can imagine."

"Why?"

"It's my job," Munn said.

"Then maybe you can tell me about J.J."

Munn took a swig of beer. "You mentioned something to De-Longpre about a piece of paper you got out of Shecksnyder's shoe. What the hell was that all about?"

"DeLongpre thought I was hallucinating, because I couldn't find the paper. Landry, the cop who hit me, must have taken it."

"What was it?"

Manion again hesitated. "Just scribbles. J.J.'s handwriting."

Munn removed a pencil and a folded sheet from his pocket and pushed them across the table. "Show me."

Manion tried to duplicate the scrawl. "Gay-no," "New At C," "Wash in Basin Bur So," "Baton Gay," "Gallig, LaP., Fur-no."

Munn scowled at the sheet. "Looks like a job for Sherlock God-damned Holmes." He put it and the pencil back in his pocket.

"Okay, now it's your turn," Manion said.

Instead of replying, Munn pushed back his chair and smiled at a large, full-bodied woman who was strolling through the club staring at faces. He insisted that the woman join them at their table. She was wearing a red wig, a short red skirt, a tight red blouse, rather large red high-heeled shoes, and stockings that had a red tinge. Her fingers, which were tipped with red polish, clutched a red drink, probably some margarita permutation, since the establishment was ersatz Mexican. Manion was amused to note that none of the reds matched.

"I was supposed to meet an old friend," she said, regarding the crowded room wistfully.

"What luck, honey." Munn pried her drink from her fingers and placed it on their table. "Now you get to meet two *new* ones."

"Your buddy looks a little grumpy," she told Munn.

"He's been sick, but he's all well now."

Manion's head throbbed. He leaned forward, ignoring the woman. "You're a lying sonofabitch," he rasped.

Munn turned from him and asked the woman, "Do you mind if I call you Red?"

She smiled. "How'd you know my name?"

He winked at her. "I'm the one they call the seventh son."

Manion had had enough. He started to stand, but Munn waved him back down, then said to the woman, "You ever hear of a galoot named Benedetto?"

She looked uneasy. "Gee, I don't think I have."

"Fat, ugly little fucker," Munn said. "About so high. Has this hand like a claw."

The woman stood up suddenly. "I see my friend now," she said. She began backing away, bumping into the Nola Olé!'s customers like a two ball with too much spin. "Uh . . . nice meeting you," she almost yelled.

Manion turned from the curious sight to find Munn staring at him. "What about you?" Munn asked.

"What about me what?"

"You know Benedetto?"

"I've heard of him," Manion said. "Fat, ugly little fucker."

"Ever have any dealings with him?"

"No."

"What about his son, Reevie?"

Manion shook his head again. "Him, I've never even heard of. Does he look like his daddy?"

Munn grinned ruefully and picked up his beer. He emptied a third of the bottle into his mouth, swallowed, and said, "You're no fucking help at all."

"People have been telling me that for years."

"The lady at our table was one of Benedetto's whores," Munn said. "I know most of 'em by sight. This is one of his dives. It's a nice friendly place where young people come to meet for only five bucks a watered bourbon or three bucks a beer. I got no idea how much that goddamn root beer's gonna cost me.

"Anyway, by this time of night, Benedetto sends in the pros to make sure nobody goes home alone and unhappy."

"Sounds like a humanitarian."

"You sure you've never brushed up against him or his kid?"

"Not since I've been clean. When I was hitting the booze, it's anybody's guess. Are you going to answer my questions?"

Munn rubbed his eyes, then stared at his beer bottle. "Yeah, sure. They found a feather under your friend's body."

"What?"

"One feather. Goose feather. Duck feather. A fucking feather."

"I don't understand . . ."

"The only person who heard Legendre shoot himself was the guy who called it in, and he didn't leave his name. The other neighbors heard nothing. In itself, no big deal. But then there's the feather. To my mind, it at least suggests that somebody might have used a pillow to muffle the shot. Pretty weird behavior for a suicide."

"But it was classified as a suicide."

"It was simpler. The note looked okay. The evidence at the scene looked okay, except for the feather. And that's not exactly hard evidence of foul play, no pun intended. So the investigating officers took the easy way. That happens when your city's going broke and there aren't enough officers to handle all the work. You don't go looking for complications."

Manion slumped. He was exhausted.

"You better hit the road," Munn told him. "You look like shit."

"I'll take the insult if it gets me out of here. Don't you want a lift back to your car?"

"Don't bother," Munn said, rolling his eyes around the room. "This is a friendly crowd. I'll catch up with you some other time."

"Sure," Manion said, happy to be away from Munn, happy to be going home.

When he parked his Mustang at Zohran's Garage, Timo was draped across his desk, snoring in time to the music of the late-night TV talk show that was blaring in his ear.

Outside, clouds were bumping into each other and piling up in the dark sky. A warm, moist wind whipped the dust and discarded cups and wrappers along Merchant Place. Manion's head suddenly stopped throbbing. He didn't seem to be in any hurry as he strolled home. He was too tired to rush.

He had the key in his lock when a figure stepped out of the shadows and asked, "Terry Manion?"

Manion released the key. The idea of trying to draw his gun struck him as ridiculous. He turned to the figure and said, "What now?"

The moon poked through a cloud, shining down on a man who was shorter than Manion but considerably heavier. He was wearing a denim jacket, rough-worn denim pants, and a T-shirt. Possibly to compensate for thinning hair, his tanned and lined face sported a full beard. He said in a rapid, curiously high-pitched eastern seaboard accent, "Sorry if I startled you, but I've been here a hell of a long time, champ."

"You're Marcus Steiner, right?"

The man nodded.

"You look vaguely like your book jacket picture," Manion said. His weariness had taken him past the point of annoyance. "What the hell are you doing here?"

"Friendly type, huh?"

"It's been a long, hard day and I'm not happy about drawing it out much longer."

"Dr. Courville told me you were getting in today," Steiner explained. "The first day can be a real bear, so, being basically a nice guy, I gave you a call. Your machine said you were out. I kept trying every hour, and at midnight I figured I'd better drive over and see exactly how shit-faced you were. I've been here a long time for a guy with a full bladder."

"C'mon in," Manion said, entering and turning on the lights inside the house.

Marcus Steiner entered, looking around the place. He walked with his shoulders bent forward, vaguely bear-like. His bald head looked polished. "Nice digs," he said.

"Thanks," Manion replied. "There's a bathroom just past the desk."

Steiner moved toward the closed door, his eyes taking in the room. When he returned, Manion was still at the front door.

"You sure you're all right?" Steiner asked.

"Sleepy."

"What've you been up to? You smell like you might have been pushing your luck."

Manion glared at him.

"Excuse me, champ. But I'm an old hand at this. I'd know that booze-and-cigarette perfume anywhere. It makes my mouth water."

"I'm sober."

"I can see that. But I get the feeling you've been tempting fate. Fate cannot be tempted. You can."

"Going to the bar wasn't my idea."

"I'm not your preacher, champ," Steiner told him. "No explanations necessary. I'm here to help, not kvetch. You need me for anything, give a call." He took a card from his pocket and handed it to Manion.

"Could you soft-pedal the 'champ' business? It sounds like something from one of your books."

Steiner was a hard man to insult, apparently. He smiled. "Oh? You've read my books?"

"One of them. *In Salvador.*"

"A good choice."

"It must have been a tough one to write, assuming that it was written from experience."

Steiner hesitated, then answered, "Yeah. A tough one."

Manion yawned. "I'm sorry, but I'm going to fall asleep right here if I don't get to bed."

Steiner said with a grin, "We'll have plenty of time to talk about my problems and yours in the weeks ahead. There's something else I want to bend your ear about. When we've both had some rest."

Manion nodded. The thickset man was descending the steps to the sidewalk when Manion said, "Didn't they make a movie of *Women of Manhattan?*"

Steiner chuckled. "Yeah, if you can call it a movie. They used three dames from the stage who were about ten years too old and some young stud with an attitude who was a boyfriend of the producer. That's Hollywood for you. It's why there never was and never will be a movie made from *In Salvador.* G'night, cha—Manion. Sleep well."

As Steiner stalked down the sidewalk, Manion shut the front door, yawned for the hundredth time, and punched on the air conditioner. When he was sure that it was actually working, he climbed the stairs and went to bed without undressing. He'd done that before, but never sober.

14
.

THE CLOCK on the dashboard of Nadia Wells's shiny green Jaguar read 10:15 A.M. as the car purred down Merchant Place and parked in front of number 332. The lady, garbed in fawn-colored dress suit and silk blouse, paused to check out the street, then exited the car. She shook her head reproachfully at the *Third Man* window display, noticed her reflection in the glass, ruffled her hair, and continued on to the dark blue door, where she affected a scowl. She pressed the door button, triggering chimes that vibrated through the building. When there was no immediate response, she pressed the button again, several times. The chimes gonged like Holy Name of Jesus Church at noon on Sunday.

She heard an upstairs window open and a voice shout down, "Who the hell is it?"

She backed to where she could see a sleepy-eyed Manion, dressed in a rumpled shirt, leaning out of the window. Instead of answering his question, she glared up at him. He blinked, mumbled something like "Just a minute," and disappeared from the window.

When he opened the front door, a white terrycloth robe was wrapped around his thin frame and he was wearing his glasses. "And good morning to you, too," he said as she brushed past him brusquely.

He followed her into his office. She was pulling the curtain that ran along the back wall. Since no light got past the storefront with its curious display, Manion had put in a French door and matching windows at the rear to brighten the room. They looked out on a small brick patio and a lush garden that, though beautiful, was on the verge of becoming a jungle.

Squinting at the glare from the morning sun, Manion asked, "Did I forget an appointment or something?"

"It's a wonder you haven't forgotten your own name," the elderly woman replied, moving on to the kitchen. "I'll put some coffee on while you get more presentable."

Manion looked down at his robe and bare bony knees. He'd thrown off the clothes he'd slept in but hadn't had time to put on pajamas to make the deception complete. The way things were going, he needn't have bothered.

He shrugged and retreated to his upstairs bath, where he shaved, showered, and dressed in just under fifteen minutes. By then the office was filled with the aroma of chicory coffee.

She stood in front of a black box attached to a wall approximately one foot higher than her five feet three inches. A black leather strap dangled from its bottom. She said, "It's about your idea of art, sonny . . ."

"Pull the strap," he suggested.

Nadia put a tentative hand on the strap, then gave it a good yank. The front panel of the box opened and a mechanical crow poked its head out. The crow was made of plastic. It was wearing a beret and sunglasses. Its head moved jerkily as if it were surveying the room. When it was finished, it said in a metallic voice, "Clean your rack, Jack," then emitted a caw that caused Nadia to take a backward step. Another side-to-side head movement and the crow withdrew as the panel closed.

She pulled the string again. This time the crow asked, "Got the juice, Bruce?"

"Very droll, Terence," Nadia said.

Manion filled his cup with black coffee and hoped that his head would eventually clear. The spot where he had been hit throbbed mercilessly. "What's on your mind, Nadia?" he asked.

"I don't believe in wasting my money, Terence."

"It's a well-known fact."

"Here's another one: I don't like to be jerked around."

Manion frowned. He could feel an anger building up within him. He knew what the problem was. "So?"

"So what am I to think? I pay good money to get you on your feet, and your first night away from the Spa, you're in a barroom until the wee smalls."

"You had me followed?" Manion's face felt hot.

"Not followed . . . exactly."

"What then?"

"I sent Felix out to Henderson Parish to help you with the law, if you needed it."

Manion tried to keep his temper under wraps. "How'd you know I was in Henderson?"

"For God's sake, sonny, you know I have friends on the force. Ten minutes after your name went into the computer for wants and warrants, I knew where you were and what was going down. Information fuels my business.

"Anyway, I told Felix not to interfere unless necessary. And it didn't appear to be necessary. That swat on your head didn't seem to be bad enough to keep you and your pal Munn from hitting the nearest bar. But Felix stuck around to make sure."

Manion's hand went to the sore spot on his head, rubbed it lightly. "Felix must be losing it. Otherwise he'd have told you the strongest thing I had to drink was a root beer."

"Just one of them, I believe."

"Then . . ."

She fixed him with her sky-blue eyes. "I never in my life heard of a man staying on the wagon by going to bars every night."

Hostility and indignation spewed to his brain on a wave of anger. Then the wave ebbed and he relaxed. Nadia was right. Sure, Munn had twisted his arm. But he had been curious about how it would feel. The boozy crowd, the jukebox, and the smell of whiskey and beer had been potent reminders of a life on the sauce. The idea of just one small cocktail had seemed quite appealing. The fact that he had not given in to the temptation was almost beside the point. If he continued to flirt with the desire, sooner or later he would give in to it. As had been proven time and again, his was an addictive personality.

"Okay. It was a mistake," he said.

"But not a fatal one. At least not yet." She finished her coffee and set the cup on his desk. "Now, suppose you tell me how you got mixed up with a stiff in Henderson Parish?"

Manion almost laughed at the question. Only Nadia could use a word like "stiff" without sounding self-conscious. He rose and, while retrieving the coffeepot from the kitchen, gave her an accurate report of everything that had happened from the time Felix dropped him on his doorstep until he and Munn left the crime scene.

When he finished, she got him to re-create the scribbles from the missing paper he found in the dead man's shoe.

Nadia made little "hum-hum" noises as she studied what he'd written. "Mumbo jumbo," she said finally. "You sure it was J.J.'s writing?"

"As sure as I am of anything." He pressed his fingers against his aching head.

"Sorta like a hangover, isn't it?" Nadia said maliciously.

"Nothing like it," Manion lied.

"You tell your good and great friend Munn about the note?"

Manion nodded. "He asked me to try and duplicate it, too."

"That's two of us smart. Where'd you boys meet anyhow? An old case?"

"In grammar school. He was the large, ominous hulk at the back of the room. I was the skinny teacher's pet in the middle of the room who tried to stay out of his way."

"Schoolmates then."

"I guess. It'd been twenty years since I'd seen him when he showed up at the Spa several days ago. He wanted my deposition on that business in Los Angeles. But he asked me about J.J."

"Now that's interesting. And then he suddenly appeared last night, about a mile past his jurisdiction." Nadia began to rub her chin. "A real odd duck, Mr. Eben Munn. I checked him out. He's supposed to be loony tunes."

Manion did smile at that. "Aren't we all?" he said.

"Not like Munn. You know, sonny, I used to believe there were only two types of cops, crooked and straight, and it was always wise to assume the former. These days you get all kinds—bad good guys, good bad guys, weirdos, boozers, law school graduates, pain freaks, wimps. All kinds. And Munn's kind hasn't been charted yet.

"Most of his career, the time he spent on Vice, he was a man you could count on. That is to say, he was reliably bent. If the price was right, Munn would do the job, look the other way, whatever. But he went into some sort of decline. Took a year's leave of absence. When he decided to work again, he requested a reassignment to Homicide and got it. But he was a changed man. Cynical, outspoken, and—here's the intriguing part—quirky. These days, if you wave a C-note at him, he'll most certainly put it away. But you can never be sure what it's buying. A guy named Tabor is in Angola right now because Munn put him there, supposedly after depositing thirty grand that Tabor had sent him to lie on the stand."

"Then I assume he's just about out of the bribery business."

"One would think so. His fellow officers don't know what the hell to make of him. They're a bit afraid of him, or maybe just furious with him, because he can't be trusted."

"The Tabor thing sounds a bit apocryphal. If the story's that widely circulated, wouldn't Munn be Internal Affairs' number one project?"

Nadia shook her head. "Who's to say he's not? The New Orleans Police Department is as politically complex and as devious as the court of the Borgias. The point is, he seems to be on your case, sonny. I'd go very cautiously around him."

Manion nodded. But he wondered if the warning had come too late.

Nadia cocked her head. "Shecksnyder and the other man broke in here two weeks ago. Right around the time of poor old J.J.'s death."

"Yes. That occurred to me," Manion said. "But as far as I can tell, the files weren't touched." He opened a drawer and removed the four newest folders. "That includes these cases of J.J.'s."

Nadia withdrew a pair of glasses from her coat pocket and put them on. The frames were fifties cat's-eyes. Manion watched her bemusedly as she peered through them at the contents of the folders.

"Nothing here to make a bishop belch," she said finally, placing the folders back on Manion's desk. "Well, sonny, what are your plans?"

"*Cherchez la femme,*" Manion said, picking up the phone and dialing the number Pos Fouchette had given him.

"Which *femme* is that?"

Listening to the rings, Manion answered, "Slo Bentine."

"I suppose that makes sense," Nadia said, but Manion did not hear her. A voice on the other end of the line was speaking a language he did not recognize. He asked to speak to Slo Bentine. The voice hesitated, lapsed into barely understandable English with an accent he identified as Asian. "No Slo Bentine here. Never heard of Slo Bentine." Pos had given him the phone number of a Chinese hand laundry.

Manion stood up. "A slight change of plans," he said. "I'll have to see Pos first."

"My morning is free. If you want some company, I'll even drive."

He wondered if she was merely curious about the girl, or if she was being overly protective of him. He asked, "Will Felix and I share the back seat?"

"I'm in the Jaguar," she said. "Felix is resting up, after the night you put him through."

"One of us put him through it," Manion said. "I'm not sure it was me."

She stared at him. "You put me through it too. But I'm tougher than Felix. You want me to drive you or not?"

"I'd be honored," he said.

As they pulled away from the curb in her green Jaguar, a black Range Rover parked halfway down the block started its engine. When the Jaguar glided past the Captain's Curse and turned right on Canal Street, the Rover lunged forward in pursuit.

15

●

SLO BENTINE sat at Pos's kitchen table, sipping coffee and staring through the window directly into the morning sun. She thrived on the sun, felt lovingly warmed by it, no matter how hot the temperature. It tanned her skin, never burned it. She snickered at all the warnings about skin cancer. The sun was health-giving and that was that.

She needed it this morning because she had not slept well. The unfamiliar bed had been uncomfortable, and the apartment stank from cigar and cigarette smoke and beer. She had been able to sleep only a few hours at a time, awakening to find Pos sitting across the room, watching her. Not staring at her in a weird way or anything, just sort of doting on her. She rather liked it. Liked him. Not enough to actually get serious about him—a dumb Cajun with absolutely no prospects. Not much more than common sense, actually. And far too little of that. She wondered if he really knew anything about J.J.'s death, or if he was just trying to scare her to keep her with him. If that was the case, she'd know soon enough. At least she wouldn't have to worry about him forcing his attentions on her. Though she was sure he was very attracted to her, he'd behaved like a perfect gentleman.

She turned from the sun, waited for her eyes to adjust to the room. Pos's skinny back was to her as he stood before the stove, frying something in a large skillet for their breakfast.

"Smells good," she said.

"Gree-ards and grits," he said buoyantly. "My mama us'ta make it with pork, but I use red veal. Don't care much for pork."

"Who was it you kept trying to call last night?"

"That sonofagun's been out with some prairie hen. But I caught him this morning. He be here soon. We get you out of this mess, I swear."

He pulled the heavy skillet from the flame and shook it, bending over to take a deep sniff of its contents. "Oh man. This is gonna be good, yeah. You get the dishes."

She'd washed the pile of dishes that had been in his sink for God knows how long. Now the sink was starting to fill up again. Pos did a lot of cooking for a bachelor. J.J. hated to cook, so they'd eaten out nearly every night. She preferred eating at home.

She found two chipped white china plates and carried them to Pos. He filled one with the grillades and grits and told her to sit down and dig in. She was starving. The food smelled wonderful.

Pos filled his plate and placed it on the table across from her. He returned to the stove and picked up a coffeepot and two cups. He poured the coffee strong and black, then took his seat. Before he ate, he closed his eyes, folded his hands, and mumbled something. Slo was amazed. She asked, "You saying grace?"

Pos nodded sheepishly. "Funny thing is, my mama still thinks I be the bad boy of the family."

Slo loved the food, loved the onion and garlic seasoning. And the grits were smooth, not like her mama's. When the meal had been consumed, and Pos had lighted his first nonfiltered Camel of the morning, she collected the dishes, placed them in the sink, and ran water over them. "I'll do these in a minute," she told Pos. "I better call my mama now. She'll be having kitty fits."

"Uh . . . better not tell her where you are," he said, worry lines crossing his forehead. "In case . . . somebody's trying to find you."

She nodded, walked to the bedroom, and flopped onto the bed she had taken such care to make not an hour before. Her mother sounded frantic, but there was nothing to be done about that. Her mother always sounded frantic. No, Slo told her patiently, she did not know when she might be home. She was with a friend, and she was fine and her mother was not to worry.

"Who's the friend?" her mother asked. Slo was trying to think of an answer when the door buzzer sounded.

*   *   *

Pos stubbed out his cigarette in a sawed-off Dixie Beer can ashtray and stood, adjusting his Levi's. He was smiling when he opened the door, but instead of the friendly, helpful countenance he was expecting to see, he was greeted by the unemotional face of the hit man whose employers had nicknamed him Croaker. From the expression on Croaker's face, Pos immediately realized he had made a seriously bad judgment call.

Another sure sign of trouble: Croaker had a gun in his gloved right hand. He raised the pistol until it was aimed at Pos's stomach. It was a Saturday night special, the one that had been nicknamed the Swamp Angel. It seemed to Pos a mark of disrespect. A Swamp Angel for a swamp rat.

Croaker gestured Pos backward with the gun until the thin Cajun was against the card table in the center of the living room. Pos shook his head sadly. He'd had it all worked out, goddammit! He just wanted to explain that Slo wasn't going to be any problem for anybody. But he wasn't getting the chance.

From the corner of his eye he saw movement by the bedroom door. Slo was standing there, holding the phone receiver in one hand, the base in the other. She seemed frozen in place. Croaker swung the gun in her direction and Pos threw himself onto the man, shouting, "Noooooo!"

Croaker smashed Pos in the face with the saw-handle butt of the Swamp Angel, growling, "Get out of my way." Pos felt his cheek swelling, but he continued to grapple for the gun. Then, just before he heard the report of the bullet leaving the gun, he found himself being lifted off his opponent by a great force. It was not until he had fallen to the floor on his back that he began to be overwhelmed by a searing pain that filled his chest and stomach.

If Croaker had not paused to check Pos's condition, the girl might not have made it back into the bedroom. By the time he pushed through the door, the phone was resting on the floor where she'd dropped it. A metallic voice like an angry bee buzzed from its earpiece. Croaker's eyes scanned the empty room and rested on the closed bathroom door.

It was locked. He raised his foot and brought it down on the door handle. Wood splintered and the door bounced back into the bathroom. He followed it, gun chest-high, ready.

The bathroom was empty. The screen was off the window. He looked through the bare frame and found himself squinting into the bright morning light. He could vaguely make out a female shape running down the cracked concrete driveway. She seemed to be running directly into the sun.

16

·

MANION'S RATHER vague directions forced Nadia Wells to drive slower than was her wont. Otherwise she might have hit the young woman who dashed into the street in front of the Jaguar. "It's her," Nadia said to Manion, though, in fact, she was not certain that the fleeing girl was the weeping creature she'd seen at J.J.'s funeral.

Manion was out of the green Jaguar immediately and Nadia watched him chase the girl on unsteady colt's legs. The elderly woman started to follow in the car, when a mild explosion came from somewhere to the right and the girl made an odd sidestep.

Nadia stared in the direction of the shot, spotted a man in a dark sport coat leaning out of a window with a gun in his hand. "Shit!" she mumbled, spinning the wheel of her car in the gunman's direction.

The Jaguar bounced up the driveway, neatly blocking the gunman's view of Manion and the girl. Nadia made a fist and banged it down on her horn. She looked for her purse and was frustrated at finding it on the rear seat, well out of her grasp. When she glanced through the windshield again, the gunman was motionless, scowling at her. Then he backed away from the window. He was coming after them!

Nadia shifted into reverse and roared backward, the front end of the Jaguar sending sparks as it nudged the cement drive. She made a wide turn and braked in the street beside Manion and the girl, who was sitting down on the asphalt like a recalcitrant child. High up on her left arm near the shoulder, her blouse was turning scarlet. Nadia shouted, "Get her in here, quick!"

She waited impatiently while Manion tore open the rear door, jumped in, and pulled Slo in behind him. Nadia let him reach across the wounded girl to swing the door shut, then spun the steering wheel and floored the gas pedal.

As they zoomed away, Nadia saw the gunman exit through the front door of Pos Fouchette's duplex. The arrogant sonofabitch didn't seem to be in any particular hurry.

Wincing from the pain, Slo Bentine moaned, "He shot Pos."

Nadia said, "My purse is on the back seat, sonny. See if there's not a fully loaded Bulldog .44 Special in it."

It was one of those leather-and-canvas drawstring bags. Manion found the gun and held it up. "Now what?"

"Now we circle the block, and if that bastard is still standing there on the front stoop, I want you to shoot his ass off."

But the gunman was gone. Driving by slowly, they could see that. The front door to the apartment stood open. Nadia stopped the Jaguar, frowning. She scanned the cars along the street, apparently looking for something. The girl stared at Manion. "Pos is in there, maybe dying," she said.

Manion made no motion to get out of the car. He replaced the gun in Nadia's purse. A thin crowd of neighbors was starting to gather. Nadia said, "Shit!" again and lowered her window. She checked to see that Slo's wound was hidden, then put on a happy face and innocently asked a bald-headed man in plaid Bermudas and a white T-shirt, "What's going on, cap'n?"

"I dunno. Sounded like shots. Drug stuff, prob'ly."

Nadia shook her head. "What kind of a world are we living in anyway?'

"Ain't that the truth," the bald man replied as the Jaguar slowly moved away from the crowd.

"You just gonna let Pos die?" Slo screamed.

"Shut your mouth and use your brain, girl," Nadia snapped. "Maybe Pos was shot. Maybe he's alive. Maybe that man with the gun is still in there. Too many maybes. Let the police take care of the maybes."

"But—"

"How bad's she hurt, sonny?"

Manion ripped the arm of Slo's blouse and pulled it away from the wound. "If the bullet missed the bone, it shouldn't be so bad. Assuming we can stanch the blood. There's a lot of it."

"Can you move your fingers, girl?" Nadia asked.

"Uh . . . yes. But Pos—"

"Hell's bells! Enough about Pos!" Nadia bounced the car into a K & B Drugstore parking lot. "Sonny, go phone the goddamn paramedics and tell them to get over to Pos's place. And pick up some gauze and unguents while you're in there. It might be to this gal's advantage if we don't get involved with organized medicine until we have a clearer understanding of where we stand."

The gray-faced man with an egg-shaped head and playful eyes ran his fingers lightly but proudly over Slo's bandaged arm, nodded to Nadia, and took the pale blue envelope she offered. "Nice doing business with you, my dear, as always," he told her.

"She gonna live, Gus?"

"I suppose so, Nadia, unless she picks up any more bits of flying lead. These pills are to knock out any infection. These are to let her sleep tonight."

His amused brown eyes returned to Slo. "There's gonna be a scar, young woman," he told her. "Nothing I can do about that. But I could recommend a good cosmetic reconstructionist . . ."

Nadia put a hand on his shoulder. "Maybe later, Gus, when she's had a little rest. Then we'll decide if she needs anything like that."

By applying only a slight pressure to his shoulder, she maneuvered him out of the bright bedroom. "Thank you, Doctor," Slo called after him from the bed.

Manion looked down at her, resting on plump pillows with her bandaged arm tan against the white and green summer quilt. "Gus isn't a doctor, exactly," he said with a smile. "He's a vet."

She smiled back, assuming he was joking. He wasn't.

Nadia returned, followed by the imposing Olivette, who that day sported a pink turban-and-slacks combination. The secretary's whiskey voice was saying, as much for Slo's benefit as Nadia's, ". . . Pos is at Charity Hospital, emergency ward, alive but barely. They've got the bullet out of him, and they're optimistic but guardedly so. Trying to notify his brother, wherever he is."

"I never heard of any brother," Nadia said. "His family's out in one of the bayous somewhere near Houma. Buddy's their cousin. He should know."

She looked down at Slo. "Well, girl. You say Pos told you that you were in hot water because some unspecified villain was worried you might know something about J.J.'s death?"

Slo moved her head up and down, looking even more girlish than usual.

"Only you don't have any idea what dangerous information you possess?"

Again the nod.

Nadia lifted her eyes skeptically to Manion. He sat on the bed beside the girl and asked softly, "You weren't with J.J. the night he . . . died?"

Her head moved horizontally this time. "That afternoon he made me pack up my things and go stay with a girlfriend who lives uptown. He said it'd only be for a few days." She was slurring from the medication.

"He send you away very often?"

"Never. When he was sort of retired, we were together all the time. Then he started working at your office and I didn't see as much of him. But he never sent me away like that before. He said something about having to concentrate on a business matter and he didn't want me around to distract him."

Manion glanced at Nadia, then back to Slo. "Was he acting strange in any way? Worried? Sad?"

"Like I told the police, he was just the same as always. Not depressed or anything. Just the opposite, in fact. When we first met at the gumbo place . . . Did I tell you how we met, about there being only one table and—"

"You told us, girl," Nadia interrupted her.

"Yes. . . . Well, anyway, when we first met, J.J. just seemed like a nice older man. And when I . . . when I started getting to know him better and started liking him a lot, he still seemed like his age was telling on him, making him move slowly and carefully. But during the last couple of months—once he started going in to your office, Mr. Manion—he began to change. He wasn't so old anymore. He, uh . . ." She blushed. "He even started behaving more physical with me, you know." She yawned and closed her eyes.

"Tell us what you all did that last day," Nadia said in a loud voice.

Slo's eyes opened reluctantly. "The whole day? Well, he was up when I woke, like always. I fixed breakfast and we went for a ride, which was a little unusual, through the Quarter and then over the bridge to McDonoghville, past the black projects to a nice little street that didn't look like it was black at all. But it was, because the guy J.J. stopped to talk to was black. I mean, not really black, like some. But he was black, I'm pretty sure. Anyway, I stayed in the car while J.J. went inside the guy's house with him."

"You remember the address?" Manion asked.

"No. Surely not. It was back behind the projects." Another yawn. She was fading fast.

She opened her eyes suddenly. "Spooner Street. I remember that." She was quite pleased with herself for a beat. Then she frowned. "But I'll never think of the number."

"What about the house?"

She shook her head. "It was a duplex, I think. And it had a big fig tree in the front yard, because J.J. stopped to pick a few before he got back in the car." She smiled. "He got some fig juice on the folder he was carrying and it made him mad. J.J. was real particular when it came to work. Liked everything to be just so. He kept trying to rub the fig juice off the folder, but that just made the stain get bigger."

"What color was the house, girl?"

"Gray, maybe. Blue gray or light gray. With white shutters. It was a nice house, I remember. Looked clean and fresh. The other houses looked nice too. Better than the one I grew up in, and this was over the river, too, and right near that project.

"Is that all, now?" she asked. "I'm really wore out."

"Get all the sleep you want, girl," Nadia said, removing one of the pillows from behind Slo's neck and easing her head down to the one that remained. "Don't you worry about a thing."

She led Manion from the room and closed the door gently behind her.

"Sort of makes you wonder what was going on in J.J.'s head, doesn't it? Getting involved with a terminally unsophisticated little child like that."

"Pos too," Manion said.

"Pos I can understand. They're a perfect match."

Buddy and Felix stood quickly when Nadia entered the living room. Buddy's eyes were red. Nadia asked him, "Have you notified Pos's kin?"

"Jus' my aunt lef' on the Bayou. She . . ." He hesitated. "She and Pos don' get along so good. She say she sorry, and I should let Fostah know."

"He the brother?"

"Uh huh." Buddy nodded his round head. "On'y I dunno where that goddamned Fostah Fouchette be. He travels all over the place. He don't answer his goddamn phone. I ain't laid eyes on him in over a year. I better get over to the harse-pital so that Pos'll have some family there when he wakes up."

He started to go, then turned to Nadia, scowling. "You saw the bastid that did it, Miz W.?" He pronounced the letter "dubba-yah."

"I got a glance at him. I suppose I'd recognize him again."

"You see him, you tell me, huh?" Buddy growled. "I'll pound the sonofabitch into the goddamn groun'."

Nadia said, "Well, you just hold that thought, Buddy. He got a good long look at my plates, and anybody with a dime can turn that into an address. When you're through at the hospital, come back. I want you and Felix to settle in here for the next few days. Maybe you'd better tell whoever's not too busy with repos to drop by too. I'll feel better with a little army."

She turned to Manion. "Guess you got something you want to do?"

He nodded. "I'll take a drive over the bridge and try to find the house on Spooner Street. None of the folders J.J. left at my apartment was stained with fig juice or anything else."

"Right, sonny. George can ferry you to your car. But let's find something to nibble on before you go."

Lou-Ruth, the new cook, let Manion sample some of the shrimp Carnival she was preparing for dinner. Nadia made herself a rather dainty ham sandwich and took it and a glass of lemonade into her office.

Olivette looked up at her over a computer screen. "Something?" she asked.

Nadia placed the sandwich plate and the glass on her desk blotter and eased into her chair. "Call Lil at the DMV. I'd like to know if anybody tries to access the Jaguar's license plate, and I also want her to find out what she can about this number." She took a folded slip of paper from her shirt pocket and passed it to the big woman. "It's presently attached to a new black and gray Range Rover."

"What's the story, hon?"

"The Range Rover was on our butts all the way from Terry's to Pos's house."

"Oh my. You think it was the gunman?"

"The gunman was shooting Pos at the time we were being followed. No, this is gonna be some pissant who doesn't know any better than to try and tail somebody in a car that's bigger and shinier and more ostentatious than anything else on the road, except maybe a Rolls."

"Takes all kinds." Olivette picked up the phone.

"Hell, if everybody was as smart as us," Nadia said, bringing the ham sandwich to her lips, "wouldn't life just be a bitch?"

17

THE DUPLEX on Spooner Street was, as Slo Bentine had described, blue gray with white shutters and a fig tree in its front yard. It stood out in sharp contrast to the cold cement-and-brick, three-story low-income apartment buildings just a few blocks away, with their broken windows and graffiti and scorched, patchy, foliage-free lawns.

Manion got out of his car and approached the apartment on his left, the one beyond the fig tree. He climbed the steps to a dark gray front porch. Three red ceramic pots filled with colorful plants flanked a screen door. Behind the screen, the front door was open. The detective could see most of a living room with gray-and-white-striped wallpaper and a white hallway leading all the way to the back of the house. An errant cool breeze stirred the curtains along one wall.

Manion pressed a brass door buzzer and wondered what it would bring. The house appeared to be unoccupied. He had started to reach for the buzzer again when a voice to his left said, "What's up?"

A light-skinned black man in khaki trousers, pink T-shirt, and white sneakers stood by the side of the house. Manion placed his age at about twenty. He was wiry, muscled but not excessively so. His hair was cut short and neat. Rimless eyeglasses were perched on his small hooked nose. Manion suddenly realized that after a decade or so of Afros and dashikis, the severe Malcolm X look had come back into vogue.

Slightly magnified by his glasses, the man's brown eyes observed Manion without much interest. "You looking for something?"

"My name is Manion."

"Oh," the black man said. "Finally made it back, huh?"

He hopped onto the porch. His shirt sleeve moved up over his right biceps, briefly displaying an amateur tattoo of some sort. "Go on in," he said to Manion. "Door's open."

Inside, the floor had been sanded and varnished, and offered such a sharp response to Manion's heels that he had a fleeting desire to break into a Fred Astaire tap dance.

The smell of lemon wax mixed with the perfume of magnolia in a vase. A white sofa faced a polished captain's table containing used textbooks and a three-ring binder. Past that, a small color television set rested on a metal stand. On the wall above the TV was an oval mirror in a brass frame. In it, Manion could see that the black man had passed silently through the door behind him.

"I suppose you've got some kind of ID?" the man asked.

Manion took out his wallet and held it so that his PI license was displayed. The man nodded. "Well, that's some disguise you've got, Mr. Manion. Not exactly Mike Hammer, are you?"

"Who is?"

An object on an end table caught Manion's eye. It was a bronzed pork chop mounted on a black plastic base. Manion picked it up to read the plaque on its base: "Leon Harris, Fastest Waiter of the Year."

Leon Harris smiled and took the award out of Manion's hand, placing it back on the table. "It's a contest the restaurants have. For charity."

"Where do you work?"

"Toody White's. That is, I used to work there. I'm starting a new job today." He looked at his wristwatch. "Soon."

"I'll try not to keep you."

Leon moved past him. "C'mon back to the kitchen."

Manion followed down a hall, past a closed door, then an open one revealing a clean contemporary bathroom. The hall ended at a kitchen with pale yellow walls and a stark white table, a no-frills refrigerator that hummed in monotone, and a sparkling sink. Leon motioned toward the two chairs at the table and asked Manion if he wanted a beer.

"No thanks," Manion said as he sat down. "But a soft drink or coffee would be fine."

Leon found two cans of diet Coke in the fridge. "Need a glass?"

Manion shook his head. Leon took the chair across from him, his back to a sunny, screened-in porch. "Through with your travels, huh?" he asked.

"J. J. Legendre told you I was traveling?"

Leon nodded. "I saw about him in the paper. That was too bad. He didn't look like the sort to do that."

"We were all surprised," Manion said, deadpan. "How well did you know J.J.?"

"How well? I just met with him the two times. At your office. And then he came here after I phoned him."

"What exactly was he doing for you, Leon?" Manion was feeling his way along.

"You don't know?" Leon Harris frowned, suspicious now. "You didn't even look at the file?"

"What file?" Manion asked.

"Why, the file that . . . What the hell's going on?"

"I'm trying to find out what J. J. Legendre was working on just before . . . he passed away."

The black man sipped from his diet Coke. Then he said, "There's a lawyer named Mettier. Ever hear of him?"

"Mettier, Fine and Abadie. I've done a few things for them."

"That's what he said. He eats at Toody's a couple times a month. I asked him his advice on hiring a detective and he gave me your name."

"So you phoned and met with J.J.?"

Leon nodded. "He said he was filling in for you until you got back from some big job that had taken you on the road. I told him what I wanted and—"

"Tell *me* what you wanted," Manion interrupted.

Leon shook his head. "It's all in the goddamned file. Besides, it's all taken care of."

"J.J. handled it?"

"No. But I was just being stupid. My uncle was an old man. Old people have accidents."

Manion waited for him to explain, but he said instead, "Look, I went over it all with Mr. Legendre. He had our conversation transcribed, I know, because he charged me for it. Sixty-five bucks. And he put it in a file folder with my name on it."

Manion said, "That file's missing. I didn't even know your name until I saw it on your trophy."

Leon's mouth dropped. "Then how'd you find me?"

"Your address. I discovered that J.J. visited this place the day before he died."

Leon hunched his shoulders. "I asked him here to tell him to drop the whole thing. He must've just deep-sixed the file."

"Why don't you fill me in on some details?"

"It's past history. It's got nothing to do with anything."

"A couple guys broke into my office the same night that J.J. died. It looks like they stole your file. J.J. would not have thrown it away. So maybe it does have something to do with something."

Leon shook his head. "That's crazy. It was about my uncle, a black man in his seventies. He had bad legs and they gave out and he fell down a flight of stairs."

"But you hired J.J. to look into it."

"I . . . I was looking for somebody to blame. But that was just grief and stupidity. I wanted to make trouble for people, just to be making trouble. End of story."

"There must be more to it than that."

Leon looked at his watch again and squirmed on his chair. "That's all there is," he said.

Manion held up his hand, fingers and thumb extended. "We've got a man who fell down a flight of stairs . . ." He brought his little finger in toward the palm. "We've got a man who was in no way suicidal who is supposed to have committed suicide. . . ." The ring finger moved in beside the little finger. "And we've got my office which was burgled, with your file being one of the things taken." The middle finger joined the others. "What do all of these things seem to have in common?" Manion's outstretched index finger and thumb formed a child's pistol, which he aimed at Leon Harris.

"Hey, now." Leon looked uncomfortable. "Don't try to drag me into your bullshit."

"When J.J. drove here on his last day alive, there was a young woman in his car. You happen to see her?"

Leon shook his head.

"Somebody tried to kill her this morning. The guy she was with is in the hospital now. They took a bullet out of him, but that may not be good enough."

"Shit!" Leon Harris exhaled. He shook his head again, more emphatically. "This can't have anything to do with me."

"Tell me about your uncle."

"Are the police going to be coming here?"

Manion didn't answer right away. He was trying to decide which reply would get the best results. Finally, he said, "That tattoo on your right arm, is it a gang symbol?"

Leon unconsciously clamped a large hand over the tattoo, as if trying to hide it. He nodded. "Ancient history. When I was in high school, I used to be an Olay. So I spent some time with the police."

Manion knew about the Olays—a teenage gang of light-skinned blacks whose name was a contraction and corruption of the expression "café au lait." He asked, "How much trouble did you get into?"

"Not much. We weren't really into the violence, just self-preservation," Leon said. "Our only reason for ganging was to protect ourselves from the Chops." That was the reigning New Orleans street gang, a mixture of blacks and Third World youths from the Tchoupitoulas Street ghetto who reputedly were guilty of extortion and murder. "To the cops we were the same as the Chops, so they hassled us."

"If the police come here, it won't be me that sends them," Manion said, standing. "You decide you want to talk to me, you know my number."

Leon stretched one leg under the table and pushed Manion's chair out to stop him. "Sit down," he said. "I don't know anything that'll make any difference, but I might as well tell you now and get it over with."

Manion slipped into the chair.

"I thought there was something funny about how Parker died," Leon told him. "But that was stupid."

"Why don't you just start at the beginning so that I can figure out for myself how stupid it was?"

Leon shrugged resignedly. "Okay. My uncle Parker looked after a family on St. Charles Avenue. He'd been with them for a long time. Maybe twenty-five years. Both he and my mother. Parker and Irma. Sort of like butler and maid."

"Where's your mother now?"

"She died birthing me,"Leon said matter-of-factly. Then, noticing Manion staring at him, he added defensively, "You have a problem with that?"

"No. It's just . . . my mother died having me."

"I don't suppose they both had the same first-time intern on the charity ward who forgot to stop the flow of blood?"

"No," Manion said. "I don't suppose so. But the result was the same. Who took care of you? Your father?"

He shook his head. "Parker explained later that my mother had lots of men friends and none of 'em exactly rushed forward to claim me. So he raised me himself. We had an okay little shack on Willow Street, in the Carrollton area, uptown," Manion knew the area well enough. He had grown up near Carrollton Avenue himself. As the activist Dick Gregory had once pointed out in the days before he left the comedy field to become a health faddist, "In the North, the white man doesn't care how big the black man gets, as long as he doesn't get too close; in the South, he doesn't care how close he gets, as long as he doesn't get too big."

Manion's mind focused again on Leon's story. ". . . there was a woman named Mildred that Parker hired to see to me during the day and some nights when he had to stay late at work. My memory is of a nice woman who liked her wine but never got so drunk that she couldn't handle me properly. I used to fantasize that she and Parker would settle down with me as their kid.

"But Parker didn't have much time to go wooing Mildred. And for all I know, she was married to somebody else, just never talked about him. She moved away when I was about six, and Parker brought in a whole lineup of substitutes that ran the gamut from drugged-out schoolgirls to a woman of eighty-some-odd years who was deaf as a post but kept me amused for hours talking about witchcraft."

"How long were you in Carrollton?"

"Let's see. . . . Until I was in the fifth grade. I remember, Parker took me out of school one morning and brought me to work with him. Only time he ever did it, and to this day I don't know why. Anyway, I was playing in the yard and that didn't sit well with the master of the house. Not at all." He stared into the tabletop as if it were a video of that time gone by. Then he snapped out of it. "As best I can recall, that was right around the time we packed up and moved over here. Lately, I been fixing the place up. It looks better now than it did then, when it was new. I get a fair rent from the nurses living next door. You sure you don't want a brew?"

"No," Manion said. "But don't let that stop you."

Leon shook his head. "I got the impression my new boss doesn't like people who arrive at work juiced." Suddenly, he frowned. He slapped his shirt pocket, ran a hand into his right pants pocket, then his left. He relaxed, removing a business card. Manion wasn't able to spot the name on it, just the drawing of a cartoon pelican in gym regalia.

Manion said, "You okay?"

Leon nodded. "Yeah. Fine. I just got worried that I'd misplaced something. But I didn't."

"Your uncle Parker—I assume his full name was Parker Harris?"

Leon nodded. "Parker F. Harris the Second," he said with a grin, sliding the business card into his shirt pocket. "Parker was very much into heritage. Both his grandfather and father had worked in rich men's homes." He paused, and a strange bemused look came over his face. "Hell," he said, "I seem to be following in the family tradition. But it's better than juggling dinner plates, which is what I've been doing until I graduate."

"Who're you working for now?" Manion asked.

Leon opened his mouth, then hesitated. "It's no matter."

"Same people Parker worked for?"

"You mean, did they give me a job to buy me off? No. Parker worked for the Gaynaud family."

The name was not unfamiliar to Manion. Lawson Gaynaud had been an acquaintance of his father.

"Did they pay your uncle well?" Manion asked in a friendly tone.

"I guess. Well enough for us both to live comfortably."

"How'd he feel about you running with the Olays?"

Leon's forehead became a mass of ridges as his long fingers traced a design on his beer can. "I was sort of on my own by that time. Parker was spending most of his time at the Gaynauds'. Had his own room there, and he never liked the drive over the bridge. So he wasn't all that hip to how I was living my life. I'm just as glad he never found out. Before he started to fade the last couple years, Parker had a pretty good punch."

"He was your legal guardian?"

"Legal? Maybe not. I'm not sure."

Manion waved his hand at the room. "But he lived here with you."

"Like I said, not so much the last four or five years. New Orleans people are funny about that bridge. They say it's always jammed up and they use that as an excuse not to drive over here. Parker always hated to drive. And with his arthritis and slowed-down reflexes, it wasn't particularly safe for him to be driving. So we went for pretty long periods of not seeing each other." Leon glanced at his watch. "Damn, I'm sorry, but I've got to get to work."

Manion followed him to the front door. "You never really told me what made you hire a private investigator."

Leon waved his hand dismissively. "Look, I was just pissed off because nobody bothered to inform me that Parker had died until nearly two months after he was buried. Hell, they just put him in the ground. Parker was a member of a burial society. He had a friend in the society who was a musician. Parker would have wanted him and the brass band to set his body free with a good send-off. But I never got the chance to arrange it."

"Who finally called you? Gaynaud?"

"His lawyer. Had a real dead-fish delivery. He told me a will had been found when they were cleaning out Parker's room. He'd left me all his possessions, including this place, free and clear, and a bank account with a couple thousand dollars in it."

Leon pushed the screen door open and stepped onto the porch. Manion followed, asking, "What'd you want J.J. to do, check the medical examiner's report, talk to Gaynaud, what?"

"I don't know. All of that, I guess." Leon's large hand rubbed the back of his neck. "Look," he blurted out, "I was mad, like I said. I went over there to Gaynaud's. A fine-looking red-haired woman let me in. I sat in their parlor for about ten minutes and this pale, prissy guy came in. Gaynaud's son. He's in politics—a congressman or senator, like that. He told me that I had to leave."

"That's all he said?"

"He said his father wasn't home and his mother was sick. And the bottom line was, I had no business in their house. That did nothing to improve my temper. And since I had a few extra bucks, thanks to Parker's will, I went to your office and met with Mr. Legendre."

"That was when?"

"Month and a half ago, more or less."

"And J.J. said what?"

"That he'd look into it."

"What'd he find out?"

"Mr. Legendre said the medical examiner's report looked okay. He had a chat with Gaynaud, who showed him the place where Parker fell."

"What was J.J.'s impression?"

"He said it all looked respectable to him but he wanted to check out a few things. Nothing specific. I'd cooled off by that time, so I told him to forget it, to just send me the bill." Leon shifted his feet. "I really can't be late to this job."

Manion stepped off the porch. "Did J.J. bill you?"

Leon hesitated, then shook his head. "No. I never got a bill."

"Maybe it's in your file folder," Manion said, walking away. "Wherever that is."

At his car, Manion experienced another of those post-rehab dizzy spells. Sitting behind the Mustang's steering wheel, he felt the heat rise from it and the dash. The leather seat was like a hot iron. It was a cloudy day, but the clouds were moving so quickly they didn't block the sun long enough to matter. The air was hot and muggy. His head hurt. He hadn't had enough sleep. He'd been knocked unconscious. He'd been shot at. Dr. Courville would not be amused.

He watched Leon shut and lock his front door. He wondered if he should follow the black man to find out the identity of his mysterious new employer. Or maybe he should visit Lawson Gaynaud.

The dizziness coursed through him again. And something else even more palpable. He shivered in the humid heat. Then he began to sweat. He leaned back and tried to breathe slowly, annoyed with his body for its reminder that he still wasn't a totally well man.

When he was more or less composed, he drove across the Bridge back to New Orleans and his home.

He tried to sleep, but that didn't work. Thoughts continued to spiral through his mind. The spinning sensation that had overtaken him earlier in the car returned. Finally, he picked up the phone and called Marcus Steiner.

18
.

THE SUN was sinking somewhere beyond Audubon Park when Manion arrived at his destination on Prytania Street, but dusk didn't signal a cooling trend. The warm air was so thick with humidity he could hardly breathe.

He found a curbside parking spot directly behind a large silver and black vehicle and parallel to a concrete wall with an intricate wrought-iron gate that led to Steiner's property. The gate's grillwork detail was impressive—lyres adorned with grapes formed a frame around a goddess, probably Roman but possibly Greek, whose flowing gown reminded Manion of the addled young woman who tried to teach him ballet when he was a boy. Beneath the woman was a demon with arms outstretched, a literal tongue of flame shooting from its mouth.

Through the gate, Manion could see a patio with large red-orange tiles that surrounded a working fountain and continued on to a two-story off-white house with antique-green trim. A huge overhanging cyprus tree protected the fountain from the sun. In lieu of a lawn or garden, bright orange and yellow and red plants and flowers grew in abundance from assorted pots that lined the fountain and the base of the house.

Manion hesitated before pressing the gate buzzer. He was feeling considerably better now and his natural tendency to fend for himself was taking over. Still, he could hardly just walk away after asking for help. He'd make it short.

His index finger touched the button. He heard movement; then something heavy brushed against the concrete base of the wall beside the gate. There was an electronic squawk followed by Steiner's voice. "Who is it?"

Conscious of the presence on the other side of the wall, Manion announced his name into the polished brass speaker below the buzzer. The heavy gate clicked open, but he did not immediately enter.

Shifting his angle, he saw an object in shadow just to his left. Then one massive, baleful eye. Manion pushed the gate open farther. A huge four-legged creature moved out of its way. At first, Manion thought it was a colt, but when it bellowed a moan-bark, he recognized it as a black and brown Great Dane, the largest he had ever seen. The dog was not displaying any signs of ferocity, but at his size, he didn't have to. Manion was uncertain how to proceed.

The front door to the chateau opened and Steiner bounded through it, his hairy body wrapped in a white silk kimono. He looked like a bouncer at a bathhouse. "Hungry Joe?" he called. "C'mere, boy."

The giant animal twisted his body sideways and trotted off to his master. Manion shut the gate behind him and followed. The dog's coat was shiny and flat. The fur on Steiner's arms and legs was curly and turning gray.

"Don't worry about old Joe, Manion," Steiner said. "He's a lover, not a fighter. Just like his master."

He led the detective into a large area that seemed to serve as both living and dining room. It was furnished with an odd combination of the contemporary and the antique. An ancient coffee table piled high with magazines fronted a large cushioned sofa covered in off-white canvas. A stereo and TV set were housed in an ancient cupboard. A rosewood bookcase ran along one wall, containing neatly stacked volumes and records and more magazines in bindings. Facing the books were walls decorated with prints by local artists like George Duro and older masters such as Gauguin and Picasso. A very modern glass-and-chrome sculpture formed the centerpiece of a sturdy Early American dining table at the far end of the area. Past that were two identical swinging doors separated by about twenty feet.

The hardwood floor had suffered from Hungry Joe's paws. There were no carpets. A central air-conditioning unit kept the room almost chilly. When Manion mimed a mock shiver, Steiner said, "Joe and I will never get used to the goddamned humidity. So I keep it frosty in here."

A woman entered the room from the rear. She was nearly as tall as Manion, a brunette with sun-bronzed skin. Her thin but top-heavy body was covered by a white kimono that matched Steiner's. She bent carefully to pet the dog. Steiner said, "Come and meet Terry Manion, Angela."

She moved gracefully across the floor, her bare feet making little pat-pat sounds. She held out a delicate hand, and Manion wondered for a moment if he was supposed to shake it or kiss it. Opting for the former, he said to both of them, "I'm sorry if I disturbed you . . ."

"Not at all, Terry. Angela and I were just discussing fucking."

Manion smiled. "Come to any conclusion?"

"We think it's here to stay," Steiner said.

Angela added rather solemnly, "Marcus was explaining the difference between Molly Bloom's sexual urgency and that of Lady Chatterley."

"I teach creative writing over at Newcomb," Steiner said with a crooked smile. "This gorgeous gal is one of my advanced students."

"Ah," Manion said. "So you've been conducting a lab project."

Angela seemed not to hear him. She cocked her head to one side and regarded Steiner adoringly. "He's absolutely brilliant."

"When the lady's right, she's right," Steiner said. "Who else but a brilliant burn-out like me could have come up with this method of recharging the batteries? I mean, once you hit the best-seller lists, you're never exactly at a loss for feminine companionship. But when you teach a course at a college for women, holy shit! Just call me pasha."

"A one-woman pasha," Angela added, covering his bare foot with hers.

Manion, who during his years at Tulane had never found the Newcomb women to be either passionate or accessible, said, "Marcus, you look like you've got your hands full. Why don't I just come back some other time?"

"Don't be a nut," Steiner told him. "Angela's gonna hop into her duds and run out for some poor boys. We'll have our talk, and when she gets back, we'll stoke up on cholesterol and calories. Give us a minute. Make yourself at home. Snoop around."

Steiner and Angela disappeared through the door to the left.

Manion and Hungry Joe listened to their bare feet climbing stairs. The dog wandered back into the living room to park himself near an air vent. Manion flipped through a stack of magazines, then strolled toward the rear of the house. The door on the right led into a neat, well-appointed kitchen.

He looked at the other door. Snoop around, the man had said.

He found himself in a small room containing a staircase and a bank of filing cabinets. And another door.

It opened into a very small office or den that was filled from floor to ceiling with books, except for a six-foot stretch occupied by a desk topped by a computer, a telephone, snips of paper with scribbled notes, and a large closed box marked "Goddess." The computer seemed to be humming, but its screen was blank.

Manion pressed the Enter key and the screen read, "Goddess" and "Manion."

He keyed in "Manion" and pressed Enter again.

The dark screen filled with amber letters—a shorthand version of his biography, from his birth on September 12, 1958 at Baptist Hospital in New Orleans to the date of his departure from Evangeline Spa; a total of fourteen entries.

He keyed the one for "Marriage—June 12, 1986." The screen changed and a new amber legend appeared: "Marriage to Gillian Coigne Duplessix. Union dissolved after fourteen weeks and two days. Ex-wife now residing in Orient with Kim Taki, CEO Taki Industries."

Manion had not known about Gillian's latest mate. The Navy SEAL had apparently gone the way of the German industrialist and the Raiders linebacker.

He returned to the biography menu and selected a more recent date. The screen filled with a duplication of J. J. Legendre's obituary in the *Times-Picayune*. Manion had never seen anything quite like that on a home computer—a tear sheet from a newspaper, complete with photograph of J.J. when his face had been less haggard. The obit covered the high points in J.J.'s life. Near the bottom, there was a brief mention that the elderly detective had returned to work at the Terence Manion Agency prior to his untimely death.

Manion was reading the obituary through again when Steiner said, "Quite a gizmo, huh?"

He was wearing khaki shorts and a T-shirt that read, "I Did!" Manion had no idea what it meant until Steiner turned around and he saw the question on the back of the shirt: "Guess who wrote the best-seller *In Salvador*?"

Steiner patted the computer and said, "They had to put a gun to my temple to get me to use one of these bastards, but I can say without reservation it is an invention that ranks right up there with the wheel and the saxophone."

"Marcus, what the hell is all this?" Manion asked.

"The Manion file, you mean?"

"Yeah. That's what I mean."

"Research," Steiner said. He waved a hand around the room, indicating the books. "All of this is research. I'm the rajah of research."

He pressed a few keys and J. J. Legendre's obit was replaced by a file marked "Goddess."

Steiner scratched his bald head and hit another key. The screen suddenly blossomed into a recognizable computerized image of Jayne Mansfield. "You're a movie nut, Terry," he said. "Maybe you can understand how I could fall in love with a woman I've only seen on the screen. Innocent. Flirtatious. Incapable of guile or complicated thought. The greatest breastworks ever created by God or man."

Manion moved away from the computer. He was rather dismayed by his appointed sponsor. Steiner didn't seem to notice. "She's my dream girl, pal. When I was struggling through puberty in the fifties in Wheaton, Illinois, it was Mansfield who spun my top. She's the one icon from that decade that has remained intact over the years. Monroe got dissipated. Presley got fat. Mansfield lives on, tits akimbo. I started digging into her in 1986. She's the one who brought me to New Orleans, to my new life."

"How's that?"

"She was killed not far from here. Automobile crash. Nasty death. Decapitation. Nasty. But it was an accident. Not like Monroe. Not like Presley. Anyway, I came here to research a sex queen, and what do I find?"

"What?"

"Ha! Maybe satisfaction. That just may be what I found."

"How long have you been living *here*?" Manion asked.

"In this house? Not long. Less than a year. Before that, I was renting in the Quarter, but the way the bottom has fallen out of the real estate market, I figured what the hell. Time to buy."

"How close are you to finishing *Goddess*?"

Steiner put his arm around Manion's shoulder and led him from the room. "Never been further from it. I'm laying it aside for a while. I've got a better idea.

"What's that?" Manion was afraid he knew the answer.

They were in the kitchen, where coffee cups had been set out on a thick oak table. Hungry Joe, tired of his own company, loped slowly into the room, his gait reminding Manion of Robert Mitchum's walk, and flopped onto the tile near the entrance to the kitchen.

Steiner said, "We'll get to that in a minute."

"Does it have anything to do with why you were following me this morning?"

Steiner did not reply.

"It's tough enough to do a good shadow job," Manion said. "You don't have to give yourself a handicap by driving a British battleship."

"So that's the reason for your visit?" Steiner asked.

"No. I couldn't see who was driving the Rover," Manion said. "I didn't make the connection until I noticed it parked out front."

"Serves me right for being too lazy to use the garage," Steiner said, not in the least embarrassed by his curious behavior.

"Did you spy anything interesting this morning?" Manion asked.

"We can get into that," Steiner said, "after you tell me why you're here."

Manion stared at him. The idea of confiding in a man he obviously shouldn't trust made no sense. But he didn't know anyone else who had been through the rehabilitation process. He said, "I'm not sure. I've been feeling a little woozy ever since I left Evangeline Spa. But today it was more than that. I got the shakes. And I just felt . . ."

"Scared?"

"Maybe. Like I was operating without a plan, not sure what the hell I was doing."

"What do you want to do?"

Manion shrugged. "The *Picayune* story about J. J. Legendre's death is in your computer, so I assume you've read it. They're calling it a suicide."

"Yeah."

"I don't believe it. But I don't know if this is a realistic conclusion, or if it's based on some kind of residual paranoia carried over from the drugs."

"Can you get a fix on what's bothering you about the suicide?"

"I've been told that there was some evidence to the contrary that the police ignored. But it's not just that," Manion said. "My place was robbed. The guy who did it has been murdered. He had a piece of paper that I think contained some of J.J.'s notes."

"You've got the paper?"

"I . . . lost it. A cop knocked me out, and when I woke up, the paper was gone."

Steiner grinned at him. "You sure do live a full life, pal."

"I'll trade you," Manion said.

"The question is: Is all this stuff really happening?"

Manion said, "It's happening. But I'm not sure if I'm adding it all up properly. Can I trust myself?"

"I don't know. Can you?"

"The reason I came here is to get an unbiased opinion."

Steiner cocked his head to one side. "Let's see where the cop conked you."

Manion pointed to the spot behind his ear. Steiner squinted at it. "Christ, it's the size of a pigeon's egg and it's sort of yellow-colored. You sure as hell got hit. I think you'd be wise to remember the immortal words: Just because you're paranoid, it doesn't mean they're not trying to get you."

"That what do I do?"

"What's your worst fear?" Steiner asked, sitting down.

"That I'm not up to the job of finding out the truth about J.J.'s death."

"Hell, Terry. It's like any job. Maybe you can do it, maybe you can't. No big disgrace if it beats you. But I would imagine that you're going to have to give it a shot.

"If you're asking me about the aftereffect of drugs on your skill as a detective, I don't have the answer. But I think Doc Courville would have tried to patch up any cracks like that before sending you off. The main thing is for you to keep away from the shit now that your system is relatively clear."

"I don't have any desire for drugs," Manion said.

"That puts you one up on me, pal. And I've been clean for a long time. Look, I've got a suggestion. Why don't we keep company for a spell. You can bunk in here. There's an extra room upstairs. Stick around until you get back your confidence."

"That's a little above and beyond the obligations of a sponsor, isn't it?" Manion asked.

"Maybe. But I know what it's like when somebody close to you . . . dies like that."

Manion recalled the scene from Steiner's novel in which the hero finds his wife who has just taken her own life. He asked, "How much of *In Salvador* is autobiographical?"

Steiner stared at him. "Some," he said. "Some always is."

"The wife who committed suicide," Manion said, a statement more than a question.

Steiner nodded. "She was a beautiful woman. Born in León. Modeled in Paris. Intelligent. Funny. Everything a man could want. We were living in this big goddamned palace of an apartment in New York. Having a hell of a good time." Steiner was on the edge of tears but beat the urge. "I haven't talked about it much. It wasn't part of the book's publicity packet. It's not something I got into with *People* magazine."

"You don't have to get into it with me either," Manion said.

"But I want you to know. It's important. I left this lovely, passionate woman and went off to Israel with the idea of doing a book about the Mossad. The PLO had killed three guys in Cyprus who turned out to be Mossad agents, and that got me interested. Anyway, it took longer than I thought and Martine—that was her name—got a little restless and went off to ski in Europe. She met up with some young stud closer to her own age who evidently had access to a lot of coke. Martine and I had been doing our share of toot, but this punk pushed her over the white line, so to speak. Then he dumped her. Strung out and alone, she . . . cut her wrists in the tub. By the time the Swiss police identified her and got word to me, nearly a month had passed.

"I arranged for her coffin to be brought back to this country and planted next to my parents in a little cemetery outside of Wheaton. For a while I tried to find the bastard that put that razor in her hand, but I was deep into the white shit myself by then, really wailing, and I had nothing to go on. So I gave it up, went in for a cure, and wound up writing *In Salvador* instead. Real life is just another form of research, right?

"Anyway, I'm clean now, with enough money to take me into the next century. So I'm here for you, Terry. You can count on it."

The bearded man suddenly extended his hand. Manion didn't take it. He asked, "Why were you following me? What's the story on that file in your computer with my name on it?"

Steiner withdrew his hand and used it to scratch his scalp. "Well, Terry, I'm interested in you."

"Interested in me how?"

"Not sexually, if that's what's on your mind. I'd like to hang out with you while you investigate your friend Legendre's death. I think there's a book in it."

Manion stared at him. "You're wrong," he said, standing.

"Hold on now. Just think about it. A true-life story about a private detective who solves the murder of his best friend."

"Maybe it's not murder. Maybe I won't solve it. Maybe I don't want my story selling for fifteen dollars a pop."

"Nineteen ninety-five," Steiner said. "Seriously, you'd call all the shots, Terry. Nothing gets put in the book that you don't approve of."

"You got *that* right," Manion said, walking out of the kitchen.

Steiner followed at a trot. "Slow down, for God's sake. Angela is coming back with poor boys."

Manion reversed his direction and stormed through the door leading to Steiner's office. "Hold on now!" Steiner shouted.

Manion approached the computer and reached out to the keyboard.

Steiner said, "Let me do it." He moved past Manion. "You sure you want it this way?"

"I'm not a public figure," Manion said, his temper cooling. "Try writing about me and I'll sue your butt."

"All you had to do was ask," Steiner said, deleting the "Manion" file from his hard disk. When he turned, Manion had already left the room. He ran after the detective, caught him at the front gate.

"Wait a minute," Steiner called. "You're still going to need a sponsor."

"I'll take care of that myself," Manion said, getting into his car and driving away.

19
•

AS DUSK deepened, Croaker aimed his black Thunderbird toward Canal Street along the Claiborne Overpass, shifting angrily. He punched the buttons on the car radio, but the airwaves seemed to be filled with nothing but the rantings and ravings of rock groups. No Verdi to ease his mood and lift his soul. No Puccini. Only twanging guitars and the occasional zydeco accordion that his father loved but that had been one of the reasons he'd moved away from home. He growled in aggravation. All that did was make his chronically raw throat feel worse. He removed a little disposable atomizer from his coat pocket and sprayed an antiseptic mist into his mouth. If nothing else, it cut the taste of bile.

To his right was Charity Hospital, where Pos Fouchette was hanging on to life. Dammit! He'd have to clean that up, too. It had been a mistake to let Reevie Benedetto involve him in something that was none of his affair. He had known Reevie for a number of years, ever since Charlie Benedetto, for whom he worked on a freelance basis, had sent him abroad to get the kid out of a "situation." The old man, as tough as he was to do business with, always played it straight and clean. Reevie worked things out like an overly complicated chess game. But in a chess game, sometimes you concentrated so hard on one objective you forgot to keep an eye on the whole board.

Croaker understood that he was a pawn. And Reevie was running the risk of losing him by not playing straight with Johnny the Wolf about the Legendre "suicide." As in the past, Johnny had been his main contact. But Reevie, for whatever reason, had made it clear that Johnny was to be kept as much in the dark as possible about the whole business. That meant that whenever Johnny had asked any pertinent questions, Croaker had been forced to go into a tap dance and play stupid. In fact, he didn't know much.

Still, he could tell Johnny was growing more and more pissed about being closed out. And since he couldn't take it out on his nephew, his wrath would probably come down on Croaker one of these days.

Even when he was working with you, Johnny was an asshole. He'd forced Croaker to work with that low-rent flake Shecksnyder, who lived like a pig and thought like a pig. It had not surprised him when the petty thief had tried to blackmail Reevie. Sure, Shecksnyder knew how to crack a lock and work over a room without scuffing up the floor. But he was scum. And he was a flake. Whatever Johnny was, he didn't belong in Personnel.

Croaker had refused to close out Shecksnyder. Though he didn't know for sure, he suspected that Johnny Benedetto had done that job himself. It had been messy and unprofessional, which fit his impression of Johnny the Wolf. If you knew what you were doing, you always tried to give the cops an out. If it was a possible suicide, and they couldn't get a handle on what had really gone down, then they could label it a definite suicide and everybody would be happy. A guy with his throat cut in a meat locker was in no way a suicide. A bush-league job.

Johnny's stupidity seemed to have rubbed off on him. The business that morning had been a total fuckup. All his. There was no one else he could blame. Even if he had taken out the girl, it wouldn't have been a smooth, clean hit he could be proud of. As it was, he'd shot the wrong person. Definitely the wrong person. And the girl was still alive and on her guard. The old lady had gotten a good look at him too. And to top it all off, some sonofabitch in a black Range Rover had followed him from the scene of the crime. It'd taken Croaker nearly thirty minutes to shake him. Dammit!

On Canal, he used his horn to blast an elderly black pedestrian out of his way and swung left, away from the downtown area. The cars were filling the street near Mandina's Restaurant. It was the drinkers' hour. He wished he could be there with them. Black Jack on the rocks. Table'll be ready in ten minutes. Breaded veal maybe, or fried trout. Shit! As hungry and thirsty as he was, he had to pin down the guy in the Range Rover and find out how he fit in.

The building he was looking for was easy to find. It was a scdate tan stucco, with a large floor-to-ceiling window disclosing a brightly lit cream-colored showroom that contained half a dozen shiny Jaguars of various colors and styles. The sign on the building, in old English type, read, "Canal Imports." Next to the building was a floodlit blacktop lot filled with an assortment of shiny European motorcars, new and used.

Croaker made a U-turn, crossing the neutral ground that split the two lanes along Canal, then drifted to the right curb and parked. He watched the lot for a few minutes, noted a salesman trying to remain patient while two young black men in short-sleeved shirts and Bermuda shorts checked out the cars.

Croaker counted four other salesmen inside the building and two women at desks along one wall. Behind the building was some sort of service department that apparently was closed for the night.

His mood darkening even more, he got out of his Thunderbird and crossed the neutral ground. A few yards from the door to Canal Imports, a bag lady was ensconced on a public bench, hugging a cloth sack while rocking back and forth, humming to herself. Croaker scowled at her. He was disgusted at the way the city seemed to be turning to crap before his very eyes.

Once he'd entered the showroom, it took a full minute for a salesman to approach him. The man was short, with a naturally sad face that he tried to brighten with an insincere smile. He was wearing a dark blue linen suit with a yellow tie dotted with ducks. Croaker didn't like the tie at all.

"Need any help, suh?" the salesman said affably.

"I'm looking for a Range Rover," Croaker replied in a voice so hoarse the salesman took a step backward.

"Good choice," he said, recovering, running his eyes over Croaker's wardrobe appraisingly. Suit, Italian cut, maybe four hundred. Shoes a hundred and fifty. The man could probably afford at least a down payment. He continued eagerly, "*Four Wheeler* magazine's 'Four-wheeler of the Year.' Now over here we have a—"

"I'm looking for a silver and black Range Rover." There was only a hint of bayou dialect in that hoarse delivery, but the salesman was a bit depressed by it.

"We've a nice black—"

"Silver and black," Croaker repeated with a tone of finality.

The salesman hesitated. "I don't think we have one on the floor right now. But I've got some really beautiful—"

Croaker opened his mouth and the salesman put up his hand. "Yeah. Right. Silver and black. Well, I think I could probably order one for you . . ."

"Isn't there one I could see?"

"See?"

"Yeah," Croaker said. "You know. Observe. Take a look at." He got out his atomizer again. Too much talking.

The salesman pointed at a black Range Rover on the floor. "It's just like that, except it has a silver stripe along the door. Heck, I bet we could even put a stripe on that one and . . ."

Croaker frowned, confused. His contact at the DMV had given him this address. "I heard you had a black and silver Range Rover here. Dealer plates. Maybe one of the guys uses it?"

The salesman shook his head. "I don't know. Maybe. Not me, though." He turned to a group of similarly dark-suited men and asked, "Any of you guys drive a black and silver Rover?"

A myopic fellow with a baby face said, "That's a lease. Friend of the owner's. Some kinda writer. Moved here from New York and wasn't sure if he really needed a car. Imagine that? The boss gave him the option to buy if he wants. I cut the papers about six months ago."

"Before my time," the sad-faced salesman said.

"Any chance I could get a look at it?" Croaker asked Baby Face. "If it's what I want, I'll let you order me one."

Baby Face winked at the sad-faced salesman and motioned Croaker to follow him. "Lemme check my files," he said. "I'll try to get the guy on the horn and see if it's okay."

In his small, glass-partitioned office, Baby Face slid open a file drawer, flipped through bulging folders, and stopped. He yanked out one folder and carried it to his desk.

Croaker easily read the name on the outside of the folder. It seemed familiar. He shifted on his feet impatiently, while Baby Face dialed a number. Croaker took note of that, too.

After the fifth or sixth ring, Croaker heard the phone being answered and a voice shouting, "Fuck off! I'm not here!"

The salesman's soft pink face registered surprise, then professional frustration, as he cradled the phone. "Uh, must have caught him at a crunch time. I'll try him again tomorrow. How can I reach you?"

"I've changed my mind," Croaker said over his shoulder, heading out. "I think I'll buy American instead."

He went directly to a Katz & Besthoff Drugstore in the next block, where he chased a nervous woman away from the pay phone by standing within inches of her and glaring. He dialed a number and gave the person who answered the name and phone number he'd gotten from the salesman. It took only a few seconds for a computer to spit out the address. Croaker hung up the receiver without saying "Thanks." But he was smiling now.

He moved to the drugstore's liquor counter and picked out a bottle of the most expensive bourbon the place carried. At the stationery section, he selected notepaper and an easy-glide ballpoint pen. Just beside the cashier, he spotted a display of his brand of throat spray, so he picked up a couple of those. He felt in control again. His good luck was returning.

The disgusting bag lady had worked her way to the front of the drugstore, where she was bothering customers entering and departing. Croaker walked around her, holding his breath. He got into his Thunderbird, turned on the air conditioner, and eased from the curb.

His destination was Prytania Street, just past the Garden District. He used Loyola Avenue, Dryades, and Louisiana to get him there as quickly as possible.

He drove past the address, noting the Range Rover parked in front of a formidable gate. He parked his car a block away and left with the package from Katz & Besthoff under his arm. As he neared the Range Rover, mulling over a few methods of getting his quarry to leave his home, the grill gate creaked open. And Terry Manion walked through it!

Croaker stepped into the shadow cast by an oak tree and chanced another look. Manion was being followed by a stocky, bearded man in shorts. The detective seemed angry about something. He turned his back on the stocky guy and got into an old Mustang that was parked in front of the Range Rover.

Croaker realized that the beard was apparently his quarry, Marcus Steiner, the Yankee who was leasing the Range Rover. And he was a pal of Manion's!

Croaker cursed under his breath. This too was to be laid on Reevie Benedetto's doorstep. If Reevie had let him do Manion in the first place, this whole mess might have been avoided.

20

•

MANION WAS too restless to go home. Besides, the Gaynaud house, where Leon Harris's uncle had worked and died, was less than ten minutes away. He turned his Mustang in the direction of St. Charles Avenue.

He liked the drive along the avenue at night, liked the warmly lit, elaborately constructed homes, separated from the outside world by fences and foliage. Liked the rattling, clanging streetcars that swayed precariously down the center of the neglected grassy neutral ground.

Manion was surprised to find a few ultramodern glass-and-concrete monstrosities sandwiched in among the crumbling antiquities. When had those gone up? In the last three or four months? The French Quarter had a governing board that ruled on any architectural change in the area, but the rest of the city, even a revered area like this, was less structured. Anyone could construct a double-decker Swiss chalet there if they had the inclination and the money. So far nobody had tried. But at the rate the bargain basement property values were being picked up by international buyers, there was no telling what the city would look like in a few years.

Manion parked several blocks from the Gaynaud home, partly out of habit, partly for masochistic reasons of his own. He strolled from the Mustang down the badly lit and broken sidewalk until he reached a tall wrought-iron fence. Set well back from it and the sidewalk was a substantial stone building that he knew very well. At ground level, two shuttered French windows flanked a front door with a cut-glass panel. A polished brass lamp illuminated a section of the carpeted porch, a still glider, a plaster cat he knew was chipped and cracked. The floor above was fronted by a balcony that could be entered by any of three French windows belonging to three bedrooms.

Manion wondered if his ex-wife Gillian was inside, in from the Orient for a visit with her family before heading on to a new lover and a new adventure. He could almost hear her laughter on the evening air.

Drifting halfway between agony and reverie, he was brought back to earth by the sound of something moving from the house toward him in the darkness. It was a collie dog, old and slow. The dog poked its long pointed snout through the gateposts and moaned at Manion. Manion petted its head and said, "How ya doing, Napoleon?"

The dog nuzzled his hand. From somewhere at the rear of the house, a woman's voice called out, "Nap-eee, Nap-eee, come in now." Manion recognized it as belonging to Gil's sister, Margee, who had sent him on the journey to Southern California that ended with his rehabilitation at Evangeline Spa. One of these days, he would have to have a long chat with Margee, but he wasn't quite ready for that. So he patted the dog once more and moved off down the street.

The Gaynaud home occupied nearly half a block of prime, albeit rapidly depreciating, New Orleans real estate enclosed by a filigree iron fence a foot taller than the average man. Huge, gnarled oak trees, garnished with Spanish moss, combined with traditional sculpted shrubs and blooming magnolias and crepe myrtle to complement a white two-story house supported by two equally white columns. The house had mint-green shutters.

Faux flambeau lamps illuminated an assortment of brightly colored plants and flowers. It seemed as if the whole place had been dragged behind a team of slow, careful horses all the way from the Natchez Trace. It was, in fact, so unashamedly retro that for as long as Manion could remember, there had been a popular local expression: "That's as old-fashioned as Gaynaud's front porch."

As Manion put his hand on the gate, he half expected to hear the happy singing of the darkies in the cotton fields out back. That dream was shattered by a red and chrome classic Corvette that cornered on two wheels and roared down the formerly peaceful avenue in his direction.

The convertible screeched to a stop, rocked back and forth, and made a wide turn, heading straight for the closed gates to the Gay-naud driveway. It halted a half inch from the wrought-iron gate.

The blonde behind the wheel clenched her jaws under her out-sized glasses and aimed a remote control device at the gate. She pressed it and it clicked, but the gate refused to open. She tried it again. Then she stood up above the windscreen and threw the object at the gate.

That didn't work either.

Manion moved to the car. "Try 'Open sesame,' " he suggested.

She glanced at him, then slumped back into the seat. "Damn stupid gate," she said.

He noted she was wearing what appeared to be a black double-breasted jacket. In lieu of a blouse, she'd tied a pink scarf around her neck, leaving her breasts almost exposed. Her hair, with its impossi-bly white-blond color, had been given added body by the windy trip. Her green eyes were magnified by her glasses.

He bent over and picked up the gate device. He aimed it, clicked it, and the gate rolled open. Without giving him another look, the plantinum blonde gunned her sports car onto the grounds, swerving off the drive and putting an end to several exotic blooms along the edge of the lawn. Manion followed in her wake.

She stopped the car near the front door but kept its engine idling. She just sat there unmoving, her eyes open, her breathing ragged. Manion reached across her and turned off the car's engine. He tossed her gate opener onto the seat beside her.

She shook her head and frowned, staring at him. Her emerald eyes were all pupils. Her thin Roman nose was chalk white, but the area around the nostrils was an angry red. Her generous mouth looked slack and raw. With all that, she was still one of the most beautiful women Manion had ever seen. He assumed that, sober, she could be heartbreaking.

It took her three tries to get the car door open. She swung her body around, giving Manion a view of exquisite legs exposed by a gathered white skirt. She tried standing, but it was beyond her.

"What are you on?" Manion asked.

"You name it," she said. "Gimme a hand, huh?"

Manion took her rather large hand in his and yanked. She came up from the car suddenly, a tall woman, bumping into him on an angle. He staggered backward as she pressed against him. Her legs, no matter how shapely, behaved like sponge rubber.

Somehow Manion kept them both upright. Her arms went around his neck, and her bracelet dug into the tender spot on the back of his head.

"Ow. Take it easy," he told her, dislodging the bracelet.

Her legs gave out completely and they did a little ballet across the lawn. She began to laugh.

"You think this is funny?" he asked.

"Who the hell are you anyway? Who the . . ."

She passed out and Manion ducked down and let her body fall over his shoulder. With some effort he stood, lifting her. She was tall but thin enough to make the trip to the front door a possibility.

There she seemed to rally and wiggled, kneeing him in the side and making noises that sounded like "Whoop, whoop."

"Let's have the key," he said.

"Key? No key." She giggled.

Manion tried the door handle, but it was definitely locked. He lowered his shoulder and deposited her beside the door. "Come on, lady, time to get straight."

"Straight? And waste all that Stoli and chemicals?" She yawned and went limp again. Manion eased her down until she was sitting on the concrete, propped against the side of the house.

He found her wallet on the front seat of the Corvette and was rooting in it for a key when the front door was opened by a large, scowling man in his sixties. Mini-jowls hung from the corners of his square, gray face. Charcoal hair was speckled with ash. Manion immediately recognized him as the man he'd come to see.

Lawson Gaynaud's hooded eyes opened briefly as his daughter fell over at his feet. Then he switched his attention to Manion, whose fingers were still in her wallet. Gaynaud's face began to glow red, except for his eaglelike hooked nose, which remained waxen white.

Manion tried to smile. "She's had a little too much," he said. He withdrew his fingers from the wallet and added lamely, "I was looking for her key."

"She has none," Gaynaud replied. "Lindsay loses her keys. Her keys, her temper, and, it seems, her sense of discretion. She even loses her wallets."

Manion handed him the billfold. "I suppose we should get her into the house," he said.

"Please," Gaynaud said, turning his back on them. He was wearing poplin pants with a web belt, a blue chambray shirt, and dark blue slippers with the Coast Guard shield on the front. Manion wondered what he'd been up to before they disturbed him. A little brightwork, maybe.

Lindsay Gaynaud seemed to be adding pounds by the second as Manion toted her down a long, dark hallway to a comfortable living room, where a giant gilt-edged mirror, perched above a marble fireplace and mantel, dominated the decor. A beige carpet matched the walls, on which were hung original oil seascapes.

Manion canvassed the room desperately until he discovered a purple velvet love seat. He dumped Lindsay Gaynaud onto it.

The elder Gaynaud shouted, "Clovis!" and continued to glare at his daughter, shaking his head in disgust.

An attractive young woman entered the room at a run. Black horn–rimmed glasses were perched on her pointy nose. She was wearing a man's button-down blue shirt, the sleeves rolled to her elbows, baggy blue denim trousers, and high-top basketball shoes. Her coppery hair was cut as short as a man's. She wore no makeup. Her body was too full and her mouth too ripe for her to successfully carry off the asexual effect she was obviously courting.

She frowned when she spotted Lindsay on the settee.

"Help her to her room, Clovis."

Clovis moved to the snoring girl. She withdrew a small glass bottle from her trouser pocket and held it under Lindsay's nose, using her free hand to close the girl's mouth.

Lindsay struggled, took a deep breath, and began to cough. She sat upright, making a gagging noise. "Holy shit!" she shrieked. "You trying to strangle me?"

"Can you walk, dear?" Clovis asked patiently, with just a hint of southern-accented malice.

"Oh, Clovis. Sweet Clovis." Lindsay tried to stand, but sank to her knees on the carpet. "Help me."

Clovis gave the girl another whiff of salts and helped her to her feet. Lindsay was wobbly but manageable. "You might want to have her checked," Manion offered. "She said she'd been mixing vodka and drugs."

Gaynaud's hawk's eyes flashed at him. "My daughter may drink to excess on occasion, sir. She is not an addict."

Clovis and Lindsay were edging slowly from the room. "She told me she's been using chemicals," Manion said. "That doesn't make her an addict necessarily. But you might want to look into it."

Gaynaud hesitated, then bellowed, "Exactly who the devil are you, young man?"

"My name's Terry Manion."

Gaynaud's forehead wrinkled. "Jack Manion's boy?"

"Yes."

"Your father was a fine man. Not that I'd ever be able to condone what he did to himself."

The sore spot at the back of Manion's head began to throb, and he closed his eyes briefly.

"Are you all right?" Gaynaud asked, more curious than solicitous.

"An old war wound," Manion muttered. "I'll be okay."

Gaynaud stared at Manion as if perplexed. "Have you . . . and my daughter been . . . friends very long?"

"We met maybe ten minutes ago. I was on my way in and she almost ran over me. She looked like she might hurt somebody, probably herself. So I helped her to the door."

"Well, I thank you for your good intentions, though I firmly believe that helping folks only makes 'em weaker and more dependent."

"That's some philosophy," Manion said.

"Isn't it?" Gaynaud mumbled as he moved to a cabinet housing two cut-glass bottles and a set of stemmed glasses. The bottles were filled with brown liquids. "Excuse me for falling down in my host's chores. It's just that I get upset seeing Linnie like that. Doesn't happen as often as you might think. She . . . uh, suffered a great loss. She was engaged to Gerry St. John. You must recall the tragedy."

"That's one I missed," Manion said.

"Ah. Well, poor Gerry. His father, Hammond St. John, and your father and I did some work for deLesseps Morrison when he was mayor. Way back before your time. I was still with Metro Mortgage." His rigid face relaxed in a smile, then tensed again as his train of thought went back on track. "It was one of those flash thunderstorms. A downpour. Water coming down in buckets. Streets were flooded, like they get. Gerry drove his sports car into the aqueduct off of Washington Boulevard. Because of the storm, the water was at least thirty feet deep. He got trapped in the little car. Some kind of foreign toy. Didn't have a chance. Awful thing. Linnie's never been the same."

"When did it happen?"

"Nearly a year ago. Just about a year. I remember because I'd just got back from Baton Rouge visiting Lawson junior—he's with the legislature, you know. Anyway, I got back just in time to get caught in the weather. Hammond's phone call woke us in the early morning. Lord, it was a ghastly thing. Linnie just . . . couldn't handle it. She's been seeing a . . . doctor, but you have witnessed all the good it's doing. She's out of control. Won't listen to anything anybody tries to tell her."

He gave Manion an odd, fixed grin. "Sorry, but I keep forgetting the amenities. Mrs. Gaynaud and I don't do much drinking . . . Sherry's about the strongest stuff we've got in the house. Care for some?"

"No thanks," Manion said, wondering why everyone seemed to be offering him alcohol since he returned. Gaynaud poured a glass for himself and carried it to a brightly patterned sofa, indicating that Manion should sit nearby in a velvet armchair.

"Your dad used to talk about you all the time. We played gin once a week at the Pickwick for nearly ten years. The golden boy," he said, toasting Manion with the sherry before taking a sip.

When he'd swallowed, he asked, "Are you in banking like Jack?"

"No," Manion answered.

"What then, stocks and bonds? You're not in real estate. I know everybody in real estate. Even if I am retired."

"I'm a private investigator."

That brought back Gaynaud's scowl. "You mean like on TV?"

"That's the general idea. Usually not so dramatic."

Gaynaud's lip curled in much the same manner as it did in response to his daughter's condition. "Jack sent you to college for *that*?"

"As hard as it may be to believe, Mr. Gaynaud, I didn't stop by tonight to chat with you about my father or my occupation, or even your daughter."

Gaynaud sat back on the couch. "What then?" he asked warily.

"I've got a few questions about Parker Harris."

Gaynaud scratched his chin and frowned. Then he pushed himself up from the couch and refilled his glass. "Old Parker, huh?" he asked. "What about him?"

"What happened to him?"

"He just lived too long. His legs gave out from under him and he fell down some stairs. Neck broke like a twig. Better that way. No suffering. No indignity of hanging around a hospital ward with tubes stuck in your veins."

"Could I see where it happened?"

Gaynaud cocked his head to one side. "Why, for heaven's sake?"

Manion tried a smile. "It's the sort of thing I do."

"You should be ashamed of yourself."

Manion shrugged. "I give measure for measure. Nothing shameful about that."

"And who's paying you to worm your way into my home?" Gaynaud's eyes were almost completely veiled by their lids. Then they opened suddenly. "Ah, the nephew. Of course. Still at it."

"Nope. No nephew."

"Then some other person of color?"

Manion was amused by the use of the antique phrase, if not by its intent. His client was Nadia, whose color was probably the only thing Gaynaud might find acceptable about her. Still, he asked, "What difference would that make?"

"None to me, certainly. But perhaps to you, if you expect to continue . . . doing what you do. There's a new mood in the city, as I'm sure you're aware. Battle lines are once again being drawn."

"I'll keep that in mind," Manion told him.

"You won't, but that's your problem. I suppose you know that another . . . member of your profession approached me a while ago, asking about poor old Parker. I was kinda hoping that would be the end of it. Now here you are."

"Was the other man's name Legendre?"

"Yes. A fine old French name. Seemed like a smart fella. He work with you?"

"He's dead."

"Oh. That's too bad. He looked healthy as a hog."

Manion wondered if Gaynaud was toying with him. "His death was rather sudden. Just like Parker Harris's."

The smile that had been playing around Gaynaud's lips disappeared. "Parker? I wouldn't call seventy-five years sudden."

"A man's alive and hearty one minute and dead with a broken neck the next. That's sudden at any age."

The older man grunted. "Well, come on. I might as well show you where it happened, if for no other reason than to be rid of you."

He led Manion to a large, round room in the center of the house. A piano sat silently in one corner, beside French windows. At least twenty folding chairs were stacked in piles along one wall. "When my wife was in better health," Gaynaud explained, "she'd give little recitals, much to the delight of our friends."

He pointed to the rear of the room where a staircase of carved mahogany made a half twist on its way to the floor above. It was a splendid work of hand-rubbed carpentry. Brass rods tucked the maroon runner into place around each stair. "That's where . . . it happened. The doctor thinks Parker may have had a mild stroke. Or maybe, like I said, his legs just gave out. He was near the top of the stairs and he fell backward. The carpet would have cushioned the fall, ordinarily, but he landed on his neck."

"Who found the body?"

"I did."

"And you called the doctor?"

"He was here at the time."

"Oh?"

"As I told you, my wife has been ill. She rarely leaves her bed. The doctor spends a great deal of time here. I have the bills to prove it, if you're interested."

Manion said, "Not particularly. But I *would* like to know the doctor's name."

"Henry De La Verne," Gaynaud replied with surprisingly little hesitation. "You can call him if you wish. He's a busy man, but I'll ask him to spare you a few minutes."

"My schedule is pretty tight too," Manion said. "But I'll keep Dr. De La Verne in mind." He decided not to waste his time with the doctor. He didn't think Gaynaud was bluffing. If De La Verne had any worthwhile information about Parker Harris's death, he would not pass it on to Manion.

The detective let his eyes wander over the room's high ceiling with its crystal chandelier, the murals along the wall. "How many people live here?"

Gaynaud did not reply. He seemed to be depressed by the room or the stairwell or something else beyond Manion's knowledge. He ushered the younger man back into the living room, where Manion repeated his question.

"People? This is a residence, not a hotel. My wife and I live here.

My daughter, Lindsay. Lawson junior stays here when he's in town, but he spends most of his time at his home in the capital. Clovis Longstreet, who makes this whole place work . . ."

". . . sleeps here?"

Manion had tried to make the question innocent, but Gaynaud's face reddened all the same. "She lives here, yes. Now, if that's all . . ."

"I'd like to talk to her about Parker Harris."

Gaynaud sighed in frustration. "She never met the man. She's only been in my employ a few months. Since Linnie's condition worsened and my wife . . . I suspect it was Linnie and her problems that prompted my wife's illness. Anyhow, as God is my judge, I simply can't handle all of this by myself. Clovis is my right arm these days. The only one I can depend on. Without her I'd . . ."

Gaynaud didn't finish the sentence. His mind seemed to have momentarily tripped off to some other location. Judging by his expression, it was not a nice place. Manion asked, "Then Mrs. Gaynaud's condition is not entirely physical?"

The older man's eyes flashed again and his mouth sharpened to a thin line. "Not entirely." Then the anger deserted him to be replaced by self-pity. "They say it's the menopause thing, but—"

Manion didn't want to hear about the menopause thing. He interrupted with, "Could I see where the dead man lived?"

Gaynaud pointedly glanced at his wristwatch. "I suppose so."

Parker Harris's room had been directly over the kitchen and well away from the main bedrooms. Food smells lingered in its corners like bad memories. There was a neatly made single bed, a writing desk, a chair, and a lamp. A small, empty bookshelf. No dust anywhere.

"Is someone living here now?" Manion asked.

"No. The maid goes over it every so often. We decided not to replace Parker. I've got a fella stops by four times a month to keep the garden and lawn in shape. We don't entertain, what with Lily . . ." He let it trail off.

Manion opened the rolltop desk, exposing several felt-tip pens and cheap writing paper. "I understand there was a will," Manion said.

Gaynaud nodded. "Dammit, it *is* the nephew who hired you. Got himself a few bucks and hired another detective. What's the plan, Terry? Is he going to try and squeeze a few more dollars out of me?"

"How much has he squeezed out of you already?"

The older man was silent for a minute, then: "I had to pay for the funeral expenses and the legal fees for the handling of Parker's will."

"That wasn't the nephew's fault. Nobody thought to tell him his uncle had died until a month after the fact. The old man wasn't even buried the way he'd requested."

"Then the boy *is* your client."

"I told you he wasn't. But I *have* talked with him."

"I bet that was educational."

Manion had no intention of playing that game. "Could I speak with your maid?"

"Why?"

"She must have known Parker. She worked with him."

Gaynaud shook his large head. "Letty is new. She started here after Parker's death." He turned off the light in the room and led Manion back through the silent house.

"Where might I find someone who *did* work with Parker?" Manion asked at the front door. "We could start with your former maid."

"She retired and went to live with family in the country. I don't have any idea where that might be." He paused then: "It sounds as if you intend to pursue your investigation."

"A little bit, I guess," Manion said. "Until I figure out why you didn't just boot me out of the house as soon as you found out what I wanted."

Gaynaud's jawline tensed. "I allowed you to remain in my house for one reason only—your father and I were very close friends."

It caught Manion offguard. He rallied weakly. "If that's true, he never mentioned it."

"Your father was a secretive sort of man," Gaynaud said, his face breaking into a victor's grin. "I bet there's a whole lot of things he never mentioned to you. Good night, Mr. Manion. I don't suppose you'll be bothering me or mine anymore in the future."

"I'd rather not, but you never know."

Manion continued to stare at the door for a few seconds after it had slammed. Then he walked away from the house slowly, his mind a jumble. So many strings, so few connections.

The night was clear and the moon bright overhead. Fireflies swooped in and out of the magnolia trees. The humid air had a sweet, decadent odor. He'd barely reached the sidewalk when he heard the front door open.

He half expected it to be Gaynaud, but it was the daughter, staggering to her Corvette. He started back. To do what? Stop her from killing herself and some other, unsuspecting driver?

The engine roared and the car made a U-turn, coming directly toward him. When she saw him in her headlights, she spun the car to the left, away from him. He leapt to the right. He shouted, "Lindsay!" as she passed. He didn't know if she heard him or not.

By the time he reached his car three blocks away, the Corvette was just a memory.

21

CROAKER HAD watched and waited while Manion drove away from Marcus Steiner's home. Then, just as he started toward the writer with his bag from Katz & Besthoff, Steiner ducked back inside his gate. He didn't shut it.

Croaker looked past the opening, checking out the grounds before entering. There wasn't much light. Finally, he took one cautious step inside the gate. The front door to the house was ajar. Steiner evidently wasn't sticking around too long.

Croaker looked over the shadowy area once again, trying to decide on the best spot to wait for Steiner to exit. That was when he spotted the battered dog bowl in the light from the open door. It was a very large bowl. Croaker beat a fast retreat to a point just outside the gate where he could keep an eye on the front door.

The dog—a fucking giant dog—walked lazily from the house, followed by Steiner, who was rattling a ring of keys. Croaker back-stepped away from the gate. The tree-lined residential street was dark, deserted. He circled the Range Rover. Through its windows, he saw Steiner exiting through the gate. The dog was at his heels. Don't let him take the goddamned animal for a walk, Croaker prayed silently. Animals were too unpredictable.

Steiner said something to the dog and patted its head. He closed the gate with the dog inside. Croaker relaxed. His luck *had* definitely returned.

When Steiner put his key into the door of the Range Rover,

Croaker moved up behind him cautiously. He touched the back of Marcus Steiner's head with his pistol and growled, "Don't turn around. Just do what I say."

Unconsciously or not, the writer chose to disobey. He got only a fleeting glance at Croaker before the barrel of the gun came down on his skull like a padded hammer: Croaker did not want to knock him out, merely teach him a lesson. "Go around to unlock the passenger door and get in," Croaker rasped as the writer staggered. "Or I drop you where you stand."

This time Steiner did as he was told. Croaker followed him around. "Now slide across behind the wheel," he ordered gruffly.

"What do you want?" Steiner asked tentatively.

"Drive to the river," Croaker ordered.

Before the Range Rover could pull away, a little BMW convertible parked just behind them. A sexy brunette got out and held up a bag bearing the name "Mother's Muffalettas." She was smiling the smile of an obedient child. The smile altered drastically as Steiner pulled away without acknowledging her.

"Marcus, where are you going?"

Croaker ducked down in his seat. "Just keep driving!" he commanded.

"Marcus Steiner!" Angela screamed. "What do I do with all this food?"

The Rover rolled away from the woman.

Croaker stayed bent over. Maybe she hadn't seen him. If she had, she wouldn't be able to identify him. But he wanted her to think that Steiner was alone in the car. "Turn as soon as you can," he barked.

When he felt the Rover make a right turn, he rose up again. He stared at his captive. "That was fine, Marcus," he said.

"What now?"

"Keep headed toward the river." Croaker looked at the writer with some amazement. He hadn't considered the possibility that the Steiner on Prytania who drove a Range Rover might be the *novelist* Marcus Steiner. But the T-shirt's message nailed down that fact. "I read your Salvador book," he said.

Steiner kept his eyes on the road. "Oh?" he asked with no hint of surprise.

That was perfect, Croaker thought. The guy just assumed everybody read his goddamned book. Croaker said, "I found it very interesting. The characters were so real I almost felt like I knew them. That only happens with the best literature."

Steiner made no effort to reply, but Croaker thought he was preening a little.

"That your woman back there?"

Steiner nodded.

"Too young. You like them young, right?"

Steiner frowned. "So what?"

Croaker said, "You go with women your own age, it makes life a lot simpler." He placed something on Steiner's lap. Steiner was familiar with the object, a bottle of whiskey.

"Think of this as a celebration, Marcus. Like finishing a new book. The drinks are on me. Take a taste."

Steiner left the bottle where it was. He said, "I don't drink."

Croaker grabbed the bottle, popped the seal, and unscrewed the cap. He held it out. "Try it, you'll like it. It's the best money can buy."

"No thanks."

Croaker started to say something, then thought better of it. "Okay," he said. "If you won't drink my liquor, maybe you'll satisfy my curiosity. Why were you following me this morning?"

Steiner said, "It was a mistake."

"No shit. But tell me about the mistake. Explain it to me."

The Rover crossed Magazine Street. Noise. Bright lights. Then into darkness, silence, a street in need of repaving. Steiner said, "I saw you come out of an apartment. I was curious, so I followed you."

"What made you curious?"

"You had a gun in your hand."

"That's a good way to get hurt, following a guy with a gun in his hand."

Steiner sniffed the air.

"Smell something bad?" Croaker asked.

"No. The booze. It smells like perfume."

"And tastes like nectar. Are you working with him?" Croaker asked.

"Who?"

"Manion."

"No," Steiner replied. "I'm not working with him. I only just met him."

"Ah," Croaker said, as if that meant something. He reached into his pocket for his throat spray. He sent two blasts of medicated mist into his mouth. He saw Steiner staring at him and shoved the spray into his pocket angrily.

"The street's coming to an end," Steiner told him.

"Take a left," Croaker ordered. "Then follow that path over the tracks, there." He indicated an area of scrub grass and shell beside railroad tracks leading to an ancient wooden building that seemed to be at least partially a warehouse. As the Rover approached, its head-lamps illuminated the open doors of an empty attached garage.

"Put it in there," Croaker said. He had driven by the building months ago, had stopped and looked it over. He hadn't imagined he'd be using it so soon.

They passed a rusty For Rent sign hanging on the side of the building. The area was completely deserted. The owner of the prop-erty was not throwing good money after bad by paying for electricity.

Steiner parked the car in the garage. He turned off the ignition and Croaker poked him with his gun. "Start her up again."

Steiner looked at the whiskey bottle and licked his lips.

"Ready for one, huh?" Croaker asked. "Not just yet. Start the engine."

The Rover began to purr. "Okay," Croaker said, opening the car door. "Out."

After Steiner obeyed the command, Croaker growled, "Help me close up."

Together they shut the garage doors.

They were in darkness, except for the little colored lights on the Rover's dash. Croaker pushed Steiner through a door into another room. The floorboards gave slightly under their weight. The air smelled of sawdust and mildew. The door separating them from the Rover slammed behind them.

For a moment Steiner thought Croaker had remained outside, but that hope was dashed by the husky growl. "Soon we'll have that drink. But first, we'll have some more conversation. You use a lot of conversation in your books. Let's have some now."

"Conversation about what?" Croaker recognized the tone of desperation in the writer's voice.

"Tell me about Manion."

"I don't know much. He got into some jam in Los Angeles and wound up in a rehabilitation center. He was just released and I'm supposed to help him when he needs it."

Croaker was silent for a while. Then he asked, "What were you doing on General Taylor this morning?"

"Following Manion. I . . . wanted to be sure he was all right."

"You're a damn good storyteller, Marcus."

Croaker could feel Steiner relaxing. A little more and he might even try some defensive move.

"How well can you see, Marcus?" Croaker asked.

"There's enough moonlight through those windows for me to see where you are."

"Could you write something?"

"Not that wouldn't look like chicken scratch."

"Okay. I want you to take this."

Croaker handed Steiner a piece of notepaper and a disposable pen. Then he fired up a lighter, holding it between them, throwing ominous shadows over the empty, dusty room.

Croaker rasped, "Write what I tell you: 'I've . . . got . . . nothing . . . more . . . to . . . lose.' "

Steiner paused after the first three words.

"Go on, write it like I said."

Steiner took a deep breath, then straightened. He said, "If you want a suicide note, write the fucker yourself."

Croaker shoved the gun closer to Steiner's face. "Write!"

"You're sort of a novelist too, aren't you?" Steiner asked. "You set the scene. The room next door. The car with the engine running. Suicide."

"It's more like a play," Croaker said. "Act one: You drink too much. Act two: You get depressed. Act three: You decide to kill yourself because you're weak and life is shitty. I'll write the note, if you want. It won't change things much."

Croaker moved the gun until it was pointed at Steiner's temple. Then he clicked off his lighter. His finger tightened on the trigger. But there was a distracting noise. The shell surface cracking outside the building.

Croaker moved to the window, looked out at two figures moving in on the building. His goddamned luck hadn't changed after all.

Steiner realized he was no longer afraid of the man. The jumble of his thoughts and memories had somehow chased away his own fear. He was too furious to be afraid.

He saw the killer at the window, outlined against the dark blue night sky. His hands moved across the floor, searching for a weapon. Then he lost sight of the man. He felt a breeze against his face, and from the garage came a tremendous crash that shook the whole building, followed by the tympany of shattered glass and lumber landing against tin.

The front door was thrown open and two figures bounded in carrying guns. Steiner could barely make out their features. The first was a thin man in his late sixties who walked bent over as if his back hurt. He was followed by . . . Steiner blinked. Perhaps the blow to the head had seriously affected him. The second figure appeared to be a bag lady in dirty tatters. She announced dryly, "Well, Mr. Steiner, if you're finished playing around in here, we might as well get going. That ornery, murderous sonofabitch has just driven your Range Rover through the back wall and taken off for parts unknown."

22

.

MANION WAS fumbling with the key to his front door when he noticed that the lock had been forced. Mumbling a curse, he pushed the door open but did not cross the threshold. Someone had turned the air conditioner on full force and it was making a groaning sound.

"Hey, Ter, don't jus' stand there. You're lettin' in all the hot air," Eben Munn called out from the office. He was sitting behind the desk, his huge dusty cordovans resting on and smudging its surface. He was watching Manion's small portable TV. It was positioned precariously on the edge of a filing cabinet with its sound off, an episode of *The Avengers* flickering silently on its screen. "I've seen these shows so many times I know 'em by heart," he informed Manion. Then he pointed to an open box of Popeye's chicken oozing grease on the desk. "Grab a thigh an' give your tummy a treat."

"As I recall, one of us lives here, Eben. And I don't think it's you." Manion wanted to be annoyed, but the best he could muster was bemusement. "What're you doing here?"

"Like the man says, everybody's got to be someplace."

"Find someplace else," Manion said, turning away. That was when he saw the other man, tied to a chair in the corner.

"You remember Mighty Mo Jobert, don't you, Terry? The steno's steno."

Jobert's eyes pleaded for assistance. His mouth was covered by a strip of adhesive that had probably come from the upstairs medicine cabinet. Manion turned to the crew-cut policeman, who was now focusing on the small screen, and inquired waspishly, "What the devil is all this?"

Munn held up a big hand. "Just a minute. I love this part. Watch the way this dame spins . . . then kicks . . . *Wow!* Beauty! Terry, if I could meet a dame who could lift her leg that high, I'd give the single life a pass." He turned to the detective. "Scarf some chicken. It's better'n all that Commander's shit."

Manion sighed. There didn't seem to be much sense in maintaining an indignant pose. He grabbed a drumstick and flopped onto the only cushioned chair in the room. "Been waiting long?" he asked.

"I don't know." Munn looked at Jobert. "What do you think, Mo? Two hours? Three hours? I knew my old schoolmate had to come home sometime. It's *mucho* important, Ter. Else I wouldn't have busted in and all. I'll get some glue and liquid wood in the morning, and that door'll look like new. I swear."

He swung his legs off the desk and hopped from the chair. Walking to the kitchenette, he said, "Time to sluice the goose."

Manion heard his refrigerator open. He stared at Maurice Jobert, who was now mumbling something under the adhesive. Manion wondered what, if anything, he should do about Jobert. He decided that the little man wouldn't expire if he were to remain tied up for another few minutes anyway.

Munn returned with a Dixie for himself and a Barq's root beer for Manion. "I remembered you were on the wagon, Terry. So I got you a six-pack of this chemistry set bullshit. But old Mo here showed a preference for it too. So there're only a few cans left."

He handed Manion the root beer, then walked back to Jobert. "You gonna behave yourself now, Mo? You gonna stop all that weeping and whining?"

Jobert glared at him. With his free hand, little finger daintily extended, Munn grasped a corner of the adhesive. He yanked hard and Jobert let out an involuntary yip, then began speaking in earnest. "He's a madman, Mr. Manion. My God, the indignities I've been through tonight—"

Munn slapped the adhesive back over Jobert's mouth. It didn't stick, but it momentarily stopped the little man's flow of words. Manion said to them both, "It'd be nice to know what's going on."

"That's precisely it," Jobert said, the adhesive hanging from his chin and his voice at least one octave higher than usual. "I have no idea."

"I guess that leaves you, Eben."

Munn carried his beer back to the desk chair, flipping off the TV set on his way. He sat down, took a swig of Dixie, and smacked his lips. "Well, boys, it's about Reevie Benedetto."

Manion frowned. "The Crawfish's son?"

Munn nodded, staring at Jobert, who seemed totally confused.

"I told you I don't know the man," Manion said.

"Then you've got a real treat in store," Munn said, grinning. "Big, good-looking galoot. Got that glow of health. And wealth. Hell of a dresser. A million-dollar education in Switzerland or some such place. Friend of Jobert's."

"Me?" Jobert's eyes seemed to be springing from his head. "I don't know what you're talking about."

"Your girlfriend does, Mighty Mo. I bet she was on the horn to him the minute I dragged you off her and out the front door."

"You . . . You're crazy!"

Munn said to Manion, "A couple times I spotted Mighty Mo and this li'l popsie splitting a poor boy at a lunchroom near Criminal Courts, and since he's not exactly the studmuffin of the steno department, I started wondering why a hot-looking lady like that would be wasting her time with a cold fish like him. So I checked her out. She was born Loretta Pruitt, but she used to be called a lot of other names when she was hookin' for the Crawfish, four or five years back. Good enough at the game to lift herself up by her garter straps, so to speak. She seems to have delusions of grandeur these days. Calls herself an antiques dealer. Of course, the shop's owned by the Crawfish.

"That's where Maurice here has been leading me every so often. He hops over there from the Criminal Courts and strolls right on in. Then, lo and behold, the *lady* lowers the goddamn blinds and puts out the Closed sign. It's romantic as hell. But I been getting a mite bored with it all, so today I jimmied the rear door to the shop. And I tell you, Manion, the sight of them in this old four-poster makin' the beast with two backs, it brought a tear to my eye. Maurice, you old dog, those two-bit Beulahs know how it's done, don't they?"

"You're crazy!"

"Now, Mo, I know it's a hard thing to swallow, that you been splittin' the sheets with one of the sweethearts of Bourbon Street. But facts are facts. For some probably diseased pro who can be had for the price of a square meal at Galatoire's, you broke your marriage vows and, worse yet, broke the laws of this proud city. You sold out your office, lied, cheated, and, Maurice, you stole. And you are now going to pay the price in full."

Jobert weighed the policeman's words, then said again with less conviction, "You're crazy."

"So I've been told in the past, not without reason. But in this instance, I am a goddamned monument to sanity. Maurice, when you Xeroxed those pages and brought 'em to your little whore, what in the world did you think she was gonna do with them?"

Jobert licked his lips. "I didn't do anything."

Manion, though mildly interested in the tableau that was taking place in his office, was growing weary and annoyed. "Couldn't you have had this conversation with Maurice at *your* place, Eben?"

"This is for your benefit, Terry. See, one of the things this little weasel passed along to his whore was a transcript of our chat at that country dryout center. Reevie Benedetto's got it now."

Manion turned to Jobert and said, "Well, that sort of changes my vote. Which one of us gets to use the rubber hose first?"

"I wouldn't mind batting him around, but I don't think he's got any answers. I was kinda hoping it might suddenly occur to you why the Benedetto kid was so interested in you."

Manion shrugged helplessly. "Could he have been involved in any way in that business in L.A.?"

"I've been keeping pretty close tabs on the lad and I'd be willing to bet he hasn't been on the West Coast in a long time. Naw, this is something closer to home. Was he tied in with your pal Legendre?"

"Not to my knowledge."

Munn stared at him for a beat, then said, "That's too bad. Either you really are in the dark, or you're pullin' my chain for a reason I can't figure. Either way, it's too bad, 'cause now I'm stuck with this pissant."

"Maybe you could pretend you're a normal cop and arrest him?"

"Hell, no. Then I'd have to explain why and how and like that. And he'd be out in the shake of a dog's tail and Benedetto'd have him killed. And what would be the sense in that?"

Jobert paled. "Killed? Why would anyone have me killed?"

"You tell him, Manion. All this yapping's made me dry as sand," Munn said, heading for the kitchenette.

Manion paused to consider the question. Then he began, "You handed the documents over to your girlfriend and she gave them to the Benedetto family. Maybe there were a couple other buffers in there between her and the Crawfish, but you're the man on the bottom. As soon as you get arrested, or prove to be a potential embarrassment to the Benedettos, you will be killed and everybody will be happy ever after. If the embarrassment has spread to your girlfriend, she'll be killed too. It's organized crime's version of the domino principle."

"But . . . but even if I'm not arrested, if Loretta has told them that Munn has . . . taken me, won't I still be . . . an embarrassment?"

Manion smiled. "This is all speculation, of course. I mean, you shouldn't bet your life on it, but being dragged from your love bed by a deranged character like Eben Munn may not be taken as seriously by them as your being thrown into the lockup. Of course, if you do know a little more about Benedetto's operation than you've told us, then they may kill you just for good measure."

Munn returned from the kitchenette with a fresh beer. He smiled at Manion. Jobert said, "I know nothing. Nothing. My God, what can I do?"

"Go fishin'," Munn said, punctuating the statement with a belch.

"I don't fish."

"You got any relatives livin' out of state?"

"My wife has a sister in Oregon. She's always complaining about the rain."

"You two ought to pack your raincoats and visit her for a while. Two or three months," Munn suggested.

"Months? But how could I? My work."

Munn removed a knife from his pocket and grinned at the nervous little man. "Your work? Why, you little shit-heel, how much did you think about your work when that whore was giving you the goods?"

"But I . . ."

Munn moved closer with the knife, raised it, and brought it down. Jobert screamed, then realized it was his binding, not he, that had been cut. "Shut up and listen," the policeman growled. "I'm offerin' you the opportunity of a lifetime. You tell your superior you've had a breakdown. Tell 'im anything. Just get 'im to give you permission to go away for a while, till I can take care of the Benedetto family. If you get canned, too damn bad. If you don't, when you get back to town you'll be working for me, too. You understand?"

"N-n-no. I don't understand at all."

"Which part?"

"N-none of it."

Munn looked annoyed. He brushed the strands of rope from Jobert's arms, then lifted him from the chair by his lapels. He began to shake him back and forth. "Get out of town! You understand that?"

Jobert nodded his bouncing head.

"Fine. Then that's all you got to know right now. When you get back to town, we'll cover the rest."

"But . . . what do I do now?"

Munn threw the little man against a wall, shaking the black box hanging there. The mechanical crow peeked out, asked, "What's the flak, Jack?" and went back into his house.

Munn blinked at the box, then turned to wink at Manion. Jobert groaned and Munn grabbed him by the collar and belt and moved him to the front door. Manion managed to precede them and open the door so that Munn had a clear path to toss the unfortunate Jobert into the night.

Jobert picked himself up but remained on the porch. "What do I do?" he asked Munn.

"Dammit," Munn growled. "I've seen some lame-os in my time but . . . What you do, jerk-off, is go up to Canal, flag a cab, go home to your wife, pack your goddamn bags, and get the fuck out of town before somebody cuts your goddamn worthless throat."

With that he slammed the door and turned to Manion. "Was I too easy on him?" he asked.

"You could have shaved his head," Manion replied.

Munn asked, "Is he still out there? I don't have the heart to look."

Manion peeked through the curtained window. "Don't think so."

"Good. Then let's you and me go talk to Benedetto's kid."

"About Jobert?"

Munn scowled. "Don't you go simple on me too, Manion. Hell, no. Jobert's on his own. He made his own bed." Munn chuckled at what he'd said, then continued. "No. I just want to check out young Reevie, see the kind of stuff he's made of."

"And you want *me* along? Why?"

"So's I can observe the dynamics of the situation."

"You mean you want to see if I was lying about not knowing him."

"Something like that," Munn replied. "Let me shag another beer an' we'll make like trees and leaf."

If they'd left immediately, it might have saved a life. But Munn paused to make a phone call. He whispered something and was about to hang up when the doorbell sounded. Manion raised his eyebrows. Munn shrugged, whispered a few more words into the receiver, then replaced it. He shifted his beer can to his left hand and slipped his right inside his coat.

Manion pushed the curtain back. Jobert, the bad penny, was on the stoop. Manion opened the door and Jobert nearly flew into the room. He was followed by a crone dressed in rags and patches, a pistol in her outstretched hand.

Manion almost laughed when he realized it was Nadia Wells under the filthy clothes. He hadn't seen her bag lady disguise before, but it had been the talk of the agency.

She ignored him. When she spotted Munn in the doorway to the kitchenette, she aimed her gun in the direction of the policeman's privates. Munn grinned at her and eased his empty hand out from under his coat jacket.

There was a tapping at the side window. Felix was there, aiming his .45 at Munn too.

"Jesus!" Munn exclaimed. "I feel like the mystery guest at a shootout."

"Nadia," Manion said. "What in the world are you up to?"

"Is everything okay in here?"

"No problem," Manion said. "Meet Eben Munn."

"Is this the famous Miz Nadia Wells?"' Munn said. "Pleased to meet you, ma'am."

Nadia put her gun away and nodded to Felix, who seemed to fade away. She said to Manion, "We found . . . Mr. Jobert, was it? . . . Mr. Jobert staggering around outside, baying to the moon about how he'd just escaped from killers."

Munn stared at Jobert and shook his head. "What a pure-d jackass you turned out to be."

Felix entered through the front door with Marcus Steiner. Manion stared at the author with curiosity.

Munn observed Steiner's T-shirt and asked, "What's *In Salvador*?"

Steiner ignored him and said to Manion, "It's been something of a memorable night . . ."

"It's a long story, sonny," Nadia cut in. She allowed her eyes to shift quickly to Munn and back again. "You and Mr. Steiner can get into it later. Right now, why don't you tell me about Mr. Jobert."

"Not in front of *him*," Manion said, pointing at Steiner.

Nadia turned to look at the writer with eyebrows raised.

"He's got it in his mind to write a book about me." Manion explained. "He shouldn't be in here, if we're going to talk."

"Just a minute, Terry," Steiner said. "Some bastard held a gun to my head. He pistol-whipped me." He pointed at the scab on his bare scalp. "I've earned the right to know what's happening."

"What do you say, Manion?" Munn asked. "Do we give Short-Pants Shorty the heave-ho?"

"Terry, please. I swear this has nothing to do with any book. That was a stupid idea and it's done with. This is a personal matter now. The sonofabitch tried to kill me."

"Why?" Manion asked.

Steiner said without blinking, "He thought I was working with you."

"What made him think that?"

"He must've seen us together in front of my house."

Manion frowned. "How did he get to your house?"

Steiner paused, then replied, "He must have followed you there."

Nadia said. "Nope. He had your license plate number, Mr. Steiner. And it got him as far as Canal Imports, where your Range Rover is registered. I know. I had your number too. Only I got there before the gunman, and when he arrived, I followed *him* to your place. That's how come I happened to be in a position to save your life.

"So what we should be asking you is: Why did you follow me and Terry to Pos's apartment this morning?"

"At the time, I was still planning to write a book about Terry," Steiner admitted. "I saw the man shoot at you both. I saw you drive away, and then he came out of the building, with the gun in his hand. He was very cool about it. Took his time. He slipped the gun into his pocket and began walking to his car, which was parked at the end of the block. When he drove away, I did too. I'm not sure what I hoped to achieve by following him. In any case, I lost him in traffic. I guess I'm not very good at remaining unobtrusive. I never dreamed he'd track *me* down."

Manion stared at Steiner. He began to say something, but Nadia broke in. "Mr. Steiner, when you were with the gunman, what else did he say?" she asked.

"Just that he was going to kill me and make it look like a suicide."

Nadia looked at the floor for a few beats, then said to Manion, "Let's keep him around, sonny. Maybe he'll think of something else that'll help. If he gets in anybody's way, we can boot him out then. Mr. Jobert, on the other hand, is not needed here. You want to walk him to the Caddy, Felix?"

Jobert was happy to go, happy to have someone tell him what to do.

When the stenographer had gone, Nadia said to Manion, "Okay, fill us in."

Reluctantly, Manion did. When he'd finished, Nadia made clucking noises with her tongue. "Why'd this Benedetto fella want the transcript of your and Munn's meeting so bad?" she asked.

"Well, ma'am, that was what I hoped to find out from that little weasel." Munn pointed in the general direction of the front door. "Only I really don't think the weasel knows."

"The weasel said you were trying to kill him."

"No ma'am. All Terry and I did was to suggest he get the hell out of town, before somebody turns him into crab melts. Not us. Somebody else."

"Like Benedetto?"

"That'd be my guess," Munn said.

"Who's Benedetto?" Steiner asked.

"Mr. Steiner, we're not gonna give you a play-by-play," Nadia said. "If you want to stay here and observe, fine. But open your yap again and it's *adios* and goodbye."

She turned to Munn. "Why not lock the weasel behind bars and toss the key down a drain?"

"Actually, ma'am, puttin' Jobert in a cage would just make it that much easier for the Crawfish to snuff him."

Nadia backed to a chair and sat. She crossed one leg over the other and grinned at Munn. "In other words, you don't trust your brother officers."

"Oh, they're great enough guys to see a ball game with. Have a poor boy and some Dixie. Play a little poker. But to trust with somebody's life, even a sorry sumbitch like Jobert? No ma'am, I would not."

"Is there anybody you do trust, Officer Munn?"

Munn popped the tab on his beer and leaned his bulk against Manion's desk while he took a sip. "That's some question. Now you, ma'am, impress me a great deal. But I don't know you well enough to say if I'd trust you or not. Terry, on the other hand, is my old schoolmate. I have seen him under pressure. Sweating under the aluminum ruler of Sister Veronica. Gettin' his finger broken trying to play soccer, a game he plainly had no aptitude for.

"But, more important, I did something . . . very dumb once, on a school trip. And he saw me. We'd never been friends. In fact, we never liked each other much. He had the perfect opportunity to do me in, and he just kept quiet. I would say that, if pressed, I might trust ol' Terry. At least part of the time."

Manion made a "humph" noise and looked away. The reason he had not informed on Munn all those years ago was that, outside of a mild curiosity as to why Munn would have wanted to steal the souvenirs in the first place, he had absolutely no interest in the matter. In those days, his main interests were movies and books, in that order. Crime and punishment were not even in his top ten.

"The more important question is," Nadia was saying, "can Terry trust you?"

"Some," Munn said, grinning at Manion. "Maybe not one hundred percent, but some."

She turned to Manion. "Well, sonny, we both know there are a number of reasons we should keep the NOPD out of our hair in this situation. But"—she waved her hand at Steiner—"the crowd of involved parties is starting to expand. And even with all the good men and true who work for my agency, I'm not sure we can cover every angle. I think we've gotta go slightly public. In case somebody else gets seriously damaged by that clown with a gun."

"Go slightly public how?" Manion asked.

"Well," Nadia answered, tapping Munn's knee with a knuckle, "I think we'd better tell the police everything we know."

Manion shrugged. "That shouldn't take long," he said.

23
.

SEATED BEHIND the wheel of his Thunderbird, Croaker
tried to control his breathing. And his temper. The day had been
thoroughly frustrating. In a career that had spanned a number of very
productive years, he had not once failed to fulfill an obligation. Now,
for some unfathomable reason, he had suddenly become totally inef-
fective. He had been unable to do the job on the Bentine girl. He had
known in advance of the complication involved and should have
taken steps to avoid it.

Then he was unable to put the bearded, jailbait-loving writer
away. The guy was fit and might have been tough to handle without
the gun. But he'd had the goddamn gun. It should have been a cake-
walk. He still didn't understand what had gone wrong. Who could
have known enough about him to follow him to the warehouse?
Maybe it had just been the luck of the draw. Some lard-ass night
watchman scuffling by at the wrong time. But there had been two of
them. With guns.

Dammit! He brought his hands down on the steering wheel with
such force it almost cracked. There was something he had to discuss
with Reevie Benedetto, and Reevie would not be happy about it. Still,
it had been one hell of a getaway. Right through the fucking wall.
That Rover was one tough machine. Just a few dents and a busted
headlight.

But just as he'd discovered a most amazing coincidence and made
up his mind what to do about it, he'd let himself get chased off! By

whom? Spooked by shadows? Or the real thing—federal cops, SWAT team? Who? He hadn't looked back, just floored the Rover to a spot within walking distance of his T-Bird.

For some reason, he was convinced that Manion had been back there. Manion was the man on his case. He was stirring up the whole thing over that old dick's death. He'd been with the grandma that morning, helping the girl get away. He'd teamed up with the writer, for Christ's sake, and now they knew much more than they should. Knew, for example, the kind of car he was driving.

He was not particularly concerned about the car's plates, which belonged to a Subaru that had been totaled on the Chef Menteur Highway six months before. It was the car itself that mattered. He liked the way the T-Bird handled—smooth, reliable. But he had no choice. He was starving, but he had to dump the car before he did anything else.

The side streets of New Orleans were, in general, in terrible shape. Potholes. Bumps. The roots of giant trees had rippled some streets badly enough to put a tank to the test. The T-Bird took the bounces hard as he pushed it along at a too-fast clip. Croaker was no longer careful about the car's shock absorbers. He wouldn't be using it much longer.

Eventually, he arrived at his destination: Ruffy's All-Nite Service Station in the Carrollton area near Dublin Park. It was unusually active for that time of night. Five cars, packed with joyous young black couples in prom gear, were lined up at the pumps.

Croaker parked the T-Bird on the street. He gave his throat a few shots of his atomizer; then he strolled toward the large hangar-shaped garage at the rear of the station. As he passed the prom cars, he watched Willie, Ruffy's night man, exchange little half-pint bottles of booze for hard cash. Old enough to drive, old enough to drink. The cars roared off, the couples happy as larks. Croaker waited until Willie noticed him. They exchanged nods and Willie went into his office and picked up the phone.

Croaker continued on toward the garage. A side door opened, letting out conditioned air and clamor. Beside it stood a sullen young woman in grease-stained overalls who watched him warily as he entered.

There were eight or nine similarly dressed men and women stripping four cars. Ruffy, all two hundred pounds of her, sat on an ancient green sofa watching her crew work. She was in her late thirties, a big, solidly built woman, in a full yellow skirt and a blue halter that barely covered her huge, shapely breasts. Scarlet-haired. Good cheekbones. Sexy, Croaker thought, even with all the weight. Her eyes were gray with flecks of green in them. They never seemed to blink.

"Well, well, long time no see, Mr. World Traveler," she drawled.

"How you doin', Ruffy?" He tried unsuccessfully to smooth out the roughness in his voice by whispering. That only made him sound more sinister than ever.

"Can't complain. Can't complain. How's the T-Bird?"

"Hot."

"Oho." She smiled. She had good teeth. Big. White. They didn't looked bonded or any of that fake crap. "How hot?"

"The tires are melting."

Ruffy shouted, "Hey, Julie. Take this gentleman's keys and bring his mobile in here, will you, hon?"

"The keys are in the car," Croaker told the sullen woman. "It's the only black T-Bird on Dante."

Julie nodded and was off.

"Well, sweetheart, what's your pleasure?"

Croaker stared at Ruffy, wondering if she was flirting with him. "Anything and everything," he answered, placing the ball in her court.

"I mean what kind of car will you be needing?"

"I don't suppose you get any Range Rovers?"

She smiled. "No Rolls neither. They're scarcer'n hen's teeth in these parts."

He looked around the garage. "Anything I can drive away?"

"Hmm. I got a Cutlass Ciera, a V-six with power front discs, rack-and-pinion steering, auto three-speed; a Volvo Turbo; a Jetta GLI; a Celica GT-S, loaded. And any minute, they're supposed to be bringing in a Porsche nine twenty-eight from Westwego."

Croaker did not seem to be impressed by the list. Ruffy pushed herself upright, her breasts almost leaping from their blue halter. Because of her boots, she was an inch taller than Croaker. She said, "You're getting hard to please in your old age."

"It's just that I got used to the T-Bird."

"Well, hell, hang on to it then. Take the Cutlass. Bring it back in two days and we'll have the Bird looking like you'd never recognize her. But it'll feel like the same car. Trust me."

Croaker smiled. "When I return the Cutlass, how's about you and me having dinner somewhere?"

Ruffy's bright, unblinking eyes studied his slender frame. "We'd be like Jack Sprat and his wife." she said.

"So we lick the platter clean. So what?"

She laughed. "Sounds like fun. But the work on the T-Bird's still gonna cost you two grand."

He shrugged.

"I'll get the Cutlass brought around for you. It's a total redo, clean as an old maid's bidet."

"Can I use the phone?"

"Use anything you like." Everything she said sounded suggestive.

Reevie's line was busy. More fucking bad luck. He'd have to go through the dumb wop. He dialed a number, and when it was answered, he said, "Hi, Johnny. I couldn't get through to Reevie, so I'm checking in with you."

Johnny Benedetto's voice rapped back, "Gimme the good news. Is everything finished?"

"Uh, I'm still working on it."

Johnny made a sound like he was swallowing something, then said, "What the fuck's it all about anyway? Reevie ain't goin' to all this trouble over a broad."

"I don't know, Johnny. I just do what you and Reevie tell me. Maybe you ought to ask him."

"I did. He gave me some shit about stopping some guy from smearing a broad he likes.'"

"Then that must be it," Croaker said.

Johnny was silent for a moment. Then, "I think you'd better take Pos all the way out."

Croaker felt the blood rush to his head. "Why? I guarantee he's not going to be a problem."

"We don't want to take the chance. Reevie started this thing and we gotta close it out. Pos and the Bentine girl. Erase, please."

Erase, please! Johnny must've been watching kids' TV again. "I'm gonna need some guys to spring the girl."

"Call that special number and tell 'im it's for me, and tell 'im what you need. You remember the number."

Did he remember the fucking number? "Yeah," Croaker wheezed. "I got a great memory."

"Call me later to let me know," Johnny said. "I'll be at the gym."

"You working out?"

"Naw. Reevie's got this little secretary mouse who's askin' for it."

"Good luck," Croaker said. He replaced the receiver, and then tried Reevie's number again. He wanted to talk to him about a lot of things. Another busy signal. One of those nights.

Ruffy had the Cutlass ready for him, engine purring. It was a light green with dark green interior, a little gaudy for his taste. But he'd only have to use it for two days. "What color you going to paint the T-Bird?" he asked the big woman.

"Whatever color you want."

"Something subtle."

"Range Rover gray?"

"Is that really a color?"

"Swear to God," she said. She made a cross on her chest and kept her finger pressing against her right breast a little longer than necessary, sort of fondling it.

"Okay, Range Rover gray," he said, staring at her breast as he got behind the wheel of the Cutlass. He had to adjust the seat and the mirror for a taller man. He studied the dash until he was sure where the lights were and the wipers. He turned on the radio and was bombarded by some bush-league Mex music, switched to FM and found a symphony orchestra. He pushed a few buttons and loaded the station into the car's tuning memory. "See you in forty-eight hours," he told Ruffy as he edged the sedan toward the garage's open door.

"I'll be waiting, lover. Me and my big . . . appetite." She winked at him.

The Cutlass felt a little spongy when he hit the street. But the car was the last thing on his mind. He was thinking about Ruffy, all two hundred pounds of her. He was thinking that if the evening with Ruffy was going to be as memorable as he hoped, he wanted nothing pressing on his mind. He'd have to put Manion and that writer under first.

Parking was always a problem at Charity Hospital. Croaker found a spot on South Villere Street and took his time easing the unfamiliar Cutlass into it. He unholstered his gun, checked its load, then replaced it in its leather holster under his right arm.

On the first floor of the antiseptic building, he found a pay telephone and dialed a number.

A woman's voice answered, "Charity Hospital."

"I wonder if you could tell me the number of Mr. Fouchette's room. Posell Fouchette."

The voice hesitated, then asked, "Are you a relative of Mr. Fouchette's?"

Croaker grinned. She was making it too easy. "Yes ma'am," he replied with a straight face.

"Well, Mr. Fouchette is still in Emergency. But his condition is improving."

"Thank God," Croaker said. "I have some . . . flowers I want to send. What room . . . ?"

"Like I said, he's in Emergency. But I think he's scheduled for a room tomorrow. You can just send the flowers to the hospital. Uh, could I ask you what relation you are to Mr. Fouchette?"

"His . . . cousin."

"Well, hang on a minute. There's a police officer who'd like to talk with you."

Croaker depressed the switch hook and broke the connection. Tomorrow was another day. And there was more than enough to keep him occupied for the rest of the evening. He fed another coin into the phone and dialed the number Johnny had given him. The operator informed him that Henderson Parish numbers required twenty-five cents more. He didn't have another quarter. He wished he were in a kid's cartoon where he could stick his gun into the phone's mouthpiece and have it poke out of her earpiece. But there was no way in the real world to intimidate a telephone operator. He would have to get change somewhere. He slammed the handset down. The machine kept his money.

24
.

STEINER SHARED the couch with Manion. Felix leaned against the door in the hall, where he could keep an eye on the Cadillac and its passenger, Jobert. Munn sat on the desktop with his legs dangling to the floor. The grease from the fried chicken container stained his pants, but he didn't seem to notice. They were all listening to Nadia Wells's concise description of the day's events—from her and Manion's arrival at Pos Fouchette's apartment on General Pershing Street until she found Steiner in the deserted railroad warehouse.

Munn chewed on the inside of his mouth. "Gee, maybe we should have kept Jobert in here to take all this down for us in shorthand. Let's see now: The shooter drives an '89 T-Bird, black, Louisiana license TB24B7. He's tall, thin, and wears a suit. Flat-faced. Excuse me if I don't rush right out and put the cuffs on him."

"It was the voice that made him unique. I've never heard a voice like that before. It's as if his throat were filled with razor blades," Steiner said.

"I suppose we could get some mug books . . . naw, screw that. Mug books are a colossal waste of time. This boy seems to be getting desperate. He's gonna make some serious mistake before too long."

Nadia sighed. "It would be nice to be rid of him before that happened. All this is starting to get a little expensive. I had to send some men to Mr. Steiner's home, just in case. Could you possibly spread the word on that T-Bird and license?"

"It's probably in some chop shop as we speak, but what the hell." He picked up the phone, dialed a number, and asked for a Lieutenant Lemack. He gave Lemack a description of the gunman responsible for Pos Fouchette's wound, and the make, model, and license of the T-Bird.

Lemack wanted to know the source of his information. Munn refused to tell him, winking at Nadia. Then his face clouded and he leaned forward. "Hey, shake it, break it, or hang it on the wall. Do whatever the fuck you want with it, Lee. It's straight goods, but if you need the name of the informant, you can keep sitting on your ass while the guy mows down half of Nola. No skin off my pension!" He slammed down the phone.

"He said he'd get right on it." Munn turned to Manion. "Well, schoolmate, let's put together whatever we've got."

Manion felt strangely at peace. He was sober. His mind was clear, and it was finally working properly. He said, "We've got a gunman with a hoarse voice who tried to kill Pos and Slo Bentine. He also tried to kill Marcus in a way that would look like suicide. J.J.'s death looked like suicide. The gunman is probably the same gruff-voiced man who accompanied Odie Shecksnyder when he broke in here, which means he probably killed Schecksnyder, too."

"What do you suppose they were looking for here?" Munn asked.

"J.J.'s files."

Munn coughed and rolled his butt on the desktop. "So which files did they take?"

Manion knew of only one, the Parker Harris file. But he wasn't ready to pass that information on to Munn. He didn't want to sic any police on Leon Harris unnecessarily, definitely not a blue elephant like Munn. "There's no way of telling," he said. "There weren't any carbons."

The big cop gave him a disgusted look. "Geez, Manion. Haven't you heard of computers?" He emitted an elaborate sigh. "I guess we'd better hope that when we catch this frog-voiced son of a bitch, he'll be alive enough to tell us something that'll link the whole goddamn mess to the Benedettos."

Nadia extended one leg and poked the toe of her dirty sneaker into Munn's knee. "Quid pro quo time," she said.

"What do you wanna know, ma'am?"

She looked at Manion. "Sonny?"

Manion stood up and moved to the desk. He looked inside the greasy chicken box and found a wing that had been overlooked. Waving it, he said. "What's the deal with you and the Benedettos?"

Munn's face closed up suddenly. "Personal matter," he mumbled.

Manion nibbled at the chicken wing, waiting for some sort of elaboration. When it didn't come, he said, "Okay, then. What makes you so sure that the Xeroxes Jobert gave his girlfriend wound up with Reevie Benedetto?"

"I, ah, got my sources."

"And why exactly did you roust Jobert tonight?" Manion asked.

Munn sighed. "Ever have one of those days when shit descends? That was today. Started with a hangover. Car battery was dead. Had my credit card cut in two at the gas station. A guy I picked up for raping and beating a four-year-old walked because the kid's still in shock and can't identify him. My aunt's givin' 'em hell at the Covenant Home. And then I find myself in the Quarter outside a goddamn antique shop, waiting like a perv while some sleazeball pinhead gets his rocks off with one of Benedetto's hookers. So I sort of snapped. *Mea culpa,* huh?"

"Hey, son," Nadia said, "Terry just asked you a question. I don't think he wanted the story of your life. It does look like you acted a bit precipitous, however."

"Unless," Manion said, "you'd decided to protect your *sources* by tossing Jobert to the Benedettos."

Munn grinned at Manion. "Why, podnah, you do have an evil mind."

"Well, that makes two of ya," Nadia said. "I'll let Terry worry about what the Benedetto kid wants with that transcript of your conversation at the Spa. My main concern of the moment is this fella with the sore throat. We know he's dangerous. We think he killed J.J. and we know he shot Pos Fouchette. I am assuming that if this felon should manage to murder someone before the arthritic arm of the law grabs him, our chat tonight will be evidence enough of our willingness to cooperate with the police and aid in his capture."

"Sure, enough. You can trust me on that, Miz Wells."

Nadia stared hard at him, then stood up, yawning. "In that case, you go to your pew and I'll go to mine. I've guests at the house. And I need a bath."

She paused as Manion moved to open the door for her. "You get yourself some sleep tonight, sonny. You've had a full day."

"You don't know the half of it," he said.

"But I will, won't I?" she asked, studying his face.

"Don't I tell you everything?" he replied, looking blandly innocent.

"I don't know about you sometimes, sonny," she whispered. She turned to Steiner. "Coming, Mr. S.?" she asked in her normal voice.

Steiner shook his head. "I think I'll stick around here for a while. Maybe Detective Munn can give me a ride when he leaves."

Munn shrugged.

Nadia stood on tiptoe and pecked Manion's cheek. Then she was gone, Felix following in her wake.

Munn moved to the door, paused there until he heard the Cadillac's door shut and the car drive away.

"Okay, Manion," he said. "Gimme a second and maybe we can make it as far as the street this time."

"You're not still planning on visiting Reevie Benedetto?" Manion asked.

"Sure," Munn said. "It's ten o'clock. You think this young hood-about-town has gone beddy-bye already?"

"Only if he's had the kind of day I have," Manion said.

"Hell, a little runnin' around is good for you," Munn said with a typical lack of sympathy. "Cleans out the cobwebs."

Actually, Manion felt awake, alert, and rather eager to meet the young Benedetto. "It's your party," he told Munn. "We'll drop Steiner off on the way."

"Drop me off?" the author protested. "Just when the fun's starting?"

"That's the spirit," Munn told him. "Damn right, the fun is gonna start."

He picked up the phone and dialed a number that Manion was unable to read, then turned his back to them. He mumbled something into the receiver, replaced it, and started for the door.

"Late date?" Manion asked.

"Don't I deserve one?" Munn said with a wide grin.

"We going to this Benedetto guy's house?" Steiner asked as he followed them from the room.

"Naw. We'll try this place he runs," Munn said, frowning at the door that he'd damaged breaking in.

"A bar?" Steiner asked, suddenly concerned.

"Hell, no," Munn said. "Would I take a wuss like Manion to a place where they serve booze? We're headed to a health club."

25.

REEVIE BENEDETTO had awakened that morning at eight
A.M. feeling well rested, invigorated, and eager to experience the day
ahead of him.

Wrapped in a silk robe, he had descended the stairs of his two-
story faux antebellum home to notify his staff that Leon Harris would
be arriving in the afternoon to assume charge of all household details.
Larue, the maid, and Chico, who doubled as handyman and chauffeur, took the news with no outward show of emotion. Marie Josie,
the cook, threatened to quit. Reevie said she was free to do that, of
course, but suggested she wait to see what life with Leon would be
like.

He'd spent the rest of the morning puttering about the house.
Shortly before noon, Emilio Vargas reported that the Farmer's mil-
lions had been received and, as they spoke, were being deposited and
redeposited, until their history would be even more difficult to follow
than the road to the Algiers Canal. The rest of the day had passed just
as smoothly.

Except for the incident in the Sports Plantation's weight room.
But even that had its up side. Reevie had been finishing his chest pulls
when a large, heavily muscled young fellow began whistling as he
exercised. An off-key, grating whistle. A small, elderly Asian asked
him politely if he would stop making the sound, and the whistler
wheeled on him and began poking his thin chest with a large index
finger.

"This is the South, Mr. Toyota, where little yellow men are not allowed to make demands of white men. You understand what I'm sayin'?"

Before the bewildered Asian could react to the outburst, Reevie moved between the two men. "Is there a problem?" he asked amicably.

"And what would make it your business?" the big man replied arrogantly.

"I own this place."

"Fine. Then perhaps you might instruct this Jap of the rules governing the disturbance of members while they're working out?"

He was the son of an oilman named Granville who had once been a man of influence in the city.

Reevie turned to the Asian. "The main rule to remember, sir, is that if any ignorant asshole annoys you in any way, please call it to my attention and we'll take care of the matter."

"What!" the big man exclaimed.

"Clean out your locker and take a hike," Reevie commanded in as soft a voice as possible. "Tell the girl at the front desk I said it was okay to give you a full refund on your dues."

"My name's Granville, pal."

"That's *your* problem," Reevie said. He turned and walked away. For the first time since he could remember, there was total silence in the room—no clanging machines, no chatter from the members. The silence was broken by the big man.

"Wait just one fuckin' minute, *pal*," he called out.

Reevie faced him, smiling. "We're not pals," he said quietly. "I doubt that we're even the same species."

"I told you. My name's Granville. As in Wesley Granville, Jr."

Reevie said, "Well, Wes junior, what's your name supposed to do, make me froth at the mouth?"

"My father is—"

"Your father is in the oil business. You have any idea what's been happening to the oil business? Wes, old man, if you keep relying on your father's dwindling influence, you'll be lucky if they'll let you into the YMCA."

"That's what you think, huh?" Wes junior tried to use his poking finger on Reevie. The smile never left Reevie's face as his hand shot out to grasp Wes's finger. Reevie bent it backward and Wes went with it, shocked, white-faced. Reevie moved his body beside the big man's and continued controlling him by the finger, turning him until he was bent back over Reevie's hip. The hip was removed and Wes fell onto the carpet.

Reevie was careful not to break Wes's finger as he dropped to one knee. He pushed the finger into Wes's left nostril, shoved it hard. Wes screamed and bucked. Reevie bent the finger another pain-filled fraction of an inch, and Wes quieted down, moaning.

Reevie said, softly into his ear. "You're bothering the other members, Wes, what with your nose picking and other nonsense. Your patronage is no longer encouraged at this private establishment, and your presence is no longer tolerated."

Wes started to speak, but Reevie jammed the finger harder into the nostril. "Don't make an even bigger mistake," Reevie told him, secretly hoping that he would. "Just get up and get out."

Wes was still. Reevie released his hold and stood up. The others in the room were watching them, shocked but fascinated. They'd have something to talk about for days.

Wes rose to his feet, squeezing and releasing his hand as if to pump blood back into his damaged finger. His nose was raw and puffy. He glared at Reevie, who repaid his hostility with a wide smile. "So long, Wes. It's been fun, but I have to get back to work now. See you around. But not here."

Reevie headed away. Wesley Granville, Jr., breathing like a walrus came to a decision. He charged forward, screaming, "No Mafia greaseball tells me what to do!"

Reevie watched Wes junior's progress in the floor-to-ceiling-mirrored wall. Without turning, he moved his head to the left, letting Wes's fist sail over his shoulder. He brought his right elbow back, sinking it into Wes's stomach, then pivoted to the left. As Wes's body lumbered by, Reevie brought the flat side of his right hand down in a chopping motion against Wes's exposed neck.

Like a dazed steer, Wes staggered forward a few steps and stumbled headlong into the wall, leaving a smear of red on the mirror as he slipped down to the carpet.

Reevie picked up a phone and told the desk to send up a cleaning crew. He wondered if Wes would try taking him to court for assault. Probably not. He would not want to call attention to his being blackballed from an establishment that was open to practically anyone. Reevie turned to the others in the room. "I'm terribly sorry you had to be bothered by all this horseplay. Please be my guests for lunch in the dining room."

He had barely taken one step out of the room, when they all started to chatter animatedly. He smiled. It had been a refreshing, even relaxing workout. Among the other attractions that the city of New Orleans offered was the presence of so many thugs and bullies who actually deserved to be beaten mercilessly. Reevie had long ago recognized in himself certain, well, sadistic tendencies. How delightful it was to give vent to them and still feel as if you were on the side of the angels. It was another of St. Croydon's principles: *Make your apparent weaknesses work for you.*

Later there'd been more good news. His father had called to cancel their nightly dinner. Reevie's first concern had been that the old man was planning to hatch some business without him. But no, the Crawfish had explained that he hadn't been sleeping well and he was going to eat "light" at home in an effort to "fuck up" his insomnia.

Reevie had taken advantage of the opportunity by arranging his own intimate dinner party.

His only guest had arrived ten minutes ago, at seven-thirty, while he was applying the final touches to his dinner wardrobe— gray piqué shirt with a tiny purple monogram where the pocket ordinarily would be if the shirt had a pocket, pleated black linen trousers, black suede loafers with a red felt band across the instep, no socks. His ankles were a bit too pale, so he'd touched them up with a bronzer.

Now he took one final look at himself in the mirror, smoothed the gray shirt over his muscled stomach, grimaced and studied his strong white teeth. Well satisfied with himself, he went down to greet the lady.

She stood in the living room beside Leon, who was dressed in dark double-breasted blazer and gray slacks. Reevie watched them both carefully. Neither seemed in any way overly aware of the other. She said, "Well, R.B. Aren't we so very southern all of a sudden, with a new butler and all?"

He smiled and asked, "Leon, are you the butler?"

Leon's face showed no emotion. He elected not to reply.

Reevie said, "Definitely not a butler. An associate, yes. Maybe at some future date a partner. But a butler, never."

She faltered, looking from Reevie to Leon. "I'm sorry I . . . I just assumed. Please forgive me."

Leon let her off the hook. "Natural mistake. No problem," he said.

Reevie said, "Lindsay, I'd like you to meet Leon Harris. Leon, Lindsay Gaynaud."

He was staring at Leon, monitoring another test. Lindsay extended her hand. Leon opened his mouth, paused, then, shaking her hand, said, "It's a pleasure." Reevie couldn't have been more pleased. The name Gaynaud had obviously registered, but Leon had chosen not to react.

He turned to Reevie and said, "Marie Josie tells me that dinner will be ready in about a half hour. Larue will be serving you. I've stocked the bar in the study and selected a few CDs for the machine. If it's all right, I'd better be running."

"Leon's attending night school," Reevie explained.

"I may never understand you," Lindsay told him as they walked hand in hand to the den.

"I'm just an ordinary guy trying to make everybody happy," he said, and she smiled sadly, as if to say she would never be happy again.

Reevie paused and stared at her. She was wearing her fine platinum hair down. It was a modified 1930s look, brushed across the scalp and cascading straight down until it twisted around her shoulders. It glistened in the light, the same way it did that night he'd first spied her at an artist's loft in the Quarter. She'd been standing alone, staring at a painting of an exquisitely muscled black man, the artist's specialty. Her idiot fiancé, Gerry St. John, had been off somewhere trying to score a vial of cocaine.

Reevie had approached a groaning board containing barbecued ribs and chicken parts, selected two drumsticks, and moved to her side in front of the painting. Holding out one of the drumsticks to her, he'd said, "Funny how some art makes you hungry."

She'd taken the drumstick with a laugh. By the time St. John returned, annoyed at having failed in his mission, Reevie had fallen in love, or something like it. St. John had behaved like a possessive, jealous fool, insulting both him and Lindsay. But even if he hadn't been such a boor, Reevie still would have had him killed. St. John had been a man in the way.

What Reevie had never dreamed was that, a year after his fatal "accident," St. John would still be in the way. Lindsay couldn't banish the lout from her thoughts. All of Reevie's boyish charm and devotion and devious manipulation had failed to turn the trick. So had therapy. So had the booze and the drugs, though they, at least, offered temporary relief.

Reevie found himself in a quandary of his own making. He wanted Lindsay as he wanted no other thing in life. But he was unable to truly possess her. The closest he could come was when she was under the influence of alcohol or cocaine. Though that was sexually satisfying, he realized that her increasing addiction would soon change her from the person he idolized to just another burnt-out dope whore. There had to be some solution to the problem, but he hadn't quite discovered it.

In the study, with its green-and-brown-striped walls and over-stuffed furniture of forest-green velvet, he paused at the stereo wall while Lindsay studied the portable bar. He pressed a button and the mesmerizing, insinuating voice of Aaron Neville floated into the room from quad speakers.

He stared at the abundance of resilient, pale pink flesh exposed by the deep V of Lindsay's double-breasted jacket, then moved his gaze upward. He wondered how much longer her beauty would last. Except for a slight puffiness around her pale green eyes, she looked astonishingly healthy.

He moved to her, took her in his arms, inhaling the faint gardenia scent of her perfume. Under the jacket, her body went rigid. She allowed their lips to touch briefly, then slipped away from him. She gracefully descended to the sofa and seemed to relax against it. He lifted a bottle of a '78 Taittinger blanc de blancs from its bed of ice. As he popped the cork, she asked, "Would you mind doctoring it a bit with Stoli?"

Obeying her request, he said, "It's a shame to put something so harsh into something so beautiful." He handed her the drink and took the seat next to her on the sofa.

She shrugged. "Like they say, it cuts the grease." She swallowed almost a third of her drink.

"Good day today?" he asked, sipping his unadorned champagne.

"Well, thanks to you, I got a late start. Played a little tennis at Martie's." She smiled. "I got through"—she looked at her watch—"seven hours without a drink. Improvement, no?"

"I don't think that's the way one cuts down."

"No, I guess not. Am I hopeless?"

She didn't really want the truth and he was certain that she wouldn't have accepted it from him. So he moved the conversation to something that might matter. "Is that what your father thinks?"

"Father very rarely thinks of me at all. He has other things on his mind."

"Such as?"

This time she took a sip from her glass. "I like this very much. What do you call it?"

"It's a Silver Stiletto," Reevie lied, creating the name as he spoke. "But we were talking about your father . . ."

"All morning long he was railing about some problem my brother was having with the legislature."

Reevie raised an eyebrow and placed his barely touched glass on a spotless coffee table. "What sort of problem?"

She shrugged. "I haven't the foggiest idea. I don't suppose we have time for another of these before dinner?"

Reevie poured her another one, and another, until the dinner went cold and the liquor prompted a flood of tears and regret over the departed Gerald St. John that even several lines of exceptionally pure cocaine were unable to check.

Finally, Lindsay got to her feet, reeling slightly. Reevie thought she was on her way to the powder room, but she said, "I'm sorry. I have to go."

He ran after her, caught her at the front door. "Please. Don't."

She put out a hand, touched his face. "You're very sweet, Reeves. You should find yourself someone who isn't so fucked up."

She turned and he grabbed her arm. "You can't drive like that."

"Like what? I'm an excellent driver."

"You're not yourself."

"I am very much myself. Very much so. I may not be who you think I am. But I am very definitely myself." She stared at his hand, which was clutching her arm much tighter than he'd intended. He relaxed his fingers and she moved through them like quicksilver. Quicksilver woman. Quicksilver hair.

He watched her stagger to the Corvette, get inside, and start the engine. She didn't turn back to wave goodbye. When she and the car had moved beyond his line of sight, he went back inside the house and closed the door behind him. He wondered what his next move with Lindsay Gaynaud should be.

She made the move herself. By ten P.M. she was back, standing in his living room, shaky, but considerably more sober than when she'd left.

"I'm sorry," she said, though she sounded more nervous than sorry. "It's just that sometimes, I can't . . . quite . . . come to grips with . . ."

He went to her and pulled her to his chest. "It will get better," he told her. "It just takes time."

"I want it to get better *now*, R.B. I want to do something *now* that will make it better."

He led her to the den, placed her on the sofa. He took the vial from his pocket and handed it to her. The vial had a special cap that sprayed a measure of cocaine into the nostril.

"Better," she said, after she'd taken a few hits. "Is there any of that champagne left?"

She had not asked for the vodka and he certainly didn't suggest it. He carried two full glasses of undefiled wine to the couch. She picked up the vial again.

He watched her, waiting to hear why she'd returned.

"Daddy is such a fool," she said suddenly.

"What happened?"

"He accused me of having an affair with a man I don't even know."

Reevie raised an eyebrow and lowered his nearly full glass to the table. "What man?"

"Somebody named Manion. He wears glasses."

Reevie face remained bland. "What made your father think you two were . . .?"

"I seem to have fallen asleep in my car in front of the house. And this Manion character helped me inside. Daddy assumes we spent the evening getting high and fucking our brains out."

Reevie analyzed the information and asked, "Manion just happened to be passing by?"

She frowned. "I'm not sure. He was walking near the house."

"What happened after he helped you inside?"

She started to raise the vial again, but he caught her hand and took the cocaine away. She looked hurt. He repeated the question.

"He and Daddy talked for a while and then he left and Daddy came into my room and started shouting at me. So I got out of there and came back here."

"What did Manion and your father talk about?"

"I have no idea. Do you know him?"

"Manion? We have mutual friends."

"I honestly do not know him at all," she said. "Anyway, I obviously was not sleeping with him tonight. I was with you tonight. Not sleeping with anybody."

"You shouldn't have tried to drive home. It's dangerous, and the cops are so tough on DWIs these days that even your father may not be able to keep you out of the clink."

"But you could, couldn't you, Reevie?" She reached for the vial and he let her take it.

"Yes, I suppose so." He touched her cheek. "But even I might not be able to get that beautiful face put back together after a head-on collision."

"I'm an excellent driver," she said. "Excellent."

"It only takes one . . ."

He stopped because she was unbuttoning her jacket. She was naked underneath. She said, "Dammit, I didn't come back here for a lecture."

26
.

AS MUNN'S unmarked car screeched into the Sports Plantation's parking lot, it passed a bright neon sign depicting a cartoon
pelican wearing gym clothes. Manion had seen the same logo on the
business card that Leon Harris had consulted in his kitchen. He wondered if he would bump into Leon inside.

It was shortly before closing time, ten-thirty on week nights. As
Manion followed Steiner and Munn through the front door, he was
impressed by the number of club members leaving the place at that
time of night with healthier-than-thou expressions. How odd that
fitness seemed to be all the rage in a city that was one of the last
bastions of self-destruction. He wasn't worried. New Orleans had
survived even more pervasive national fads.

Two physical specimens of opposite gender sat behind the front
counter, wearing the cartoon pelican on their white T-shirts. They
were blond, robust, and strangely asexual. Their only purpose in life
seemed to be to take membership cards, run them through an electronic slot, and study the results on a television monitor before grant-
ing entry.

The male member of the reception team flexed his neck muscles
and showed Munn his wristwatch. He said, "Sorry, guys, but—"

Munn cut him off. "We're here to see Mr. Benedetto."

The blond man turned to his partner. "Is Reevie in tonight?"

The girl shook her head. "He is sometimes here this late, but not
often," she said.

"Where's his office?" Munn asked.

Both blondes stared at him with their blue eyes. Brother and sister? Manion wondered. The male leaned forward and said, "Like she told you, he's not in."

Munn took his leather-encased badge from his pocket and flashed it. "We'll wait. Where's the office?"

"Uh, maybe I better call back there . . ."

Munn took the phone from the young man's hand and replaced it on its cradle. "Just be a good kid and let us do our job, huh? You say the office is where?"

"Through the turnstile, all the way to the rear of the building," the girl said. "What's going on?"

"Nothing to worry your pretty head," Munn answered over his shoulder. He moved so quickly he was already entering Reevie Benedetto's office when Manion and Steiner caught up to him.

The first thing Manion saw when he stepped through the doorway was a broken antique lamp that had fallen from the desk, scattering shards of colored glass across a pale blue carpet. The top of the desk was bare; like the lamp, a clock, answering machine, and telephone were all on the carpet, along with a vase no longer filled with flowers or water, a purse, pens, and assorted bits of correspondence and business papers.

A dark-haired young woman was on the carpet, too, her dress around her hips, struggling with a wiry middle-aged man who had managed to rip his way though her pantyhose. He paused in his unwelcome pursuit to look their way just before Munn grabbed him by the hair and belt and tossed him across the room as if he were a beach ball.

The man bounced off the wall onto a white couch, arms flailing. He tried to get his feet under him. Munn hit him once in the stomach and once in the neck, hard punches that had a paralytic effect. Then he grabbed the front of the man's face in one hand and began banging his head against the wall so hard the plaster flaked.

Manion helped the woman to her feet. She was sniffling. The underside of her lip was swelling where it had been bitten. Her right eye was closing and turning purple. He placed her in a chair, then ran across the room to try to stop Munn from killing the would-be rapist.

When he failed to pry Munn's fingers from the man's head, Manion made a knuckle and used it to deliver a short jab to Munn's face, just where the cheekbone meets the jawline.

Munn's eyes shut in pain and his mouth opened. He dropped the unconscious man into a bloody heap on the couch. Steiner, who'd been observing every detail since he entered the room, said to Manion, "Very effective."

"It works on dogs, too," Manion informed him.

Munn shook his head. "Jesus, you like to bust my jaw." He turned and spotted the brunette girl, now weeping softly in the chair. He moved to her and opened and closed his hand helplessly, staring down at her with an expression that mixed pain and frustration.

"Shit, honey, but I'm sorry!" he said.

She waved him away. "Nothing for *you* to be sorry about." She sniffed and seemed to get control of herself, pouting while she held back tears. "I . . . I'm okay. He wasn't able to . . ."

Manion picked up the phone, but Munn grabbed it from him and slammed it back on its cradle. "Not just yet," he said.

"A doctor should look at her. At both of 'em."

"Later," Munn said. He opened an unmarked door.

"That's Mr. Benedetto's private office," the brunette said flatly.

"Good," Munn said. "Are you expecting him?"

She shook her head.

"Better call him then. Get him over here."

She took a deep breath. "What about *him*?" She pointed at the unconscious man as if he were something a dog left on the carpet.

"If he starts to get frisky, Manion can handle him. Manion's a regular brute, he wants to be." He rubbed his jaw.

The brunette looked at Manion. "He's kidding, right?"

"He's quite the clown," Manion said.

She cocked her head. "You have a cigarette?"

"Nope. No minor vices."

"That figures." She stared at him so long Manion grew uncomfortable. Then she shifted her attention to Steiner's T-shirt and asked, "Did your friend really write *In Salvador*?"

Steiner was studying a group of framed documents on the wall. "I'll go ask him," Manion said.

Steiner didn't seem to notice him approach. The documents included operating licenses, certificates of public service, and a small, comparatively discreet diploma, the plainest that Manion had ever seen, stating that Reeves M. Bennett had graduated with honors from St. Croydon's College in Switzerland in 1985.

The battered brunette chose that moment to pick up the telephone and punch out a number. Munn was back in the doorway before she'd finished, watching her carefully. Her breathing was so deep the exhalations sounded like sighs of resignation.

She said into the phone, "This is Lonnie, Mr. Benedetto. I . . . I'm sorry to bother you, but there's been some trouble here at the office." She paused, then added, "You'd better come. It's a mess."

She replaced the receiver and leaned back in the chair.

Rubbing his hands together almost gleefully, Munn said, "Well, this is all very interesting. I better go calm down those rocket scientists at the front desk."

As the policeman stormed through the door, Manion sat on the couch and asked, "Work for Benedetto long, Lonnie?"

"A while," she replied, picking up her purse and rummaging through it for a cigarette. Finally, she found one, ancient and bent. She smoothed it out and looked at him. "Naturally, you don't carry matches either?"

Steiner moved toward her, flipped out a gold lighter, and used it with a flourish. She smiled at him, but his mind seemed to be elsewhere. He snapped the lighter shut and strolled into Benedetto's inner office. Lonnie watched with mild curiosity.

Manion said, "Is this your boss's brother? It says here his name is John Vincent Benedetto."

She saw that he'd removed the wiry man's wallet and was poking through it. "Uncle," she said. "Good old Uncle Johnny."

Manion dug a packet from the wallet, an ancient contraceptive sealed in foil. "Well, at least he's an advocate of safe sex," he said, looking at her innocently.

The brunette shook her head. "You're as funny as strep throat," she said.

The reply and Munn's return ended that conversation. "Where's the beard?" the policeman asked.

Lonnie indicated the inner office and Munn moved quickly to the door. Steiner met him there.

"Find anything interesting?" Munn asked.

"What are we looking for?" Steiner asked.

Johnny Benedetto groaned and tumbled from the couch onto the carpet. Munn walked over to him and placed his right foot on the thin man's chest. "Johnny the Wolf, huh?" he chuckled. "Your piss-elegant nephew's gonna be real unhappy with you."

27.

"ENOUGH OF these goddamn courtesy calls," Nadia Wells told Felix as they pulled away from Steiner's house. "Take us on home."

Since leaving Manion's, she'd had an unpleasant time of it. First, she'd had to deal with Maurice Jobert's truly terrible wife. In the course of many years in both of her chosen professions, she had seen a number of men brought low by overbearing women, but Lady Jobert was a past mistress of the art of psychological castration. When the woman had finally ceased flailing her husband with words, Nadia tried to explain the necessity of their leaving New Orleans. Mrs. Jobert was not convinced. Nadia shrugged, told her it was her decision, and got out of there without a backward glance. She didn't think enough of Mrs. Jobert to care if the Benedettos did a job on her, and as for Maurice, death would probably be a relief.

With thoughts of a hot bath on her mind, Nadia had asked Felix to take a fast swing past Steiner's place on Prytania Street. Studying the area, she suggested that he drive alongside a dark Ford Probe that rested against a curb with two of her operatives inside.

She rolled down her window and stared at the man behind the wheel, veiled in a plume of cigar smoke. He had a long face that was mainly forehead and chin. His partner, chubbier and with a mustache, chewed on the cigar that was causing all the smog.

"Everything quiet?" she asked.

"Yes ma'am," they answered, almost in unison.

"Girl in the house with a big dog. She the guy's daughter or something?" Long Face asked.

"Or something," Nadia replied. "You realize that undetected observation is the operating order?"

"Yes ma'am," they replied again, obviously products of the parochial school system.

"Then what's that goddamn cigar doing in your mouth, Slim? You can see the smoke for a mile and smell it for ten miles. Kee-rist."

The chubby man began to say something, but Nadia cut him short. "Please! I been listening to people talk bullshit all night. Just douse the butt and do your bloody job, or you'll be hitting the bricks come morning."

She pushed the button that raised her window and told Felix of her desire to be gone.

They'd just driven onto the Broad Street overpass when Felix announced unemotionally, "Somebody following."

Nadia turned to look through the small black window, but it was impossible to see much of anything with the headlights shining into her eyes. "What makes you think so?" she asked.

"Right headlamp's a little high. Turned with us onto Claiborne, then up Canal, and he's still back there. Can't tell the make."

"Pull over and see what he does."

By the time the Cadillac stopped at the side of the overpass, Nadia had her .44 Special in her hand. Felix had his gun ready, too, his eyes never leaving the rearview mirror. "Here he comes," he said.

A green Oldsmobile passed them without slowing. "What do you think?" she asked.

Felix shrugged. "Guy in a suit behind the wheel. I don't know. Maybe I'm a little spooked."

"Well, goddammit," she said, putting the gun away. "We're all spooked. Spooked is a healthy reaction in this sort of situation. Stay as spooked as you want. Only get us home!"

When Nadia strode into her living room, she found Buddy sitting on a couch with his shirt hanging loose and his belt unhooked, watching two talking heads trying to explain the day in sports. Buddy clicked off the machine and attempted to gather his shirt around him.

"Relax," Nadia told him. "I've seen bellies before."

"Tha's some outfit, ma'am," he said, indicating her bag lady disguise.

"Bright of you to notice. How's Pos?"

"He's outta intensive," Buddy said. "Got that tough Cajun hide, I guess. I wanna go see him t'morra, if it's okay."

"Sure," Nadia said. "You tell the girl Pos's gonna make it?"

Buddy shook his head. "She been sleepin' since you left. Every couple hours, I look in on her. She's a sweet li'l thing. Pos is a lucky man."

"Pos was nearly a dead man."

" 'S what I jus' said. Instead of dead, he's on the mend and got hisself a fine little lady."

"You must be sleepy yourself. Catch a quick snooze and Felix'll spell you."

Buddy hesitated. "I was jus' gonna investigate the icebox. Your new girl made some real fine swimps Cardinal for dinner and they's some leftovers."

Nadia yawned. "Keep eating 'swimps' with béchamel sauce late at night and the only place you'll be sleeping is in the cardiac arrest ward."

She yawned again and marched off into the inner recesses of the house, where her husband, George, would be asleep on his back, mouth open, making a sound like a buzz saw tearing through metal.

Felix had just finished checking the Caddy for dings when he saw the two men reflected in the polished rear bumper. They were moving in on him from the trees. With a mild grunt he straightened, his hand rising inside his coat.

"Don't!" A third man was standing to Felix's right, his arm straight out, aiming a gun. A diamond earring in his right lobe caught the moonlight.

Just as Felix was wondering what the Wells Agency guards were doing with themselves, they rounded the side of the house, hands on their heads. Behind them was a little Mexican holding a gun.

Felix studied the gunmen, their unshaven faces, red-rimmed eyes, rumpled sport jackets. Earring reached past the older man's coat to remove his weapon. "Where's the girl?" he asked.

"What girl?"

"You're right on the goddamned edge, Mac," Earring said. "You're holding a material witness in that house against her will. I can have half the fucking NOPD here in a second to level that place, but I'm trying to be nice."

"You sayin' you're a policeman?"

Earring used his free hand to find and flash a worn leather pouch containing a Henderson Parish Sheriff's Office badge. Felix memorized the number and nodded. "You guys are a little off your beat, aren't you?"

"We're heading to the back door now and you're gonna take us inside. And maybe nobody'll have to bleed."

Felix smiled. "I'm twice your age, boy. I stopped being impressed by tough-guy talk when you was still on mama's milk. You can book me or you can put that popgun away. But I ain't taking you anywhere. Not if all you got to show is that Henderson tin."

The old man leaned against the bumper of the car. Earring glanced at him for a beat, nodded, and put his gun into his shoulder holster. Then, in one fluid motion, he detached a leather sap from his belt and brought it down against the side of Felix's skull. He pulled the swing at the last moment, but caused enough damage to send the older man to his knees. "I don't mind cracking your nut, old-timer. If that's what it takes."

Felix shook his head. He was having trouble seeing and he couldn't catch his breath. Earring tried to drag him to his feet. When that didn't work, he drew back the sap once more.

Before he could use it, a huge, squat object leapt from the bushes. Buddy, a napkin still tucked into the top of his shirt, grabbed Earring's raised arm, twisting it back until the sap fell. He pushed the man between him and the other guns and pressed something cold and sharp against Earring's throat. It was a fork, stilly carrying a shred of shrimp Carnival.

Suddenly, the area was flooded with light. Nadia's amplified voice shouted, "You men are completely surrounded. Throw down your weapons and put your hands on your heads."

Earring's associates spun around, trying to identify the direction of the voice. But there was at least a quartet of loudspeakers in that area.

One of the gunmen shouted, "We're police! Come outta there with your hands raised!"

Nadia countered with, "Throw the guns down, *now*, or we open fire."

Buddy dug the tines of the fork deeper into Earring's neck. "Maybe you bettah second the emotion," he growled nastily.

"Yeah, okay. Do it," Earring yelled out. "But these people better know they're in deep shit."

The men dropped their handguns. And for a few slow seconds nothing happened. Then Nadia's voice shrilled, "Will the idiots on my payroll please pick up those goddamn guns, or do I have to come out there and do it myself?"

28

IT TOOK a lot to shake Reevie Benedetto's composure. But when he entered his office at the Sports Plantation that night, he was at least momentarily startled. The place was a mess. Lonnie, his secretary, was seated on one of the visitor's chairs, puffing nervously on a cigarette. She had a cut lip and a swollen eye. Her blouse was ripped.

His uncle Johnny was on the couch, bleeding from the nose. Beside him was the annoying cop, Munn, wiggling his eyebrows obscenely. The tall, blond man with the bespectacled pale blue eyes and the amused, almost detached expression was a total stranger. But the other man—the bald, bearded fellow in the T-shirt and shorts—he recognized immediately. He'd read all of the man's books.

What the devil was Marcus Steiner doing in his office? Except for that question, Reevie had figured out the scenario immediately. He glared at his uncle Johnny, his mind working quickly to determine how to take control of the situation.

He moved to his secretary. "Are you all right, Lonnie?"

"As well as can be expected," she said.

"So you're the Crawfish's kid?" the policeman asked.

Reevie turned to him, ignoring the use of his father's nickname. "And you're Lieutenant Munn, I believe."

"You know me?"

"My father pointed you out once. He speaks of you often," Reevie said. He squatted before the bleeding man on the couch. "You okay, Johnny?"

Johnny Benedetto nodded, putting his wrist to his bloody nose.

Reevie stood up, adjusted the crease in his trousers, and turned to Manion and Steiner. "I don't believe I've met these gentlemen, though I recognize Marcus Steiner." He put out his hand. "I'm Reeves Benedetto."

Steiner just stared at him with a half-smile on his face. Manion didn't bother to smile. Neither seemed interested in shaking Reevie's hand.

Munn was observing the dynamics very carefully. He said, "Makes a fella wonder why, doesn't it?"

"Why what?" Reevie asked.

"Why you'd be so interested in a guy you obviously don't know."

Reevie shrugged. "I'm afraid you lost me," he said.

"This here's Terry Manion," Munn drawled. "You're familiar with the name, aren't you?"

"Me? Whatever gave you that idea, Lieutenant?" Reevie asked. But he stared at Manion for a few extra beats, as if to convince himself that this tall, apparently mild-mannered man was indeed Terry Manion.

"Maybe I was misinformed," Munn said. "Like maybe your uncle's a drag queen in disguise."

Johnny Benedetto started to stand, and Munn yanked him backward so aggressively that he hit his head against the wall again. "Jesus," he growled. "Get me away from this psycho sonofabitch, Reevie. Call Chawlie."

Reevie said, "Was that really necessary, Lieutenant?"

"This miscreant attacked that woman, molested her, tried to rape and sodomize her. I wouldn't be surprised if he wound up spending the next ten to twenty taking it in the rear himself."

Johnny's eyes danced nervously. "Don't believe that shit, Reevie. The broad's been comin' on to me. I didn't do anything she didn't ask for."

Reevie glanced at his secretary. She said, "He hit me, threw me to the ground, and tore my clothes. He tried to rape me and said he would do more. Sound like anything I'd ask for?"

Reevie took a deep breath and faced Steiner and Manion. "You gentlemen just happened to be passing by?"

"They're with me," Munn said.

"And what brought you, Lieutenant?"

"Actually, I was looking for you."

"Me? Here? At this hour?"

"It's the only address I had for you. In any case, here you are."

"Yes. And what was it you wanted?"

Munn patted Johnny on his head. "That's not so important, now that we got the Woofer's fate to discuss."

Johnny's eyes narrowed. "He didn't phone it in, Reevie."

Lonnie leaned forward anxiously. "What's that mean, he didn't phone it in?" she asked.

Reevie knelt beside her, took her hand, and looked into her eyes very sincerely. "Tell me how you feel," he said,

"I'll live."

He smiled. "Let me get my doctor."

"Later," Munn said. "Right now we keep the party at its present strength."

"All right, Lieutenant. How do we proceed?"

Munn got to his feet and handed his Police Special to Manion. "Shoot that slimy rapist if he tries to run out," he instructed. "Reevie 'n' me are stepping into the next room for a little palaver."

"Wait a minute . . ." Lonnie protested.

"It'll be fine, Lonnie," Reevie assured her. "I swear I'll make it up to you. If you need a doctor, you'll have the best. Any way you look at it, you're going to be well taken care of."

"Jesus Christ, Reevie, you ain't gonna take that lyin' cunt's—"

Reevie wheeled on his uncle, his face momentarily flushed. He opened his mouth, then hesitated, letting himself cool off. When he spoke, he said. "You just sit there, Johnny. You don't say anything. You don't do anything. Just . . . sit . . . there. Capish?"

"Please don't make me stay in the same room with *him*," Lonnie pleaded, prompting a frown from Manion.

Munn said, "There's a dining room out there. Why don't you go get yourself a cup of coffee or something."

"It might be better if we all stayed just where we are," Reevie said, bending down again and reaching out his hand tentatively toward Lonnie's shoulder. When she did not draw away, he touched her. "Nothing can happen to you here. Johnny will never touch you again. If he is foolish enough to try, Mr. Manion has a gun. And we'll be right in the next room. Be a good kid, okay?"

She nodded. Her cigarette had gone out. Reevie found her lighter on the floor and relit the cigarette for her. Then he and Munn walked into his private office, shutting the door behind them.

* * *

After a few minutes of silence, Johnny said, "I'm gonna take that psycho cop's head off. Make book on it." He aimed the statement at Manion, the man with the gun.

Manion did not bother to reply. He knew that by the time Munn and Benedetto were finished with their negotiation, whatever it was, Johnny would be lucky if he could take the head off a glass of beer.

Steiner yawned and strolled near the closed door. "Hear anything good?" Manion asked him.

Steiner shook his head. "What do you think?" he asked. "Is Munn making a deal?"

"That's not the question," Manion replied. "The question is: What kind of deal is he making?"

Lonnie exhaled a plume of smoke. "Gee, aren't we all so very sophisticated, sitting around here as if nobody had tried to rape anybody."

"Shut your fuckin' mouth, you . . . you fuckin' cocktease lesbean," Johnny snarled, leaning forward.

Manion pushed the barrel of the gun to within a few feet of Johnny's head. "This would not be a good time for you to die, Johnny. I can't imagine who would bother attending your funeral except your brother. And think how embarrassed he'd be, standing there with you in a closed coffin."

"Fuck you, too, you fruit," Johnny spat. "You and the guy in short pants."

Manion shook his head sadly. "I've been sick," he said. "Maybe I'd better take a little catnap. Would you mind holding this for a while?"

He presented the gun to Lonnie.

"Wait a fuckin' minute!" Johnny yelled. He pushed himself from the couch and grabbed for the gun. Manion, with surprising agility, tossed the weapon from his right hand to his left. As Johnny's hands clasped empty air, Manion hit him near the base of his skull, roughly the same spot where he himself had been sapped. Johnny fell to the carpet, unconscious.

"Now doesn't that make it a little less tense in here?" Manion asked.

Lonnie smiled. "I thought he'd never leave," she said.

Steiner had barely noticed the brief tiff. His complete concentration was centered on the closed door.

The door opened fifteen minutes later. Johnny was still on the floor. "What happened?" Munn asked.

"He tried to grab the gun from Terry," Lonnie answered.

"Terry, huh?" Munn looked from the girl to Manion, who gave him a smile of childlike innocence. "Well, maybe Terry better give me my piece back now."

The policeman holstered his weapon, then used his foot to nudge Johnny. "C'mon, Woofie. Time to put on your travelin' shoes."

"Where's he traveling?" Steiner asked.

Reevie stared at him. "Away."

Johnny sat up with a groan. He pressed his fingers against the spot where Manion had hit him and gave a little grunt of pain. Reevie helped him to his feet. "C'mon, Johnny," Reevie said. "Time to go home and pack."

"Huh? Pack? Pack what?"

"All your possessions. The lieutenant is being kind enough to let you stay out of jail."

"I'm not going to any fuckin' jail," Johnny growled.

"That's what I just said, Johnny. No jail. Instead, you're going to live with relatives."

"What relatives?"

"The ones in Sicily."

"Sicily? That's bullshit. Who the fuck wants to live in Sicily?"

"You do, Uncle. It's much nicer than Angola this time of year."

"Fuck all this. Lemme talk to Chawlie. Chawlie'll take care of this."

Johnny staggered to the telephone, but before he could pick it up, Reevie grabbed him by the shoulder and spun him around. "Listen to me, *Uncle*. They've got you dead bang on assault and rape. Charlie can pull a lot of strings, but he can't do the impossible. I've been able to convince the lieutenant that you'll be a good boy and leave the country. In a few years, maybe you can come back to the U.S., get a place on the West Coast, the East Coast. Maybe even Florida. But not in Louisiana. That's part of the deal. Never again in Louisiana."

"I ain't going to no fuckin' Sicily. They don't even have no blondes there."

"We'll send some over for you. Of course, if you don't want that, you can always take your chance in the courtroom. But you'll lose there. And you'll wind up in a place where a lot of Charlie's enemies are hanging out, and if *they* don't get you, there's a whole cast of characters ready to make Sicily look like heaven on earth, even without blondes."

"I . . . I gotta think about it. I gotta talk to Chawlie first."

"No. Either you leave here with me or you leave with the lieutenant."

Johnny cocked his head, and his eyes brightened. "Okay, then Sicily it is. I go with you." He pushed his hands out from his chest, wrists together as if bound. "I'm all yours."

Munn said, "He thinks you're kidding."

Reevie suddenly drew back his hand and brought it full force against Johnny's face, knocking him off his feet. "I gave my word, Johnny," he said. "And I give you my word: if you leave with me, you do it my way."

Johnny, a welt forming on his cheek, stared at his nephew with a mixture of confusion and fear. He nodded his head somberly.

Manion, Munn, and Steiner watched from the nearly empty Sports Plantation parking lot as Reevie drove off with Johnny in his shiny Porsche. It was nearing midnight on a muggy, starless night. A warm breeze floated in from the east. Manion asked Munn, "Why was Benedetto checking up on me?"

Munn shrugged. "He said he wasn't. Claims it was his father who wanted your transcript. He didn't know why, but he'll see if he can find out."

"Yeah. And then he'll see to it that Uncle sets sail. What are the odds?"

"That the kid will deliver? Hell, one hundred to one in favor."

"I might take that bet."

Munn shook his head. "That's 'cause you don't know the kid."

"Why don't we start with what you're getting out of all this?"

Munn grinned. "Think I'm lining my nest?"

"I'm only asking a question. What's in it for you?"

"I'm just the class clown. You're the valedictorian. How do you figure it?"

Over Munn's shoulder and through the glass doors of the building, Manion could see Lonnie leaving the ladies' room and heading toward them. "I suppose you'd want something that would let you put the screws to Charlie Benedetto. But I can't see the kid throwing his father to you to save his uncle."

"Ah," Munn almost chuckled in glee. "But that's what we couldn't have figured. Johnny's gonna get a roommate in Sicily with him. His big brother, Charlie. The kid wants them both out of his hair. He's decided to shoot the moon for the family business."

Manion liked the way Lonnie walked, purposeful but not aggressive. Feminine but not fragile. He said to Munn, "So you're going to help him take over?"

"Awww. You think I'm gonna hop into bed with the boy, cut me off a chunk of the dope trade, or the hookers. Is that any way to judge an old Mater Dolorosa man? Look, I got the kid cold. I can put him away. Or . . . I could let him run a limited operation."

"How would that work?" Lonnie paused to pick up a sheet of paper from the floor and place it on the front counter. Good legs.

"I let him run the business. Only instead of expanding, it starts to lose ground."

"Why not close it down entirely?"

"Because then they'd just open up another shop. Like the man says, it's better to do business with a devil you know than a devil you don't."

Lonnie turned off nearly all the lights in the building and pushed through the front door, which she then locked. She stared at them, shook her head in disgust, and made a wide circle around them, heading for her car. Munn said, "Think she'd like us better if we'd deballed ol' Woofie?"

"Don't kid a kidder," Manion said, walking after Lonnie.

"Hey, where you runnin' off to?"

"To catch a lift," Manion said.

There was a frown on Munn's face as he watched Manion meet up with Lonnie. After a brief conversation that he couldn't hear, they both got into her car. He turned to Steiner and said, "Well, it's you and me, Shorty. What say we cruise Jazz City, get loaded and try to score a couple of waitresses?"

Steiner shook his head. "I haven't cruised since I was in my twenties, and I have an exceptional girl waiting for me at my place."

"Girl? How old is she?"

Steiner frowned. "Old enough."

"She like you referring to her as a girl?"

"She likes whatever I do."

Munn shook his head. "She must be something, this *girl*. Maybe the three of us could have a quick snort."

"I've been dry for nearly five years."

"Geez," Munn howled. "Everybody's on the wagon but me. What happened to all the heavy boozers?"

"They reformed or they died," Steiner answered.

Munn didn't say another word to the writer all the way back to Prytania Street.

29
.

NADIA WELLS was bringing her lecture to a close. ". . . then, after that roughneck with the earring, Landry, brutally beat my driver, I forced him and the other thugs you call policemen to turn over their revolvers." She pointed to an assortment of handguns, knives, and saps laid out on a coffee table.

Officer Frank Billet filled his notebook with shorthand scribbles and Lieutenant Joe DeLongpre ran a hand through his sparse gray-blond hair and tried to keep his temper. He glared at the men sharing the screened porch with the uniformed officers he'd brought with him. "And how precisely did you accomplish that, Mrs. Wells?"

Nadia was wearing a pale yellow Chinese silk robe over her white pajamas. Brooks Brothers had made the pj's for a small male, but they were the brand and make she preferred. "Why, Lieutenant, I'm afraid I did threaten them. But I did not know they were police at the time. Not the way they looked and behaved."

DeLongpre studied the other occupants of the Wellses' living room. A fully dressed man in his sixties sat on the sofa next to a large, turbaned woman in a caftan who was holding an ice pack against the man's head. A birdlike young black woman in a pink terry cloth robe kept busy filling cups with coffee from a porcelain pot. It smelled wonderful, but DeLongpre had refused it twice in anger and now felt embarrassed to change his mind. Instead, he thanked Nadia, faced the porch area, and shouted for Landry.

Landry answered the call with a poker face. DeLongpre studied him as if he hoped to learn something from the flicker of an eyelash, the twitch of a lip, the glint of an earring. He said, "Let's make sure Billet has this correct, Landry. What exactly was it that made you and Copas and Robideaux and Hurrell drive at least twenty miles over the parish line to give these folks a hard time?"

"It was a phone-in, Lieutenant. An anonymous tip."

"Okay, it was an anonymous phone-in. Pray continue."

"The, uh, party said that a woman was being held against her will on these premises, that she was a witness to a shooting that took place a couple days ago."

"What shooting?"

"On General Pershing."

"This caller a man or a woman?"

"Yes."

"Yes, what?"

"Uh, man, I think."

"Okay. So you get this anonymous tip pertaining to something that was going down in Orleans Parish. And so instead of calling the proper precinct, you and Robideaux and Hurrell and the Mex come barrel-assin'—excuse me, Mrs. Wells—come roaring over here throwing your weight around. I don't understand that at all, not at all."

"Uh, the guy said time was of the essence."

"He use that term, 'of the essence'?"

"I'm not sure. Maybe. Look, Lieutenant. We didn't come roaring in. We took it real quiet. We then attempted to survey the exterior of the house. That, uh gentleman there"—he pointed to Felix on the couch—"was outside near a car. I approached him, identified myself, and ordered him to accompany us inside for a search."

"Without a warrant."

"Well, I was hoping we could get him to agree to let us come in without one."

"Was that when you sapped him?"

"That was a mistake, I admit. I was using it as a sort of intimidation tool. He tripped and I went to grab him and sort of hit him by mistake."

DeLongpre looked heavenward. "Je-sus, Landry, that's the lamest crock of—"

"Well, what about this?" Landry interjected, turning to the light to display four puncture marks in his neck.

"What the hell is that?"

"I was attacked by this fat guy with a fork."

Billet stopped writing and looked questioningly at DeLongpre. "Put it all in there," the lieutenant told him. "Fat guy with a fork."

He turned to Nadia. "Would it be possible for me to speak with the, uh, gentleman who attacked Detective Landry with an eating utensil?"

"As I was telling Sheriff Tiberian—a very old friend, by the way—as I was telling him about this deplorable situation, I mentioned that some of my employees would have to take care of certain business obligations. I'm afraid that the man who stopped your Detective Landry from cracking my driver's head again was needed elsewhere. But I can make him available at your convenience."

"Thank you, ma'am," DeLongpre barely got out through his clenched teeth.

Nadia saw Felix staring at her, with raised eyebrows. He was wondering where Buddy was. Nadia ignored him, focusing in on DeLongpre. "Do you suppose we can cut this short? We'd like to get us a little sleep in whatever is left of the night."

Landry said, "Before we go, don't you think we should make sure that the tip wasn't straight, Lieutenant? Maybe they *are* holding some innocent woman here."

"This place is full of innocent women, you low-life scum," Olivette's throaty voice replied. "But we're all free to come and go as we please."

"Well," DeLongpre said, "we don't really have a search warrant."

"Look all you want to," Nadia said. "Then get the heck out."

DeLongpre sighed, then called to a couple of the men in uniform. He ordered them to go through the house looking for Landry's mystery hostage.

In less than half an hour, they returned to report that the only other human on the premises was an elderly man in one of the bedrooms snoring so loudly they couldn't think.

"That's my husband," Nadia told DeLongpre. "He's free to come and go also."

Felix was glaring at Nadia now. She knew what was on his mind. Buddy was not in the house. Slo Bentine was gone. And where was his precious Cadillac?

Nadia couldn't look him in the eye. Instead, she addressed De-Longpre. "I think we've been very patient with you, Lieutenant. As long as you're satisfied this so-called anonymous tip was a hoax, I would appreciate it if you would cart these reprobates off to jail now, so we can sleep. I'll be glad to drive down tomorrow to sign the complaint."

"Complaint? Jail?" DeLongpre asked.

"Of course," Nadia said. "With no call, these ruffians invade my privacy, harm my employee, and then have the gall to lie about it. Indeed there will be recriminations. I don't want these hoodlums merely to get their wrists slapped. I want them put away and for a damn long time."

"Now wait a minute . . ."

"Think, Lieutenant. What kind of a policeman has Landry been up till now? Reliable or not?"

"Damn reliable. A solid member of the department, which is why—"

"So you figure he suddenly got stupid, started wandering all over hell and gone getting into trouble, hitting unarmed men, trying to break into the homes of law-abiding citizens?"

"We all make a mistake—"

"If you don't start using your brain, Lieutenant, I'm gonna lift that phone and call Sheriff Tiberian one more time. He hates to be waked up even more than I do. And I'm gonna tell him that he's got a lieutenant so fog-brained that he doesn't check the weapons his men are carrying to see if they're the ones they're supposed to be carrying. Or if their pieces"—she moved to the table containing the recovered guns and knives and picked up a .38 Man-Stopper—"have the serial numbers filed off."

"What!"

"And check some of the loads. Since when were hollow-points standard issue?"

DeLongpre was astonished, but he was watching Landry warily now. Landry was looking at Nadia Wells, and his lip was beginning to twitch.

"What you're saying," DeLongpre summed up, "is that my men came here with the intention of performing an illegal act."

"It sure as hell looks that way to me. Of course, maybe they've got a tape recording of that supposed anonymous call. And maybe those guns won't have any history of sudden death when you run 'em through ballistics. But I wouldn't bet the farm if I was you."

Suddenly, a Police Special appeared in DeLongpre's hand. "Okay now, Landry. We'll just do this slow and by the book. Let's us just walk calmly out to the porch and talk to your pals."

The lieutenant and Billet followed Landry to the screened-in porch, where Hurrell, Robideaux, and Copas stopped chatting with the uniformed policeman to look desparingly at DeLongpre's gun.

DeLongpre ordered his uniformed men to handcuff the four suspects. Though the reading of their rights, Copas, Hurrell, and Robideaux stared at Landry for guidance. He simply shook his head from side to side, once—a gesture of silence.

When the weapons had been collected and marked, and the suspects loaded into squad cars, DeLongpre asked Nadia, "Any idea who hired them?"

She shrugged. "Somebody with more money than brains."

"Maybe we'll find out," he said, halfheartedly. "I don't suppose you know what they were after?"

She sighed. "I could be getting deluded about my own self-importance in my old age, but I suspect they were gonna bump me off."

DeLongpre hadn't heard anybody use that particular phrase since he was a boy, watching gangster movies at the Fox Theater. "Why?" he asked.

As soon as Landry had described Slo Bentine, the witness to a shooting whose existence was known to only a very select group, Nadia Wells had realized the rogue policeman had been sent by the gunman or his employer. But it was too complicated a story to waste on a dunderhead like DeLongpre. "Hell, Lieutenant. When you've lived as long as I have, and you've been engaged in the kind of businesses I have, you make a whole mess of enemies. Especially if you've been doing things right."

"I'd appreciate a list of those enemies."

"You'll have it. And now, good night, Lieutenant," she said, shutting the door on him.

Felix was alone in the living room, waiting for her with a sour look on his face.

"How's the head?" she asked.

"How could you have done it?"

"Done what, you ornery old goat?"

"Let Buddy drive the Cadillac."

"He had to get Slo away from here, and that was the only car not blocked in by those bozos."

"He could have taken a cab."

"The idea was for him to get her away without witnesses."

"What if he has an accident?"

"Good Lord, man, that Landry snake *did* scramble your brains. Buddy can drive. He doesn't have accidents."

"He'll be showing off for the girl."

"Forget about him. Get yourself some sleep in the room the girl was using. I'm phoning for a couple extra hands to keep us company in case we get more visitors."

"Damn. Did you see that Buddy?" Felix asked, offering one of his rare smiles. "Ran right out there and grabbed that sonofabitch, with nothing but a fork for a weapon."

"That he did," Nadia replied.

Felix's smile turned into a frown. "I sure as hell hope he uses more caution with the Cadillac," he said.

"Keep this up," Nadia told him, "and I'll go get my own sap and use it on you."

30.

MANION CONTINUED to stare at Lonnie's profile as she concentrated on the French Quarter traffic. "Don't do that," she said, but she was smiling.

"Do what?" he asked.

"Don't stare at me like a goggle-eyed perch."

"Have you ever seen a blue-eyed goggle-eyed perch?"

"What are we doing?"

"Going to my place."

"I know that. But what are we *doing?*"

"You know that, too," he said.

"Whew. Rape and romance on the same night. Too much."

He finally forced himself to look away. "Yes. About the rape. How long did it take you to push poor old Johnny over the edge?"

"What!" She chanced a glance at him before refocusing on the road. "What are you talking about?"

"If we are going to get anywhere, we might as well start out vaguely straight with each other. You and Munn are working together. I'd like it better if you were a cop. But Munn hates the Benedettos enough to pay or coerce a civilian to keep tabs on Reevie."

She did not reply. From her expression, she might not have heard him. "Okay," he said, "let's start with the basics. Is Lonnie your real name?"

"Look," she said. "I don't know what you're talking about. Maybe I'd better just drop you off at a bus stop or something."

"This late at night? Besides, something has happened and it doesn't happen that often. Not for me at least." The image of his ex-wife flitted through his head like a rose petal floating on a hot wind.

She tensed, edged forward to the wheel. He could almost hear her mind whirling. "Who are you?" she asked.

"Munn must have given you a little background. Replay it in your mind. While you do, I'll just list a few observations: One, Munn phoned somebody tonight just before we left for the Sports Plantation. Two, when we got to the place, he seemed to know you. Three, you didn't act like a rape victim. And you initially deferred to Munn, who neglected to identify himself as a policeman. But it was four, the timing, that was the real payoff. We drive up to the place just as Johnny the Wolf is making his moves on his nephew's secretary. That's a pretty strong coincidence, especially when you realize it gives Munn a powerful club to hold over Reevie's head."

"It's Lucille," she said suddenly.

"Ah, progress. Fine. Policewoman Lucille?"

She shook her head. "No."

"Just a hired hand?"

"Not exactly," the woman whose real name was Lucille told him. "You're about to start an affair with Eben Munn's kid sister."

Manion was momentarily at a loss for words. When the power of speech returned, he asked, "What sort of lout would send his *sister* into a situation like that?"

"Nobody sent anybody," she said, her face coloring. "Getting a job there was my idea, not Eben's. I hate the Benedettos as much as he does."

"Why?" he asked.

"It's personal," was her immediate reply.

"That's what your brother said, too."

They were silent for a while. Lucille concentrated on the traffic. They were on Canal moving into the Quarter, and at that time of night, every other driver was probably drunk or on the way. No matter how tough the Driving While Intoxicated laws might get, New Orleanians would always feel it to be their inalienable right to drive under the influence.

Munn's sister navigated around a weaving blue Buick and turned onto Merchant Place. Manion thought the street looked especially gloomy. Even the Captain's Curse seemed deserted. When Lucille stopped the car in front of Manion's home, she didn't look at him. He was certain that the moment for them had passed.

He was trying to formulate a plan to put them back on track when she asked, "Will I get a ticket if I leave the car here overnight?"

"Probably not."

"What about break-ins?"

"According to my neighbor, who's a respected fence, thieves stay away from here because they're afraid of his dog."

"What kind is it?"

"Little but deadly."

"Well, lock your door anyway," she said. "It's not much of a radio, but it's all the company I have when I drive."

She paused before his picture window and studied the faded *Third Man* poster in the moonlight. "Is the decor this strange inside?" she asked.

"Just about," he replied, opening the front door her brother had splintered earlier.

She walked past him into the dark hallway. "I did set up that creep Johnny," she said. "It wasn't all that difficult. I mean, you really don't have to do much more than sneeze for him to take that as permission to start pawing you. Anyway, the setup was my idea, too. Eben hated it. But I convinced him it would be safe if we timed it right. I didn't know Johnny had such a short fuse."

"If Eben didn't like the fake rape, what *was* his plan?" Manion asked.

"It wasn't very clearly defined. He wanted me to poke around Reevie's private files for something that would put the whole family away. But Reevie must keep the really interesting stuff somewhere else. Maybe his home. The best I could come up with was the transcript of Eben's interrogation of you at Evangeline Spa. It's in a locked drawer of his desk."

Manion had been turning on the lights and the air conditioner. He paused. "He didn't pass it on to his father?" he asked.

"Not that I know of."

"Then your brother lied to me."

She followed him into the office/living room, where she sat down on the couch. "You can't expect Eben to behave well when it comes to the Benedetto family."

He stared at her and eventually he smiled. "So you've seen the transcript and you know a great deal more about me than I do about you," he said, moving to the kitchenette to heat the pot of coffee he always kept on the stove.

She followed him into the small room. "Not much more," she said. "I'm twenty-eight, stand five nine in my stockings, and weigh . . . never mind what I weigh. I've had three varieties of measles. I hate football, but I let myself get dragged to basketball games. Celery gives me hives. Have you ever been married?"

The image of Gillian appeared again and abruptly vanished. "Yes. Briefly. You?"

She shook her head. "No. But I lived with someone for several years. In Boston. I went there with my mother after my father died. Eben was old enough to stay here on his own."

"No other brothers or sisters?"

She shook her head. "Just Eben and me."

"What brought you back to New Orleans?" he asked, patting the coffeepot to see if it was heating.

"A combination of things," she said. "I had worked my way up from secretary to marketing associate for an advertising agency and I was tired of my job. My lover, who was vice president of the agency, was tired of me. And I was worried about Eben."

Manion turned off the gas flame and started to pour her a cup of coffee, but she held up her hand. "No, please. I'm jumpy enough."

He said, "I'm afraid I don't have much to calm you down. No wine or whisky."

"I don't need anything, thanks." She moved closer. "Well, maybe one thing. Could you hold me?"

He took her in his arms. She seemed to be shivering. He moved to kiss her but she said, "No. Not yet. Let's just stay like this for a minute."

He smelled the pleasant shampoo scent of her hair. She was taller than Gil and more solidly built. She lifted her face to him and they kissed.

It was the least impulsive kiss Manion could remember. Probably because of her cut lip, it began as a very tender kiss. But as her mouth opened under his and their tongues touched and probed, he found himself almost weakened by passion.

They broke, raced up the stairs like children, then paused at the rumpled bed that he wished he'd made earlier. But this had been so unexpected. With the sweetest of smiles, she began to undo the buttons of his shirt while he busied himself with the clasp at the back of her blouse. His hand brushed the material where it had been torn in the scuffle with Johnny, and a shiver ran through her. Suddenly, she grabbed him with all her strength and pulled him to her.

This time the kiss was like sunlight invading a dark house. It emptied his mind of all its shadows, including the one that had rested there for far too long.

He remembered tumbling on the bed. So many buttons. Buckles. Zippers. Then the thrill of flesh against flesh. Hands. Tongues. Their bodies moving together, finding the right rhythm, losing it, finding it again. He and Eben Munn's sister! He wanted to laugh, but his happiness wouldn't let him.

31
•

CROAKER HAD not waited for the final act of the comedy at Nadia Wells's home. He'd given the four Henderson Parish cops the address and found a good observation point on an elevated plane less than a city block away from the target area. He had not seen them park, but he did spot the quartet moving in on the house from separate directions. The Mexican guy had strolled up to the car containing the jagoffs from the Wells Agency and with minimal effort disarmed them.

He'd prodded them to the rear of the house where Landry and the others had been swallowed up by trees and foliage. It seemed to be going down smoothly when, suddenly, all hell broke loose. Floodlights lit up the night like a goddamned carnival and he could hear the old lady's voice ordering the badges to throw down their guns. At that point, Croaker had been convinced that the cops would hold their ground and plow right over the old lady. Then he heard the old bitch telling her men to pick up the discarded weapons.

He should have known better: these were guys Johnny Benedetto had told him to use. Naturally, they were unreliable punks.

He cursed Johnny all the way back to his place, a small house on Clara Street previously owned by a dope dealer who had used some of his profits to install state-of-the-art security devices. The irony was that the guy had been taken off in his car, well away from his fortresslike house. Croaker had bought the place from the dealer's girlfriend, who had decided to relocate to Vegas, where she hoped to pursue a career as a showgirl or a hooker or most likely both.

Croaker liked the idea of all the security gizmos, but not the inconvenience of them. He'd just punched the second set of numbers and heard the bolt that controlled the metal front door click, when his phone began to ring. He waited impatiently for the bolt-retracting gears to disengage, then pressed his thumbprint against a plastic window under the useless doorknob. The phone rang again while the scanner studied the whorls, loops, and arches. Satisfied, the machinery gave a little hum and the door popped open.

Croaker caught the phone in the middle of its third ring. It was that fuckhead Johnny. "I need you here, at my place," Johnny ordered him.

Croaker did not like Johnny's tone. "It's late," he said.

"It's gonna get later. Be here in ten minutes." Johnny hung up on him.

Croaker held onto the phone, frozen by anger. Then he replaced the handset and moved to his stereo. He flooded the room with Mozart's *La Finta Semplice,* a relatively new CD acquisition. Fifteen minutes later, the phone began to ring again.

Scowling, he clicked off the music. He paused by a mirror to straighten his tie and put on his suit coat. Before leaving, he reactivated all of the security devices.

Johnny the Wolf lived in a Mediterranean eyesore on a large parcel of land near Lake Vista. It was a squat, sort of orangy structure he had purchased while he was still living with his wife and kids. The fact that the wife let him keep the house should have told him something. The only thing it had going for it was a picture window with a view of Lake Pontchartrain. Croaker had been there only once before, for one of Johnny's so-called parties. Two washed-out bimbos for every guy, grocery-store-brand booze, and loud rock music from the radio. A Johnny Benedetto Production.

Croaker parked on the street behind the property and gave his throat a spray before working his way through a neighbor's driveway and pool area to approach Johnny's house from the rear. He hadn't liked Johnny's phone manners and he wanted to check things out a little before strolling through the asshole's front door. Usually a guy wouldn't try anything in his own house, but with Johnny nothing was certain.

Johnny's pool was covered with leaves and scum and it smelled

like a sewer. Croaker skirted it and homed in on a lit window at the
rear of the house. Through an inch gap where the blinds didn't quite
reach the sill, he saw Johnny angrily throwing clothes into a suitcase.
He was grousing to somebody Croaker couldn't see.

Eventually, Reevie came into the room, holding a drink of some
kind. Probably Coke, since Reevie wasn't much of a boozer. Croaker
felt a little less apprehensive with Reevie on the scene. Just as he was
backing away from the window, he heard Reevie mention his name.

He moved closer.

"I dunno where the fuck he is," Johnny was saying. "You heard
me tell him ten minutes. That was nearly an hour ago. He's got a real
fucking attitude problem. What makes him think he's good enough to
have a fucking attitude? Like he's not just another two-bit asshole
with a gun. You're the one who keeps saying to use him."

"He was the first guy to ever take care of a problem for me,"
Reevie said. "He took care of it very well. Or so I've assumed."

"Yeah. That was then and this is now," Johnny said, hoisting
another empty suitcase onto his bed. "Aw, do what you want. Me, I
don't count anymore. I'm going to fuckin' Sicily. And if he puts the
chocks to that fuckin' gonzo cop, I'll love him like he was Faye
Dunaway."

Wonderful! Now they wanted him to kill a cop! Afterward,
maybe he could join Johnny in Sicily, whatever that was all about.

He circled the house and approached the unlit front door from
the flagstone walkway. He put out his finger to touch the doorbell and
noticed that directly underneath it, somebody had pinned a scapular
medal. He hadn't thought about the Benedettos being Catholic, but it
made sense, of course. That was what was so beautiful about a religion based on faith—if you believed you were clean, you were clean.
His own father could screw around with every bayou bimbo who fell
for his bullshit, but that didn't stop him from going to mass every
Sunday morning. Johnny probably went to Sunday mass too. And
took communion. Even if he'd clipped that low-life Odie Shecksnyder, Johnny would've rationalized the whole thing somehow so that
a murder wound up a venial sin.

Croaker had put the Church behind him the minute he completed his first job. He shook his head to chase away the thoughts of
both religion and bygone deeds. Then he pressed the doorbell.

He heard the heavy footsteps approaching, and Johnny's voice
asking who was there. He replied and the door was opened slowly,

Johnny suddenly being cautious for the first time in his life. "C'mon in," he said.

Croaker entered a living room that was littered with boxes and plastic wrap. He said. "Place could use a woman's touch."

Johnny shot him an evil eye. Reevie entered from the back of the house and shook his hand. He offered him a drink, but Croaker refused. "It's past my bedtime," he said pointedly.

"There's a fucking cop you gotta take out," Johnny blurted.

Reevie gave his uncle an exasperated look and said, "Just keep packing, Johnny. I'll explain the situation."

"Yeah. Keep packing." Johnny turned to Croaker and asked, "You got any fucking idea what the weather is like in Sicily? Do I pack winter or summer?"

"Why not both," Reevie replied. "You're going to be there awhile."

Johnny raised a defiant middle finger to Reevie—a meaningless gesture, since he eventually did as he was told. Reevie indicated that Croaker should sit on an ugly purple armchair. He sat on an even uglier matching sofa. "My uncle is going away," he said. "From now on, we'll be talking directly, no middleman."

Croaker relaxed a notch, slumping back in the chair.

"He asked you here tonight at my request." Reevie lowered his voice slightly. "I wanted to make sure that the problem with the Bentine girl has been handled.'"

Croaker took his time replying. He wondered if Johnny could hear them from the back room. "The guys I used," he said, "the Henderson Parish cops, they blew the job."

"Blew it how?"

"From what I could see, they let the old lady bluff 'em down."

"That's fucking bullshit!" came Johnny's cry as he rushed in. "Landry's a stand-up guy, a performer." He glared at Croaker. "He must've been set up."

"Johnny," Reevie said quietly, "there's no need for you to worry about any of this. I'll handle it. You just get ready."

"Something smells here," Johnny said, looking from Reevie to Croaker. "Something's not kosher." He stormed back out of the room.

Reevie turned his head to observe the telephone on the coffee table. He brought his finger up to his lips, a request for silence. Then he lifted the receiver very carefully.

He replaced the phone almost immediately. "Well," he said. "We haven't much time. He's whining to my father. I don't want the old man to find you here."

Croaker didn't want that either. He said, "There was no setup. Those guys were lame."

"I'll have to find out their situation. Should we have to remove them, would you underwrite the job?"

"Not if they're on the inside. Your old man's got a bunch of guys on the payroll better positioned for that sort of thing." Reevie nodded. "Since Johnny seems to be in love with that punk Landry," Croaker continued, "I assume that's not the cop he wants killed."

"Don't worry about that," Reevie said. "You have enough on your plate as is. If you don't think you can take care of the girl and Pos, I want to know now."

"I'll take care of them. But the way I see it, getting rid of Manion would work just as well. He's the only one beating the bushes about the Legendre guy. And he's more accessible."

"Why don't we make sure and get rid of them all. If you feel you can. The girl, Pos, and Manion."

If he said no, Reevie would simply send out somebody else to do the job. He said, "I'll take care of it."

"Good. If there's nothing else, you'd better be going."

There was something else. He started to tell Reevie about the writer, Steiner, suddenly showing up. But Johnny picked that moment to stroll back into the living room with a nasty grin on his face. "You gonna take care of that fucking cop Munn for me, old buddy?" he asked Croaker.

Croaker looked to Reevie for guidance. "First things first," Reevie said.

"But if Munn's in the ground, Johnny the Wolf stays home and the broads of New Orleans won't have to go into mourning."

Reevie said to Croaker, "Take off, now. We can talk more to-morrow."

Croaker was happy to get out of there. The last place he wanted to be was in the middle of a Benedetto family squabble. But it might be interesting to observe one without being observed himself.

*   *   *

Less than ten minutes after Croaker found a comfortable, se-
cluded spot near a living room window, the Crawfish's black limo
braked in front of Johnny's house. Rillo, the bodyguard/chauffeur,
got out, opened the back door, and then preceded Charlie Benedetto
down the walkway. Benedetto walked slowly, wincing with each step
as if he had corns.

Rillo positioned himself just inside the front door, standing. The
Crawfish sat next to his son on the couch, and Johnny sat across from
them.

Johnny seemed so jumpy, Croaker wondered if he'd been packing his nose with something. He started in right away. "Your kid,
your snotnose kid there, made some fucking deal with a fucking cop
and I'm on my way to some fucking Mamma Mia Motel in Sicily,
where the women are all fat as pigs."

"Calm down, Johnny," the Crawfish said.

"Calm down? Jesus, Chawlie, it's me, Johnny the Wolf, you're
talking to. A cop has given me twenty-four hours to get out of town
and this . . . this *gavronne* you call a son slaps me in the face and tells
me I gotta go—"

The Crawfish turned to his son. "Well?"

"Johnny tried to rape my secretary," he said.

"So?"

"So he got caught."

"By who?"

"By a fuckin' cop," Johnny said.

The Crawfish scowled. "This broad is your secretary," he said to
Reevie. "Tell her to say it was a mistake."

"The bitch wanted it—"

"Shut up, Johnny!" the Crawfish suddenly bellowed. "Well?" he
said to Reevie. "They got no victim, they got no case. *Finito.*"

"The girl's not going to change her story. I've got a feelin the cop
planted her there. And he showed up with two other witnesses."

"They got names?"

"A private investigator named Manion and Marcus Steiner, a
writer."

The Crawfish shook his massive head. "Christ, Johnny, you
dumb dago, you shoulda sold tickets." He sighed. "So this is gonna
cost me, right? How much does this fucking cop want?"

"His name is Munn, Dad, Eben Munn."

"Shit! Well, I figured we'd have to kill that sonofabitch sometime. Might as well be now."

"See? That's what I said," Johnny chirped up.

"And the other witnesses?"

"Kill them, too. Cheaper by the dozen." Charlie Benedetto chuckled.

"And my secretary?"

"I guess so."

"And the five or six people at the front desk who saw her bruises? And the doctor who treats her? And the photographers who take pictures of her black eye? And the legal secretary who probably has taken down her deposition?"

The Crawfish looked exasperated. "What are you saying, Reevie? That we should let 'em run your uncle out of the country like some fucking bomb thrower?"

"Nobody's kicking anybody out of the country," Reevie said. "He's leaving the country of his own volition rather than stay and stand trial and unquestionably be sent to prison."

"I don't get it," the Crawfish said. "This Munn, who's got some hair up his nose about me and who's been trying to put me in a box for years, sets Johnny up for a fall, then lets him go?"

"Reevie made a deal with the whacko," Johnny whined.

"Oh?" The Crawfish gave his son a suspicious look. "What's his end of it? What's he get?"

Reevie smiled. "He gets to take Johnny's place in jail."

The Crawfish relaxed. "Explain."

"He laid it out for me like this: Johnny goes to prison unless he agrees to leave the country." Reevie paused, then added: "And you go with him."

The Crawfish took a minute to digest that one. Then he chuckled. "Me? Leave the country? I was born here. So was Johnny. That Munn *must* be crazy. How's he plan on getting me on the boat?"

"I'm going to help him."

The Crawfish's eyes narrowed.

"You see, Dad, he thinks I want you out of the way so badly I'm going to provide him with enough evidence to force you to take the trip."

"Yeah?" The Crawfish was looking at Reevie with a strange

mixture of curiosity and disbelief. Johnny sat there with his mouth hanging open.

"So here's my idea. Johnny leaves the country. Munn takes this as a sign of my good faith. A couple days from now, I call him and tell him I've got something—canceled checks, a ledger of accounts, whatever—that will give him all the leverage he needs to send you to Mars if he wants."

"And then what happens?" the Crawfish asked. "I go to Italy. My ambitious twerp of a son takes over and everybody's happy ever after?"

"Not exactly," Reevie said. "We get somebody to deliver this material to Munn in some well-populated spot. We notify our guys on the NOPD—and by the way, Johnny's Henderson Parish screwups are in hot water and we have to pull the plug on them."

Johnny jumped up. "No fucking way. Not on just the say-so of that fucking Croaker, a goddamn Frog who can't even shoot straight no more."

"Siddown, Johnny, or I'll knock you down," the Crawfish growled. "Reevie's telling us a story. Okay, boy, we got this material being handed over to Munn. And . . ."

"And we send our cops in. They open the envelope and find not canceled checks but cash, cocaine, and a thank-you note from your friend Emilio Vargas. Goodbye, Lieutenant Munn. Welcome home, Johnny.

The Crawfish thought it over. He smiled, then he chuckled, and eventually he began to laugh uproariously. "I love the shit about Vargas," he said wiping his eyes. "Maybe they'll boot *him* out of the country."

Johnny was frowning. "This means I don't stay in Italy?"

"He's my brother, but he ain't so bright," the Crawfish said, messing Johnny's hair. "It means you go to Italy and spend a couple weeks and then you come home."

"If you want blondes," Reevie said, "take an SAS flight to Sweden."

As the idea sank in, a smile spread across Johnny's face.

"The only problem I see," the Crawfish said, "is what happens to the jamoke who delivers the package to Munn. He's gotta be one hell of a stand-up guy because he's gonna do time. In fact, maybe he's gonna have to be put away."

"I know just the guy," Johnny said. "Mr. Fucking Bad Attitude, the guy who got Landry in the shit. What do you say, Reevie, we dump that fucking Croaker?"

"Maybe," he said. "Maybe that'd be okay."

Croaker had heard enough. He moved quietly away from the house. He was concentrating so hard on his options that he passed Johnny's swimming pool without even noticing its stench.

32.

MANION CARRIED a tray of coffee and beignets up the stairs and into his bedroom just as Lucille was opening her eyes. At least one of them opened. The other was puffy and discolored. And her lip was more pouty than Brigitte Bardot's in her prime. "You look beautiful in the morning," he told her.

"Sure I do. I can't even see out of one eye. I'm probably about as beautiful as Rocky Gazarra."

"Who?"

"Rocky whatever-his-name-is Prizefighter. Is that breakfast, I hope I hope?"

"The de-caf coffee you asked for is from Ragusa of Royal Street."

She stared at him with her good eye and frowned. "You're dressed."

"Ragusa refuses to serve anybody who drops by naked. Claims it's a reserved right."

"Must be part of that conservative element in the French Quarter." She shifted her glance to the plate he was carrying. "Are those beignets from last night? I though we devoured them all."

"Not all," he said.

At a certain point, their hunger for food had replaced other appetites and they'd thrown on their clothes and wandered off into the night. At Morning Call they'd purchased a dozen powdered beignets and a half-gallon of milk. Despite Lucille's protests, they also visited an all-night drugstore for a tube of salve for her eye.

Back at his home, they'd lounged on the bed, mainly undressed, drinking milk and eating the crisp, sweet beignets. He'd asked her, in a moment of seriousness, what Charlie Benedetto had done to make the Munns hate him so.

She'd hesitated, then explained. "Our father owned a neighborhood bar and grill on Cambronne Street. It was called Buckley's. I'm not sure why. I guess my father bought it from somebody named Buckley, but that was before I was born."

"I know the place. I even had dinner there," Terry said. "There was an iron claw machine that could not be beaten. It never occurred to me that it was owned by the father of one of my classmates."

"Then you know it was nothing special. Red beans on Mondays, fried trout on Fridays. Oyster poor boys anytime. It was a rather sweet little place, at least in my memory.

"Johnny Benedetto came in one night. To get cigarettes or to use the phone. For some reason. My mother used to wait tables. Johnny did something or maybe just said something. Eben knows the story better than I do. I was still a kid. Anyway, my father came around the bar and grabbed Johnny—threw him out into the street.

"The next night, just before closing, some guys came in and chased all the customers away. They tore the place up a little and then they went after my father. He tried to defend himself. He was a big man, and so was the guy who worked with him, Claude LaBarre. But those bastards knew what they were doing. They held Claude at gunpoint while they took turns beating my father with a baseball bat.

"They did something to his head. He never really recovered. And after a few months, he just died in his sleep. Mother sold the restaurant, such as it was. After paying Daddy's medical bills, we were barely able to move to Boston, where Mom had a sister. Eben sent us money to keep us going."

"Where's your mother now?"

"She died several years ago. It was a blessing. She didn't really want to keep going. She'd always blamed herself for what happened. Eben took her death pretty hard."

Manion wondered if that was when the cop had his semibreakdown and conversion. "How old was Eben when your father was attacked?"

"I was thirteen, so he was nineteen. He was there when the men entered. He tried to fight them, but they held him back and made him

watch every blow that Daddy took. Then, Eben told me, the door opened and Charlie Benedetto walked in—a bloated, strutting little man. He took one look at my father and told his thugs that they hadn't done enough.

"He took the bat from one of the thugs and gave Daddy one last, final hit. Eben went off his head. He started laughing. Benedetto and his men were confused; then they grew uneasy. They left him there, laughing uncontrollably beside my father's battered body.

"I asked him what had made him laugh like that. He told me he was thinking about revenge."

"I'm going to be late for work," she informed Manion. It was eight A.M. and she was still in bed. He was standing beside the bed, adjusting his tie, trying to overcome the urge to join her.

"You can't go back there," he said. "Reeves Benedetto isn't what you'd call slow. He'll have figured out that you and Eben suckered him."

"But today's payday. I have to get my check." She polished off a small beignet and picked one just a little larger.

"Have them mail it to you."

"But Eben said Reevie's happy with the deal they struck. He's glad to be rid of his uncle and his father. It's not a lie. I know that he's ashamed of them."

"More likely he thinks they're slowing him down," Manion said.

"He's not like the rest of the family," she replied. "Eben hates all Benedettos, but he could be wrong. From everything I've seen, Reevie's a kind, generous, and politically correct man."

"It's a danger to think all politically correct men are honorable. Some of them are just as intrinsically evil as conservatives."

She frowned. "Are you laughing at me?"

"No. I'm trying to convince you that guys like Benedetto never let you know how they really feel about anything. You have to be a little wary of them."

"I need that check. It was for two weeks' work. Nearly nine hundred dollars. It may be a while before I get another job, even if Reevie gives me a good reference. And I'm not sure he won't."

"Let Eben get your money for you," he said.

She grinned. "He might enjoy that. Well, if I'm not working today, why are *you* dressed?"

"One of us has to make a buck."

"You're certainly Mr. Romance in the morning." She shifted on the bed, the linen falling from her freckled breasts. She looked up at him with mock innocence. What was so important, Manion thought, that it couldn't wait for another hour or so?

He stepped out of his trousers, removed his glasses, sat down beside her, and leaned forward. She made a muffled noise and held up an uneaten portion of beignet that had been trapped between them. She took her time munching and swallowing. Then she circled her arms around his neck and pulled him down onto her. He offered no resistance whatsoever.

When he awoke, he found her bathed and dressed and seated in his reading chair studying a piece of paper. He swung his long body upright, let the cold wooden floor against his feet wake him nearly all the way.

"You have one of these, too," she said, waving the paper.

It was his reconstruction of J.J. Legendre's cryptic note that had been taken from him at the scene of Odie Shecksnyder's murder. "Who else do you know who has one?" he asked.

"Eben. Isn't he supposed to? He showed it to me yesterday."

Manion was disappointed. He'd hoped that the original might have found its way to Benedetto, making a clear link between him and J.J. "I gave your brother a copy. Why'd he show it to you?"

"He said it was some sort of shorthand and asked if I could make any sense of it, I guess, because I know shorthand and he doesn't."

"And did you make any sense of it?"

"I think the 'Gay-no' refers to a woman named Gaynaud."

"A woman?" Manion asked.

"Yes. I've spoken to her several times. She's Reevie's girl."

Manion forced himself not to smile. "What about the other scribbles?"

"Well, 'Gallig,' 'LaP,' and 'Fur-no' could refer to Gallighan, LaPorte, and Furneaux. Legislators, or something. I've put in a bunch of calls to them. Their offices are in Baton Rouge, so the 'Baton Gay' probably has something to do with that city too."

Manion wanted to kiss her again. And did.

When they broke apart, he said, "Now moving on to the main prize, what about 'New At C' or 'Wash in Basin Bur So'?"

She shook her head. "Nothing. I'm afraid you'll just have to work on those yourself. What is this anyway?"

"Notes a friend of mine wrote in a hurry."

"Why don't you ask him what they mean?"

"He's not available."

She shrugged and, turning to go, asked, "See you again sometime?"

"Tonight?"

"Dinner. My apartment?"

He frowned. "Talk to your brother. I think you should stay away from your place for a while."

She shook her head. "You're fixating on Reevie, and it's nonsense. Just because his father is a pig . . . He's embarrassed by his family. I'm sure that's why he's being so cooperative with Eben about getting them out of the country."

"Okay. He's a prince. But would it hurt to humor me for a couple of days?"

"I promise to be careful," she said, returning to kiss him on the lips.

He watched from his upstairs window as she crossed the sidewalk to her car and drove away. "Speaking of being careful. . ." he said to himself, picking up his Colt. He rooted around in a closet for a few minutes and found an ankle holster, an impulse item he'd purchased at a gun shop years before. This was as good a time as any to break it in.

He descended to his office and consulted his notebook before picking up the phone. An out-of-breath Leon Harris answered on the third ring. "I was almost out the door," he said. "I'm late for work."

"Just one quick question," Manion said. "When we talked, you told me your uncle had a friend in one of the burial societies. Would that have been the Basin Street Burial Society?"

"Yes," he replied, curious. "Marvell Washington. He worked with my uncle at Gaynaud's."

"Any idea where I can find him?"

"Can't help you. I only met him once or twice. Big, solemn man. Why?"

Manion started to reply, but Leon cut in, "Jesus, I'm sorry, but I've gotta run. Can we talk later?"

Manion told him they could and probably would.

*   *   *

There was only one Marvell Washington in the Greater New Orleans phone book, but he wasn't at home. A woman's monotone voice informed Manion that her husband might be found at a club called the Grin and Bare It on Bourbon. Manion knew the place, a dark dive that offered a continuous round of low comics and even lower strippers.

According to a hand-scribbled sign at the door, that morning's attractions were "Matty Mason, star of *The Chuckle Corner* on Orleans Cable, Lorraine ('The Southern Pearl') Lane, and Dixie Tracy ('She's Arresting')."

There were no customers in the dark lounge. It smelled of pine oil and stale cigarette smoke. There was a doughy stripper seated on the empty stage in her pasties, ignoring the loud recorded music while reading the *Times-Picayune* and sipping coffee from a thick white mug. Spotting Manion, she sighed and started to put away the paper. "Relax," he told her. "I'm just browsing."

The morning bartender had just blown his nose and was studying the result in his grayish handkerchief. He sniffed, shoved the kerchief into his back pocket, and said, "What can I do you for?"

"Is Marvell around?"

"Marvell who?"

"The Marvell whose wife said I could find him here."

"Oh. That Marvell. What do you want with him?"

"Just talk."

"Hey, Dixie, the guy wants to t-t-talk with M-M-M-Marvell." He laughed. The stripper shrugged and went back to the paper. Manion wondered what could be that interesting, unless it was the Vic 'n' Natalie cartoon.

"Talk about what?" the bartender asked.

"The secret of this place's success," Manion said. He pointed to a doorway leading to the rear of the building. "Is he back there?"

The bartender looked him up and down, then shrugged. "Should be in the alley. You can go through there," he said.

There was a garbage can holding the club's rear door ajar. Past it, a big black man in a black suit, white shirt, and black tie sat on a low brick wall holding a cornet in his lap. A white uniform cap with a black bill and a band reading "Basin St." was perched on his large head.

"Marvell Washington?" Manion asked.

The man stared at him, saying nothing. Manion could see red in the corners of his eyes.

"I'm a friend of Leon Harris's," the detective lied.

"Ah, P-P-P-Parker's li'l nephew." The big man relaxed slightly. "And how be Leon?"

"Fine. Could we talk a minute?"

"Ab-b-b-bout what?"

"Parker Harris."

"That's what I f-f-f-figgered."

Manion nodded at the lounge. "You play for the girls?" he asked.

The man made a "hrumph" sound. "N-n-n-no sir. That's what I d-d-d—do here." He pointed his horn at the stack of crates filled with empty beer, booze, and champagne bottles. "Got to be piled j-j-j-jus' so, else the trash trucks drive on b-b-b-by, l-l-l-leave 'em here," he explained. "How c-c-c-can I help you?"

"You worked for the Gaynaud family?"

He ducked his head in a nod. "Twelve years, on and off. I d-d-d-did heavy work, when they n-n-n-needed it."

"That's where you and Parker met and became friends?"

"Yes sir. Least, we m-m-m-met there. We was never what you call f-f-friends."

"Leon said you were."

"No b-b-b-big thing. P-P-P-Parker was okay, b-b-b-but he had his m-m-m-mean side."

"Like what?"

"Oh. He liked to strut himself. M-m-m-made it hard on some f-f-f-folks worked with him."

"You?"

He smiled. "No. See, P-P-P-Parker and me was in the B-B-B-Basin Street B-B-B-Burial Society. An' he knew I p-p-play cornet with the b-b-brass b-b-band, and P-P-P-Parker figgered that made me some kinda musical talent an' he respect that. B-b-b-but he gave the rest of the staff a hard t-t-t-time all the t-t-t-time. Even M-M-Mr. Gaynaud he gave a whole lot of lip. And that m-m-m-man t-t-t-took it. Never knew why."

Manion asked, "Do you still do any work for Gaynaud?"

"No sir. Not since P-P-P-Parker died. We was all let go."

"Were you there the night Parker died?"

"Oh, yes. See, they had this p-p-p-party earlier. And I cleaned up after the p-p-p-parties. So I was there."

"Did you see Parker take this fall?"

"No sir. I was in the k-k-k-kitchen. The m-m-m-missus started screaming and I and the m-m-m-maid run in and p-p-p-poor P-P-P-Parker is d-d-d-dead."

"Where was Gaynaud?"

"He there. The m-m-m-missus is howling, shouting off her head, and he t-t-t-try to quiet her down." Marvell shook his head sadly.

"Was her doctor there?"

"Not at first. He come in later," Marvell said.

"What was Mrs. Gaynaud yelling?"

"Oh, c-c-crazy stuff. Saying that m-m-m-mister bring shame to the house. Stuff like that."

Manion sensed a presence to his right and turned. The bartender was standing in the doorway, watching them. He said, "If you finished stacking them crates, Marvell, I need some beer for the bin."

Marvell said, "I j-j-jus' got dressed, Mistah J-J-J-Jim. They c-c-coming for m-m-m-me any m-m-m-minute."

The bartender nodded. "Okay, just get back here after they plant the poor son' bitch." He gave Manion another glare, then strolled back into the building.

"Mr. Alphonse Lagarde be buried t-t-today," Marvell Washington said to Manion. Lagarde had been a local entertainer, a cabaret singer who'd become a fixture in the Quarter. Manion remembered him from his college days. "Mr. P-P-P-Pete Fountain be p-p-p-playing with us. Other c-c-c-celebrities also."

"Has anybody else asked you about the night Parker died?"

"Nope. Nobody asked me n-n-n-nothing that night. And nobody asked me nothing since b-b-b-but you."

"Could somebody have pushed Parker down those stairs, Marvell?"

The black man's face showed genuine sadness. "Mistah, we live in a world p-p-p-people apt to do anything."

Manion cocked his head to one side, his mind spinning. "Did you know Parker's sister, Leon's mother?"

Marvell shook his large head. "No. Never had the p-p-p-p-pleasure."

A car horn echoed down the alley. An old Lincoln had stopped on the side street. Marvell hopped from his perch and waved at the men in the car. He turned to Manion. "Say hello to Leon for m-m-me. He seem like a nice b-b-b-boy."

As he went off down the alley, the black man stood taller and he walked faster. He swung his cornet. His friends in the Lincoln yelled something at him and they all laughed. Manion felt a sudden urge to run to the car himself and ask if he could tag along. He wanted to march behind them as a member of the second line—the nonmusical mourners—to help give Al Lagarde a final send-off. But he had other spirits to lay to rest.

33.

"HI, POS." Slo Bentine's voice came to him as in a dream. He was afraid to open his eyes, afraid that he would still be in the hospital ward with the night moans and coughs and the odd scream of torment or despair.

"Oh," he heard her say, "I thought I saw his eyes flutter."

He opened them then to a room rich in sunlight. He remembered. The night before, he'd been moved into a smaller ward. His bed was the closest to the window.

Two figures were between him and the sunlight. One of them said, "Hey, Posell, the doc says you as well as any man took a bullet in the gut. Welcome back to the worl'."

Pos smiled at his cousin Buddy. He was groggy. His mind floated somewhere above the bed. His stomach felt as if he'd swallowed a cup of pins. He saw the figure beside Buddy move back from the bed. "Wait," he called out.

His eyes focused and she was there, smiling tentatively at him, wearing a summer dress that Buddy had finally persuaded her mother to provide. An inch of bandage showed under the sleeve. "You're hurt," he said.

"I'm fine," she said. "Especially since the doctor told us how well you're doing."

"They wanna make sure you ain't bleedin' infernally, *cousin*. Then they gonna kick your Cajun butt out of heah, make way for some sick people."

Pos reached out a hand and Slo took it, brushed it with her lips. "I think I'm ready to get out of here now," he said.

"You hang on now. Another twenty-four hours and we got a private ambulance to take you to this hidey-hole we rentin' in Kenner. You gotta stay off your feet for a while. Let them clamps and things do their work."

"I ain't going to no Kenner. I'm going to my place."

"Don't be a dumb coonass. They ain't caught the guy who shot you, and Miz Wells wants you to lay low till they do."

Pos began to feel discomfort. He moved on the bed, and his stomach seemed to catch fire. "Lie quiet," Slo ordered him softly and he obeyed.

"You still don't have nothin' to tell us about who did this to you?"

"Like I tol' the cops and everybody else who's been askin', it was just a big guy with a gun. I can describe the gun better than him. That's what I saw most of."

"Oh," Buddy said, moving closer, " 'fore I forget. I finally got through to Fawstah last night. I been tryin' his place, but nobody been answerin'. Last night, I finally got him and tol' him about you bein' in here and all. He wanted to come see you right away, but I tol' him to let you rest. He should be here soon."

Pos's mouth felt dry. "Buddy," he said, "could you maybe get me a coke? They got a machine somewhere."

"I'll get the nurse."

"No. You do it. And take your time. I want to have some words with Slo."

Buddy grinned. "Yeah, I getcha."

As soon as he had gone, Pos began to push himself upright.

"What in the world are you doin'?" Slo asked in alarm.

"Help me, please, girl."

She helped him sit up, then awkwardly swing his legs out. "We have to get away from here," he said.

"That's crazy, you—"

He felt dizzy from the combination of painkillers and pain. He took her face in both his hands and said, "Look at me, girl. I know what I'm doin'. You and me's in big trouble, unless we get out of here."

"But you're not suppose' to walk."

"Check and see if they's a wheelchair round here."

They were cut off from the rest of the room by a dark green curtain. She looked past it to where nurses, orderlies, and visitors ebbed and flowed. Not far away was one wheelchair. She moved down the row quickly and began to drag the chair toward Pos's bed. It refused to move. She searched the machinery, found the wheel locks and released them.

He had slipped into his robe. With difficulty, she managed to help him into the chair. His naked knees stuck out past the robe and hospital gown. "Where are your clothes?" she asked.

"I don't know, but the hell with them. We don't have time."

She pushed him through the ward door into a long hallway that smelled of floor wax and ammonia. At the far end of the hall, Buddy leaned against the information desk chatting with several nurses and the uniformed policeman who'd been stationed to keep an eye on the gunshot victim. Slo pushed Pos in the opposite direction.

They took a service elevator to the second basement, where visitors' cars were parked. She found the Cadillac they'd arrived in. Fortunately, she had forgotten to lock the passenger door. She helped Pos onto the rear seat, where, by drawing up his knees slightly, he was able to lie on his back.

He told her precisely what she had to do to jump-start the car. She was surprised to discover how easy it was.

There was a moment of panic when she realized that it would cost three dollars to pay for the parking. But Felix kept a collection of change in the ashtray.

On the street, free from the hospital, Slo stopped the car, turned and asked, "Where do we go?"

Pos felt more discomfort than pain. He smiled up at her sweet, worried face and said, "We're goin' home, *cher'*."

34.

"THAT'S SOME conclusion you've drawn, sonny," Nadia Wells said to Manion as they sat in a small room just off the main hall of the newly constructed Huey P. Long Memorial Library in the French Quarter. Elsewhere in the library, dedication ceremonies were taking place, with most of the state's civic and social leaders in attendance. Manion had been amused but not surprised when Olivette informed him of Nadia's participation in the event. She had never let her somewhat infamous previous profession—or her present one, which was questionable at best—stop her from moving in whichever social circle she chose.

She raised one eyebrow and said, "You really think Lawson Gaynaud killed his butler, Parker Harris, because the butler was blackmailing him?"

"Gaynaud's wife claimed he'd brought shame to the house."

She pursed her lips. "That's fuel for the fire, I suppose. But where does Reeves Benedetto fit in?"

"He's involved with the Gaynaud daughter, Lindsay. I think he's the guy who turned loose the hit man who killed J.J. and shot Pos and Slo Bentine."

"Hmm. Maybe it was Reeves who bounced Parker Harris down those stairs."

Manion shrugged. "According to Marvell Washington, only the Gaynauds were there when Harris fell. My guess is that Benedetto is just helping his future father-in-law with a sticky problem. The thing I can't quite figure is why he's putting Parker's nephew to work."

"What kind of work?"

"I don't know, but it won't be hard to find out."

She shook her head. "Benedetto has to be getting something out of it. Unless, of course, we're guilty of blaming him for his daddy's sins. He put up some of the loot that went into this place, by the way. Maybe he's a real fine fella who goes around doing nice things for people."

"Why, Nadia. Is that cynical shell of yours starting to crack?"

She chuckled. "When it does, I want you to come arunnin' with grout and plaster."

"Your 'real fine fella' Reevie B. has been making a lot of phone calls to the capital—to Lawson Gaynaud, Jr., and three men named Gallighan, LaPorte, and Furneaux. They were all included on J.J.'s shorthand laundry list. Mean anything to you?"

Nadia's face broke into a smile. "Hell, I was just chatting with Jimmy LaPorte. Drove down from Baton Rouge for the dedication. And I think I see a bit more of the big picture. He and Gallighan and Furneaux are all members of the state legislature. They're all working on that new gambling initiative."

"Legalized gambling? Aren't the lottery and the gambling ships enough?"

"There are folks who don't want it to stop there. They'd like casinos along the lakefront, slot machines in the drugstores. They'd turn this paradise into another Atlantic City and grin like jackals while they're doing it."

"A New Atlantic City," Manion said. "That was the final bit of J.J.'s doodle, 'New At C.'"

"It's got to be that," Nadia said. "The truly fascinating thing is that the one member of the legislature who almost single-handedly has been opposing the gambling amendment is . . . guess who?"

"Not young Gaynaud?"

"None other. So now we know what Benedetto is getting in return for his help in laying Parker Harris to rest once and for—"

She was interrupted by the opening of the door. A short woman in her thirties entered. She was wearing a black cocktail dress and a frown that left her pleasantly plump face when she saw Nadia. "Oh, Miz Wells," she said. "I been lookin' for you. Your office is on the line, but just sit tight, hon." She crossed the room to a telephone. "I'll get 'em to transfer the call over heah."

That accomplished, she handed the phone to Nadia and, after gifting Manion with a mildly flirtatious smile, left the room.

Nadia removed her earring and lifted the receiver. "Yes?" she said in a soft, dignified manner. Almost immediately, she sharpened its edge to snap, "It's me, dammit, Buddy. Don't you recognize my voice by this time?"

She calmed somewhat while she listened to what Buddy had to say. Then she issued a curt "Stay there" and hung up without the customary goodbye.

"Evidently Pos's wound was not as severe as we all thought," she told Manion. "He and Slo have snuck out of the hospital, taken the Caddy, and hit the high road. You better get over there and pry Buddy off the ceiling. I'm gonna phone home to break the news to Felix about his car."

Buddy was standing by the nurses' station talking with two policemen—one uniformed, one in plain clothes—when Manion signaled him from across the room. He slapped the plainclothes cop on the back and, shaking his head as if in wonder, moved toward the men's room. Manion joined him there.

Checking first to make sure the stalls were empty, Buddy explained that Slo had wheeled Pos down to the parking area and driven away. He had no idea why, unless it was because they wanted to get laid.

Manion sighed and asked, "What's the situation with the police?"

"They pretty p.o.'ed. Pos was a, uh, material witness. But he was th' victim, after all, and not th' guilty party. Still, they plenty p.o.'ed and they wanna know what th' deal is. Hell, *I* wanna know what th' deal is."

"What'd you tell them?"

"That Pos is my cousin. Nuthin' else. You know me better than that, T-bone."

"Any idea where Pos and the girl might have gone?"

"His apartment? Her house? I called her mama. She ain't seen 'em she says."

"I'll try his place."

"Fawstah went over there already. You might run into him."

"Pos's brother?"

"Yeah." Buddy shifted his weight from one foot to the next. "He's the reason we found out they was missing. He came by to see Pos, only they wasn't no Pos to see."

"Are the cops through with you?"

"I guess so. Lemme go say goodbye and make sure."

Fifteen minutes later, Manion's Mustang was parked in front of Pos's apartment on General Pershing and he and Buddy were at the front door. Someone had broken the police seal, and the door was ajar.

"Anybody heah?" Buddy yelled as they entered the apartment. "Pos? Fawstah?"

A tall man in a tan suit entered the room from the kitchen. He had a square jaw and a high forehead. He was nearly a foot taller than Pos, but the dark eyes and the full lower lip were identical to his brother's. Foster Fouchette said, "They're not here, Buddy." His gruff voice had only a hint of a Cajun accent, as if it were something he'd tried very hard to eliminate. "I don't think they've been here. I broke the seal myself."

"Fawstah, you remember Terry Manion?"

"I don't think we've met," Foster Fouchette said, shaking Manion's hand.

"Any idea where your brother might have gone?" Manion asked.

Foster frowned. "Dressed in a robe? Friend's place maybe. A motel."

"What about your place?"

"No way for him to get in."

"Have you talked with him lately?"

Foster shook his head. "I've been traveling. Just got back last night. Buddy told me about the shooting."

"Looky here," Buddy said, pointing at a stain on the carpet. "That's Pos's blood. Not three feet from th' cawd table where we was playin'."

Manion glanced at the rug, then back to Foster, who evidently had no curiosity about bloodstains. "You must have some idea where your brother would go. Someplace he'd feel safe."

Foster smiled suddenly, softening the hard lines of his face. "Yeah!" he said. "Sure. That dumb Cajun'd go back home to the Bayou."

Buddy grinned. "I'd love to see Tante Nona's face when he shows up," he told Manion. "She's gonna take a broom to that busted-up Cajun's hide, comin' home with a hole in his stomach and a little gal young enough to be his baby sistah."

Foster scowled. "Maman always did rag on poor Pos."

"She and old Georges thought the sun and the moon set on this guy, but Pos couldn't do nuthin' right." Buddy chuckled.

Manion asked Foster, "How long a drive is it?"

"The cabin? Three hours by car to Houma. Another hour by boat. If you know where you're going. The bayous can be tricky."

"But *you* could find it," Manion said, making it sound like a request.

Foster stared at Manion. "You wanna go?" he asked. "I'll take you."

Manion handed his car keys to Buddy. "Let Nadia know where I've gone. I'll call her tomorrow."

The three men left the apartment together. Manion closed the door behind them and reaffixed the police seal as best he could. By the time he caught up with the others, Buddy was sliding behind the steering wheel of the Mustang.

"Where you want me to drop this tin can, Terry?"

"Zohran's Garage, near my place."

"Fos, you tell your mama hello for me now," Buddy shouted over the engine noise. "Tell her one of these days I'm gonna come by for some étoufée. And tell that sonofabitch Pos what I think of him for runnin' out on me like that."

They waved as he drove away. Manion pointed to a silver Acura Legend a few feet away. "Is that yours?"

"No," Foster said. He led Manion down the block to Galvez Street, where his sedan rested under a chinaberry tree. Manion waited while Pos's brother unlocked the doors and let the heat from the midday sun escape.

When they were under way and heading for the Jefferson Highway, Foster asked, "You know much about the bayous, Manion?"

"Not much."

"My daddy used to say, 'De bayous, dey ain't no vacation spots for strangers, no.' "

"When was the last time you were home?"

"When the old man died. Six years ago."

"Well, I hope you remember the way."

Foster said grimly, "I can't forget it, no matter how hard I try."

Living around Cajuns most of his life, Manion had heard his share of the tall tales about giant 'gators and other swamp monsters. He asked Foster how dangerous the bayous really were.

"They're the hunting grounds for all sorts of critters that can kill a man faster than any human could. Cajuns call it 'goin' one-on-one with nature.'"

"Sounds a little daunting."

"Well," Foster said, "it's for damn sure more people enter the bayous than come out again."

35

•

AT THE Shell, a short-order restaurant on University Place in downtown New Orleans, Emilio Vargas stared in a floor-length mirror at Reevie Benedetto being handed an oyster poor boy sandwich on a cardboard plate by a counterman.

It was lunchtime and the place was packed with men and women from the workday world. Vargas watched Reevie weave around them, purchase a draft beer, and head toward the high wooden table where the Latin stood, nibbling a roast beef on a kaiser roll. Without turning to Reevie, Vargas said, "Your father knows of our enterprise."

"That's why you had to see me? Because of some rumor?"

"The Farmer doesn't think it's a rumor," Vargas said. On the table beside his food was a folded copy of that morning's *Times-Picayune*. He pushed it a few inches with a manicured finger so that Reevie could see a small headline: "Six die as Bastrop Farm Burns. Arson Suspected."

Reevie turned his attention to his sandwich. He took a bite, chewed slowly. "You talked to the Farmer?"

"No. And I won't. At this point he would be no more communicative than a blackened redfish, which I suspect he must resemble."

"So? We have his money."

"Money?" Vargas's voice was a low hiss. "One must be alive for money to be of any use. The fire is a message from your father."

"He's not that subtle," Reevie said. "In any case, you don't have to worry about my father. He's going on a long trip."

"Where?"

"To Italy. He and my uncle Johnny. They'll be leaving soon and they won't be returning. Unless they want to go to prison."

"I doubt that your father would enjoy prison. Still, when do they leave, precisely? I think I shall make myself unavailable until they are safely departed."

"Johnny should be leaving momentarily. He has to take care of a few business matters first. My father will be gone by the end of the week."

Vargas stared at the confident young man's reflection. Could he really dispose of so powerful a figure as Charlie Benedetto that easily? If so, how dangerous might *he* be? "How was this accomplished?" he asked.

Reevie shrugged. "Maybe the police are getting more efficient."

Vargas stared at him a beat longer, then smiled. Without bidding him farewell, he placed the remains of his roast beef sandwich on his plate, turned, and left the Shell.

He crossed University Place and bounded up the steps to the revolving front door of the Fairmont Hotel. There, a young Latin with a ponytail fell in step behind him, turning to scan the street before entering the building.

The young Latin had seen and disregarded a row of parked limousines that was usually to be found in front of the hotel. But that day, one of them was a privately owned stretch limo. In its back seat, Charlie "the Crawfish" Benedetto sat in silence. He stared through the Shell's display window as his son casually polished off his sandwich and sipped his beer.

"What now?" Rillo asked.

"You got something pressing?" the Crawfish rapped back.

"No sir."

"That fuckin' kid," the Crawfish said, with some regret. "Goddamn bright boy. He figures he and that spic can pull stuff in my state behind my fucking back?"

"Maybe it's not what you think," Rillo said. Actually, he hoped the kid *was* trying to duke the old man. That way the number three spot, after Johnny the Wolf, would be wide open.

"Not what I think?" the Crawfish roared. "I think he's plannin' on sending me to Palermo to suck olives. And because that's exactly what he *is* doing, I'm gonna have to put the boot to him. That's what I think, you fucking dumbhead wop!"

Rillo took the insult, as he'd taken insults in the past. It was his own fault for speaking out. There were times when you couldn't win with the Crawfish.

36
•

FOR TWO hours Manion had been idly watching the marsh-lands as the car sped along Highway 90, past towns named West-wego, Boutte, Paradis, and Des Allemands. Every now and then the marshes gave way to lakes, then gathered again.

Though he had not lied to Foster Fouchette about his ignorance of the bayous, the drive was not unfamiliar. His maternal grandfa-ther, a jovial man who had never let his inability to drive a car stand in the way of his occupation as a traveling salesman, had been chauf-feured along 90 every other week to Morgan City, New Iberia, La-fayette, and other capitals of the Cajun empire. He had returned along Highway 10, the so-called Swamp Expressway, pausing to visit clients in Port Allen and Reserve. When Terry's grammar school schedule permitted, he would accompany his grandfather, thrilled to be going somewhere, anywhere, fascinated as the highway cut through the soggy landscape that could move swiftly from pastoral farmland to dark and ominous swampland with its nightmare forest of gnarled black, leafless trees.

They would stop at little towns, and Manion would tag along into hardware stores and machine shops and listen impatiently to discussions of mill problems and mechanical solutions. Then he and his grandfather would dine on crab or shrimp or oysters and return to the car, where a series of ever changing taciturn black chauffeurs would be waiting patiently, sometimes napping.

A curse from Foster Fouchette pulled him back to the present.

Pos's older brother seemed to be growing more agitated, the closer they came to the swampland. He twisted in his seat and glared at the road behind them in his rearview mirror. "Fucking country drivers," he said.

Manion suggested he relax, listen to some music on the radio.

Foster grumbled. "Probably can't pick up anything but that goddamned zydeco."

"I sort of like it."

"That's because you didn't grow up with it. Goddamned accordions and washboards. Part of the reason I left home."

"You said you traveled," Manion said. "What do you sell?"

"Machinery," Foster answered.

"That's a coincidence. My grandfather used to travel for Louisiana Tool and Dye."

Foster nodded. "Good company."

"This was his route."

"I bet he's not still working it," Foster said. "Computers and phones are all anybody needs. No people."

"Does that affect your job too?" Manion asked.

"No. What I do, they'll always need the personal touch."

"What kind of machinery do you handle?"

"Weaponry," Foster said. "You can't demonstrate the product over the phone."

"Do you do much of your traveling by car?"

"Some," Foster replied.

"But not this one."

Foster looked at him, puzzled. Manion pointed to the odometer. "A hundred and forty-eight miles. Not much mileage for a guy who's been traveling."

Foster nodded. "This is a loaner. Mine's in the shop. I pick it up tomorrow evening." He coughed, reached into his pocket, and withdrew an atomizer.

"Laryngitis?" Manion asked.

"Another Cajun memory," Foster said without expression. "I was fifteen. A boy named Beau Sislock tried to hang me."

"Why?"

"He thought I killed his dog. Pos killed the fucking dog. He didn't mean to. He was carrying it to our pirogue and dropped it into the water. Went down like a rock. Something, a 'gator probably, dragged it off. Beau and his brothers grabbed me one day. The brothers held me down while he tied my hands and hoisted me on a winch that his father used to hoist their boat out of the water. I hung there for a few seconds; then I started kicking, and the rope broke and I fell into the Bayou. Beau's brothers got scared and dragged me out and cut me loose. I couldn't do anything but grunt for a month. Finally, this old doctor who used to boat by every so often took a look at my larynx, shook his head, and gave me some cough medicine.

"It never really healed. Not a day passes I don't think about Beau Sislock."

"Ever meet him again, as an adult?"

Foster stared at the road. "Fell on bad times, I guess. I heard he killed himself."

"Plenty of that going around," Manion said. He leaned forward and turned on the radio. He pressed the presets. The second button brought in a clear channel station that was sending a noonday opera out across several states.

"How's this?" Manion asked. "Better than zydeco?"

"Much," Foster said, relaxing slightly. "Rossini's *The Marriage Contract*. Opera's the only thing the wops do right. I love it."

"I thought you might," Manion said genially. His Colt pressing against his ankle was uncomfortable and comforting at the same time.

When the divided highway ended at Houma, Manion and Foster Fouchette drove on along a paved road for another ten miles. There was not much traffic, but Foster seemed overly attentive to it.

Finally, Manion turned to look back through the rear window. He saw several sedans, a semi. He asked. "Something the matter?"

Foster raised an eyebrow. "Like what?"

"You seem to be interested in what's going on behind us."

"You better look back," Foster replied, "or you never know what's gaining on you."

"I think the advice was not to look back," Manion said.

"Bad advice," Foster told him.

Just past Boudreaux they spotted the stolen Cadillac, seemingly none the worse for wear, parked near a wharf facing Lake Penchant. Nearby, a wooden platform roughly the size of a small house was active with shrimpers drying and preserving their catch.

Foster walked past them along the wharf to where an assortment of flat-bottomed boats lay moored. A sign read "Etienne Dupre Boat tours. Bayou Cruises. See Blue Bayou. See Reptiles. Alligators. Cajuns." Foster approached a dark-skinned, wiry man of indeterminate age who was spread-eagled in one of the boats, his head resting on a pink polka-dot pillow. A red kerchief was tied around his neck. A dirty white cap with the legend "Tarpon Rodeo, Grand Isle, 1985" covered his face.

"How much to rent an outboard?" Foster called to him.

The man's hand went up to remove the cap. His eyes opened and his head came off the pillow, leaving a grease-stain reminder. He raised the cap with thin fingers and adjusted it on his head so that his eyes were shaded from the sun. "Well now, that be for an hour or a day, or what?" the man was speaking slowly, trying to use words they could understand rather than the rapid Cajun that was all but indecipherable.

"Day."

"Oh, I dunno I kin get you a guide for a whole day."

"No guide. I was born in Terrebonne Bay."

"Oh yeah? You don't sound like it, no."

"Ah been abody coonass since 'fore you be boon. Now all dis waitin' here in de hot sun is puttin' me in a bad way."

The man leapt from the boat, his grin revealing several missing teeth. He grabbed Foster's hand and pumped it. The next part of their conversation was completely lost on Manion, though he did hear the name Fouchette mentioned once or twice.

Eventually, Foster and his new pal walked to a badly painted blue and white flatboat with an outboard motor attached. Foster handed the man two twenty-dollar bills and hopped into the boat. Manion was surprised at how gracefully he did it.

Foster removed his suit coat and tie, folded them neatly, and placed them on the boat's rear seat. He started the motor with only two tries and checked its capability. Apparently satisfied, he signaled for Manion to come aboard.

Manion climbed on awkwardly. Foster grabbed his arm and helped him get comfortable on the mid-boat seat. Foster slipped the aft line free from the wharf. The man in the Grand Isle cap freed the forward line and shoved them away. Foster adjusted the rudder, turning them until the wharf was at their rear. The boat cut west through the green waters.

Manion looked back at the man in the cap, who was scratching his head quizzically at the sight of the two of them in business suits heading into deep bayou. "Was he Etienne Dupre?"

"No," Foster said. "He's mostly Indian. A Houma. Largest surviving tribe in the state. Lot of 'em settled in these bayous. Can't hardly tell 'em from Cajuns anymore."

The boat was moving swiftly through the water, its spray misting Manion's glasses. Carefully, he turned so that he sat facing Foster at the tiller. "How far are we going?" he shouted into the wind.

Foster smiled. "As far as it takes," he said.

Foster maneuvered the small craft through lake and canal and inlet, where they moved easily past oyster fishermen and shrimpers heading home with their catches. Manion tried to keep a mental chart of their journey, but he had a rather poor sense of direction, even on dry land.

"Welcome to Blue Bayou," Foster said suddenly, with no small amount of sarcasm.

Manion twisted on the seat. They were turning into a narrow canal that seemed indistinguishable from others they'd passed.

"It's real name is Ciel Bleu Bayou. Bayou Blue Sky," Foster said. "But somebody got the bright idea that Blue Bayou sounded catchier, and when the song 'Blue Bayou' got popular, it seemed like they'd made the right choice. Not that any of the Cajuns ever got a penny. . . . Hey, Manion slide to starboard, huh?"

Manion did as he was told, and the boat made a sharp turn to the left to avoid a small, flat barge loaded with moss that an ancient Cajun was poling into the open sea.

"What's his story?" Manion asked as their boat leveled off.

"Asshole is harvesting moss," Foster snarled. "That's a promising occupation. When was the last time you slept on a moss pillow?"

Manion didn't reply.

"The whole idea of Cajun is like that old fool." Foster cleared his throat and worked the tiller with one hand while he sprayed his throat with the other. "It's past history. The farms and the oil fields brought the big bucks into the area long ago. The wealthiest Cajuns began to feel bad because the rest of the world still treated 'em like poor white trash. So they stopped their children from speaking Cajun French at home. They were the style setters, and the language started dying out. The culture too. Now the oil money has dried up and there's not even heritage to hang on to."

The air was turning hot and humid. Mosquitoes began to hone in on them. Manion slapped at his neck. "What about Paul Prudhomme and the Cajun food craze?" he asked. "I hear it's gone all the way to Europe. That must have done something for the morale down here. Not to mention the income."

Foster shook his head. "It's like renaming this place Blue Bayou. Hanging on. Prolonging the agony. The quicker these throwbacks join the twenty-first century, the better. Look at that, for Christ's sake."

Near the banks an odd-looking bird, possibly a pelican but with a long, skinny neck, was hanging from a sturdy tree, waving in the arid breeze. "What is it?" Manion asked. "Voodoo?"

"Just about as stupid. A 'gator trap. Baited with a bayou chicken. You put it on a large hook and drop it low enough so maybe a 'gator'll be dumb enough to get himself caught. Or you can get a gun and shoot the fucker in the head and be done with it. But that wouldn't be Cajun style."

Nearly a mile down the canal, Foster cut the motor so that they were barely moving in the water. He gestured with his chin. "Guidry's," he said.

Manion twisted around until he was able to see a little shed and a wharf on their right. Beyond the shed was a small house of unpainted wood. In front of the shed, a man stood bare to the waist. His cotton pants were streaked with blood, wet and dry. Nearby were four teenage children, three boys and a girl, all equally bloody. At their feet, and covering most of the slope of mud and crabgrass, were animal corpses, with and without pelts.

Foster waved and the man waved back with a pelt in his hand. "Lou Guidry," Foster said to Manion. "He's younger than Pos, but he looks like he's in his sixties. This place can do that to you."

"What kind of animals are those?"

"Nutria."

"They look like giant rats with floppy ears."

"Smell like 'em too," Foster agreed. "Twenty-five, thirty pounds. Teeth three inches long. Come all the way from Australia. Guy had a private zoo over to the west at Avery Island. A hurricane took down a portion of the zoo, and the nutria escaped into the swamp and never looked back.

"Trappers started noticing something was eating the muskrats out of their traps. And when they weren't eating, the big rats were fucking. They overran the place. Got as far as New Orleans. Then somebody—must have been an outsider, because the Cajuns would never have changed their ways—figured: Screw the muskrats, let's trap nutria. The state helped out by putting a bounty on 'em. But even with that, they can't kill enough of the damn things to dent the nutria population. They may wind up taking over the area."

He swallowed, winced, and sprayed his throat again. "Talking too much," he said, gesturing to the right. "Good thing we here."

The Fouchette cabin was set back several hundred feet from the water, shaded by two giant oak trees whose branches seemed to be intertwined over the building. A tractor tire hung from one of the larger branches on a rope as thick as a child's wrist. An ancient washing machine seemed to be planted beside the house.

Slo Bentine stood at the machine with her back to them. She was wearing cutoff Levi's and a tan shirt from which the sleeves had been removed, exposing the bandage high on her arm. She was scrubbing clothes by hand in the tub of the washing machine.

Foster brought the boat in beside two others tied to a post at the end of a short dock that seemed as stable as a cork on water. He stepped easily from the boat onto the dock. Manion followed, a bit less steadily.

Slo did not hear them approach, until Foster was only a few steps behind her. That was when Manion said, "That's far enough."

She turned, saw Foster, and took an involuntary step backward, emitting a fleeting cry of alarm. Foster looked around, and satisfied himself that Manion was, indeed, pointing a pistol at him. He had sensed a vagueness about the blond private detective, but there was nothing vague about his stance or the way he was holding the gun.

Foster raised his hand slowly and used his index finger to tap a spot between his eyes. "Put it right here, Manion," he said. "If you got the guts."

"Do I have to?"

Foster said, "I never meant my brother any harm."

"Brother?" Slo's mind was having trouble assimilating the information.

"Search me, Manion," Foster snapped. "If you find a weapon, use *it* on me."

Slo circled them and ran to the cabin's rough wood porch. From the corner of his eye, Manion saw another figure standing in the doorway—a small, thin woman in bib overalls and a sweatshirt.

She had something in her hands. Manion hoped it wasn't a gun.

He changed his position until Foster was standing between him and the woman. Then he moved closer. Foster's hands were behind his neck, fingers interlocked.

"Turn," Manion ordered.

Affecting a bored pose, Foster obeyed. He saw the little woman and called out to her, "Hay, Maman, yo' fave-rite boy come home."

The woman was carrying a rifle. She raised it menacingly.

"No, Maman. This man be fran'. We just be tak-tak."

The woman looked skeptical, but she lowered the gun. She said in singsong Cajun, "You been away too long, Fos. You sound like some damn Yankee, that accent."

Manion moved behind Foster. Bending his knees, he kept his gun trained on Foster's back and used his left hand to pat the man's legs, crotch, chest. When he was satisfied that Foster was not carrying a gun or a knife, he backed away.

"I'm not here to kill anybody," Foster told him. "It was a mistake Pos got shot."

The little woman bounded down the steps. Holding on to her rifle with one hand, she threw her arms around Foster. "Damn, boy. I miss you so."

It happened too quickly for Manion to stop her. He watched helplessly as Foster spun her around between them, his fingers grabbing the rifle. The woman's happiness faded into a frown and she began to struggle in Foster's arms.

Foster said to Manion, "Put that thing away! It's no good to you now."

Manion pondered the situation.

He was not an expert marksman. If he fired, he might hit the woman, or Slo. Considering his skill, he might even shoot some stranger in the swamp. He lifted his right pant leg and slipped the gun into the thin leather holster strapped above his ankle.

Foster had the rifle stock trapped between his side and elbow. He raised his arm, and the rifle barrel swung down in a clockwise arc until it was pointed at the earth. Foster held it out to Manion. "Here, take this so I can hug my maman."

Feeling rather silly, Manion took the rifle. "What games you and yo' fran' playin', you big big 'gator?" the little woman asked Foster, putting an arthritic fist next to her son's cheek and pushing it as if delivering a slow-motion punch.

Manion walked past them and up the steps. The front of the house had been waterproofed by tar paper and painted battleship gray. He rested the rifle next to the front door. Slo was standing there. "You and Pos all right?" he asked her.

She nodded, her eyes never leaving Foster. "He's Pos's brother? He tried to kill us."

Manion shrugged. That was how he had figured it. Foster's habit of parking his car well away from his destination had suggested he might be something more than just an innocent brother. He'd shown no curiosity about that spot where Pos had been shot. And there was his voice, like a nutmeg grater on a tin can.

Then there had been Foster's playful description of his occupation—weapons salesman. Finally, he loved opera. Whoever had broken into Manion's home had listened to opera on the radio.

But with Slo corroborating his suspicions, he still was not able to get a fix on Foster. Hit man, loyal brother, what?

"Maman, this is Terry Manion from New Orleans."

"You a city boy, sure 'nuf," the little lady said, her expression clearly signifying what she thought of city boys. "Why you put yo' gun to mah Fos?"

"At the moment, I'm not sure."

Foster smiled. "Let's go see how my idiot brother is healing."

Inside, the house was dark and cool. Wall-to-wall tan linoleum covered the floor. A large space running from the front of the house to the rear served as both the living room and kitchen. The walls had been covered by imitation pine paneling. The furniture was old and battered but had a comfortable look. Several childlike finger paintings had been preserved behind glass and frame, and hung on the walls. The house was immaculately clean.

There was a strong odor from the kitchen stove that nearly lifted Manion from the ground. It was not the aroma of tomato paste or scallions or peppers but some other pungent smell he could not identify. It came from a large skillet on the back burner. Mrs. Fouchette saw him staring at the simmering mix. "We fixin' some Blue Bayou 'Gator Sauce Piquante fo' dinner. Was gonna carry some of it over for tomorrow, but if you as hungry an eater as mah boy Fos, that plan sure's not gonna work."

Manion followed Foster into another section of the cabin. There was a short hall with two doors leading to small bedrooms. In one, obviously Mrs. Fouchette's, Manion spied an altar containing candles and a chipped plaster statue of the Blessed Virgin, a kneeler, a four-poster bed covered with a dark brown quilt containing an assortment of green cloth alligators, no two of which seemed to be alike.

Pos was in the other bedroom, occupying one of two single beds. It must have been the room where he and Foster grew up. Everything in it was a duplicate— two small chests of drawers, two desks and chairs, two open closets. On the walls were holy cards depicting various VIPs from the history of the Catholic Church.

Foster moved to his brother's bed. Pos looked up at him apprehensively. He was covered to his neck with a quilt that had "Posell" stitched in one of its squares. Foster drew the quilt back, exposing his brother's bare chest. Someone had removed the surgical dressing. A poultice that looked like a mixture of cobwebs and wet tea leaves had been placed over the gunshot wound.

Foster asked, "Maman got the *traiteur* here that quick?"

Pos nodded, smiling weakly and nervously as Foster placed the quilt back over the wound.

"How you doing?"

"I'll live," Pos said. "If that's okay with you."

"You ran at me, asshole," Foster growled. "You brought that on yourself."

Pos looked at the door, where Slo Bentine now stood. His eyes went back to his brother. "Please don't," he said.

Foster shook his head. "No need. It's us against them."

"I wish I could trust you, but you betrayed me, bro'. I called to ask you to he'p, to tell us what to do, so Slo could be safe. An' you come with a gun in your hand."

Foster's face turned red. " I had an obligation. Fuck if I have to explain myself to you." He took out his atomizer and sprayed his throat angrily.

Pos licked his dry lips. "Get me some water, honey."

Slo moved from the door. When she was gone, Pos whispered, "If you got to shoot her, I want you to finish me, too. Okay?"

Foster glared at him. "Listen to me, coonass! I'm here to keep you both from being killed. I don't work for the Benedettos anymore. They want us all dead."

"All?"

"You, the girl, Manion. Even me."

"I'm not gonna be much use for a while," Pos said, his eyes shifting to Slo as she approached the bed with a jelly glass full of water. Pos pointed his chin at Foster, who took the glass and gulped its contents. "How they gonna know where to look for us, bro'?"

Foster wiped his mouth on his shoulder. "Reevie knows we hail from Blue Bayou. They'll come."

"Wal, they ain't gonna get much cooperation from anybody in the Bayou," Pos said, waving the girl away. "They'll probably never find the cabin by theirselves."

Foster shook his head. "Stop being a jackass all your life."

Pos said to Slo, "Go help Maman, *cher*. Me and Fos gotta talk." She didn't want to leave, but she did.

Pos painfully withdrew his arm from under the quilt. He grabbed Foster's wrist. "You knew how much I love that woman," he said, "yet you was gonna shoot her dead."

"I didn't know until you came at me," Foster said. "I didn't know until you forced me to shoot you."

"Dammit, don't you lie to me, Fos. You knew. Else why did you kill J.J. Legendre?"

Foster's glance met Manion's across the room. Behind his glasses, the detective's blue eyes seemed oddly dreamy.

Foster said without emotion, "I did it because I was paid to."

"By Reevie Benedetto?" Manion asked.

Foster nodded.

"Why'd Reevie want him dead?"

"I don't know. Reevie said to take him out and remove any information I could find in his place or yours about the Gaynaud family and some old black guy who worked for them."

Pos clutched his brother's arm again. "That's the truth?" he pleaded.

Foster frowned. "Why the fuck would I make up a story like that?"

Pos fell back in the bed, laughing. "Oh man. I thought you shot him to give me a chance with Slo."

Foster glared down at him, furious. "You thought I'd kill a man for *that*?"

He shook loose of Pos's grip and stormed from the room. Pos looked up at Manion and said, "You heard him, Terry. It wasn't me caused J.J.'s death." He was ecstatic. "Where's that girl of mine?"

"I'll get her," Manion said flatly. He didn't share Pos's good mood.

Slo was cowering on the ancient sofa in the front room while Foster paced angrily. "Pos wants you," Manion told her. She seemed relieved at the excuse to leave.

Foster stared at him. "Forget revenge, Manion. Maybe later. But first, I'm going to need you."

"For what?" Manion couldn't keep the bitterness out of his voice.

"Let's go outside."

As they passed Mrs. Fouchette at her stove, she said, "Not too far, darlin'. Food smells like it's 'mos' ready."

The screen door slammed behind them and they took off across the moist grassland, moving fast as if hoping to escape the situation. They walked swiftly past a barn where a rusted '48 Buick sedan was being used as a bayou henhouse, past a cinder-block-and-sheet-metal outbuilding housing the generator that supplied the cabin's electricity. When they were far enough away so that their voices would not carry to the cabin, Foster said, "I never knew Legendre. It was nothing personal."

A flush of anger coursed through Manion. He waited, hoping it would build enough for him to raise his fist to Foster. Or curse him. Or kill him. When it didn't, he felt as if he'd somehow betrayed J.J.

He turned and walked away from Foster, who shouted after him, "Don't be a fool. The main thing now is for us all to stay alive. I need you."

Manion kept going until he arrived at a barbed-wire fence marked with a sign reading, "Stop! Hungry Marsh." Beyond it was a boggy area that contained a bayou brand of quicksand.

Manion had no idea how long he stood there staring at the wet, muddy surface without seeing it.

Suddenly, Foster's gravel voice came from just behind him. "You ever kill a man in cold blood, Manion?" he asked.

"Not yet."

Foster stood beside him. "My first was when I came back here to bury my papa," he said, looking off across the swamp where shimmery lights seemed to dance on the top of the marsh grass. "I'd just started selling guns in those days. Colts. Mainly to police departments. I was as straight as. . . as you think you are.

"Anyhow, I came back here to bury the old man, who they said had gotten tanked up one night in Houma and driven his car into a tree. I was, after all, the favorite son. We planted him just up the Bayou in St. Paul's Cemetery. Friends and neighbors turned up. And Beau Sislock. He hadn't changed much. He'd divorced a woman and left her with kids, that kind of guy. He called me aside and showed me a paper that had my father's signature scrawled across the bottom. It said that Beau was the owner of this piece of the Bayou. It was dated the night my father died.

"The old man was a fucking lush. And he'd go into Houma or Morgan City and play bourrée until his pockets were empty. But to gamble away his cabin and land? No fucking way. Still, the IOU looked genuine. And Beau expected to take immediate possession.

"I said nothing to either Maman or Pos. The next day I took Beau out here to show him around the property. I brought a bottle, and he drank most of it. He began to brag about how he took advantage of my father in the game. 'Everybody cheated the old bastard,' he told me.

"He expected me to believe that he'd won the bayou property and then my father obligingly killed himself the same night. I'd seen enough of life by then to mistrust that kind of coincidence. I asked him point-blank if he'd killed the old man.

"Beau wasn't drunk enough to admit it, but he was drunk enough to have trouble lying about it. He was standing not far from where you are, and I was right here."

Foster took a step closer to Manion, until he was almost brushing against him. "I moved behind him, very calmly," Foster continued, "circling his neck with my right hand, cupping his chin, then pushing the back of his head with my left until his neck snapped. I had never dreamed of killing anyone before. It was so easy. It was getting rid of the body that was hard. But I had an idea to make the punishment fit the crime. He'd used a car on my papa. I'd use a car on him.

"I barely remember getting him back into the pirogue and taking him along the waterway to Morgan City, where we'd left his car. It was dark. The dock was fairly empty, and the little shit was easy to carry. Nobody spotted us.

"I took back Papa's IOU and placed Beau's body in the passenger seat. He'd been keeping a mileage log and it told me he made a fat-bodied *I* and didn't close the top of his *g*'s. So I sat down and wrote a little suicide note to give the law something to think about if they didn't assume he'd died in an accident; 'I got nothing more to lose.' And I signed his name."

Manion said, "You used those words on J.J.'s suicide note, too. You'd better think of a new line or somebody's going to start to wonder."

"The words are from a Cajun song, 'Final Lament.' Very sad song. But you're right. You shouldn't overdo, unless you're looking to get caught." He grinned. "In any case, I sent the bastard and his car off the blacktop and it smashed into a tree. Beau's body flew out into the swamp. Better than I had planned. By the time they found him the next morning, some critters had had a good portion of him for breakfast. And I was just waking up in my bed in Morgan City. I never had a better night's sleep."

From the cabin Mrs. Fouchette's voice commanded, "Come on in heah now, 'fore dis 'gator dries out. Wipe yo' feet on de mat."

"This thing about murder," Foster said, "either it's the hardest thing you ever do or it's the easiest. You find that out when you do it. But maybe it's something you never really want to know."

Manion was suddenly tired of him. He said, "I'm supposed to think that an unpremeditated killing led to your career as a hit man. But if Beau's death was so unpremeditated, why'd you buy the booze, unless you were planning on getting him drunk?"

Foster smiled but said nothing.

"Did you kill Parker Harris, too?" Manion asked.

Foster frowned. "The old spade who worked for Gaynaud? Never met the man. Reevie could have done it. He killed a guy last year, made it look like he'd drowned in a flooded aqueduct."

"And my father, was he another one of your goddamn suicides?" Manion didn't know where the words had come from. His mind must have been playing with them for a while.

Foster frowned. "What are you talking about? Your father?"

Manion waved him away. "Wishful thinking," he said. He walked past the confused killer and strode into the cabin. He wiped his feet on the mat first.

Slo took her and Pos's plates into the bedroom. Manion and Foster sat on opposite sides of Mrs. Fouchette, who insisted that they both join her in prayer. When they only politely dabbed at their food, she

grew angry and, eventually, grabbed their plates and took them to a
sink that was just outside the back door.

"Time to go," Foster told her.

The old woman stuck her head back inside. "Where you goin' dis
time of night?"

"Manion and I have work to do."

"What kinda work won't wait 'til daylight?"

"Our kind of work," Foster said.

Manion watched as he grabbed the rifle from beside the front
door. He held it out to the old woman. "You keep this near you," he
said.

As she watched him, fear took the place of annoyance on her
face. She came inside the cabin, wiping her hands on the front of her
blouse. She hugged Foster. "First your no-good baby bro' gets hisself
shot. Now you want me to keep a gun handy. What's going on, Fos?
What's dat dumb coonass Posell got us into now?"

"No! I'm the dumb coonass who caused all this. Some people are
on their way to kill Posell and his girlfriend. Manion and I are going
to stop them. But maybe tomorrow some other people will come. You
be ready for them."

He started for the door.

"You not gonna say goodbye to your brother?"

"Say it for me. Be nice to him for a change. You and Pa always
had it wrong about us. Pos was the good one."

She started to cry. "You think I don't know what kind of men my
sons are? He comes here all shot up, dragging along a little mouse girl
half his age, and you tell me he's worth anything?"

Foster's face darkened. "He's your own flesh and blood. If you
can't feel anything for him, at least try to keep the poor bastard
alive!" he roared.

She recoiled as if he'd slapped her. Then she turned her back to
them both. Foster coughed and used his throat medicine. He walked
out and down to the dock. Manion followed.

"She'll never change," Foster growled bitterly. "It goes with this
fucking territory. C'mon, let's go fix things."

"Maybe Reevie didn't send anybody."

"Dream on, Manion."

"But if they're out there, why haven't they come in by now?"

"Because it only just turned night. And if you get the choice, you
wait until night. Preferably when everybody's asleep."

"That's how you'd do it?"

"Yes," Foster said.

He retrieved his coat and tie from the boat in which they'd come and boarded an aluminum-hull canoe, lowering himself onto a seat at its stern. Then he moved the paddle and steadied the craft for Manion.

The canoe was quieter and faster than the other boat, but it also had a livelier roll. Manion charily picked his spot amidships. Foster used the paddle to push them away from the other boats and into the canal.

The moon had started to rise in a starry sky. Blue Bayou was cooling off. In another few hours, it would be quite chilly. The night was filled with new sounds—crickets, frogs, vaguely eerie water splashes. The one thing that made no sound was their canoe as it cut through the Bayou toward the entrance to the canal.

As they passed Lou Guidry's home, they could hear a television commercial for a European automobile that would make a nice, expensive lawn decoration in the swamp. Manion glared at Foster. He opened his mouth to speak, but Foster stopped paddling and shook his head.

They rounded a bend and Manion heard the sound of male voices, then a slap. A boat with an outboard had been tied to the branch of a tree that was growing half in the water, half on a narrow strip of land.

Foster gave the canoe a hard push and ducked down. They glided silently past three men seated around a fire. Two of the men were coatless, wearing holsters over their city clothes. They were slapping at bugs, real and imaginary. The third man was the wiry Indian from Etienne Dupre Boat Tours. There was dried blood near his hairline, and his hands were tied behind his back.

The gunmen would have had to be searching the canal to see their canoe as it passed. They were being kept too busy by the mosquitoes and gnats. Foster waited until bushes and other foliage were between them and the men and their fire. He used his paddle again to propel the canoe, angling it in toward the raised land. It bumped lightly against brush growing at the water's edge and Foster was out, steadying the hull's roll for Manion.

He secured the canoe to a branch, then led Manion around the brush until they could see the fire's glow in the near distance.

Manion removed his pistol from its holster. Foster spotted it and put out his hand.

Manion kept the gun. Foster whispered, "I'm better with it than you."

Manion compromised by tucking the pistol into his belt.

They were now about fifty feet from the fire. Foster sighed resignedly and picked up several objects—an assortment of dried branches and a large rock. He tossed one branch into a bush to their right.

"What the hell's that?" one of the men yelled. He was a swarthy youth wearing a blue-and-white-striped shirt and black silk pants that were streaked with mud. He seemed fairly unnerved.

The other man, in tan gabardine pants and white-on-white shirt, was older, more confident, less prone to jitters. "Probably some lizard or something."

Foster tossed another branch.

"Jesus!" the blue-striped shirt said. He turned to the Indian. "What is it?"

The Indian shrugged. "Night bird. Critter. Maybe giant bayou bear."

White-on-white stood up, took his gun from its holster, and slammed it against the Indian's head. "Don't fuck with us, Frogface," he said.

A third branch rattled the bushes.

"Goddammit! Something's out there!" Blue Stripe shouted.

"Then go see," White-on-white told him.

"You go. You're the fucking brave dude."

Shaking his head, White-on-white moved to the bush, aimed his gun at it.

Foster threw another branch, luring White-on-white closer to where they were waiting. The man was positioned only a few feet away, his back turned to them.

Foster leapt forward, bringing the rock down against the man's head and rolling with him behind the brush, out of sight of both Manion and Blue Stripe.

Blue Stripe jumped to his feet. "Hey, Lou. What the hell . . . Lou? Don't screw around."

He backed away from the fire, staring at the spot where his partner had apparently disappeared.

There was more rustling. Manion watched as Blue Stripe closed in on the bushes. He wondered what Foster expected of him. Was he supposed to attack Blue Stripe, or just sit still?

The question became moot when a branch flew through the air and landed at Manion's feet. When he looked up from it, Blue Shirt was aiming his gun at him, notably relieved to be dealing with a human problem. One that could be handled easily.

"Where's Lou?" the man asked him nastily.

Manion didn't get a chance to tell him. Foster moved up and grabbed the swarthy man, twisting his arm until the gun dropped. Then Foster brought his fist down against the back of the man's head where the skull meets the neck.

"He's yours," Foster said to Manion. "Load him in their boat."

The young man was no lightweight. Manion had to drag him most of the way. He dumped him into the hull. Foster threw Lou in on top of him.

"You tossed that stick at me back there," Manion said. "You set me up."

Foster shrugged. He had two pistols in his belt. "I told you I needed your help."

"Help? You used me for bait, like one of those bayou chickens."

"We got our 'gators." Foster hopped into the boat with the unconscious men. He pushed free and started the outboard engine.

"I'm taking them into another bayou. They won't find their way out. The Indian'll get you back to Boudreaux. How you make it to New Orleans is your own problem."

"Wait a minute!"

"No time to wait," Foster said. "Got debts to pay. There's a big, beautiful woman I owe a dinner. And there's a man I owe too. So long, Manion." He waved. "*Bon chance.*"

His boat made an arc out into the canal. Manion pulled his gun from his waistband and aimed it at Foster, but it was a futile gesture. They both knew he wouldn't use it.

When Foster's hull had disappeared into the night, Manion released the Indian, who guided him back to Fouchette's wharf. There they traded the canoe for the boat he and Foster had come in on. By the time they arrived at Boudreaux, Foster's car was gone. Manion jump-started the Cadillac and headed back to New Orleans.

It was nearly seven A.M. when he crossed the Mississippi River

Bridge, surrounded by truckers, the early working shift, and ambitious young business types eager to get an hour's jump on the competition. His initial plan had been to drive directly to his home and sleep till noon. But his address was no secret to the Benedettos, and he'd had enough jeopardy to last a while. So he exited at Broad Street and drove in the direction of Nadia Wells's home. There would be guards there and, with luck, an empty bed.

He wondered where Lucille Munn had spent the night. He hoped she would not criticize him too harshly for standing her up.

37
.

IN THE early hours of the morning there had been what Reevie thought of as a "disturbance" at his home. He had handled the immediate situation in his own distinctive manner, of course. But Lindsay had been awakened and seriously unnerved, which caused him some dismay. And there were a few loose strings to be tucked away. Along with that unexpected problem, there were expected ones that he would have to handle. His father's suspicions, for example.

Instead of spending the day at the Sports Plantation, he decided to visit Gaynaud's as soon as he had finished his morning workout. He wanted the old man's assurance that all was well in Baton Rouge. And he also wanted to make sure that Lindsay would keep her promise to remain silent about the disturbance, at least for a few days.

Later that night, he would arrange a meeting with his father and his uncle Johnny at one of the clubs in the Quarter and promote a little family solidarity. His father could not have any real evidence of his disloyalty. It was just a matter of unruffling feathers. The disposal of the mess he'd left behind at his home was a much more serious problem. Busy day.

The little blonde at the Sports Plantation reception desk gave him her brightest smile. "Mornin', Mr. B. Gonna put all those beautiful muscles to work?"

"Not all of 'em, Annie. I'm saving one for a special workout with you one of these days."

She giggled. "I'm ready when you are."

As he passed the business office, he spotted the woman he knew as Lonnie waiting by a desk in Accounting. "What are you doing here so soon?" he asked her, noting the rim of a bruise peeking from behind her dark glasses.

"Picking up my check." She seemed nervous.

"Working today then?" he asked.

"I could," she said.

"Good. I'll see you when you're finished here."

He continued on to his office. He had not given Lonnie much thought since the supposed rape. He knew that a sexual attack was not beyond the realm of probability as far as Johnny was concerned. But he also knew that something was wrong with the whole set-up. For one thing, why had the cop Munn been there at that precise time?

He wished there were some way he could be wrong about Lonnie being a plant, but he knew he wasn't. Therefore, much of his office work had been compromised. He had been careful to keep most of his plans for the real estate and casinos at his home, along with certain other files containing material that he had copied from ledgers in his father's private safe. Lonnie had been privy to crucial phone calls, of course, but he would worry about that later. The manner by which he would reward her disloyalty was something that could keep for a day or two.

His phone was ringing. He hated to answer his own calls, but his plans were reaching the critical stage. He grabbed the receiver and identified himself.

He recognized the caller's voice immediately. He listened for a few seconds, his initial apprehension giving way to bemusement and finally to curiosity. Then he muttered, "Sure. I'll meet you in five minutes. But why don't you just come to the office . . . ?"

The caller offered no explanation, merely broke the connection.

Intrigued, Reevie placed the receiver back on its cradle. Five minutes, eh? He opened his wall safe and took out a small gun. He hefted it, then slipped it into his pants pocket.

Four minutes. He heard the outer door open.

Lonnie was standing at her desk, the phone in her hand. "Everything okay?" he asked.

She jumped. "Oh. I thought you were . . . in the gym."

"I'm running late today." He stared at the phone.

"Just calling a friend," she said. "Lunch date."

"Lucky guy," he said. Three minutes.

"Just a friend," she said. "But he doesn't seem to be answering." She replaced the phone awkwardly.

"You sure you're all right?"

"I'm still a little shaky, but I'm much better. I stayed in bed all day yesterday."

"If you feel up to it, I'd like you to stick around for a couple of hours, just to catch the phone."

"Of course," she said, sliding into her chair.

"I'll be back shortly," he said on his way out of the office. "Just going down to the massage rooms."

She nodded and gave him an uncertain smile.

The Sports Plantation had eight massage rooms. They were empty until noon, when Manuel and Gloria and their merry masseuses and masseurs arrived to pound and beat and unravel the knots of stress and strain. On occasion, Reevie used the windowless rooms for early-morning meetings that he wished to be free from either watchful eye or wiretap. He had his office scanned for electronic devices every so often, and invariably the result would be negative. But, as one of his professors noted, "The wise businessman realizes that paranoia has its positive side."

Reevie was surprised to find the massage area dark. He paused in the doorway, groping for the light switch. But even after he found it and pressed the buttons, the room remained in darkness.

A voice said, "Hello."

Reevie jerked around, momentarily startled. "Oh, you're here already. We're going to have to take this somewhere else. The lights seem to be off in here."

Reevie backed to the door. Before he got there, he felt a slight stir of air. Then a solid object smashed against his head. An explosion of reds and yellows danced before his eyes. He felt another blow and tumbled forward onto the tile floor.

He was vaguely aware of being turned over. There was the sensation of being moved. The tiles felt cool. He'd had them imported from Spain. He heard running water. Someone was drawing a bath.

38

.

"IT WAS pretty much as we figured," Manion was saying to
Nadia Wells. "Reeves Benedetto felt that J.J. was a danger to the
Gaynaud family, so he hired a hit man, Foster Fouchette."

Nadia shook her head sadly. "Murder then. Not suicide. You got
your job done, sonny, and I thank you."

They were seated on the side porch. It was nearing noon, but the
sun had not yet burned off all the dew, and the lawn and shrubbery
glistened. Manion sipped a café au lait and watched the two Wells
Agency operatives read the *Picayune* in their sedan parked in front of
the house.

"There are strings hanging," he said.

"Foster Fouchette? I gathered from what you just told me that he
has severed his employment with Benedetto."

"I'm not certain what he's up to, or capable of," Manion said.
"But even if he's no longer our problem, Benedetto will just put
another pistol on the payroll. You don't want to have to keep your
bodyguards out there indefinitely."

"It does a proprietor good to sample the service from time to
time," she said. "Anyway, let's just get your childhood chum Eben
Munn to tell Reeves to lay off."

Manion shrugged. "Another string," he said. "There is a possibility that Munn and Reevie have struck a deal for more than just the
removal of Charlie and Johnny Benedetto."

"Not our problem," she said. "Nothing more is, now that J.J.'s death is accounted for. It's over for us. Go into the spare bedroom and get some sleep. You've earned it."

"Maybe I'll catch a nap later."

"You look like the hinges of hell right now."

"Thanks.'

"I make myself tired telling you to get some rest."

"Munn's coming here any minute to pick me up."

She shook her head. "Foolish boy. What'd you have phone him for?"

"I was trying to reach his sister, actually."

"Sister? Older or younger?"

"Younger."

"You mean to tell me that after having him, his mama and papa had the gall to copulate again?"

When he didn't smile or respond, she asked, "Am I sailing into dangerous waters?" He spread his hands in a gesture of helplessness. "My God," she said, "you haven't got yourself involved with a cop's little sister? Does she have a fine thrusting chin like his?"

Manion, in spite of himself, had to chuckle. "No," he said. "A nice rounded one. She's pretty round all over. And before you ask, she doesn't have a crew cut either."

"She lives with Munn?"

"No. As a matter of fact, he didn't know where she was."

"Try her house," she said.

"I did that before I phoned Eben."

Nadia stood with her coffee cup and stared at him. Then she shook her head and walked from the room. She had just returned with a fresh cup when a squeal of brakes signaled Munn's arrival. The two Wells operatives leapt from their car and intercepted him.

Manion watched bemusedly as Munn flashed his badge and stormed across the lawn. "Get your butt in gear, Manion. We don't have much time," he shouted through the screen.

He spotted Nadia and gave her a two-finger salute. "Morning, ma'am."

"We were sort of hoping that your little sister would be with you," she said.

Munn glared at Manion. "She should never have broken her cover. Goddamn amateurs."

"Have some coffee?" Nadia asked sweetly.

"No thank you, ma'am. Terry and me, we have to hotfoot it across town before my ace in the hole gets played. C'mon, Manion."

Manion sipped the sugary dregs from his cup. Nadia said to Munn, "I take it you fear that Foster Fouchette is planning to put an end to Reeves Benedetto?"

"Something like that," Munn replied as Manion bent to kiss Nadia's cheek. "I put out an APB on Fouchette."

"But if he were to croak Reeves Benedetto, wouldn't that solve a lot of problems?" she asked.

"Not mine," the policeman replied with feeling.

39

MUNN SPUN the wheel as they bounced onto the lot of the Sports Plantation, barely missing a black and silver wagon that was exiting. "You drive like I used to," Manion said.

"Speed counts," Munn replied, bringing the car to a jouncing halt near the front door.

The two men got out and started up the path. Suddenly, the front door opened and a stream of people flowed toward them. Manion stopped a tall man whose warm-ups were dripping with sweat.

"What's going on?"

The sponge shrugged. "They're clearing the building. Gas leak or something."

Munn moved to the side of the disgruntled crowd. "Let's try the back," he told Manion, running a fist over his stubble of beard, "get the lay of the land first."

They rounded the building and moved very carefully down a narrow walkway, ducking under windows as they passed. When Munn reached the windows to Reeves Benedetto's office, he paused, raised his head to take a quick peek, then pushed Manion back and away.

Munn whispered, "Two guys going through the files. It looks like Lucille's down."

"What!"

"She's on the floor."

Manion was already moving around the building when Munn hissed, "Go in slow."

Manion ignored the request. He pushed past the departing jocks and would-be jocks. The blonde receptionist was putting on a windbreaker while studying her teeth in a hand mirror. Behind her, the other members of the staff were busily locking drawers and closing down the counter. The blonde stared at Manion and said, "You must have missed the word. We're closin' up. Little problem. But we'll be open tomorrow, same as always."

She turned away and continued on as if she didn't exist. As he approached Reevie Benedetto's closed office door, he removed his gun from its ankle holster and, in one motion, threw open the door and bounded into the room.

The first thing he saw was Lucille, lying on the carpet, unconscious. He raised the gun, pointing it at two expensively dressed Latins who were standing beside an open cabinet. The one with papers in his hand was middle-aged and conservatively garbed. The other was in his twenties, expressionless, in a loose black silk suit with padded shoulders. There was a tattoo of a teardrop on his cheek. His long, straight hair was gathered into a ponytail.

Manion felt the artery in Lucille's neck, keeping his eyes on the two men. She moaned and he turned to her. The man with the ponytail reached inside the front of his silk suit jacket and took out a gun. The window behind him exploded and he was thrown forward onto his face on the carpet, landing only a few feet from Manion and the girl. There were two holes in his silk jacket.

Eben Munn stood just outside the window, peering in through the broken glass. "She's tough as tiger meat, Manion," he said. "Comes from good stock. Next time, pay more attention to the bad guys."

He addressed the remaining Latin, whose cheek had been nipped by flying glass. "Hey, mees-ter, can Reevie come out to play?"

The man did not reply.

Manion carried Lucille Munn to the couch.

"Yo, Terry, which one is Foster Fouchette?"

"Neither," Manion answered over his shoulder. He was trying to listen to Lucille's breathing.

Munn raised an eyebrow. "Then who *are* these guys?"

Manion shrugged. "I've never seen 'em before."

"Well," Munn said, scowling, "cover this oily bastard for me so I can come around and join the party. And watch out for Reevie. He may not be our buddy anymore, now that we've shot his office all to hell."

*   *   *

"They just seemed to appear," Lucille told them while her brother prowled the office, glaring at the well-dressed Latin. "The one with the tattoo,"—she indicated the bloody body on the carpet, shuddering,—"pointed his gun at me and asked me where Reevie was. I was too startled to speak.

"He pressed the gun against my temple and asked me again. I . . . I told him that Reevie was down the hall in the massage rooms. I'm sorry, but I didn't think they were bluffing."

"And what was this bozo,"—Munn flipped open the wallet he'd taken from the dapper Latin—"this Seen-yore Emilio Vargas, doing while Pony Boy was scarin' you to pieces?"

"Just watching silently, like he's doing now. Until I told them where Reevie was. Then they forced me to phone the front desk and clear the building. Then the . . . one on the floor hit me with his gun and I passed out."

"Been a rough couple of days for you," Manion said. "Time to get into a less hectic business."

Her eyes narrowed. "And where the hell have you been, by the way?"

"Skulking, dodging bullets. The usual. Sorry I missed our date, but I was lost on Blue Bayou."

"Hey, spare us something, huh?" Munn growled. He turned and suddenly grabbed Vargas's lapels and pulled him toward the door. "Let's go see if Reevie's still hanging out in the massage rooms."

"The woman should not come," Vargas said, finally breaking his silence.

Munn looked at his sister. "It's up to you, but maybe he's right."

"I'll pass. I've had enough."

Munn shrugged. "You coming, lover boy?"

Manion nodded, and followed as Munn dragged Vargas out of the office, down the hall, and into the massage rooms.

Munn stood in the center of the well-lit main room and looked around. "Well, here we are," he said.

"In there." Vargas indicated a door marked "Massage A."

Inside was a shelf containing towels, a clothes rack, a massage table, and a bathtub. Reevie Benedetto was in the tub, still in his clothes, his lifeless body resting in a mixture of artesian well water and his own blood. His wrists had been slashed. A razor blade lay on the tiles beside the tub. A folded sheet rested on the massage table.

"Shit!" Munn said in disgust.

Vargas sighed. "He was attempting to betray his father. Such a thing can lead a man to suicide."

"Suicide?" Munn bellowed.

"There is a note," Vargas said, pointing to the folded sheet.

Munn removed a ball point pen from his pocket and used it to poke the note open. "I'm afraid I touched it," Vargas said.

" 'I have got nothing more to lose,' " Munn quoted. "Handwritten, with his signature."

Manion was not surprised. He said. "It's from an old Cajun song."

"Suicide? Dammit!" Munn moaned.

Manion looked at the tiles. He pointed to the black streaks on their shiny surface. "Suicides don't usually drag their heels. Somebody lugged the body from the main room into here."

Munn brightened.

"Perhaps the young man's father, then," Vargas said as if the matter were something that did not concern him. "He was aware of Reevie's disloyalty."

"Oh, say that it's so!" Munn prayed, eyes to heaven.

Manion said, "It looks like one of Foster Fouchette's jobs. Faked suicide. The note. Exactly like his work. Except for the scuff marks on the tile."

"Maybe he wanted us to know he did it," Munn said. "Like a calling card."

Manion nodded. "Maybe. Fouchette said something about not repeating yourself unless you wanted to get caught."

"Then again," Munn said, turning to Vargas, "we could simplify matters and hang this on you, seen-yore."

"He was like that when we arrived."

"What the hell were you doing here, anyway?"

"Mr. Benedetto and I had . . . a certain business arrangement that was not working out."

"Involving legalized gambling?" Manion asked.

Munn gave him a curious look.

Vargas said, "I know nothing of such things. I was hoping to establish a chain of these fine fitness clubs throughout my country."

Munn glared at him. "The members of the coke cartel getting out of shape?" he asked.

Vargas shrugged. "In any case, I saw that our relationship was becoming . . . awkward. And I wanted to end it. By force if necessary. But murder would not have been the wise course of action."

Munn looked at Manion questioningly. Manion took a deep breath and removed his glasses, cleaning them with a handkerchief. "Reevie and Señor Vargas were involved in a scheme to put legalized gambling on the ballot. It sounds as if they were planning to cut the Crawfish out of the action. Somehow the old man found out." Manion replaced his glasses and stared at Vargas. "And what did he do, señor? Threaten you?"

Vargas remained silent.

Manion continued, "For whatever reason, Señor Vargas felt the need to pull out of the deal and remove any files or documents that Reevie might have been hoarding to keep him in line."

"Maybe the seen-yore made his own deal with the Crawfish," Munn suggested. "With Reevie left holding the bag of dog moot."

"I shall say nothing until I have conversed with my attorney," Vargas informed them.

"Spoken like a true, guilty-as-hell scumbag," Munn muttered, and led them back to the dead man's office.

There, Lucille asked, "Is Reevie dead?"

"Compared to him," Munn replied, "the guy on the carpet is doing the Lambada."

He lifted the phone and turned to Manion. "I've gotta call this in. Then you and me will . . . Uh, hello, this is Munn. Lemme speak with LeRoux." He hummed a little melody that Manion identified as "Sittin' Here in La La, Waitin' for My Ya Ya," then said into the telephone, "Hey, Luche, I got a couple dead guys over here at the Sports Plantation on Poydras. One of 'em I'll claim; the other, it's your guess. I also have a Colombian gentleman named Vargas who's in it all the way up to his mustache. He's asking for his lawyer."

He waited until the shouting on the other end of the line eventually quieted. Then he added, "You might tell your guys to go easy in the si-reens, Luche. Let's try to keep the TV cameras away till we can make some sense of the whole mess."

But that didn't happen.

The TV news crews were assembled outside the building only

minutes after the police arrived in full force. Munn spotted a minicam snout poking against a window of the office where Lieutenant Lucien LeRoux was telling him exactly how much he hated guys who didn't go by the book. Dropping the venetian blinds in front of the camera, Munn turned and said, "Luche, I realize you think I'm a little unorthodox, but—"

LeRoux, an oddly dapper cinder block of a man with a permanent tan and slate-gray hair, cut in, "You're not unorthodox, Munn. You're nuts. Everybody knows that. So don't give me any of your crazy man bullshit. Just lay it out plain."

"Okay," Munn said, his face as serious as a schoolboy's in church. "I was forced to blow that asshole with the ponytail away because he was gonna shoot a civilian, Mr. Terry Manion. He's right outside with your guys."

"I don't give much of a crap about the ponytail guy. He's an illegal anyway. Tell me about the Benedetto kid."

Munn shrugged. "I don't know. He was playing a dangerous game, helping me nail his old man. Maybe the Crawfish got hip to it."

LeRoux's eyes glazed over. "He was helping you put the Crawfish away. His own father."

"Don't tell me you buy all that 'Godfather' blood-is-thicker-than-vino bullshit? You know how these guys are, Luche. The tide turns and they show all the loyalty of a muskrat with a hard-on."

LeRoux sighed. "Maybe so. Anyway, I tried to get word to Benedetto that his kid was dead, but he wasn't at his place."

"He probably knows, one way or another," Munn said.

"Meaning what?" LeRoux snapped back.

"Meaning that the hit man probably told him when the job was done," Munn replied.

LeRoux said, "I thought you were hinting that one of my men might have tipped him."

"Oh, hell no," Munn said, with a sarcasm that LeRoux either didn't recognize or chose to ignore. "Look, Luche, you got a lot to do here. I don't want to get in your way. How's about I take off and drop by your office a little later to get the paperwork done?"

LeRoux glared at him. "The thing about you, Munn, is that nobody really knows what you're capable of. I mean, maybe *you* did the Benedetto kid."

Munn smiled at him. "If I had, Luche, you'd never find a clue.

But, as it so happens, I arrived here after the guy was slashed. I got a witness to that—Manion. And speakin' of him, since he's not actually involved in any of this business, suppose we just take off now? Like I said, I'll be in to see you later."

LeRoux nodded his head. "I'll be waiting for you."

40.

"WHERE DO you think we're headed, Manion?" Munn asked as the car turned a corner on two wheels.

"I suppose to Reevie's house to sneak a look at his files."

Munn slapped the steering wheel with his hand. "Dammit. You were like that in school, too. Always had the right answers."

Manion kept his eyes on the road. "The thing you never understood, Eben, is that a bluff is as good as a right answer if nobody knows more than you."

"No shit! All these years I been figuring you for just some wimp with clean fingernails. But you're as sneaky and evil as the rest of us."

"Praise from Caesar," Manion allowed as Munn aimed the car down the street leading to Reevie Benedetto's antebellum home.

A black limousine was parked in front. Munn drew his dusty sedan to the curb directly behind it and rolled forward until he tapped its rear bumper. He got out, grinning. "Guess whose claw-like mitt we're gonna catch rooting in Reevie's files?"

Leon opened the front door a crack to Munn's knock. "Yes?"

Munn flashed his badge and identified himself. Manion said, "Difficult day, huh, Leon?"

"It was on the news an hour ago," Leon said. "I sent the staff home. I'm not sure what else I'm supposed to do."

"What you're supposed to do is open the goddamned door," Munn grumbled.

Leon lowered his eyes to the floor and stepped back. He was

wearing a dark blue blazer and taupe trousers. Manion thought the coat fit him a bit too tightly across the chest.

Munn pushed the door open. Rillo, the Crawfish's chauffeur, stood in the center of the room, his hand moving toward his jacket. The hand stopped when he saw Munn's fierce grin. "You're not supposed to come in here," Rillo said. "Not without a warrant."

Munn shook his head. "Official police business. I'm here to notify next of kin of a death by violence." He walked past Rillo, suddenly spun around, drawing his own gun. He moved behind Rillo, fished the bodyguard's gun from its shoulder holster, and tossed it to Manion. Then he pushed his face within inches of Rillo's. "Where's the grieving father?" he asked.

Rillo didn't answer.

Leon's eyes went from Munn to Manion.

"Do I have to repeat the question, meatball?"

More silence. Munn sniffed the air, then shouted, "Dammit," and pushed Rillo into the next room.

They followed the smell of smoke to an upstairs bedroom that had been converted into an office. Charlie Benedetto was seated at a desk, pawing through an assortment of manila folders. His brother Johnny was on his knees, using a lighter to burn papers in a metal wastebasket.

They both looked up as Munn shoved Rillo into the room. Manion grabbed a throw rug and draped it over the wastebasket. The Crawfish shot him a venomous glance.

Johnny tried to stand, but Munn pressed down on his shoulder, keeping him on the floor. He brought his heel down on the hand holding the cigarette lighter, and Johnny let out a yell that could have been heard in Shreveport.

The Crawfish's eyes shifted, but his face remained frozen.

"Get the fuck outta this house," he ordered.

Munn said, "It is my painful duty to inform you that your son Reevie is dead meat, Charlie. He's over at the coroner's now, getting sliced up like Sunday's cold cuts. Organs removed, that sort of thing."

Charlie Benedetto stared at him.

"I could give 'em a call, have 'em make a death mask for your wall before they crack open his skull. Maybe I could get 'em to snip off a little finger, put it in a bottle of formaldehyde as a souvenir."

"Get outta here, you fuckin' creep," Johnny spat from the floor, nursing his hand.

Munn shifted his body and sent the thin man sprawling forward on his face, knocking over the rug-covered wastebasket and spilling ashes and scorched papers onto the floor and acrid smoke into the room.

"Gee," he said as Johnny pushed himself to his knees, coughing, "aren't you supposed to be halfway to Italy by now?"

The Crawfish's mangled fist reached out for a phone on the desk. "I'm callin' my lawyer, Munn. Get you off my case once and for all."

"Be sure to tell him where you are—in the home of a murder victim. Tell him what you're doing—going through the murder victim's private files. Burning stuff. Then listen hard for the advice he gives you."

"This is all mine!" the Crawfish shouted. "It was my boy's. Now it's mine."

"Not according to the only law we go by in Louisiana, Crawdaddy. Maybe it'll be yours some fine day. First we make an effort to locate a will. Failing that, we consider *all* the living relatives—father, mother, and maybe some others we haven't heard about. Nothing gets touched until then. So shy away from the desk right now, or I may have to use force."

Charlie Benedetto's eyes narrowed into slits, but he slid carefully away from the desk, rising to his feet with a wince. He carried a folder with him, holding it casually, as if it were of no importance to him at all.

Munn asked, "I don't suppose you saw Foster Fouchette today, maybe to pay him off for services rendered?"

"It was Fouchette who killed my boy?"

"It's his MO," Munn said.

Benedetto's hooded eyes shifted to Rillo. "Then he's a dead man."

"He said much the same thing about you," Manion offered.

Benedetto stared at him. "Just who the fuck are you, buddy?"

Manion opened his mouth to reply, but Munn said, "He's with me."

"His name's Manion," Johnny said. "He was with Munn when that bitch tricked me out."

Benedetto stared at Manion from head to toe. Then he said, "Nothing special here, huh, Rillo? Just another blade of grass waiting for a lawn mower."

"The only gardening you're gonna do, mudbug, is at 'Gola or

Texarkana. And that's only if you behave yourself." Munn suddenly reached out and snatched the folder from Benedetto. "Let's see what's so important."

The label read, "Benedetto, Père." Inside were Xeroxed sheets containing names, dates, and amounts. Rather large amounts. "What's all this?" he asked Benedetto.

Johnny looked up at his brother in alarm. "You see, Chawlie!" he squealed. "The punk was gonna sell you out, totally. Maybe you'll believe me he and Vargas were in that deal with Farmer Brown. We shoulda burned all three of 'em."

Charlie Benedetto exclaimed, "Shut your fuckin' mouth, you fuckin' idiot!"

"I love these family squabbles," Munn said. "But why don't I just tell you your rights, so we can go on record from this point."

The Crawfish moved a few steps toward the open door leading to the hall. "It ain't gonna be that easy, you bastard," he said, backing through the door. "Keep 'em here, Rillo."

Rillo, staring at Munn's gun, blocked the door while his boss ran down the hall.

Munn stepped forward and Rillo tensed. "C'mon," Munn snarled. "Get serious."

When Rillo refused to move, Munn shot him in the right leg and kicked the left out from under him. As the policeman tried to step over him, the hood, in obvious pain, reached up to grab him. Munn looked at him pityingly. "There's loyalty and there's stupidity, Rillo," he said, and kicked the man in the head.

A hall door was just closing as Munn approached it.

He entered the room. It was another reconverted bedroom, with French doors that opened onto a narrow balcony overlooking the rear of the building. That was all Munn saw as he entered—the room in shadow, the open French doors, and beyond, cloudy sky and the tops of trees. His immediate thought was that Benedetto must have opened the doors and exited through them. By the time he had rejected that nonsense, it was too late. Something smashed against his wrist with such force he lost the use of his fingers. The gun bounced onto the carpet.

He saw the weapon swinging down at his head, shifted, and felt its force as it struck against his right deltoid, sending him careening against a wall.

If Charlie Benedetto had been in his prime, Munn would have had no chance. But the Crawfish was old and ill and overweight. And adrenaline can only do so much. He stood in front of the fallen Munn, panting and puffing, and drew back his weapon for another, possibly fatal swing.

To Munn, it was as if the years had flown away and he was once again watching Benedetto swing a baseball bat against his father's skull. With an unpremeditated animal growl, Munn lowered his head and butted the fat man in the stomach.

The Crawfish made a noise that sounded like air escaping from a pressurized can as he backpedaled toward the open French doors.

Munn, on his knees, reached out a hand to grab the fat man. This only forced Benedetto to increase his backward motion. At the doors, he stepped on a small object resting near the carpet's edge and stumbled onto the balcony, his arms still raising his weapon over his head. His rear end collided with the iron balcony rail and he paused for just a second. Then he toppled over the rail with a scream.

Munn dragged himself to the balcony. He wanted to see, to make sure. He used the rail to pull himself upright and stared down on the motionless body that was sprawled on pink tiles beside the sky-blue waters of a swimming pool. He sat down on the cool concrete of the balcony and began to cry.

"This is what tripped him," Manion said, using the toe of his shoe to push a small plastic atomizer across the floor.

Munn was leaning against a wall, waiting for his fingers to stop tingling. He wiped the tears from his face with his sleeve. He felt foolish. "I can't believe you let that jerk-off Johnny run out on you," he complained to Manion.

"You sounded like you needed help. Anyway, where's Johnny going to go without his brother to lead him?"

"Maybe Italy," Munn said, chuckling in spite of himself. He wiped his eyes again and looked around the now-lit room. Apparently, Reevie had an idea of converting it into a mini-gym. An exercise mat rested on the carpet in front of a mirrored side wall. Several sets of barbells were on a rack at its foot. A rowing machine was beside it, facing a portable TV set. The other wall was taken up by a long closet. Its far door was open, displaying an assortment of sports equipment—baseball mitts, running shoes, archery material. "I thought he was using a baseball bat on me." Munn said.

"It was a golf club," Manion said. "A putter, I think."

"I would have sworn it was a bat."

Leon Harris came to the door. "Maybe I should phone the police?" he asked.

"I *am* the police," Munn growled.

Leon moved into the room. He was staring at the atomizer on the floor. He bent over and put out his hand.

"Don't touch it," Manion told him. "There should be some rather interesting fingerprints on it."

Munn squinted one eye and looked at him. "Meaning what?" he asked.

"Meaning that Reevie may have avoided one death threat before he succumbed to another. The squeeze bottle belonged to Foster Fouchette. He wouldn't have dropped it on purpose."

Manion moved to the closet and pushed open its folding doors. In its center was a curious mound, covered by a tarpaulin. He pulled it free, exposing the body of Foster Fouchette.

Munn suddenly forgot his tingling wrists and stuffy nose. Leon moved closer, staring at the dead man. "What the hell!" he exclaimed.

"It looks like his neck's been broken," Manion replied. He bent down and patted the dead man's pockets. No gun. Foster would have had one. He was clutching something in one hand. It looked like a woman's handkerchief.

"What do you figure?" Munn asked. "Could the Crawfish have done this?"

Manion shook his head. "He's been dead awhile. Probably came here straight from the Bayou this morning. Tried to do away with Reevie, only Reevie turned it around somehow."

"But if Reevie killed *him,* then who . . . ?" Munn asked.

"Who indeed?" Manion echoed.

"I'm not sure I give a damn," Munn grumbled, flexing his fingers. "Except that LeRoux is gonna want to know the answer. And I'd like to be the one to tell him."

Manion said, "There's a pretty large field to choose from, but old man Benedetto seems to be the best bet."

"Geez!" Munn exclaimed. "I'll drink to that."

*   *   *

The drink was late in coming. It was another four hours before they were finished with the Metairie police and LeRoux and his people. It was nearly seven P.M. when Munn went out to his car. Instead of following, Manion detoured into the dining room, where Leon sat at the main table, looking tired and rumpled.

"Was your boss home when you got here this morning?" the detective asked.

"Like I just told them, he was."

"Alone?"

Leon stared at him for a beat. "Yes," he replied finally.

"But he hadn't spent the night alone."

Leon's eyes frosted over. "I wasn't here then."

"You'd have an idea. The maid would know."

"Ask her." He turned away to observe two policemen who were sauntering through the room like a pair of bored and angry dogs. Manion stared at his profile—the cheekbones, the proud hawk-like nose. He opened his mouth to say something, then thought better of it.

He left the house. Munn was in the car, waiting for him impatiently.

"Forget me out here?" Munn asked angrily.

Manion took a long look back at the house. "Families," he said. "In this part of the country, it's always about families, isn't it?"

Manion asked Munn to drop him at Nadia Wells's home. Munn had been trying without success to cajole him into a celebratory night on the town.

"What's so important it beats the barbecued shrimp at Manale's?" he asked, making a final try as Manion got out of the car.

The detective stood on the still, dark street, listening to the crickets and night birds and idling car engine. "Just some errands," he said.

"You're not taking Lucille out somewhere?"

"If I were," Manion said, "I'd be sure you were the last to know."

"Gawddammit, Manion. You two are goin' out on the town and I'm gonna be stuck all fucking alone. I'll wind up with the damned TV on, some newscaster . . ." His voice dropped an octave. " 'In Louisiana today, organized crime suffered a severe defeat when crusading police lieutenant Lucien LeRoux discovered the corpses of the state's worst scum-sucking swine spread all over the goddamned Greater New Orleans landscape . . .' "

He sighed, put out a calloused hand, and winced when Manion shook it. "You ought to have that wrist X-rayed," Manion said.

"Yeah, sure. I'll get right on that," Munn replied. "See you around, schoolmate." And he disrupted the calm night by gunning the engine and roaring down the street.

41

NADIA WELLS'S chef Lou-Ruth, was not happy. The scalloped crabs, which had been ready for serving for forty-five minutes, were drying out. "Why is it whenever that man shows up, eating gets delayed?" she inquired of Olivette.

"You're very observant, Lou-Ruth," Olivette replied, staring at the closed door to Nadia's office. "Miz Wells has established a set of unvarying rules that are followed to the letter. Except when Terry Manion is around."

"Much longer and I'm gonna have to toss this dinner and begin again."

"All we can do is wait and see," Olivette said, scowling now at the closed door.

In fact, the dinner would be saved. Manion had completed his report to Nadia on all that had transpired at the Sports Plantation and at Benedetto's home. She stared at him for a few seconds, then said, "Well, chow's waiting. Who killed young Benedetto?"

Manion shrugged. "What's the difference? The main thing is that you can cancel your round-the-clock guards. There's nobody left to worry about."

"Except Reevie's murderer. Was it Eben Munn?" she asked.

"Eben? I was with him when we found the body."

"Yes," she agreed. "But you said Reeves went to the massage room at around eleven. Munn had time to bump him off before coming here to pick you up. He seemed to be pretty frazzled."

Manion shook his head. "A real stretch," he said. "Can you see Munn killing somebody with a razor blade? He'd use a meat cleaver."

"It's just a thought." She grinned wickedly and added, "Guess it wouldn't do to have a homicidal cop for a brother-in-law."

"Brother-in-law? I only met the woman two days ago," Manion said with as much indignation as he could fake.

"You don't suppose *she* killed Reeves?"

He sighed. "Do we have to play this game?"

"I know how curious you can be, sonny. So your lack of enthusiasm about guessing the culprit makes me suspect you know who he is."

He stood up. A bug, attracted by the light, flew headlong into a windowpane. The air conditioner whirred. Manion said, "I remember a very wise woman once telling me, 'Never give the client any information you can't back up with enough proof to satisfy a loathsome, mealymouthed liberal judge.' "

"Now, sonny," she cautioned. "You know I'd never use the word 'loathsome' in that context. C'mon, between you, me, and the lampshade. Who the hell slit that boy's wrists?"

So he told her.

Nadia waited a beat, expressing neither surprise, nor disbelief, then asked,"Got any proof?"

"Nothing that a mealymouthed liberal judge would accept."

"Let's hear your conjecture then." she said.

"Suppose we start with the fake suicide note and the reason the body was placed in the bathtub. . . ." He went on to build his case quickly. When he was finished, Nadia smiled and said, "Maybe we've got something more substantial to toss in the pot."

She stood up and walked out of her office. In a few minutes, she was back carrying a stack of her field operatives' daily logs. She pulled one free and handed it to Manion. "Fits right in," she said.

He studied the log and nodded, handing it back.

"Should I save this for your pal Munn?" she asked.

"I don't think so. I'm not even sure he cares."

"Well, you do what you feel is right. What I'm gonna do is feed my face. Sure you won't stay?"

"No. I have several . . . previous engagements."

"Well, then," she said, offering her cheek to be kissed. That accomplished, she added, "Tell that little Munn vixen I want to meet her."

"I will," he replied, wondering how long that meeting could be avoided.

"Say tomorrow at six?" Nadia Wells suggested in a very demanding manner.

42
.

IT WAS approximately eight-fifteen when Manion parked his Mustang in front of the Gaynaud home. The side gate was open and Lindsay Gaynaud's Corvette was parked in front.

He was about to press the door buzzer when he heard Lawson Gaynaud's unmistakable voice cutting through the still night air. "Stay where you are, dammit!" he was shouting.

Manion strolled to the rear of the house, where Clovis Long-street, clad in a soft cocoa-brown Polo shirt and cream slacks, stood shining a watchman's flashlight up into an oak tree. A ladder had been placed against the tree, and Gaynaud's Topsider-shod feet were visible on its top rungs. The rest of his body was lost in the shadows and leaves and branches.

As Manion approached, he was aware of movement at a lit window on the second floor of the house. A very thin, gray-haired woman in what appeared to be a nightgown stared down at Gaynaud and the tree.

"Gotcha, you little bitch." Gaynaud exclaimed. "Scratch me and I'll wring your scrawny neck."

He began to descend with a tiny orange and white kitten in his hand. As he stepped from the ladder, he brushed against Clovis Long-street, paused, and pushed in on her body. She responded, just for a second. Then they drew apart and Gaynaud held up the kitten so that the woman in the window could see it. "Safe and sound," he called up to her, smiling broadly.

"Good job," Manion said. And Gaynaud almost fell over backward spinning in his direction. The kitten emitted a sharp cry, and the elderly man realized that his grip had tightened on its tiny body. He threw it casually to the ground and said, "Clovis, Lindsay must've left the gate open when she came in this afternoon. Please see that Mr. Manion leaves the way he came in."

He turned his back and went about the task of folding the aluminum ladder and carting it away. Clovis Longstreet took a step toward Manion, shining the flashlight in his face. Shading his glasses, Manion said to Gaynaud, "Reeves Benedetto was murdered today."

Gaynaud paused briefly, then continued toward the back of his house.

Clovis Longstreet said, "The family is aware of that, Mr. Manion. It's been on the news."

"But there has been no mention of 'the family,' has there?"

The old man paused, rested the ladder on the ground.

Manion said, "No mention that Lindsay Gaynaud was Benedetto's girlfriend. No mention of the hold Benedetto had over the family."

Gaynaud turned wearily and said, "Come inside, Manion, if you must."

Manion looked up at the window. The thin woman was no longer there.

Lawson Gaynaud picked a chair to the right of the marble fireplace in his living room. His back was bent and he stared listlessly at the beige carpet. Clovis Longstreet asked him, "Can I get you anything?"

"Like what?" he said, annoyed.

"Like the after-dinner coffee you didn't have because of the goddamned cat," she said through her teeth.

Gaynaud stared at her, mouth agape. Then he attempted a feeble smile and said with considerably less irritation, "I'm sorry, Clovis. Guess we're all a little jumpy. No coffee for me. Maybe Mr. Manion . . . ?"

She shot a hostile glance at Manion. "Just a few answers," he said.

Gaynaud swung his large head in the direction of Clovis Longstreet and said, "You leave us alone, hear?"

She hesitated, blessed Manion with another venomous look, then walked swiftly from the room. As soon as the door closed behind her, Gaynaud said resignedly, "Please begin."

"How long have you known Reeves Benedetto?"

"Less than a year. Since he and Lindsay started . . . seeing one another."

"Did you think he was pretty good son-in-law material?"

Gaynaud's eyelids lifted briefly. "Surely you're joking. A dago, with a gangster father?"

"But you couldn't stop Lindsay from seeing him?"

"It wasn't that simple. After Gerry St. John died, she became a basket case. At least the Benedetto boy was able to get her back on her feet. Or so I thought. At the time, none of us dreamed that Gerry's death was anything but an accident."

Manion raised an eyebrow. "You knew that Benedetto murdered St. John?"

Gaynaud's head dropped onto his chest. "So my daughter informed me today."

"Where is she?"

"She's . . . sedated. She arrived home in a terrible state. Like a goddamned sleepwalker. Wouldn't say anything. Just wandered to her room. Then she began screaming. Horrible things. Upset her mother terribly. Hell, she upset *me*. All about Reeves Benedetto, how he killed a man this morning. Snapped the man's neck. But before the fellow died, he whispered to Lindsay that Reeves had murdered poor Gerry."

"And now Reevie's dead himself."

"Good goddamn riddance."

"I don't suppose you or Lindsay called the police to report Reevie's actions?"

Gaynaud exhaled loudly through his nose, like a horse. "And get Lindsay mixed up in that mess?"

From the corner of his eye, Manion saw the living room door open slightly. He waited, but no one joined them. He asked, "What time did Lindsay get home?"

Gaynaud lowered his eyes. "Around noon," he mumbled. "Clovis and I were just sitting down to lunch."

"Benedetto was murdered sometime between eleven, when his secretary last saw him, and one, when his body was found . . ."

"You're implying that Lindsay killed him?"

Manion shrugged. "Only that she had the motive—he'd murdered her fiancé—and she had the time. But let's move on to Parker—"

"Wait a damned minute! With a man like Benedetto, half the goddamned city of New Orleans had a motive."

Manion's eyes grew dreamy behind his glasses. "What kind of man was that, Mr. Gaynaud?"

"You know goddamned well. A murderer. A . . . a gangster."

"A blackmailer?"

"I wouldn't know about that."

"Oh, sure you would. He was blackmailing you, blackmailing your son, forcing him to use his influence to get a gambling initiative on the ballot. Reeves had a vision of himself as gaming czar of all the Southland."

"Foolishness," the old man blurted. "As if my son would—"

"Did you know that Parker's nephew, Leon, was Reeves's butler?"

Gaynaud's hooded eyes popped open. "His *butler*? No. But what of it?"

"He was an odd duck, Benedetto. The people who worked for him say that he was an extremely fair man, a true liberal, politically speaking. They'd seen him take on bullies in defense of racial equality."

"He was a goddamned murderer."

"I didn't say he was perfect. But he went out of his way to give Leon Parker a boost up in life. Any idea why?"

"I'm sure I don't know."

"Benedetto kept a file on you and your family," Manion said.

"What kind of file?"

"The kind that might give the NOPD all sorts of ideas if they were to see it. For example, in his own handwriting, he described the events surround Parker Harris's death. Excuse me, Parker Harris's murder."

Gaynaud blinked. "He . . . No! You're full of crap!"

Manion removed a folded manila envelope from his inside coat pocket. Gaynaud's eyes followed it as if he were mesmerized. "I suppose that's for sale?" he asked.

"No," Manion said. He put the envelope on the table in front of Gaynaud. The old man leaned forward but Manion placed his hand on the envelope. "When I go, I'll leave it with you."

Gaynaud was puzzled now. "What do you want from me?"

"Parker Harris was a blackmailer too, wasn't he?"

Gaynaud blinked slowly. "You seem to know all about it. You tell me."

"I know his sister bore your child, Mr. Gaynaud," Manion said. "Café-au-lait skin color. Leon Harris even looks like you. Has the Gaynaud nose. Maybe Reeves Benedetto realized it would be the only thing he was likely to inherit from you, so he decided to be Leon's patron. Or maybe he was simply amusing himself by having two of your offspring hanging around his house, both of them ignorant of their blood tie."

Gaynaud stared dolefully at the envelope. "You should have seen his mother, Manion. She was a beauty. She flirted with me. And we did it. Right here in this house, in my own goddamned bed. I can't deny the pleasure . . . My God, she was . . . sensual.

"And the fact is, Irma was a good nigger. Never asked me for a goddamned thing. A good woman, Irma. I tried to get her a fine doctor. I thought I had. A colored doctor, of course, but the best in the city."

"In Charity Hospital?" Manion asked.

"I was told he was the best, Charity be damned. Unfortunately, he was unavailable at the moment of delivery. Parker got her to the hospital, but she wound up in the hands of some young hack intern who saved the baby but let Irma die. It was a tragedy. She would never have made any demands on me. But Parker took advantage of the situation. For twenty years he bled me. Said he'd tell my wife if I didn't pay up. Hell, I had no objection to taking care of the boy's upbringing. But Parker wasn't satisfied with only that. He wanted more and he knew he had me."

Manion's mouth felt dry and his eyes itched behind his glasses. He had told Lucille Munn that he'd meet her at eight-thirty. He hoped he wouldn't be more than an hour late. But he had one more stop to make. He removed his glasses and rubbed his eyes. "What I don't understand is why you waited twenty years to kill him."

"Me?" the old man jerked forward. "You treacherous son-of-a-bitch!" he shouted, grabbing the envelope from the table and tearing at its flap. Inside, he found only blank pages.

The living room door swung open and the thin woman Manion had seen at the window stepped haltingly into the room. The ceiling light formed a halo on her wispy pink hair. Her frail nightgowned body was wrapped in a fresh cotton robe and there were fleece-lined slippers on her milk-colored feet. Her chalky pallor and wrinkles made her look older than her husband and quite ill. She said to him, "You told me that Parker lied, Lawson." Her voice was as shaky as her footing.

Gaynaud was up from his chair and moving toward her. "Now, Lily . . ."

"That filthy black man, that Judas, you said he'd lied about you and Irma."

"Please, Lily." Gaynaud tried to touch her, but she pulled away from him, almost falling. She turned to Manion, who was on his feet and edging close to her. "I didn't mean to harm him. I just tried to brush him away, as one might brush a cobweb from one's own face. He was shouting at my husband, outside my door near the top of the stairs. I left my room and he began shouting at me. All sorts of horrible things about Lawson and Irma. I just tried to brush him and his words away. And he took a step backward and disappeared."

She whirled on her husband. "You told me he lied, but you . . . You're the . . ."

She began to sway; then her body folded. Manion was close enough to catch her and ease her to the carpet.

Gaynaud knelt beside his wife and pressed his hand against her cheek. He started to sob.

Manion went to the door and shouted for Clovis, who arrived within seconds. Lindsay, looking almost as pale as her mother, was at her heels. She was wearing a denim skirt and a man's oxford shirt. She asked her father shrilly, "What did you do to her, you bastard?"

"Linnie girl, I didn't . . ." he protested halfheartedly. His daughter was kneeling on the carpet, holding her mother's limp hand.

Clovis asked, "Is she . . ."

"No," Manion said. "But she may want to be. You'd better get her doctor over here."

Clovis rushed to a phone near the sofa.

Manion knelt beside Lindsay, who was weeping at the sight of her still mother. "You saw Reevie kill a man this morning," he said.

She drew back, her wet eyes wide and frightened. "Oh, God, he broke the man's neck. Then he left me with him. But the man wasn't quite dead. I wiped his face with my handkerchief. His voice was a whisper. He said Reevie murdered my Gerry."

"Did he say anything else?"

"He repeated a name, Ruffy, several times."

It meant nothing to Manion. He'd hoped Foster Fouchette might have made a confession of some kind.

Mrs. Gaynaud stirred and Lindsay leaned forward anxiously. But the old woman did not open her eyes. Her breathing was ragged.

Manion stood and backed away to the door. He'd had enough of the Gaynaud family.

Lindsay called his name. "I just remembered," she told him. "The last thing the man told me before he died. He said his throat felt fine."

43
•

WHEN MANION arrived at Steiner's home, his statuesque brunette student, Angela, was on the patio, outlined by the light from the open front door. As he drew closer, he saw that she was trying to feed the Great Dane, which was lying on the patio watching her balefully.

Angela was having a difficult time because she needed both hands to spoon the Cajun Canine Chow from its can into the immense dog dish and one of her hands was occupied with a handkerchief she was using to blow her nose.

She was crying. Her eyes were red. In between sobs, she said, "Marcus isn't here."

"What's the matter?" Manion asked, taking the can and spoon from her.

"He says he's going away." She blew her nose. "He's leaving us. Me. Hungry Joe. His work. Everything. He's just going."

Manion stared at the dog food. It smelled of liver and file powder. He bent down and scooped half the can into the dog's bowl. Hungry Joe gave him a forlorn look, so he dumped in the rest of the can, too.

"Where's Marcus now?" he asked, straightening.

"He said he was going to his spot," she said, sniffling. "His precious spot."

Manion watched the dog consume the food. "What's his spot?"

"On the levee at the foot of Carrollton," she said. "He goes there at night to 'contemplate the river's force.' He's so full of shit."

Manion put the spoon into the empty can and handed them back to Angela. As he started away, she asked, "You going to find him?"

He nodded. "Well, when you do," she said, "tell him. . . tell him . . . Never mind, don't tell him anything."

It had been years since Manion had been on the levee. As a kid, he and his pals had biked there every few weeks, sometimes with BB pistols to shoot at cans bobbing on the Mississippi, sometimes just to sit and gawk at the tall, thin black man who dressed in white robes and carried a white staff as he baptized people in the dirty river water.

As he trudged up the moist, grassy hill to the top of the levee, Manion was surprised at how little it had changed. The man-made embankment that for centuries had kept the waters of the Mississippi from flooding the city, looked the same by the light of a particularly bright moon. The river seemed higher. Some of the old shacks that had existed on the river side had disappeared.

Steiner sat in the grass just over the rim of the levee, staring out at the moonlit muddy waterway. Like the old soul saver, he was dressed in white. But his clothes were a bit more stylish. White linen suit. White pique shirt. White tennis shoes without socks. There was a dark-colored canvas bag at his side. And a bottle of Jack Daniels in his lap.

Manion was almost beside him when Steiner jerked his head around to look at him. "Terry," he said. "Pull up some grass and sit." His voice was remarkably clear.

Manion took off his coat and sat down. Steiner held up the whiskey bottle. "Celebrating," he said.

"Celebrating what?"

"I don't know. The end of an era. The beginning of another. Something earth-shattering, that's for sure. I'd offer you a drink, but I'm your sponsor."

"No you're not," Manion said.

"You've got my number, champ. I just don't want to share the booze." He took a swig. "Mmm. Smooth as mother's milk."

"Angela tells me you're leaving town."

Steiner nodded. "Yeah. There's nothing for me here anymore. You won't let me write about you. Miss Mansfield's biography no longer holds its allure. The semester's almost over. Time to de-part."

"Angela seems a little upset."

"She'll get over it. Youth is goddamned resilient. I'm thinking of leaving her the dog."

"Generous."

Steiner's eyes narrowed. "What the hell are you doing here, Terry? What's on your mind?"

"The man who tried to kill you the other night is dead," Manion said. "His name was Foster Fouchette and he was a hired killer."

Steiner's eyes lost some of their moon sparkle. "Munn nail him?"

Manion shook his head. "No. It looks like he was murdered by one of his former employers, Reeves Benedetto."

"The wiseguy we met at the sports place?"

Manion nodded. "And here's the odd part. Benedetto was murdered too."

Steiner stared at the river, then sampled the Jack Daniels again.

"Anyway," Manion went on, "you don't have to worry about hit men anymore. And Nadia Wells has sent your bodyguards home."

"Bodyguards?" Steiner said. "I had bodyguards?"

"Two guys in a dark blue Ford Probe," Manion said. "They weren't very good. They lost you today around ten-thirty. At the library."

"I was there returning some books, going through a few magazines. I sure as hell didn't notice any bodyguards."

"They saw you go into the library. When you weren't out in twenty minutes, one of them went inside and couldn't find you. Then both of them went through the building, and when they came out, your banged-up wagon was gone."

"I'm sorry," Steiner said. "I didn't know. I would have waited for them."

"Where'd you go after the library?"

"Home. Then over to Tulane. I had a bite at the Student Union. Why?"

"Research," Manion said.

Steiner smiled. "Don't tell me *you're* writing a book about *me*?"

Manion shook his head. "What was your opinion of Reeves Benedetto?" he asked.

Steiner stared at him. "Arrogant. Self-confident. Too damned opinionated."

"A ladies' man?"

"Possibly. He was handsome. Wealthy."

"Well educated," Manion added. "Went to school in Switzerland. Didn't your wife meet some—how'd you put it?—some 'young
stud' while she was skiing in Switzerland?"

Steiner didn't reply. He looked back at the black water. A boat
that resembled an old paddle wheeler was passing. It was draped with
lights. Pop music blared from its decks and there were couples danc-
ing.

Manion said, "I suppose it'd be too big a coincidence for Reevie
Benedetto and your wife to have met."

Steiner exhaled heavily. "I never found out who the bastard was
who . . . left her to die like that."

"So you said. But you're a guy who does his research. Suppose
you discovered the 'bastard' had ties to New Orleans? You might've
come here to poke around. That'd make it less of a coincidence if your
paths happened to cross. Maybe you even had a name—Bennett—but
you didn't know that the guy had decided to change it back to his real
family name. So you weren't able to locate him."

"They say anybody can be located," Steiner replied.

"That's true," Manion said. "If the guy doing the looking has
patience. And luck. You had the latter. One day, a death notice
appeared in the *Times-Picayune* about an apparent suicide. The paper
actually printed what were supposed to be J.J. Legendre's last words.
Remember what they were?"

Steiner remained quiet, staring at the river.

" 'I've got nothing more to lose,' " Manion quoted. "Sound familiar?"

Steiner nodded, but his face showed no expression. "I was just
kidding, Terry, about the drink," he said. "Have one." He held out
the bottle.

Manion ignored it. "The dying woman in your novel, the one
based on your wife, used those same words. Were they the words that
your wife . . . ?"

"It's your fantasy," Steiner growled. "Don't expect me to help
you with it."

"I understand they're from a Cajun song. Was your wife a fan of
Cajun music, Marcus?"

Steiner shook his head. "Not to my knowledge. But there was a
lot about my wife I didn't know."

"But both she and J.J. put the same thing in their suicide notes. There were several possible conclusions. Maybe they were recalling the same Cajun song. But there's no reason to think your wife ever heard that song. I suppose J.J. could have read your book and taken a fancy to the line and used it when he made up his mind to kill himself. But I know he didn't kill himself.

"That brings us to the most interesting possibility. Maybe something else linked the suicides of J.J. and your wife. Maybe neither was a genuine suicide.

"If that's the case, let's take it one step further. You saw in J.J.'s obituary that he was associated with my detective agency. So you decided to become my sponsor."

The writer stared at him and said disgustedly, "You're delusional."

"Then you explain how you just *happened* to become my sponsor."

"On the advice of my doctor," Steiner said in a dull voice, "I looked up Courville when I got out here. We've kept it more personal than professional, have dinner every now and then. A while ago, I told him I was feeling a little restless, and he suggested I reaffirm my commitment to sobriety by sponsoring one or two of his patients from Evangeline Spa, help 'em over the rough spots. Good for them. Good for me. He's the one who suggested I hook up with you."

Manion frowned. "Courville wouldn't have even told you my last name, but you've got a whole file on me."

"Jesus, Terry, that's what's still got you spooked? Courville gave me your phone number. Your answering machine gave me your last name. And the rest—the research—just sort of happened once I discovered you were a private detective. It was all coincidence."

Manion hesitated, running the facts through his mind again. Then he smiled. "I can give you a better sequence of events. You tried to reach me by phone. When that didn't work, you went to J.J.'s funeral, assuming I'd be there. You casually asked one of the mourners to point me out. It was a small crowd and almost any one of them know where I was.

"So you phoned your old pal, Dr. Courville, offered to sponsor one of his patients, and when he mentioned the name Terry, you told him to stop right there."

Steiner managed a tight smile and said, "You know, Terry, I

think you're right to be worried about your paranoid fantasies. You really do need help, pal."

"Not on this, Marcus. This is clear as crystal. But maybe I will phone Dr. Courville, just to see how you and I really got together."

"Do what you have to." Steiner was staring out at the Mississippi again.

"You've been following me in the hope that I would lead you to the man responsible for your wife's death. And I guess I did. When Foster Fouchette took you for your ride, did he recognize you and confess, assuming you weren't going to live to tell anyone? No, that wasn't his style. But he must have said or done something to give himself away. Still, you realized he was only the paid assassin. The guy you wanted was the 'young stud' who bankrolled your wife's murder. And Munn and I inadvertently introduced you to him, Reevie Benedetto.

"I bet you came up with the plan that night in his office. You'd kill him and make it look as if his hired hand, Fouchette, had done the job, leaving the same bogus suicide note he always used. Unfortunately, Foster was already dead by the time Reevie was taking his blood bath."

Steiner smiled. "If you'll excuse my indulgence . . ." He brought the bottle to his lips again and held it there until it was empty. He breathed deeply and, with a boyish grin, tossed the dry bottle high through the air into the river.

When he turned to Manion, he seemed to be stone sober. He said, "So the note is the crux of it. If the guy with laryngitis didn't kill Benedetto, the existence of that note limits the number of suspects to only two."

"Two?" Manion asked.

"Yes. Me and you, Terry. We both knew about the words of the suicide note and we both had the same motive. Benedetto and his pet killer murdered people we cared for."

Manion smiled back at him. "But one of us knows for sure that he didn't kill Reevie."

"What does any of us know for sure, Terry?" Steiner asked. "We've both used substances that could make us forget weeks. Months. A little thing like the killing of a low-life slug could easily escape a clouded mind."

"Let me put it another way," Manion said. "Reevie Benedetto—

Reeves Bennett—died in the bathtub with his wrists cut. That has a significance that would appeal to only one of us."

Steiner nodded his head. "Good point."

"There are those who would tell you that Reevie was a solid citizen who believed in the rights of man," Manion said. "But I don't think his death was such an awful loss. He was a sociopath. On an impersonal level, he understood the difference between right and wrong and acted accordingly. But when it came to personal matters—his life, his career, his greed—there was no wrong. Anything that got in his way he was willing to remove. A rival in romance. His uncle. His own father. A woman with a cocaine habit became a possible threat to his post-college plans, so he had her killed without a second thought. Still, I don't believe in vigilante justice, Marcus. And since you're sitting here going off the wagon in such a big way, I assume you don't really believe in it either."

Steiner's hand went into the book bag. Manion thought he was reaching for another bottle. But it was something a little faster-acting, a military automatic pistol with a long, fluted barrel. "I picked this up in Saigon a long while back, Terry," he said. "All this time, I considered it nothing more than a souvenir."

Manion watched the barrel of the gun move his way. "If you're going to kill me, Marcus," he said, "at least you could have saved me a last drink."

"I'm not sure it's you I'm going to shoot. That's only one of two options."

"Three options," Manion corrected him.

"You mean I could give myself up," Steiner said. "End my literary career by winding up the page two story in supermarket tabloids everywhere. I'm not that drunk. No, I'm just trying to think it through. It doesn't seem possible that anyone other than you could figure out I killed Reeves Bennett."

"C'mon, Marcus," Manion told him. "You believed you were justified in killing Reevie. But it still drove you back to the bottle. I don't think you can talk yourself into shooting me."

With great care, Manion got to his feet. The pistol remained pointed at his chest. Steiner's voice was chillingly calm. "Remember, Terry, a guy on booze or drugs is capable of anything."

Manion turned his back to Steiner and took a step toward the top of the levee. The grass was slick with dew. In the distance, the music from the paddle wheeler still echoed. Behind him, the writer asked quietly, "Did you tell anybody, Terry?"

Manion didn't reply. He took another step. He was almost to the top of the levee now. The stars above. The lights of Carrollton Avenue below.

"Do you *have* to tell anybody?" Steiner asked. Then he pulled the trigger.

Epilogue

●

NEITHER THE police nor the press linked Marcus Steiner's suicide to the murder or Reeves Benedetto, and Terry Manion felt no need to make the connection for them. On the day the writer was being laid to rest a thousand or so miles to the northeast, Manion stood beside the banks of Blue Bayou watching Buddy and five other pallbearers carry Foster Fouchette's coffin from a little Presbyterian church with a steeple that looked like a dunce cap. The funeral procession went down to the water's edge, where the coffin was placed on a flat-bottomed boat. The pallbearers then boarded the boat. The minister and Mrs. Fouchette, two elderly figures in black, moved unsteadily to a place at the front of the boat.

One of the pallbearers started the outboard, and the boat cut across Blue Bayou, with various forms of water life slithering and scurrying from its path. The funeral barge's destination was a small cemetery surrounded by a white picket fence on the opposite shore, where Fouchettes for the past two generations had been laid to rest.

There were approximately fifty mourners. All were Cajuns except for Manion, Lucille Munn, and Slo Bentine, who, standing beside a wheelchair-bound Pos and doting on his every need, seemed to be in the midst of converting.

Near the end of the church service, which had been long and in rapid Cajun French, Lucille whispered to Manion, "What are we doing here, city boy?"

He had no answer for her at the time. It wasn't until much later that he'd realized why he'd come. By then the mourning had given way to laughter and food and drink and song—not the opera that Foster Fouchette loved but the French accordion music he loathed—and the sun had been replaced by a velvety blue moonlit night.

Manion and Lucille had devoured crawfish étoufée and barbecued shrimp and heard tall tales about the mystical and romantic properties of Blue Bayou. And they'd danced by candlelight to melodies with names like "Flumes dans Faires" and "Le Pauvre Hobo" and "Rooster Blues." When Buddy, their bayou tour guide, approached with the sad news that the evening was ending, Manion knew what he had to do. "Wait a few minutes," he said.

An elderly guitar player, who reminded the detective of John Wayne at his most grizzled, seemed to be the band's leader. Manion went to him and requested a song. The old man stared at him, then at Lucille, and shook his head. "Oh, podnah, you got such a purty gal an' all, what you want a sad song like that for?"

"For a man who was my best friend and for a man who wasn't a friend at all," Manion told him.

The guitar player shrugged and turned to let the other musicians know what they would be playing. The song started slowly, a forlorn ballad about a hapless guy who owned the world but failed to enjoy it. Manion waited through three verses before the old guitar player sang the final line with painful poignancy, "I got nothing more to lose."

Manion felt all tension leave him, like a dark spirit exorcised by the song. He was healthy again in mind and body and dangerously optimistic. He didn't think he'd ever felt quite this elated before. Certainly not sober. The moonlight danced on the water. The moonlight danced in Lucille's eyes. Blue Bayou magic.

"Hey, T-bone," Buddy called, breaking the spell. "You got your song in. You satisfied now?"

Manion told him that he was.